PRAISE FOR HELEN F

'A super-tense, in-your-face thriller that will ke
The Sun

'Fields at her compelling best as a mistress of suspense and tension.'
Daily Mail

'What a read! This has potential for a TV series.'
Prima

'I was on the edge of my seat.'
Yours

'This twisty, claustrophobic thriller is ideal for fans of *The Sanitorium*.'
Candis

'Fields has written yet another haunting and absorbing thriller.'
My Weekly

'Brilliant! The novel finds author Fields, a master of psychological suspense, in top form as she spins a harrowing, non-stop story populated with complex, fully formed characters – notably Connie Woolwine, a true hero for the ages! I'd say the novel is the perfect weekend read, except it won't last that long; you'll consume it in one sitting.'
Jeffery Deaver

'Quite simply, wow! One of the best high concept thrillers I've read in forever. I can't decide which is my favourite character, Dr. Connie Woolwine or *The Institution* itself. Tense and terrifying. From the opening chapter, I raced through this riveting thriller in a single, breathless session of oh-my-God-what-is-going-to-happen-next.'
***New York Times* bestselling author, Lisa Gardner**

'A claustrophobic, two-fisted, nerve shredding locked-room thriller that will keep you guessing, right until the end. Dark, disturbing and compelling.'
Neil Lancaster

'Dark and atmospheric with some brilliantly horrific characters and some excellent twists. Compelling and unputdownable.'
Catherine Cooper

'A wonderful, compulsively gripping rollercoaster of a read.'
Liz Nugent

'Absolutely AMAZING. Tense, engrossing and gripping with a truly unique main character in profiler, Connie Woolwine.'
Angela Marsons

'A non-stop thriller with a mind-bending twist.'
S. E. Lynes

'*Watching You* is a taut psychological thriller that plunges you into the dark mind of a stalker. the hunter is always watching, and the most terrifying threats come from within. Unmissable!'
Suzy Quinn

'Twisted, tense, and totally addictive.'
Caroline Mitchell

READERS LOVE HELEN FIELDS

'Fantastic. Excellent. Incredible. I could not put this one down for the life of me.'
5☆ **Reader Review**

'What a rollercoaster ride this was. I love it when a book shocks me the way this did.'
5☆ **Reader Review**

'Brilliant, intense, thrilling and unputdownable.'
5☆ **Reader Review**

'I highly recommend *Watching You* but be warned you will be looking over your shoulder during and after reading.'
5☆ **Reader Review**

'Breathtaking. Twists and turns galore. I couldn't put it down, I loved it.'
5☆ **Reader Review**

'I was completely blown away by this book it was sheer brilliance!'
5☆ **Reader Review**

'A tense, twisty, phenomenal read!'
5☆ **Reader Review**

'Helen Fields is the queen of suspense.'
5☆ **Reader Review**

'Haunting. Breathtaking shocks, horror, unforeseen twists, and an emotionally shattering conclusion.'
5☆ **Reader Review**

'Twisty, unpredictable and kept me guessing the whole time.'
5☆ **Reader Review**

'Disturbing, gripping and totally brilliant!! Helen in in her stride.'
5☆ **Reader Review**

WATCHING YOU

Helen Fields studied law at the University of East Anglia, then went on to the Inns of Court School of Law in London. She joined chambers in Middle Temple where she practised criminal and family law. After her second child was born, Helen left the Bar, and now runs a media company with her husband David. Many of Helen's books are set in Scotland, where Helen feels most at one with the world. Helen and her husband are digital nomads, moving between the Americas and Europe with their three children and looking for adventures.

By the same author:

Perfect Remains
Perfect Prey
Perfect Death
Perfect Silence
Perfect Crime
Perfect Kill
The Shadow Man
One for Sorrow
The Last Girl to Die
The Institution
The Profiler

WATCHING YOU

YOU

HELEN FIELDS

avon.

Published by AVON
A division of HarperCollins*Publishers* Ltd
1 London Bridge Street
London SE1 9GF

www.harpercollins.co.uk

HarperCollins*Publishers*
Macken House, 39/40 Mayor Street Upper
Dublin 1, D01 C9W8, Ireland

A Paperback Original 2025

2

First published in Great Britain by HarperCollins*Publishers* 2025

A catalogue copy of this book is available from the British Library.

ISBN: 978-0-00-853357-1

Set in Sabon LT Std by HarperCollins*Publishers* India

Printed and bound in the UK using 100% Renewable Electricity at CPI Group (UK) Ltd

MIX
Paper | Supporting
responsible forestry
FSC™ C007454

This book contains FSC™ certified paper and other controlled sources to ensure responsible forest management.

For more information visit: www.harpercollins.co.uk/green

For Sharon Avery,

with thanks to the universe for crossing our paths once more.

Chapter 1

Body One of Eight

29 September

Death wasn't wearing a hooded black cloak when it came for Dale Abnay. It wasn't holding a scythe, nor did it beckon him towards a reassuring light. Death, Dale realised, as he was pulled by the feet, face down, his chin gathering leaves while the tide of his life ebbed, was a devious scumbag who'd cheated by sneaking up behind him. It hardly seemed fair. He'd always imagined himself staring death down, being given the chance of a fair fight. But death was a coward wielding what Dale guessed was a rock and saying precisely nothing as it stole his life. Bastard.

The single blow to Dale Abnay's head had set off a biological bomb inside his skull, and now there was one river rushing out through his ears and another issuing from his mouth. His consciousness retreated through the arteries of his brain to a small, private space in his memory that looked an awful lot like his childhood bedroom. It was the one place in the world that he'd loved and where he'd felt truly safe, until the day his father had run off with his aunt. After that, it had become a sanctuary

1

from his alternately weeping then screaming mother, who'd called her sister words Dale had never heard before, words that got him in trouble at school aged only seven, when he'd shouted them at a girl in his class.

Somewhere beyond the walls of that childhood room, a red haze was incoming. The wind that brought it closer howled with the sound of a fox fighting hounds, and blew in the stench of maggots devouring a carcass. Dale made sure the door to his room was locked and slid under his bed. He didn't fit there quite the way he had as a child – his feet stuck out of the end and his back hit the underside slats – but the important thing was that his notebook was still there.

In the notebook, he remembered, were the musings of a pre-pubescent kid who'd dreamed of only two things – a career as a professional footballer, and receiving all the latest computer games at Christmas. For a while he'd wanted a puppy too, until an elderly neighbour had rescued a dog from the animal shelter. Dale had watched her walk the scruffy mutt every day, stooping awkwardly to pick up its crap in little black bags, then swinging the steaming package as she went. That had made him rethink his wishlist. He'd never been good enough to make the school football team either. At least as an adult he'd been able to buy all the games he wanted.

The room bounced up and down. Dale's head hit the underside of his bed hard enough for his ears to ring as a crack appeared in the floor. That had to have been an earthquake. Imagine that, an earthquake in Scotland! It was the first he'd experienced. Dale reached up and pulled the cover over the side of the bed to curtain off the destruction, vaguely aware that something really bad was happening but determined to finish reading his notebook come what may. That was a better idea. Why concern himself with the things he couldn't change? That had been a favourite of his mother's sayings, some jumbled version of it anyway. It was the first time Dale could recall it actually applying to a situation he'd found himself in, and he decided he didn't like it.

Dale opened the journal, rubbed his eyes, closed the cover once, waited a few seconds, then opened it again. Gone were the scrawled imaginings of a kid who'd had big dreams for a boy whose school report often noted that he struggled to concentrate and was rude to teachers. The tiny cartoon figures he'd liked drawing in the bottom right-hand corner, so he could flick the pages and watch them move, were gone. The list of who his friends were at any given time was gone. The special name he'd written over and over again – Lucy Ogunode – had been erased completely.

He'd loved Lucy. She'd started school with him on day one and been there still when his education had ended at eighteen. She'd never once pulled a face upon being asked by a teacher to sit next to him, and had never called him names like the other kids. Lucy was kind and sweet and lovely, and her smile had been a candle in the darkness of childhood. Until it wasn't any more, and thinking about that made his face burn and his stomach ache, so he decided he wouldn't.

Dale looked around for a pen or pencil. There had always been one somewhere under his bed for making late-night additions, and occasionally writing notes when he'd awoken from dreams. Not today, though. Today, all his fingers found as he reached around the dark corners were leaves and twigs, and that couldn't possibly be right because his mother would have given him hell if he'd let his bedroom get that dirty, and he was never, ever allowed to wear his outside shoes into his bedroom.

Two wires tried desperately to connect inside his head. They very nearly made it, but then the lights went out. Dale wasn't even sure where the light had been coming from because the curtains had been drawn and he hadn't actually seen a ceiling, but now it was pitch black beyond the bedcovers, yet somehow he could still see the pages of his book. The source of that light, he realised, was a small torch shining from behind him. He hadn't noticed it before, but it was providing just enough illumination for him to see instead of forcing him to curl up, alone, with nothing to do but wait.

He looked back at the notebook, wishing he could write Lucy's name onto the pages again, but now every page was filled with thick black scribble, cancelling out every good thought he'd ever recorded there and transforming each page into a bottomless hole. Dale pulled his fingers back from the paper, certain that if their tips touched that graphite mass they would disappear and he would immediately be sucked in after them.

He flicked on through, careful to touch only the very corners of the paper, until a drip from above distracted him and his hand trailed across the page, his fingers coming away not black but green, the darkest shade of moss, and textured like – he had to think about it for a moment, and thinking was painfully slow – the stuff his mum used to arrange flowers in. It came in a block and would crumble if you grabbed it too hard . . . Oasis, that was it. He rubbed the infected fingers on the floor, but the stain wouldn't shift, so he tried again. That time there was movement. He watched open-mouthed, with his skin flaking away as if he were rubbing his fingers on a cheese grater. It should have hurt, but it just didn't. That, in itself, might have been a mercy save for the fact that he realised he couldn't feel anything. Not anything at all. Dale pinched himself. Then he bit his bottom lip with his upper teeth. Then he punched himself in the thigh.

'Nothing,' he whispered.

More drips hit his head from above, and that was an awful

lot of liquid to have got through the duvet, and the sheets, and then the mattress. That water, slime-laced and icy cold, smelled of mud and worms. He hadn't ever thought about how worms might smell until that moment, but his journal was getting wet which was bad news because it was the only thing he had left to hold onto, and if he let go of that – if he *lost* that – then he knew perfectly well that it would be the end.

Lucy's name had appeared on the pages again, but there were no hearts or flowers decorating the letters the way they used to. Instead, the script was starting to run, leaving streaks of grey tears on the paper. He dropped the book, startled by the sudden scent of smoke and the flames spiking out from the spine. That part of it was real, he remembered, not a hallucination, which was good – better than good – because it meant there was still a chance that he wasn't losing his mind after all. Maybe the fire would be enough to wake him from his nightmare and return him to reality.

Of course he couldn't be reading his notebook again, because in the real world, he'd burned it. He'd tried at first to rip it in two but failed, then thrown it into the fireplace in disgust, squirted lighter fluid over it and revelled in the blaze. Lucy had ruined everything. He'd spent so many years loving her from afar but keeping his distance, knowing the teenage pecking order would never permit him to be with her, before making contact once school finally finished, doing his best to befriend and charm her, and finally finding the strength to ask her out. All of which was met with nothing. Just a bland, polite rejection, which he'd found worse, in fact, than if she'd slapped his face or told him she was a lesbian or declared that she'd found Jesus and was off to join a convent. But nothing was what she'd given him, and it had been amazing how much the absence of something could be such a force.

He'd pursued other women since Lucy, of course, but none who'd warranted having their names written in his book. As quickly as it had burst into life, the fire reduced to mere embers. Paper ashes formed a shifting, twisting haze in the slowly fading torchlight.

Women weren't for Dale, apparently. They were either too good or not good enough. And he'd heard somewhere – was it in a movie or on a TV show? – that the lesser women were the ones he should be approaching because they were more grateful for the attention and thus more likely to let him do the things he dreamed about. The logic of that was unacceptable to him. Why should he be relegated so young to the company of women with imperfect bodies and average faces? Why did beautiful women with high, bulging breasts and tiny, tight waists not want him the way women seemed to lust after men in the videos he'd watched in that very space, beneath his bed, in the small hours when his mother was fast asleep and couldn't catch him?

The torch flickered a few times. Dale grabbed it and shook, trying to jolt the batteries into a second wind, but it was no good. There was, eventually, nothing but the darkness. Dale tried to call out, but drips splashed onto his tongue and the sourness made him gag. The water was creeping in now from all sides. He wanted to speak, to be allowed a few last words, but his tongue was a useless, clumsy flap of meat in his mouth, and was the bed pressing down harder on his back or was he imagining that? He felt sad that he hadn't always been a particularly nice person, but he'd recently put a plan in motion to rebalance the scales. He'd wanted more. He was working on being better. Now it was too late.

He tried to roll onto his side, intent on pulling his knees up to his chest, to find those last few shreds of foetal comfort, but the leaves from the corners had multiplied and amassed around his body, pressing in like a dank blanket. The air was thick in his mouth and tasted of death. In his final seconds, as his conscious mind opened his bedroom door and allowed him to understand where his earthly body really was, he had just enough time to wonder if Lucy Ogunode – wherever she was – would hear about his death. And if she'd care.

As Dale faded from the world a few too-long-too-short minutes later, five girls watched and wept.

Chapter 2

Body Two of Eight

5 May

Detective Sergeant Lively from Edinburgh's Major Investigation Team was sitting in a church and hoping he didn't spontaneously burst into flames given the fact that he'd spent decades telling anyone who'd listen what he thought of religion. Still, there were days when the job took its toll, and recently it had taken far too many people he cared about, hence the visit. He hadn't quite managed to get as far as actually praying when his mobile started playing 'Black Hole Sun' which meant the call was coming from the station.

'Give me strength,' Lively muttered. 'Can a man not get a single moment of peace?' He answered the call. 'It'd better be fucking good.'

'Define good,' DS Christie Salter replied. They were of equal rank in spite of their age difference – Lively in his fifties and Salter in her thirties – but he'd taught Christie all she knew and rarely let her forget it, something she secretly loved.

'Either I've won the lottery or Scotland has become a territory of the Bahamas and we all have the right to move there in our retirement,' Lively said, already moving out into the graveyard and resenting having his personal time cut short. There were grave markers close by that belonged to some of his former colleagues, and he'd wanted to pass a few minutes with them, too. Paying his disrespects, as he thought of it. Dead friends didn't want to be respected, they wanted to be remembered in their best moments.

'You'd get bored of the money and sunburned on the beach. Besides, we need you here now that the squad's down a couple of members. Actually I was hoping you were free to go to St Columba hospital. A homeless male was found with multiple stab wounds. Paramedics are blue-lighting him there for surgery.'

'Multiple stab wounds and he's still alive?' Lively picked up the pace to his car.

'Probably due to the number of layers he was wearing, which seem to have prevented deep penetration by the knife. Even so, it must have been a frenzied attack. Looks to have happened last night. He was found against the fence of an industrial unit car park in Bankside this morning by the early shift security guard.'

'All right, I'm on my way. And how did I pick this particular short straw, given that you're the one calling me about it?'

'I'm heading to Juniper Artland,' Salter said. 'A dog walker found some remains. I don't have many details yet, only that the pathologist is unhappy about the scene.'

'Unhappy as opposed to which other emotion, given the pathologist's chosen career path?'

Salter ignored him. 'Just get there fast, would you? I don't know if the stabbing victim will make it, and no one's got a coherent word out of him yet.'

'I'll be there in ten,' Lively said. 'Make sure they're expecting me. I'll see if I can get anything from him before he's anaesthetised. Some first week back for you, isn't it?'

9

'It's Edinburgh,' Salter said flatly. 'I wouldn't have expected anything less.'

St Columba hospital, a new build, should have been an architectural atrocity, but Scotland understood a thing or two about maintaining the integrity of landscapes. The only requirement not properly catered for was parking, in true Edinburgh tradition, and so it was that Lively abandoned hope before even entering the visitor car park and simply pulled his car up onto a patch of grass and took his identification from his pocket before the security guard was within shouting distance.

'Police,' he said. 'I've not got time.'

'There's a sign,' the security guard blustered.

Lively turned his head to read it.

'Aye, but it only says not to walk on the grass. I drove on it. Totally different thing.'

'That grass has only recently been planted. I'll get hell for this,' the guard said, dropping his head.

Lively sighed, reached into his pocket, and tossed his keys to the guard. 'All right then, I don't want to get you in trouble. Feel free to move it for me. I'll find you for the keys when I'm done. Which way's A&E?'

The guard sighed and pointed. Lively checked his watch, tried to run a few paces to make up for lost time, then decided better of it. Any more of that nonsense and the only way he'd be getting to accident and emergency was on a stretcher with someone pumping his chest. It really was time to lose those extra few pounds – stone, his brain whispered maliciously – he'd been promising himself for the past . . . well, he'd lost track of that one.

The exterior of St Columba was Scots baronial, and might have been built in a different century with its miniature spires, sandstone blocks, multitude of windows and carved details that could make the most stoic of stonemasons weep. The few steps from outside to inside were an exercise in time-travel. It might have been a medical facility on a new planet, with an atrium four storeys high, lighting that bloomed ahead of you as you walked and dimmed behind, a series of balconies with designer couches and large areas of planting, each with its own spray keeping the soil just damp. It smelled of pine needles and nutmeg, and the sounds of birdsong and bees buzzing was being piped in from some secret speaker. Lively felt the familiar murk of the police station slip from his shoulders as he strode as briskly as he could manage to find the man who, he hoped, was still clinging to life.

He was directed through doors that excluded the general public, down a long white corridor and into a scrub room where he was given shoe covers, a surgical gown was draped over him, and finally he put on gloves. It occurred to him that there wasn't really all that much difference between a modern-day crime scene and an operating theatre.

'Dr Hall, the anaesthetist, is already in the prep room and the surgeon's on her way,' he was told. 'She gave permission for you to enter but you'll only have a minute. The patient's in bad shape. And don't touch anything as you're not scrubbed in.'

Lively walked through an automatic door. Through a window to his left he saw a team of eight people preparing for surgery, getting implements into trays, adjusting lights, tying gowns and hooking up monitors. In stark contrast, the patient on the trolley in front of him looked to be in his forties with a mess of matted ginger hair and the inevitable scars of long-term outdoor living marking his face and arms. He might as well already have been dead for all the colour in his cheeks, and his breathing sounded like a clogged whistle.

As Lively stepped towards the man's head for a few vital

seconds of conversation, a woman walked through an opposite door, smiling gently with quiet good cheer and an aura of absolute calm.

'Thank you, everyone, I hope we're good to go. We have a visitor so let's give him the space to do his job.' She nodded in Lively's direction and he couldn't help but smile back at her.

'DS Lively,' he said.

'I'm Beth Waterfall, trauma surgeon. You don't have long, I'm afraid. Go ahead, just try not to cause the patient too much stress. I understand he's been slipping in and out of consciousness since he was brought in.'

On the trolley, the patient's eyes flew open. He looked up at the anaesthetist, then to Lively and across to the surgeon.

'No, no, no!' He began shaking his head and flailing his arms, snatching at the tubes attached to his arms. 'Help me. Someone help.' It came out as a mush of sounds, spittle flying from his mouth.

'He's tachycardic, acidotic with high lactate and low haemoglobin,' Dr Hall insisted. 'We're losing time.'

Beth Waterfall shook her head. 'We've got to get in there and stop the bleeding. Detective, you have only seconds.' Waterfall adjusted her mask and moved to the patient's bare abdomen where three wounds were bleeding through temporary dressings.

Lively didn't hesitate. He positioned himself above the man's face and tried to make eye contact.

'Sir, I'm a police officer. Can you tell me anything about the person who attacked you?'

'You fuckin' crazy?' the man mumbled. 'Gonna die here. Ge' me out!'

'Anything you can remember at all will help,' Lively said.

'Blood pressure's dropping!' Dr Hall's voice was raised.

'He's been bleeding too long. Get him under now,' Waterfall said. 'Ten seconds, detective.'

Lively leaned in closer to the man's thrashing head. 'Give me something. Anything.'

The man grabbed Lively's hand with surprising strength as the anaesthetic flowed into his veins. He opened his mouth to speak, then his eyes rolled and his head drifted sideways.

'Patient's ready,' the anaesthetist said. 'Blood pressure's borderline and his heart rhythm is weak. If I keep him under long, chances are he won't wake up.'

'Detective, no offence, but I need you out of here,' Waterfall said. 'You can wait in the café and I'll find you afterwards if it'll help.'

'It's a date,' Lively said.

'Oh, you don't want to date a surgeon,' she said as a surgical assistant handed her a sheet of paper that she began reading as she spoke. 'We're workaholics who do antisocial hours, come home with our hair smelling of blood, and all our stories feature bodily fluids. Damn it, he's been bleeding into his abdomen for hours. Hang some more O neg and prepare for some serious suction.'

'Sounds like we're soulmates.' Lively gave Waterfall a smile she didn't see as she walked through into the operating theatre. 'I'll be waiting.'

Chapter 3

5 May

Dr Waterfall reappeared four hours later, her hair in a soft bob around her face, brown eyes shining warmly. He assumed she was a few years younger than him, albeit in rather better shape. Lively headed straight for the till to buy her a coffee. She sat gratefully as he handed it to her.

'I'd ask if he made it but I've three decades of experience in reading faces,' Lively said.

'His chances weren't good from the second he was brought in, but my motto is there's always hope. The surgical team fought to keep him alive, longer than we probably should've if I'm honest. I hate losing the fight. My first thought was that I'd have to go and inform his family. Took me a minute to realise I couldn't and somehow that's even worse.' She sipped her coffee, and Lively let her enjoy it in silence for a minute. Beth Waterfall had a serene face that seemed at odds with the tenacity it took to do her job, with smile lines that radiated from the side of each eye like a child's drawing of the sun, and a firm figure that reflected hours spent on her feet. The difference between her self-care and his made his cheeks feel hot. He reverted to work talk to cover his embarrassment.

'What can you tell me about his injuries?'

'I'm no pathologist, so please don't rely on my expertise from a crime perspective,' she said. 'But from a medical point of view, there were three main puncture wounds, all about the same depth and the same width at the point of entry, plus some smaller ones that looked like attempts that got snagged on material, pockets et cetera. His clothing has been bagged and is being held for you to take. The doctor who first examined him said the weapon went through several layers, which might be what kept him alive for so long but it's also what finally killed him. A more shocking presentation might have come to someone's notice sooner.'

'You sound pretty expert to me.'

'I suspect a first-year medical student could have reached the same conclusion,' Waterfall said. Her voice was low-pitched and silken, and she smiled as she spoke. Lively tried to look at his coffee cup instead of her mouth. 'The wounds were probably bad enough to stop him from walking to get help, or even to have prevented him from calling out to passers-by depending on where he was, but they weren't deep enough to cause an immediate bleed-out. Instead he leaked blood internally over a period of hours.'

Lively sighed. 'Did you notice any other injuries, to his hands maybe?'

'I didn't look carefully, I'm afraid, but certainly none that needed surgical intervention. He suffered one wound in a kidney and that was largely self-contained. Another hit an omental vein beneath the fatty layer of the skin and that was our slow bleeder. The problem for us in surgery was that the third wound perforated his bowel, causing peritonitis. The infection alone made it unlikely he would survive. I made sure my team handled

15

his body as little as possible to preserve evidence for you, although obviously the area of the incisions had to be cleaned thoroughly as did needle entry points and his face, as that was exposed for the anaesthetist. If you can trace his next of kin, I'd like to talk to them myself. It can be frustrating for family members not to have an opportunity to ask questions.'

'How long do you think it would have taken for him to bleed out?' Lively asked.

Waterfall gave a slight shrug. 'Hard to say. Several hours, but less than a whole day. In the end, cause of death was the massive haemorrhage that meant the patient suffered a cardiac arrest.' Waterfall reached out a hand and laid it gently on top of Lively's. 'I hope you catch the person who did this. The homeless community accounts for far too many deaths. We could be doing much more to help.'

'Aye, well, pay rises for politicians have to take priority,' Lively murmured. 'How else would they afford their summer holidays in the Maldives?'

'I should go,' Waterfall said, pulling her hand back slowly. 'Thank you for the coffee, detective.'

Lively found he didn't want her to go, which felt oddly like having a golf ball stuck in his throat. 'Waterfall's an unusual name. Where's it from?'

'My father was from Staffordshire. There's a village there called Waterfall. Goes back a way. My mother was from Portree. They met on a trip to Paris as students. They'd each entered a poetry competition and the trip was the prize for the winners. Love at first sight, my father said. My mother claims she made him work a bit harder than that, but I believe his version.'

Lively felt his cheeks burning again and he wondered if he might have caught some sort of virus since entering the hospital. He felt in his pocket for a card with his number on and handed her a rather crumpled item of stationery. 'In case you think of anything else,' he said.

'Do you have a pen?' she asked. Lively handed her one and she wrote a number on a serviette. 'Here, I'm guessing you'll need to speak with me again to take a statement. That'd be our second date, of course, so I'll be expecting flowers for that.'

'I'm not sure I'm allowed to do that,' Lively mumbled. 'Police budgets don't tend to stretch that far.'

'That's a shame,' she grinned briefly and Lively instinctively sucked in his gut and tried to sit straighter. 'Well, don't be a stranger. Not under these circumstances again, though, preferably.'

Lively was still trying to figure out a response when she got to her feet and walked away.

Chapter 4

Jupiter Artland was an idyll. Its architectural landscaping, with grand swirling features and stretches of water, offered a haven both for city dwellers and tourists sick of the sight of plastic and tartan trophies. The acres of parkland closed from October to well into spring, giving the land time to breathe through the rain and frosts, untrampled by human feet.

In the hours that Lively had been at the hospital, the parkland had been transformed. Vast areas had been cordoned off, tents constructed, equipment had been laboriously brought in on foot to minimally disturb the evidence and avoid damaging the grounds. Outdoor body recovery took time. It wasn't just the corpse that needed moving and preserving but quantities of earth around it, and a huge area would be minutely combed for a weapon, clothing and anything else that might have been discarded as the killer fled the scene. Lively was pleased he'd been on hospital duty indoors.

He took his time traversing the pathways to the leafy bowers that were home to the Weeping Girls. They stood, the five of them, hair cascading over their faces, against trees or free-standing, in the throes of emotions so strong you could hear them crying and screeching in spite of their cold stone hearts. He stared at the girls in horror. They were somehow so much more affecting than the human remains to whose decay they had presumably borne witness as the winter had given birth to spring.

Christie Salter stood watching Dr Nate Carlisle, Edinburgh's new pathologist, as he worked. Lively had to admit that Carlisle was a striking figure in the midst of the crime scene investigation crew who were preserving the evidence and immortalising the gruesome discovery into Scottish crime history.

'So do you fancy him too, then?' Lively whispered from behind her.

Salter's hand flew to her chest. 'God in heaven, sarge, a man's been brutally murdered here. This isn't the place to be taking people by surprise. And for the record, I'm happily loved-up.'

'Ach, you can still look, girl. You're married, not dead.'

'Distasteful in the circumstances,' Salter murmured.

'Oh come on, this is what we do. Have you never thought that without people getting knocked off in unfortunate circumstances, we'd be out of a bloody job?' Lively mused.

'I can't believe you just reframed murder as our employment currency.'

'Just telling it like it is. Admit it, you missed me, Salter.' He gave her a nudge with his elbow.

Nate Carlisle – well over six feet tall, lithe and sinewy, and sporting a hairless skull that looked better on a black man than it ever would on a Caucasian – took a few steps back from the body and glanced across at them, motioning for them to join him. 'Stay on the steps please,' he instructed.

They approached slowly and carefully. The spectre of a

defence barrister making hay with a misplaced foot or a dropped mobile phone was always lurking.

'Just how dead is this one then, doc?' Lively asked.

Nate Carlisle sighed and raised his eyebrows at Lively, which made Salter smile. It was refreshing that Carlisle wasn't amused by Lively, given the boys' club nature of so many aspects of policing.

'I'm DS Christie Salter,' she introduced herself. 'What can you tell us?'

'The remains were discovered by an employee preparing to reopen the site to the public. It's a male, I'd say around five feet ten inches tall. I'm sure you're both experienced enough to know that a body in this state of decomposition has been outside for several months. It'll be difficult to be precise without reference to some factual information that tells us when he went missing. I'll be calling in a forensic entomologist to help as there's a lot of insect life infesting the remains. Given that we're largely down to skeletal parts, death occurred a minimum of four months ago.'

'Can you rule out natural causes or suicide?' Salter asked.

'Lean over, mind your balance and try not to breathe in,' Carlisle said.

As one, Salter and Lively filled their lungs and bent for the best view they could get. Carlisle used a gloved finger to pull back a clump of hair from the blackening skull and directed their gazes to a crack along the bone.

'A fracture?' Lively asked.

Carlisle nodded. 'Temporal bone, and the fracture is clear enough that the impact would have caused an acute intracerebral haemorrhage followed shortly by unconsciousness. He couldn't have done it to himself.'

'Could he have fallen and hit his head on a rock or a tree trunk?' Salter asked.

'He could, and the mechanics of that sort of death would have resembled a skiing accident. He might even have been rendered comatose by the blow, possibly with a brain bleed that would have stopped all meaningful neurological functioning,' Carlisle said. 'But that wouldn't explain what happened next.' He motioned behind them to a technician who was moving individual leaves with metal pincers and infinite patience.

Beneath the leaves, furrows in the damp earth provided a pathway into dense bushes beneath a heavily canopied tree. A photographer on a stepladder was capturing the image of the drag marks that resembled the tracks of a sleigh in snow.

'There's a pair of walking boots deep in the undergrowth, wedged under a branch, partially buried. I'm assuming that an animal dragged the corpse out into the open, but only when it was so rotten that the ankle joints gave way. The feet stayed where they were in the boots and the remainder is in front of you. We're missing an arm, and it's possible we just haven't found that in the vicinity yet, or potentially a predator took that back to its lair.'

'Filling up the freezer for a late-night snack,' Lively chimed in.

'Christ, would you stop it, man? I'm sorry about him,' Salter muttered.

'No apology necessary. DS Lively and I have worked together before,' Carlisle said. 'It's a good job he's such an impressive detective.'

'All right you two, point taken,' Lively groaned. 'Did your lot find any other clothing?'

'No jacket, and the rest of it was lightweight cotton. Looks to me like shorts and a T-shirt, largely rotted but we've checked everything we found for identification. We've no phone, wallet or keys as yet,' Carlisle said.

'Is the skull in good enough condition that we've got a shot at facial reconstruction?' Lively asked.

21

'Give me a second and I should be able to answer that. We're about to lift the remains.'

Carlisle disappeared to where a specialist stretcher and body cover were being positioned to take the remains to a van and from there to the city mortuary. Lively turned around on the step, getting his bearings within the wider geography.

'This place has been closed for months. It's a fair bet he was killed late summer, early autumn. Strange place for a robbery, don't you think?' He stuck his hands in his pockets and frowned.

'I agree,' Salter said. 'It's not a robbery, or if it was then they weren't after anything as simple as money or a phone. Normally I'd be wondering if this was drugs related, but hiking isn't a known pastime of our local drug lords. What are you thinking?'

'Feels like an argument,' Lively said. 'Two mates, husband and wife, business partners. Maybe a money dispute. Hey, doc!' he called out to Carlisle. 'You said the feet were partially buried. How deep?'

'Just a few inches,' Carlisle replied.

'Impromptu then,' Lively said. 'Not a professional job. If it was a hit they'd have brought a spade and tidied up. No self-respecting Scottish assassin is this sloppy.'

'Nice,' Salter commented. 'Look, they're moving him. Let's follow.'

Out in the open, a tent had been erected to give some shelter and allow for dry storage of the necessary equipment. The stretcher was moved inside and Carlisle gave them both gloves and face masks before they got close.

As bodies went, it wasn't the worst type to have discovered. Lively knew from bitter experience that a newer corpse was by far the more upsetting. Once the liquefaction process was done, everything began to dry out. After that, the resemblance to a person faded remarkably quickly.

Whoever the dead man was, he was unrecognisable now. There would be no identification by family members or friends. There was enough left to get reliable DNA and possibly dental records, but naming the victim was still not a certainty.

The bones were folded and mangled, with leathered flaps of skin and brown sinew connecting them. The skull, though, was intact, in spite of the crack in it.

'Do you think the head was buried more carefully than the rest of him?' Salter asked.

'No, the skull's in better shape than the other bones because our native wild animals don't have sufficiently wide jaws to get their mouths around it and bite down. Every other part has been subjected to predator or carrion-feeder approaches.'

'All right,' Lively said. 'Give us a call when you're done with the postmortem. We'll get started looking at missing persons. Cause of death was the blow to the head, right?'

'I wouldn't jump to that conclusion,' Carlisle said, stripping off his gloves and pulling the body cover back over the victim. 'There's every chance the blow didn't kill him immediately.'

'Fuck it,' Lively murmured.

'So you think he might have been buried while he was still alive?' Salter asked quietly.

'I'm afraid so,' Carlisle said. 'With so little lung tissue left it'll probably be impossible for me to reach a definitive conclusion.'

'You think he was hit on the side of his head, dragged to an improvised, shallow grave, covered in earth and leaves, then left to suffocate or choke to death while unable to move,' Lively said. 'Probably didn't expect that when he was eating his cornflakes, did he, poor bastard?'

Chapter 5

10 May

Salter was at her desk contemplating her decision to leave her beautiful, adopted baby girl with a child-minder, to facilitate her return to work. No matter how many times she told herself it was good for her daughter to be with other people and doing everything from swimming lessons to baby ballet, those long afternoons on the sofa with a sleeping child on her chest still felt like the best dream she'd ever had. Now she was stuck with pictures of insect larvae, a soil report and a list of hiking boot retail outlets to work through. She yawned for the hundredth time that morning and stretched as Lively, dressed in joggers, a formerly-white T-shirt and running shoes, all but fell through the doorway of Edinburgh's Major Incident Team briefing room.

'Medic,' one of the squad cried, earning a round of applause.

'Defibrillator!' came the reply. 'Clear!'

Lively managed to get himself fully upright, wiped the sweat from his eyes and growled at the team. 'You all know that every one of your girlfriends comes to me for sex advice, right?'

The women in the room grimaced and tried not to gag while the men laughed.

'All right, that's enough,' Salter shouted. 'Back to work. You need a shower, sarge, or do I have to talk to you through your body's natural defence mechanism?'

Lively sniffed one of his armpits and reeled. 'Give me five minutes.' He returned a quarter of an hour later sipping black coffee and wrinkling his nose at every sip.

'No milk and sugar today! I'm impressed. Made a few life-changing decisions then?' Salter smiled.

'Just choosing to be a bit healthier,' he said. 'We never know when we're going to be put to the test, physically speaking. My resting pulse wasn't as low as I like it to be.'

'Good for you. Any particular reason for the timing?' She tried to contain her grin but lost the battle. 'Only, now that you're fresh from the shower, it also appears that your hair is a few shades darker than it was yesterday.'

Lively huffed. 'Is that the extent of the detective work you figure on doing today, or are we here to solve at least one of the two bloody murders on our patch before the superintendent has another tantrum?'

'Fair enough!' Salter raised her hands in mock surrender. 'I'm just sayin', if you should find yourself needing any advice, you know, about women or dating or the like, you can ask. I won't even take the piss.'

Lively folded his arms and sat back in his chair, mouth firmly shut.

'All right, you win. Just remember that grooming expectations are considerably more evolved than they were in the 1980s.' She picked up her own mug of coffee. 'Your homeless stabbing victim's been identified, by the way. His name's Archie Bass, well known in the community as a chronic alcoholic but apparently

25

he'd been off the drugs of late. Been on the streets for years but he uses the shelters in winter. A soup kitchen volunteer recognised the image we gave the uniforms to pass around. So I'm thinking, either he got in a beef with someone or we've got another sick fuck out there who's taking his psychosis out on what he regards as disposable humans. Want to hit the streets with me? I've got some info about the places he used to hang out and identities of a few of his regular drinking buddies.'

'I'm actually meeting his, um, surgeon, the doctor, at the, um, mortuary. She offered to help talk us through the surgical process, you know, just to cover bases and whatnot.'

Salter took a deep breath and folded her hands into her lap. 'You're stumbling over your words more than you usually would. And now that I think about it, I can't recall seeing you in a shirt for a very long time, and that one, if I'm not mistaken, has actually been ironed. That surgeon wouldn't happen to be female by any chance?'

'That's it. I'm late. And when we meet here later to debrief, I'd better not hear any more of this crap. If it were me asking you those questions, I'd be up in front of a disciplinary panel for sexual harassment in a heartbeat.' He stood up and brushed down his trousers.

Salter's smile was genuine. 'For what it's worth, you look very nice. And I'm not sexually harassing you. They sure as hell don't pay me enough for that.'

'Fuck you very much,' Lively said. 'And ask about Archie's knife. Get the best description you can.'

'Archie's knife?'

'Aye. Anyone who's lived on the streets for any period of time carries something to defend themselves. It's too dangerous out there not to.'

Chapter 6

The Watcher

12 May

Sitting in the car he'd hired using a fake driving licence ordered off the internet, he watched the entrance to the doctors' car park at St Columba hospital. He couldn't get distracted or look away. Gone were the days when cars had to pull up at the barrier. The new hospital was all mod cons. Number plate recognition meant that the woman he was there to see would breeze straight through into the multi-storey then enter the hospital from an internal corridor he couldn't access. A couple of years ago, things were simpler. Now everywhere you looked it was two-factor verification for social media and emails, thumbprint access to laptops and facial recognition security systems. Technology was sucking all the fun out of stalking.

His target drove a Tesla. It was such a quiet car that he'd been inspired to hire only electric cars himself whenever possible. You could, he'd found, follow someone at no more than a few metres behind, and as long as they had their mind on other things, they really didn't notice you until they happened to turn around.

There she was now, driving slowly, presumably out of

respect for the elderly attending their endless attempts to prolong their useless lives, mindful of the hard-of-hearing or the blind, or whoever else the hospital klaxon-called to its tax-funded doors.

He slipped a little lower in his seat, in spite of the baseball cap on his head and the fact that he'd recently shaved his hair and learned how to use make-up to disguise his face. He'd been able to sit at the table next to her in the hospital café just a week earlier when she'd been chatting with a man he'd quickly realised was a police officer. In the circumstances, that wasn't just bold, it was outrageous. He hadn't liked how friendly they were getting. It had been hard to hear much of the conversation with other people clattering cups and shouting sandwich orders across him, but Dr Waterfall had appeared to be flirting by the end, and the policeman was practically panting at her. He didn't like it. Not one bit.

A police officer involved in Beth's life would make it infinitely more difficult for him to get near her, and proximity was everything. Being familiar with her routine, her preferences, her pleasures and irritants was useful for making plans, because sooner or later he was going to have to really do something about her, but also the act of spying on her, passing her unnoticed in a corridor or stealing a tiny trinket from her handbag in the supermarket helped with his rage. Breaking into her house and climbing between her cool, cotton sheets was even better.

Rage, he knew now, was so much more than just anger. True rage was cold at its centre. It was a complex structure that resembled Escher's *Relativity* to a much greater degree than Dante's *Inferno*. It was impossible to climb out of because its gravitational pull was irresistible. He had to get rid of that fury somewhere, and he'd found the perfect escape.

But also, he had to admit that he sort of liked the hospital.

The people he saw there were weak, and that made him feel strong. Other people's losses made him feel more human. Best of all, it was too busy for him to think.

His daily headache flared, and he winced. He was used to the pain but not the wave of nausea that came with it. The painkillers he took only made his stomach worse, but without them the pain in his head would leave him bedridden and unable to look at a screen, and he had to be able to trade. Stocks and shares purchased from a life insurance policy payout on his mother – low risk, steady return – made his life possible. The carer's allowance he got for his father wouldn't even cover the bills. But he had no office, no boss, no nine to five. His time was pretty much his own, provided he watched the markets and adjusted his portfolio accordingly.

Speaking of his father, he ought to get back to him, and anyway, Beth had long since gone inside. He had things to do at home until the carer's shift started again. He'd decided to order another deep-fake video through the darknet. He'd done it before and been amazed at how easy and cheap it had been. Later on, when he was free from his domestic obligations, he would drive to the good doctor's house. He'd long since figured out how to avoid the security cameras that covered both back and front doors, but that weren't positioned to fully show the conservatory or the whole garden. Disengaging the alarm was so much easier than people realised as long as you were willing to commit the time to learning the various systems that were the most popular on the market. He'd use the skeleton keys he'd trained with. Move an item, take something or leave something.

Some days, even that was boring for him, and yes, occasionally it felt like a real job. He'd had jobs in the past, before his mother's death and his father's stroke. He wasn't stupid. Maybe he'd never be a surgeon like Dr Beth Waterfall, but he learned fast and he had skills.

More importantly, he had a score to settle. A couple, in fact.

She was spiralling out of control, losing a little more of herself every day, and given that he'd already taken her daughter, there really shouldn't have been anything left to lose. There would be a reckoning. But not yet.

For now, Beth Waterfall was still his plaything.

Chapter 7

Body Three of Eight

20 May

There was a car following her. Divya Singh thought it was the same car she'd peered into earlier in the supermarket car park, but she couldn't be sure in the dark. It was the same colour and roughly the same size, but she paid very little attention to the various makes and models.

She'd been looking for someone to point her in the direction of the bus stop. The route had recently changed thanks to a new building estate, and now she wasn't sure how to get to where she needed to be. If the car creeping along behind her was the same one she'd peeked into, the lamplight and silvered windows had conspired to prevent her from seeing if anyone was inside, and she'd shuffled away deciding to walk the two miles home instead. Her bag wasn't too heavy and, for once, it wasn't raining. Fifty years living in Scotland and she still couldn't bear the cold or the grey sky. Her husband-to-be had travelled from Scotland to meet her in New Delhi full of promises of a better life, their families in harmony, and her parents had been attracted in no small part by the idea of their twenty-year-old daughter marrying an accountant who would send money back to help support them in their old age.

Scotland had been nothing more than a dream when their marriage had been arranged, and there had been a summer honeymoon period as she'd discovered the captivating beauty of Edinburgh, the friendliness of the Glaswegians and the wild freedom of the countryside. But then the rain had started and it seemed not to have stopped for more than the odd day ever since. She imagined a time when her husband might agree to spending what remained of their lives in India, with some relief from the arthritic pain in her hands and toes, and the joy of blue skies, at least beyond the city smog. But her husband's family was in Dundee, and Divya knew the chance of her seeing India's streets again was diminishing by the month.

The car was right behind her. Divya wished she'd bothered learning to use the awful mobile telephone thing. Now her husband was in France with friends at some sports tournament, their son was in London working every hour he could to support his three children who were all at university, and she was alone walking down the sort of street where all the houses were set back from the road with tall shrubs shielding the inhabitants from having to see the real world beyond their front gardens.

She considered whether or not the driver might simply need directions. That was possible. Perhaps they were just as lost as her. If she stopped and looked back perhaps, rather than following her, they'd draw up next to her and speak.

No, her brain said. Don't do that. You know better. Keep walking. Or better still, walk up a driveway into one of those nice houses, ring the doorbell and explain that you're lost and concerned. Someone will help you. Most people are kind.

Only that hadn't always been Divya's experience of life. Moving from India to Scotland had been a baptism of fire, and anyone who thought racism was a thing of the past had never lived anywhere as a minority. More often than not it was teenagers shouting insults or calling her names, but there had been women who should have known better at the school gates, whispering foul things, excluding her from coffee mornings and forgetting to include her son in birthday invitations. Then there'd been a GP who'd asked endless questions about her hygiene and her sex life, as if she were some alien species he was investigating. A neighbour who hadn't managed to learn her name after a decade. A bank where she was spoken to in notably less friendly, polite terms than other customers. Then there was the odd person who assumed anyone not white was a criminal. Sometimes those people had spat at her. Sometimes they'd beaten up her son. Divya didn't want to knock on a stranger's door.

All of which, it turned out, was no longer a problem. The car that had been following her had pulled over and stopped, and she was now some way ahead of it. The driver had obviously been looking for a specific address. It was hard to see house names – they didn't have anything as lowly as numbers on that road. Divya turned a corner into an avenue that was even more sparsely populated, with just a handful of houses set widely apart by their vast gardens and so far back from the road that the homes were hidden behind trees. She let out the breath she'd been holding in a dramatic burst of air that misted up in the chill evening. Even May in Scotland could be cold. She wished she'd worn gloves. The shopping bags were wearing little creases into her palms and her shoulders were aching.

As the worry dropped away, Divya realised where she was. She'd once attended a school prom meeting at the house in the distance, having offered to join the decorating committee. Her son had pestered her to get involved, and she'd offered in spite of knowing how it would go with little groups of women who were already close friends, not wanting anyone else in their subcommittee with their in-jokes and side-eyes. The memory wasn't a good one, and she felt ashamed of her negativity. Scotland had been good to her husband and her son. As a family they'd lived comfortably enough, even if there seemed to have been a natural cap to how high her husband could climb through the company ranks. Her son, though, had grown up in a new world untroubled by the colour of his skin and without the accent she'd brought with her halfway across the world. He'd been sporty and that brought a solid group of friends which had attracted girls. He'd enjoyed Edinburgh but longed for London. At eighteen, he'd headed for the London School of Economics and never looked back.

And if she didn't see her grandchildren all that often, she really couldn't complain. Her own parents had barely ever seen her son. That was the price of progress and generational success. Still, her son's wife was good about sending photos regularly. There wasn't a shelf or a windowsill in her home unadorned by silver-framed photos of a child clutching a trophy or a certificate, celebrating with their team or in costume on a stage. Those photos hadn't a speck of dust on them, so often did Divya pick them up and polish them. It was about time she visited. Her son invited her all the time but she was worried about being a bur—

The car hit her so fast, she didn't even have time to close her eyes as she flew through the air. Thus it was that Divya Singh saw one of her sensible shoes go flying off into a tree. She saw a kitchen roll from her shopping shoot across the road like a rocket. She watched her handbag open in the sky above and scatter tiny precious things, each catching glints of headlights and shining momentarily, beautifully, like man-made stars – a

34

lipstick her granddaughter had given her for Christmas that she'd never been brave enough to wear, a mirror that was her mother's, a keyring in the shape of India that brought her strange comfort for a plastic trinket. She felt her arm, as if it belonged to someone else completely, fly through the air to smash into her face and break her nose before she could even hit the ground. The crackle of her fracturing pelvis was a gunshot that boomed up her spine and echoed through her skull. And when her head whipped back on her neck sufficiently fast and so brutally that she'd never have walked again even if she'd survived the impact, she could see the ground beneath her from the most unnatural angle imaginable.

The force with which she hit the ground set off a series of miniature explosions inside her body that would rupture organs and push ribs into lung tissue. Divya wondered what her granddaughter's wedding dress would look like. She imagined her son getting the promotion he was working so hard for, and heard his voice on the telephone as he called to give her the news. She felt her husband taking her hand and telling her that she had been a good faithful wife, and that he'd loved her every day even if he hadn't said it enough. Divya felt the warmth of the Indian sun easing the pain from her joints, and finally she was back there, chasing through the bustling streets with her sisters, laughing at nothing, with her whole life ahead and the sure knowledge that everything would be well. Everything would be well. Everything would be well.

Divya Singh, devoted wife, mother and grandmother, died with blood in her mouth and a smile on her face in a patch of just-fading tulips.

Chapter 8

21 May

At 12.02 a.m. Nate Carlisle arrived at the scene of Divya Singh's death. He'd been at the cinema with his mobile off as he wasn't on call, so it wasn't until after 11 p.m. that he'd been notified of the accident. His assistant had attended the scene and taken stock of the level of the damage to the body and concluded that something much more concerning than a road traffic accident had taken place, and called Carlisle even though there was nothing more he could do than had already been done. He'd attended anyway. That was what you did when an elderly member of the public had been mowed down at high speed on a dark residential street at night. You turned up, you bore witness, and you made absolutely sure that nothing was missed and nothing was mishandled, to give the police the best possible chance of catching the bastard who'd treated a human life with such disdain.

DS Christie Salter arrived while they were still photographing the body in situ and trying to get accurate measurements of how far away each grocery item had flown in which direction to calculate the speed and point of impact. Carlisle didn't need much information to know a few things already.

'Dr Carlisle,' Salter said. She was stifling a yawn and her eyes were red. 'Can you give me the headlines while you work?'

Nate Carlisle liked Salter. She was one of those naturally calm police officers who cut to the chase with a gentle, controlled knife.

'I can tell you that you don't want to look at the body at this stage unless you're really feeling up to it,' Carlisle said.

Salter pulled her shoulders back. 'Because I'm a woman.'

Carlisle didn't even blink. 'Because you're a human being, and I wouldn't wish these memories on anyone.'

'Oh. I appreciate that, actually. It's harder doing this now that I have a little one at home. Everything's more personal. You have kids?'

'I don't. I want them though. I can imagine it changes everything.' He folded his arms. 'You're going to look anyway, even though the photos and a postmortem visit would do just as well, right?'

'It's the job,' Salter said. 'Tell me what you know.' She put on a suit and shoe covers then followed Carlisle over to the covered body.

Carlisle pulled back the scene preservation sheet and Salter reeled backwards, putting a hand to her mouth to stopper the cry that wanted to escape.

'What am I looking at?' Salter asked.

'The victim has been bent backwards. Her head has dropped down her back and her legs are doubled up from the hips in the wrong direction. Sort of an opposite foetal position.'

'How?' was all Salter managed.

'She was hit fast. There are tyre marks that indicate the car mounted the pavement back there,' Carlisle pointed backwards, 'but no brake or skid marks.'

'It was deliberate.'

'It was murder. I rarely reach that conclusion myself, but at the speed the vehicle must have hit, the driver couldn't possibly have believed anything except death would follow. There are two sets of injuries, one from the collision and one when the body hit the ground. I know that already because I can see impact marks to the backs of her legs but there's also a skull injury to her upper forehead and into the hairline which couldn't have happened at the same time.'

'She flew up so high she landed on her head?'

'It's not science at this point, but my preliminary estimate is that the car was going a minimum of forty miles per hour on impact. Most likely more than fifty.'

Salter let that sink in. 'How the hell are we supposed to break that sort of news to her family?'

'Very quietly,' Carlisle said. 'Come with me.'

They walked to a driveway across the road where marker flags were being pushed into the grass.

'What is that?' Salter screwed up her eyes.

'It's a bag of carrots,' Carlisle said. 'From one of the shopping bags the victim was carrying. And I can't stress this enough – I've never seen objects fly that far in the context of a vehicle to pedestrian collision.'

'It's like an assassination,' Salter said. 'Hold on.' She pulled gloves from her pocket and trod carefully in the direction of a patch of long grass bordering a hedge. Crouching, she gently pulled out a compact mirror from the weeds and opened it to reveal the shattered glass inside. She sighed and set it back down where she'd found it. 'Poor thing got her seven years of bad luck all in one go.'

Chapter 9

24 May

Detective Superintendent Overbeck stood at the door of MIT's briefing room and hit an empty metal mug against a desk.

'I don't know what you animals do in here all day but it smells like a cattle barn in Texas. Open some windows for God's sake and leave your sandwiches in the fridge when you're working. Who the hell still eats mushed-up egg? You, get me a coffee.' She held out the mug to a detective constable who stood up so fast that he knocked his own drink all over his desk. 'Ah, Scotland's finest,' Overbeck muttered as she stalked into the centre of the room. 'Where's that ballsack Lively?'

As if by magic he appeared in the corridor, leaning over and coughing, and dripping sweat onto his trainers.

'Detective Sergeant Lively.' Overbeck took her time pronouncing his name as if he were a newly discovered species with which she was familiarising herself. 'Has the zombie apocalypse started?' Lively managed to straighten up but the panting was preventing him from speaking. 'Only it appears that you have engaged in actual physical exertion. Exertion that gives the impression that you moved at speed. A feat, I suspect, that you have not attempted since there were only a handful of television channels. So I'm assuming threat to life, at the very least, was the cause of your sudden burst of muscular engagement.'

'Very funny,' Lively muttered, heading into the room.

Overbeck held up one carefully manicured hand with nails that had cost more than Lively's trainers. 'Under no circumstances,' she said. 'You will stand in the corridor until I have finished speaking, at which time you will head directly for decontamination.'

She perched on the edge of a table, her sheer tights showing legs that an eighteen-year-old would have been proud of, at the ends of which were heels that would have put the fear of God into an orthopaedic surgeon. Overbeck was stick-thin. Her ex-husband used to say it was because even calories were terrified of her and got out as quickly as they possibly could. Only she knew that insomnia was the real reason. Daisy Overbeck hadn't slept more than four consecutive hours since she'd first joined Police Scotland three decades earlier.

'I'm going to keep this brief. We have three bodies at the mortuary and three separate open murder investigations. I haven't seen anything even vaguely approaching a motive or suspects in any of those cases. That's no progress from any of the three teams currently working on this floor. Somebody tell me why those facts have forced me to visit you today.'

People avoided making eye contact with her and shuffled paper on their desks until someone too junior to know better raised their hand.

'Because that's more dead bodies than we normally deal with in a twelve-month period, if you exclude domestic murders.'

There was a sufficient mass intake of breath that some of the air was sucked out of the room.

Overbeck stood and, as one, officers pressed themselves back in their chairs, shrinking away from her. She walked slowly to the detective constable who'd just spoken, picking up a metal ruler as she went and holding it out in front of her.

'Go and fetch the first aid kit from the kitchen,' Lively told a uniformed officer who was passing in the corridor.

'Domestic murders,' Overbeck said softly. Her voice was a dart flying towards the bull's-eye. 'Like a domestic animal. Something tamed that we hit with a rolled-up newspaper if it pees on the carpet. Domestic like the cleaner we pay less than the legal required amount per hour in cash because then they don't lose their paltry benefits. Domestic like men buying their wife a vacuum cleaner in the 1950s because shouldn't the little woman be thrilled with that?'

'Errr . . .' The detective constable was having problems controlling the undulations of his Adam's apple. 'Errr . . .'

'Do you think it hurts less somehow because it's only a domestic murder, constable?' She pointed the ruler at him. 'Hold out your hand.' He put it on the desk palm up. Lively ran his fingers over his eyes and swore silently. 'It's like this. When we add the word domestic in front of a noun relating to violence, we soften it.'

No one moved a muscle.

'In my hands, this simple item of stationery might function as a weapon. If I bring it down hard enough on your hand it will hurt a great deal. It would be an act of violence, am I right?' There was enthusiastic nodding from the officer. 'But if I rename this a domestic ruler, the blow I issue with it hurts less. Correct?' An equal amount of head shaking.

Overbeck turned round holding the ruler in the air. 'Learn the statistics and think about them every day. Every year only about six per cent of women are killed by a stranger. The others, these atrocities we call domestic, are committed by people women know. Boyfriends, fathers, husbands, brothers, former partners. Sixty-eight per cent of those deaths occur where women should feel safest, in their own home.' She returned her focus to the detective constable who hadn't dared move his hand from the table. 'If I had my way, we'd remove the sexual organs from every man who killed a woman, but apparently I'm not allowed to express that sentiment publicly. So I'll settle for this. No one in this police station is to preface any violent noun with the word domestic. Not if you don't want to experience the difference between a normal knee to the testicles and a domestic knee to the testicles.' She dropped the ruler and flicked her ponytail before returning to her desk perch.

'What was it you wanted to talk about, specifically, ma'am?' Lively asked from the safety of the hallway.

Overbeck brushed a speck of dust from her lapel. 'To help, in fact. We're short-staffed, I appreciate that, but the recent spate of deaths is attracting some unfortunate media attention. I know we have two notable officers missing at present and that you're all having to act in more advanced roles. With that in mind, I'm bringing in some outside help.'

'Does it come in the form of a pay rise and better overtime rates, because I think that would be what we really all need right now, ma'am,' Lively said.

'What you need is a personal trainer with no sense of smell,' Overbeck snapped back. 'I've actually diverted some of our media budget into engaging a team we worked with some time ago. Dr Woolwine, a forensic psychologist, and her partner, Brodie Baarda, who's a former Met officer, are specialist investigators. Woolwine's a profiler by trade but she's experienced in all types of criminal investigations, has worked extensively with the FBI and she's familiar with the territory. She'll be consulting in all three murder investigations in the absence of Detective Chief Inspector Turner and DI Callanach. Make Woolwine and Baarda welcome. They've been granted full security access. DS Lively, you've worked with Dr Woolwine before. Did you need a moment to rail against the idea of having her brought in to oversee your work, or are you going to play nicely with the other children?'

'My sandpit, my rules,' Lively said.

'It's good to know who's in charge here. Cancel the entire squad's leave until someone has been arrested in each unlawful killing case. I want a progress report on my desk at six p.m. every day from you personally. Liaise with the media office because it's going to be your face the public associates with these, as yet, unsolved crimes. Any problems, officers, refer them directly to your leader DS Lively.'

She made for the door and put on a show of pinching her finger and thumb over her nose.

'You set me up, ma'am,' Lively muttered.

'If you don't like it, you shouldn't make it so easy. Your first report is due on my desk in just a few hours so you should probably get one of the younger members of your team to show you how to switch your computer on. And God help you if any more murders occur on this patch before you've solved the outstanding ones.'

Lively felt the tempting of fate like the lure of a pub on a Friday night and crossed his fingers in his pocket as Overbeck's heels clattered away down the corridor.

'So what's this Dr Woolwine like then, sarge?' someone shouted, once Overbeck was out of earshot.

'Imagine an all-American cheerleader with Einstein's IQ but who enjoys the company of the dead more than the living, and who thinks no rules apply to her at all. That's Woolwine in a nutshell.'

Chapter 10

Dr Connie Woolwine wandered through the woodland where the Weeping Girls had witnessed a man being attacked, dragged and buried in earthy airlessness, and wondered what had been in Laura Ford's beautiful, brilliant mind when she'd designed the statues.

Crime scene tape, that flimsiest and most arresting of barriers, warned visitors away from the death site, and it was due to be removed as soon as Connie had spent all the time she wanted there. The crime scene technicians had worked their magic, and a flag marked the spot where they'd found a solitary blood spatter on a rock at the base of a tree that had, miraculously, remained protected from the elements throughout the winter. DNA testing had linked the blood to the victim so that was where she stood, waiting for Brodie Baarda to approach her from behind.

She whirled around to face him. 'You're still five metres away. Were you not trained to be quieter than that in the police?'

'You were waiting for me and listening. Plus you were

standing in place, so not making any noise with your own feet. And I was a kidnapping specialist. When I wasn't negotiating, we were entering buildings by force rather than silently.'

Connie was being unfair and she knew it. Baarda was several inches over six foot tall, with broad shoulders and feet of a size ill-designed for silent passage over twigs and leaves. Since she'd started working with him, he'd lost the soft edges of a too-comfortable but bad marriage, and reclaimed the body of his younger self who'd played rugby for his county and lifted weights to exorcise his daily demons. Baarda, his short hair curly if not regularly cut, with cheekbones that women stared at even if he never saw it, was entering his prime in his fifties. He made Connie feel safe in a way she refused to admit even to herself.

'Pick up a stick,' she said, turning her back on him. 'And make it a good one.'

Baarda sighed. 'You know I hate re-enacting these things.'

'The victim's dead,' Connie said. 'You think he's looking down on us, disapproving?'

'I think if anyone walks up and sees us doing this, it's going to cause one hell of a scene.'

'Better not waste time then. Stick, approach, hit me – carefully, obviously – and you know the rest.'

Baarda picked up a good-sized stick that nonetheless looked non-lethal and sneaked up behind her. Connie listened to him approach and imagined the options. The victim might have had headphones in or been on a call. He might have been distracted by taking a photo or simply been deep in thought. His attacker might have been wearing the softest of trainers as opposed to Baarda's standard boots. Or he might have known the person who'd struck his skull so hard it had knocked the consciousness

46

right out of him. Known and trusted. Perhaps even liked. Maybe loved.

The stick tapped Connie on the side of the skull and she let her body tumble forward and diagonally away from the direction of Baarda's mock blow. She fell face first into the dirt, aware as she collapsed that the autumnal leaf bed would have made for a softer, more hushed landing.

Looking at the tree to one side of where the victim's blood had been found, presumably from his mouth or nose, she realised it might have been nothing more than a contact splatter as he'd hit the ground. She could see the base of a tree, hedgerows and the imprint of footsteps that had trod the path before. The earth tasted rich and peaty in her mouth, not altogether unpleasant save for the grittiness of its texture. She tried to spit it out and succeeded only in sucking the dirt further back in her throat.

'Drag me,' she ordered Baarda. She didn't need to see his face to know that he'd be rolling his eyes and clenching his jaw.

He took hold of her feet, though. It was part of her process, immersing herself in the whole of the crime, seeing what the victim had seen. Baarda had worked with her long enough not to attempt to persuade her out of it. She knew he still thought of her as something of a curiosity. They were from different worlds – his blood was aristocratic, his education from Eton. She hailed from Martha's Vineyard, Massachusetts. Her family had money too, but America wielded its finances in yachts and automobiles rather than boarding school places.

The difference in height between them meant that Baarda had to bend to avoid hurting Connie's back as he dragged her, but she still felt the full force of the movement through the mud, every sharp stone and piercing twig catching on her chin and her hands, and pulling her top upwards to leave marks on her stomach. She didn't fight it. The victim hadn't been able to. It took a disconcertingly long time to reach the shallow grave in the bushes, and she was relieved when he dropped her legs to kick a second demi-ditch with his feet next to the real gravesite.

'You okay?' Baarda asked her.

The victim would have been incapable of speech, she thought, refusing to answer. Baarda muttered to himself as he kicked dirt this way and that.

The birds had stopped singing. The woods were disturbingly quiet now. Nature had a consciousness, Connie thought, that went beyond startled animals fleeing and insects rolling into balls. Nature knew when bad things were happening.

Baarda stopped preparing the ditch, picked up her feet again and began pulling her backwards into the grave without issuing another word. Connie was working, and while it wasn't voodoo, it was a deep delve into psychology. She let her body go limp, took several deep breaths, and listened closely as Baarda fought his way through undergrowth, pushed straining branches aside, and got her in place before tossing leaves and earth over her.

Connie managed a full two minutes without breathing before heaving upwards, throwing off the soil blanket and gulping down oxygen.

'Stay still before all the dirt gets in your eyes,' Baarda said, kneeling in front of her and brushing the mess from her face. 'Connie, can you catch your breath?'

'Tell me how that felt for you,' she demanded, because that had been the point all along. Not the victim's perspective – although there was something wrong with the attack that Connie couldn't quite put her finger on yet – but the attacker's.

'Ah, that's why you made me do this. Well,' he was quiet

for half a minute, 'even though I'm bigger than you, and you don't eat enough, it still wasn't easy manoeuvring your body. Your clothes kept catching on things, and an adult human with arms out over its head is long and awkward. It's hard not to be aware of every bump and scratch your head took. God almighty, Connie, you're bleeding in five different places.'

'Ignore it,' she demanded. 'I need to know.'

'It was . . . functional,' Baarda said. 'Easier to think of it like a job than to let myself feel anything. Moving into the undergrowth was difficult because of the surface roots and vines. And I could hear you gasping for breath as I dragged you, that was the worst bit.'

'How did you feel when you were getting me into the grave?'

'It was annoying, I guess. Your body was so floppy that fitting all the bits in without more time and a spade was difficult. I wanted it to be over. It was very personal, pushing your limbs into the ground. Close contact. Especially when your body was still warm, that was odd.'

'Good,' Connie said. 'That's good.'

'It was a relief to step out of the bushes because then the branches sprang back into place and I wasn't fighting them any more. Your chin really is bleeding badly, and an infection from plants or bushes is actually much more likely than from a wire fence. We have to get you cleaned up.'

'Relax, my tetanus is up to date. So, good way to kill someone or bad way to kill someone?' Connie flicked leaves out of her hair and stood.

'Messy. Intimate. Not for the faint-hearted. You're aware of everything – twigs underfoot, insects attracted by hot bodies, the sound of your own breathing – and I ache, even though you're light and the victim would have been heavier.'

'And our actual attacker took the time to strip the victim of his personal effects, to cover their tracks as best they could, then they'd have had to tidy themself up before heading out, in case they bumped into any other visitors,' Connie said, pulling a small pack of wipes from her pocket and cleaning the grazes on her stomach, face and hands.

'Indeed,' Baarda said. 'So the perpetrator is organised, thoughtful, fit, and they didn't have time to pause or panic.'

'Yup. They'd thought this through just enough, but not to the extent that they'd hidden a garden spade here or pre-dug a grave. I think using this place was impromptu, but the killer knew what they were doing.'

'It's likely not a wife, partner or close relative of the deceased or they'd be having to answer questions about the disappearance to friends and family.' Baarda walked to the backpack he'd set next to a tree, took out a bottle of water, twisted the cap and handed it to her.

'You know, Baarda, I'm never going to want to get into an intimate relationship when you're already this thoughtful. What more could I ask for in a man than someone who's willing to haul me into a shallow grave then take such good care of me afterwards?'

'When you put it like that, I realise just how close our relationship is to being emotionally abusive,' he said. 'Did you get what you needed from this whole, horrific exercise?'

'Not enough,' she said. 'Still more questions than answers. But I know one thing. Someone wanted our victim dead. They needed to be done with him. There was nothing left to chance, from the blow to the head, to hiding the body and leaving him sucking in dirt. And when death is the aim, not robbery, not lashing out, not a passionate argument, it's usually because the attacker knew the victim in some way. So now we just have to figure out who the victim was. That's the only way this'll start to make sense.'

'Good. Can we go to the hotel now? I'd really like to shower before heading for the police station.'

'Sorry, no time.' Connie marched ahead of him. 'We have a date with a corpse.'

Chapter 11

26 May

Nate Carlisle studied Connie's reaction as he drew back the cover from Divya Singh's body.

'You don't have to worry about me, Dr Carlisle. Can I call you Nate? I've seen my fair share of corpses.'

'Please do. And I don't doubt it – your reputation precedes you – but the bodies here are my responsibility. Until I can be sure a visitor's not going to faint or vomit on a body, I'm careful.'

'Oh boy, you've had people vomit on a corpse?' Connie pulled a face fit for a playground. 'I would not want to clean that up. This carnage has to come a close second, though, right? Her body looks like it's been concertinaed.' She took hold of Mrs Singh's hand and stroked it with her thumb.

Her arms and legs were crooked in places no limb should ever be. The skin, in addition to the normal mottling that came with the after-effects of a lack of blood flow, was a battle-zone of bruising, cuts, caving and pressure. The flattened top of her skull had caused her face to compress. The result was the distortion of a fairground mirror, her features too wide and too close. If Divya Singh's life had begun as a blank piece of paper on which to write her story, now she was a crumpled ball of scrap, tossed carelessly away. She was the essence of a broken woman, and whoever had killed her was a living, breathing, hate-consumed monster.

Connie cautioned herself to knock off the hyperbole before she compromised her investigative edge.

'That was no way to end a life. Do you want to tell me what happened?'

'Well, the vehicle struck her at—'

Connie gave a short, low laugh. 'Sorry, I should have seen that coming. Not the vehicle, though I get the confusion. I was talking to my friend here.' She patted Divya Singh's hand.

Carlisle stared at her. 'Er, okay, did you want some privacy?'

'Depends how open-minded you are. I try to establish a close relationship with my clients, and I don't have time to persuade you about my methods or expertise. So, you in or out? No pressure.'

Carlisle studied the woman who was holding the hand of a corpse as if she was visiting a beloved aunt in hospital and comforting her. Connie was somewhere in her early thirties, hair pulled into a ponytail that looked to be more about efficiency than style. She was around five foot six and carrying not an ounce of spare weight, and it looked to him as if that was probably to do with living a life where she didn't stand still for a single moment. There was no make-up on her face, and granted she'd had to go and wash the second she'd arrived at City Mortuary having attended the Jupiter Artland murder scene, but he didn't think she was someone who bothered much with artifice. Dr Connie Woolwine was as much a force of nature as gravity, but with added attitude.

'I'll stay,' Carlisle said.

'Good. Because Mrs Singh seems lonely.'

'She was married with a son and grandchildren,' Carlisle said, walking across to stand the other side of the body, the closer to watch Connie's inspection.

'She might have been part of a family and living a comfortable existence, but her nails are ragged and slightly bitten and the skin on her hands is rough. The damage to her skull is appalling but even so I can see she hasn't had a haircut in forever. The hyperpigmentation on her face would have been easy to treat with high street products. There's no self-care happening, yet I checked out her postcode in your file and she's living in a middle-class area of the city. It's as if she didn't matter to herself. No one was buying her hand cream or treating her to a spa day. There was no loving younger generation keeping an eye on the softer parts of her life. She was just existing. That usually indicates an element of loneliness, don't you think?'

'I met with her husband and her son. They were devastated. I had no reason to think Mrs Singh wasn't loved.'

'Ah, you see, that's the thing. People loving you isn't the same thing as actively being loved. Ask any woman who looks after a house, kids, runs errands, holds down a part-time job, fights to make Christmas perfect, organises birthday parties, then everyone forgets when it's Mother's Day and she's supposed to smile and not make a fuss. Loving someone can be passive or active. The gulf between the two is light years.' She smoothed Divya's hair and tried to make it more shapely around her distorted skull.

'I get it. Tell me how that helps,' Carlisle said softly, curious rather than challenging her.

'I don't believe in random victim selection, Nate. Human

54

beings having free choice is something of a fallacy. Every single thing we've seen and experienced in our life pre-determines the choices we make later on. The brain is the ultimate blueprint for artificial intelligence. Learning is layered and mostly subconscious. I could ask if you want to meet me for a drink later. Your options are yes, no or rain check. You might think you need a few minutes to consider, but your brain has already selected its preferred pathway whether you know it or not. Mrs Singh's killer chose her. Whether it was a daughter-in-law who didn't like the way she was being treated or a group of empathy-free teenagers who wanted to know how it would feel to take a life, there was a selection process. It's the same thing with the Jupiter Artland victim. So the better the connection I have to a victim, the closer I get to the people who hurt them.'

Carlisle crossed his arms.

'I'm sorry if I made you uncomfortable. I do that. And no, I'm not asking you on a date over the body of a woman who didn't live the life I'd have wanted for her. The more emotional the decision, the more we strive to find the answer. It makes us explore our decision-making process more closely. If I'd asked if you preferred brown, granary or rye bread your neural response would have been much less sharp.'

'You like making people uncomfortable,' Carlisle said.

'Not like; it speeds up the knowledge process for me. I find it necessary to get to know people quickly to communicate with them effectively. Breaking barriers, reading faces, triggering responses, that all helps. Mrs Singh's body is so badly broken that it's hard to figure out exactly what was happening at the moment of impact. What did her cervical spine tell you?'

'I can show you the x-rays,' he said, walking over to a

computer and opening a folder. 'Here you can see the fractures that occurred when her head was snapped backwards with the force of the blow. Mrs Singh has relatively little body weight or muscle to protect from impact injuries. Her head flew straight back. It's a linear fracture of C5.'

Connie hadn't moved from her place at Divya Singh's side.

'What would the fracture have looked like if she'd been craning her neck at the moment of impact, to look back? Or if she'd turned her whole body and was facing the car as it hit her?'

'Her head would have gone to the side or forward, in which case the break would have been at more of a diagonal line. Or the start point of the break which has the widest part of the fracture would have been at the front of her neck, not the rear.'

Connie reached down and stroked Divya's Singh's cheek. 'How's your hearing, sweetheart?' she whispered.

Carlisle went back to the table. 'Her husband said it was fine. No hearing aid. She'd never complained about it.'

'Maybe it's better that you never saw it coming.' Connie ran a gentle hand down to the shattered legs, almost entirely blackened, which still bore the impact marks. 'Can we turn her over?'

Carlisle helped. Connie sighed as she took in the damage. Nate traced the line of the car's front bumper with his finger, straight across the backs of both thighs.

'It didn't clip her, didn't come from the side. The vehicle was right behind her and not braking at all. The multiple fractures and tissue damage have made it hard to get an accurate postmortem height, but her husband says she was only five foot two.'

'You were a feather,' Connie said. 'I bet you almost drifted down on the breeze. What do you know about the car?'

'Not much. Top of the number plate is about two inches up so not a four-by-four. There are no markings on Mrs Singh's body. Annoyingly the speed helped in that regard, because the impact was so sharp and severe that her body was thrown instantaneously. We've got some tyre substance on the pavement where the car mounted and that's being processed, but the chemical make-up we get back will likely apply to multiple car makes,' Carlisle explained.

'And the physics – what damage would the car have sustained?'

'The postmortem report will be referred to a vehicle collision specialist, but in the interim I can say a broken number plate is possible and a substantial dent in the front of the vehicle is certain. I doubt Mrs Singh even hit the windscreen. The pavement blood spatters show conclusively that she landed directly on the ground, not on the car first. Ultimately, it depends on the make of the car and how tough it is. Mrs Singh only weighs eight stone.'

'Okay,' Connie murmured. 'That's all I needed. Could you turn her over again, please?' Carlisle obliged.

Connie took both of the cold, dead hands in her own, pulling them across into the centre of the body and leaning over to look at her face. 'Divya, I hope you don't mind me calling you by your first name. Dr Carlisle and I are going to do all we can to find the person or people who hurt you. You're going to be taken care of, and as soon as possible, returned to your family to find you some peace. Dr Carlisle is a good man, and I'm happy leaving you here in his care, albeit that I'm sorry you have to wait here until this is resolved.'

Carlisle gently pulled the cover back over the body.

'Can we do some actual police work now or were you wanting to talk about feelings some more?' Lively asked from the doorway.

Connie swung round to face him, looked him up and down, and took her time responding.

'Long time no see, DS Lively. We didn't really get to know one another last time, did we? So let's see . . . you're in your mid-fifties, no wedding band, no white mark where a band once was. Your accent says you didn't grow up in one of the more affluent areas of Scotland. You probably have been married because thirty years ago marrying young was still a thing. Divorce rates being what they are in the police, though, I'm thinking early divorce, not friendly, and the wife was glad to see the back of all that overtime and the macho boys' club bullshit. It's all a distant memory for you. You don't have any kids, because kids wear the rough edges off people, and while the younger generation irritates those who've experienced parenthood, it makes them more tolerant.

'You've recently started exercising because your belt has just been pulled in a notch, and you're conscious of your body because even now you're trying to hold your gut in. I'm guessing that's not for my benefit or Dr Carlisle's. So there's a new woman on the scene, but from the pinched look on your face now that I've mentioned it, you're not in a relationship with her yet, probably haven't had the guts to ask her out. You do actually want to talk about your feelings because it was the first thought you had when you came in here, and the things we blurt out without thinking – even while being a smartass – are usually lodged in truth. Tell me again how talking about feelings and doing police work are two different things.'

She stripped off her gloves and suit, ditched them in the bin next to the door, and went to find Baarda who was in a meeting in a different part of the building.

'Fuck me, that woman's terrifying,' Lively said. 'We used to burn witches in Scotland. Does she not know this is dangerous territory for her?'

'Well, that might have been some sort of dark magic, or she might have been on a call with DS Salter for fifteen minutes earlier this afternoon. Either way, she shut you up, so I'd say that's one woman you don't want to mess with.' Carlisle slapped Lively on the shoulder and left.

Chapter 12

Lively was in a corner and there was only one way out. He grabbed the nearest weapon, picking up an axe, gripping it hard, and flinging it with every last vestige of the muscle he'd let soften over the years. He'd grown up knowing how to win a fight, and that knowledge meant he'd never had to spend hours in a gym or purchase illicit steroids to bulk up and look tough.

When he'd invited Beth Waterfall on a date, he'd pictured a bar, hopefully followed by a meal, or maybe a Sunday afternoon walk to a countryside pub, perhaps even a trip to the coast. He'd asked what she'd most wanted to do, and she'd replied by text with an address, a date and a time. It had taken him a full one minute checking and double-checking her text to be certain he was at the right place, until Beth had appeared beside him and asked if he was having second thoughts about the date.

Fifteen minutes later, after a cursory training session that would have given any health and safety training officer a fit of the screaming abdabs, he'd found himself standing at the end lane of a hall with a bar at one end and multiple targets at the other, each separated by netting that really didn't feel as secure as it should.

'Damn. If I'd known you were an expert, I'd have suggested a macramé class instead. I might have stood a chance at that,' Beth joked, picking up a smaller axe, more like an ice pick, and lobbing it at the far end of the lane. It bounced against the target but didn't take. 'To be fair, I'm better at precision work with blades,' she said. 'You got a bull's-eye first time. I guess that's the police training.' She took a sip of a non-alcoholic cocktail and grinned at him. 'I don't know whether to feel safe with you or scared of you.'

Lively thought the jocular smile she gave him didn't quite reach her eyes, and wondered if she'd ever had a reason to be afraid of men. It was far too early to ask such a personal question, but she'd made a point of not drinking alcohol and had arranged their date in a crowded, public place from which she could easily get a cab home. It was the sort of sensible advice for meeting a relative stranger that he'd give any woman. Faith in police officers to be decent human beings had reached an all-time low, a fact that hurt Lively's soul more than he wanted to admit. Personally, if he ever came into contact with a fellow officer who thought it was all right to put his hands where they weren't welcome, he'd rip their head off first and worry about what his defence was later.

'You all right?' Beth asked. 'You were a million miles away.'

'Sorry, this place has got my reactions all messed up. For the last thirty years, if I've seen anyone throwing anything with a passing resemblance to a weapon, I've tackled them to the floor and bundled them into a police van.'

'We can go if—'

'Absolutely not,' he said. 'I'm going to book the place out for my squad to let off steam. Besides, it looks like you need the practice.'

'I'm just getting warmed up,' she grinned. 'Step aside and let me show you how it's done.' She threw again. Lively took the opportunity to stand back and look at her.

Dr Beth Waterfall wasn't traditionally pretty. Lively's mother would have called her handsome, but that wasn't fair and it wasn't accurate. Her hair, when it wasn't restrained by a surgical cap, was greying at the roots but still brunette laced with red where it reached her shoulders in a practical bob. She had an angular jaw leading to a square chin, deep-set eyes and a straight nose that in profile made her appear both no-nonsense and chiselled. When she smiled, though, her eyes crinkled in a way that made Lively feel disorientated and vulnerable. He hated and loved feeling that way. It was a sensation from his teenage years, when girls had been mystical creatures that were terrifying and alluring in equal measure. The years and the job had desensitised him, he knew that. But then Beth Waterfall had smiled at him across . . . well, across a bleeding body, if he was being accurate . . . and if he was ever going to meet a good woman, wasn't that the only way it was ever going to happen for him?

The only mystery left was that she'd looked back at him the same way. A doctor – a surgeon no less – with all those years of book-learning behind her and all those letters after her name, had smiled at him as if they'd known one another instantly. Two days after Archie Bass's death, they'd met again at the mortuary on Cowgate to discuss his injuries. Dr Waterfall had listened to Lively asking endless, probably very stupid questions, and smiled at him through it all. Afterwards, they'd found themselves pausing outside a café without thinking about it, him holding the door so she could go ahead, then perching on tall stools to consume their drinks minus the awkward consideration of whether they wanted to dash off to their respective jobs or homes. It hadn't been a date, but it hadn't been work exactly, because when they'd concluded their coded, careful public chat about the body they'd just seen, they'd talked about themselves just enough for the other to know a few key things: they were both single, they were both workaholics, they were both people who found themselves living outside of social norms, and they liked each other.

'Your turn,' she said, offering him an axe, handle first.

'Okay,' he said, taking the axe and getting into position. 'But if it's another bull's-eye, I get to ask you a question. Still want to play?' The flirting felt clumsy, like wearing shoes several sizes too big, but he figured if he didn't at least try it, he'd be headed directly to what the younger officers called the friend zone.

'Deal,' she said.

Lively's aim was true. Beth folded her arms and gave him a challenging smile.

'Make it count,' she said.

'Fine. I guess my question is, are we two people who're involved in a case together and who're now passing a bit of free time together or is this—' The words croaked in his throat and he was reminded of all those painful school days when his voice was breaking. He tried again. 'Or is this what you might call an actual date?'

'Well, I guess it's only a date if we both think it's a date, although I'm out of practice so I could be wrong. I think the last time I went on a date was, um, maybe twenty-eight years ago with the man I ended up marrying. He left me after a decade, moved abroad and I almost never hear from him. My turn, but you have to answer my question if I get this within twenty centimetres of the board.'

Lively was grinning before she picked up an axe to throw. She managed to wedge it in the lower edge, and it stuck there for a few seconds before tumbling to the floor.

'It still counts,' she said. 'So what about you? When was your last date?'

'Depends what you think of as dating. I was married too, a very long time ago. I wasn't the best husband and I don't blame her for leaving me. Young police officers have a way of getting caught up in the job, the squad, and in the immediacy of it all. I didn't make enough time for the home stuff. Nobody tells you that's all that matters at the end of the day when you're busy living for the moment.' He shrugged. 'After that I had . . . I guess you'd call it a fling . . . on and off for a while with someone at work. No dating. She and her husband had an understanding. I was convenient for her and she was an excuse for me not to have to meet anyone in the real world. I didn't expect to be doing this again.' Beth offered him another axe that he took from her but laid back down on the weapons table. 'I'm glad I am, though.'

'I am too.' She smiled at him and bit her lower lip.

Lively's breath caught in his throat and he found himself unable to say a word.

A man brushed Beth's back from behind and she pulled away, shoulders up.

'Sorry love!' the man called.

Lively stepped forward and reached for her. 'I'm fine,' she said. 'Just, er, not used to so much noise and so many people. Ignore me.'

'Of course,' Lively said. 'How about we get out of here? We'll call it a draw.'

64

'That'd be good.' She grabbed her coat and bag.

Lively offered her a hand to lead her through the crowd that stood between them and the door, and when Beth Waterfall took it, he could have sworn that hers was shaking.

Chapter 13

Three Years Earlier

Molly Waterfall, Mol to her friends – and that accounted for almost everyone she met because life was fun and people were generally lovely – had started an online account selling her oil paintings. It had taken her a long time to overcome impostor syndrome but when she finally figured out that if no one wanted her art then no one had to buy it, nothing could stop her. She found an app, designed her sales page, settled on a price point that made her feel valued while remaining affordable, and went live.

She'd been a happy child. There had been a brief blip when her father had left, but the truth was that at ten years old, she'd been more worried about the effect it would have on her mother, Beth, than on his absence in her own life. He'd always been absent in the ways that mattered – at work, project managing large builds, or watching Aussie Rules football because that was where he was born and had lived until he'd moved to study at Edinburgh University and just never gone back. He'd played golf obsessively because that was his 'me' time, and at home he'd just been sleepwalking until the day he left. It was a Saturday. Mol and her mother had gone food shopping which they did every weekend if her mum wasn't on call at the hospital. They'd left the house for an hour and a half, during which time her father had packed all the clothes he wanted, his passport and important documentation, his vinyl records, a few of the trinkets he'd collected over the years, then left.

One hour and thirty minutes.

No note.

No forwarding address.

Mol remembered her mother assuming he'd gone to play golf before noticing that the record collection had gone. She'd started looking around more closely and spotting objects missing from shelves, notable only for the dust rings around the spaces they'd filled. The wardrobe had been what had really brought it home to her. Her poor mother, trying to make everything all right for Molly. Telling her she was sure he'd be back. Saying that people quite often went through a period when they felt the need to run away from the banality of their lives, but that sooner or later they returned home. Mol didn't care, as long as her mother was okay. She worked so hard, and not just in medicine. Dr Beth Waterfall was a parenting wonder. Every single day was about putting Mol first – uniform, homework, school trips, sleepovers, baking together, doing arts and crafts, admiring the endless (often terrible) paintings that Mol did as she found her path to a style that really suited her. Her mother was a ball of endless, calm energy and the sun, moon and stars in Mol's life. Her father had only ever been a silent, watchful spacecraft passing through their atmosphere.

Over the years, they'd not only recovered from his exit, but thrived. They were happier, closer and more grateful for one another than they'd ever been. It had been Mol's idea to go back to using her mother's surname. The day it had been made official – her father having been in touch through his parents briefly to consent to both that and the divorce – they'd travelled to London to go to the theatre, shop, have afternoon tea at the Four Seasons and stay for two nights at The Savoy. Life was not just sweet – it was a whole rainbow of flavours, each more surprising and exciting than the one before.

Her mother's career had blossomed without a man to make herself smaller for, and Mol was proud of the work her mother did in a way that filled her stomach, heart and head every time she thought about it.

In return, her mother's eyes would fill with tears on seeing each new painting or sketch, and it was a rare week when her mother didn't deliver more art supplies, get a piece framed, or bang another hook into a wall to display Mol's work. Theirs was a relationship built on mutual respect, admiration and absolute adoration.

Which was perhaps why the website and all its necessary social media and publicity had been such a shock.

Orders were slow to begin with. The ratio of time spent engaging in publicity exercises versus visitors to Molly's sales page was pitifully low. But then she'd joined a Facebook group resulting in a frenzy of amazing feedback. Some members of that group had shared her work elsewhere, and like bamboo roots, once word had started to spread, the coverage was unstoppable. She was invited to show her work at a local abandoned factory that had been converted into an uber-cool gallery with a DJ and a fire pit. From there, she'd joined an Edinburgh artists' group that met once a month by invitation only, a fact she was a little unhappy about because her friends were excluded from accompanying her, but better not to bite the hand that was feeding her. Then she was long-listed for an international prize, and suddenly she wasn't worried about her webpage getting hits any more. The problem was how few hours there were in a day and how much new work she could produce in line with demand.

She wasn't making a fortune, but for once the thing she loved as much as her mother loved saving lives was putting enough money in her pocket to pay a little towards the bills at the home she still shared with her mum, to put half aside into her savings account, and to allow for the prospect of a holiday. She'd always wanted to visit Byron Bay in Australia, to swim, breathe deep and watch the sunset spill all her favourite colours onto the sea. It was one of the few places her father had talked about with real passion.

At twenty-four years of age, Mol Waterfall was an artist. A professional artist, to her never-ending surprise, with a growing reputation, a studio, and a body of work that was well-regarded by people who knew a thing or two about brushstrokes. The *Sunday Mail* did a photoshoot in her studio. She tied her wayward, curly blonde hair up and stuck a paintbrush behind her ear, which was how she could be found most hours of the day, and the journalist called her work unique, timeless and deeply moving. A radio station invited her for an interview. A podcast called *For Artists Only* dubbed her Scotland's Turner-in-Waiting.

And that was when things started getting weird.

It began with a message from a stranger telling her how amazing her paintings were. It was always nice to get feedback, especially when someone took the time to write a personal message with details about her work. She'd answered briefly but gratefully. There was another message the next day, which she answered again equally respectfully. The third time, she kept her response short and polite but final in tone. He replied asking for her mobile number as texting was easier than social media, and at that point she'd stopped communicating but took a moment to look up the sender. Karl Smith was a common enough name for her to be unsure if it was really his or just an assumed identity. He hadn't specified his age or job, and the photos he'd posted were generic and probably copied from elsewhere. His profile was a dead end. For a week, he'd left her alone and she'd thought that was the end of it. Then there were more messages, demanding then flattering, bordering on childish then lofty and literary, a bizarre musical e-card sent to her business email address featuring a singing guinea pig. Mol ignored them all.

Then came the barrage.

'Dear Mol, You got bored fast. I put in so much time looking at your so-called art and giving you the confidence you need. You accepted that, then cut me out. You used me. The least you owe me is a conversation and an explanation. Please send me your personal email address and I'll let you have my number so you can call. Karl.'

She'd blocked him then deleted the message before anyone else could see it, feeling irritated and unsettled for an hour, before forgetting about it, because the following week was her mother's birthday and the present she'd ordered had arrived by courier.

That evening, on a different platform, another message arrived. It took her a moment to piece it together, because here the profile picture was different, and now he was spelling his name with a C, but there was no doubt as to the sender.

'Mol, really? You fucking blocked me? It's fine. If that's how you want to play this, then game on you arrogant, ungrateful bitch.'

She was crying before she reached the next sentence, and only the fact that some iota of self-preservation told her she needed to know just how bad it was getting kept her reading at all.

'Don't try blocking me again. You don't need to give me your number. I've got it. And a lot more besides. Soon. Carl.'

From the second she finished reading that message, nothing in Mol Waterfall's life was ever quite the same again.

Chapter 14

1 June

DS Salter jogged up the four flights of stairs to Lucy Ogunode's apartment on Leith's up-and-coming shoreline. The area had been transformed, albeit that there were plenty of locals concerned about the lack of affordable accommodation and starter homes. The sea views, good jogging paths, and growing village of Instagrammable restaurants and bars had turned the former dock area into a haven for thirty-somethings with good jobs and enviable mortgage capacity.

Lucy was standing at the door when Salter reached it and ushered her in with a finger over her lips.

'Baby's asleep,' she whispered. 'Can we talk in the kitchen?'

'Of course.' They crept through the lounge, past the Moses basket complete with sleeping angel, and into the compact but spotlessly clean kitchen.

'How old?' Salter asked, taking the seat Lucy indicated to her at the table.

'Four months. Coffee or tea?'

'Coffee, thanks. I have a little one at home myself. My place never looked as tidy as this though. I don't know how you do it.'

'My wife's the organised one. She's at work, so I try to minimise the chaos. Usually means a frantic half hour before she walks back through the door. Here you go.' She handed over a steaming mug and sat down opposite Salter. 'So you want to know about him?'

'Please.' Salter took out her notebook. 'You said you were ninety per cent certain it was a boy you went to school with?'

'Yeah, I mean, it's difficult because it's a reconstruction I guess, but it looks a lot like Dale. He lived just round the corner from us in Buckstone. Could I have another look? Do you have the picture with you?'

Salter took the printout from her pocket, unfolded it and slid it across the table. She had the digital version on her mobile, but her experience had always been that people trusted their eyes more when it came to paper images rather than digital ones. She let Lucy take her time considering it.

'I'm sure,' Lucy said. 'I just wish I could remember his surname. It started with an A, I'm positive. He really hasn't changed very much even though I haven't seen him for maybe fifteen years. We finished our Highers at the same time, then I went to uni in Stirling, but I don't know what he did.'

'So the two of you weren't close?'

She shifted in her seat. 'Not at all. No one was really close with him. I barely saw him in my last two years as we didn't have any subjects together. Before that, people kind of avoided him.'

Salter let that sit for a minute. Lucy had something to tell her, and it was best not to interrupt.

'Sorry, I just want to check on the baby.' Lucy got up, popped into the lounge, then sat back down. 'He was a bit creepy. And that's a horrible thing to say because he's dead now – assuming it's him – so I feel like a bit of a bitch.'

'That's not your responsibility,' Salter said. 'Why don't you tell me everything you—'

'Abnay!' Lucy cried, slapping a hand over her mouth immediately and looking in the direction of the lounge. 'Dale Abnay. That's it! I remember feeling sorry for him at primary school because he was always alone, and I was raised to be kind. Not everyone was. They called him "Horsey", which was horrible.'

Salter looked back at the picture taken from the specialist skull reconstruction and could see where the nickname had originated. Dale Abnay's face was long and thin, with a hooked nose that seemed to extend the length of his face. His eyes were slightly wider set than the average, and his jaw was very rounded at the bottom. Abnay hadn't had the easiest start to life.

'Do you know anyone who might have stayed in touch with him?' Salter asked.

'No one, definitely no females. He got a bit strange. Obsessive, you know? That's the only reason I recognised him. For a while, he used to hang around in the hallway between lessons and watch me. I don't mean he ever did anything, and most of the time he was just smiling. Sometimes he'd try and talk to me, but I was too embarrassed and struggling to come to terms with the slow realisation that I was gay. One day – he might have turned up at my house, but the memory is really vague – he asked me out and I just sort of blanked him. I think I was polite, but I don't really know. I was stupid enough to tell my mates about it and they took the piss out of me for ages. I don't think I ever saw him again after that.'

'Is that the last thing you recall?'

'There were rumours of him behaving weirdly towards other

girls after that. He didn't seem to take a hint or be able to read body language.'

'And how accurate is this facial reconstruction? It's relatively easy for us to get the basics right but we often get lips, eyes and the tip of the nose wrong.'

'I'd say the nose is right, but the skin is wrong. He suffered badly with eczema which was painful just to look at and also resulted in a ton of bullying. He had thinner lips than you've given him, and his eyes were a sort of tawny almost yellowish colour, like an animal's. I don't mean to sound so awful.'

'You don't,' Salter said. 'Did he have any particular hobbies? Was he on any sports teams at school, or was he part of the drama club or chess club?'

'He was more a watcher than a doer,' Lucy muttered. From the lounge, her baby began a rapid, reedy cry that Salter recognised as hunger.

'I'll let you go. Thanks for calling this in. We appreciate the help.'

'Did anyone else call after it was on the news? I mean, it's odd that he wasn't reported missing or anything. Makes me feel bad for him.'

'We'll try to figure that out,' Salter said.

She called in the identification as she headed back down the stairs. By the time Salter reached her car, they already had an address.

Chapter 15

1 June

'No one home,' Lively told Salter as she pulled up at the unit in the caravan park near Buckstone. 'Looks like you might have found our man.'

'We should let the superintendent know and ask her to expedite the entry warrant.'

'It's a caravan, not a house, and the man who lives there appears to be dead. Plus, he's on a database.'

Salter climbed out of the car and put on a fresh pair of gloves. 'A caravan is a house. We still need a warrant. And what database are you talking about? Does he have previous?'

'No convictions, but we have intelligence from an undercover online unit.'

'Sir,' a uniformed officer, who looked like they should still have been on the school football team Dale Abnay had avoided, called to them. 'I've knocked on a few doors. The other residents say Abnay lived here alone. The site manager hasn't seen him for a few months but his rent was paid by standing order so as long as no money was owed, no one was chasing him.'

'Good work. Now find me a flathead screwdriver,' Lively said.

'Sarge . . .' Salter broke off then sighed. 'Fine, whatever. I'm not going to talk you out of it, am I?'

'You've as much chance of stopping me as getting a drunk man to stop pissing halfway through his leak. Shall we?' He mock bowed and let Salter go first up to the caravan door.

Blackout blinds prevented them from seeing inside, and the young constable who was now on top of the caravan confirmed that even the roof window had been covered up.

'What was the database flag that Abnay's name came up on?' Salter asked.

Lively took hold of the screwdriver and wedged it into the crack between the door and the lock.

'He was a regular user of a website called WATFOR,' Lively said, putting his weight behind the screwdriver. 'Pull the handle.'

'You damage it, you'll have to make sure it gets fixed,' Salter said, getting a grip and making sure she was standing out of Lively's way. 'What's the website? I haven't heard of it.'

There was a metallic screech and complaining plastic, then Lively flew backwards and Salter took the full force of the door opening at her. She landed on her backside, with Lively laughing as he extended a hand to help her up.

'WATFOR stands for Women Are There For Our Recreation. Works in more than one sense, I guess.'

'Gross,' Salter said, brushing herself off.

Lively had already walked inside the caravan. 'Gross doesn't even start to describe it,' he replied.

Inside, the caravan was plastered in images of women, as if every edition of every adult magazine had been crammed into the tiny space and layered over one another. The only surface not covered in breasts or female genitals was the floor, and that was strewn with rubbish. At one end of the caravan was a small bedroom and at the other was a bathroom. The middle featured a kitchen unit to one side and a put-up table opposite with a computer. The only other furniture was a set of metal shelves crammed with old videos, DVDs and magazines.

'I don't even want to look,' Salter said.

'It ain't gonna be Shakespeare, that's for sure,' Lively muttered. 'This boy must have destroyed half the Amazon rainforest with all the tissues he was getting through.'

'Please shut up,' Salter said. 'Look, his computer's here. Let's see what we can find.'

'Good luck with that. We'll need a password. It'll have to go to the nerds.'

'Is it any wonder the tech department hates you?' Salter asked. 'And actually, we might not. Look at this.' She peeled a grubby Post-it note off the top of the computer screen and waved it at Lively. 'Apparently Mr Abnay struggled to remember his many passwords.'

'That'll be the only thing he and I have in common,' Lively said. 'Let's see then.'

Twelve different passwords with a variety of numbers and special keys in different places had been scrawled next to web addresses, but at the core of them was always the word Thailand.

On the home screen, Lively began typing a variation of the word with different digits. 'Thailand01!' released the holding image and revealed a page with quick links to a jumble of different sites.

'Girls Being Bad, Girls Being Punished, Girls Taking a Beating, Girls Getting What They Deserve, Girl Slaves . . .'

'It's incel central,' Salter said. 'I suddenly feel a lot less sorry about him being shoved face down into a shallow grave.'

'And we suddenly have several million suspects. I'm not sure there's a woman in the UK who wouldn't have wanted to put

78

this dickless wee bastard into the ground. Hold on, I'm into his email. He was a food delivery driver. Probably left him free most days, working evenings and weekends.'

'With access to lots of women's addresses,' Salter said. 'What do you know about the undercover operation? They can't compile intelligence for website use alone. He must have been suspected of committing a criminal offence.'

'They were planning a party,' Connie said as she entered. 'You got into his computer already? I didn't have you pegged as that technologically knowledgeable, DS Lively.'

Both Salter and Lively automatically stood. Connie exuded something undefinable that made people respond that way.

'He left us his passwords,' Salter explained. 'Dr Woolwine, about the entry, we were concerned that vital evidence was in danger of being lost if we didn't enter immediately so there wasn't time—'

'Hey, you're not answerable to me. I'm only here to deal with the offender side of things. But warrants don't matter if there's no risk of defence counsel striking out a charge, and given that Mr Abnay is never going to be arrested for anything, even though he clearly should have been, I really don't care how you got in.' Connie gave a low, appreciative whistle as she looked up at the crudely decorated ceiling. 'This man was never breast fed, and he never got past first base with a girl. It's like an Oedipal crisis centre in here. Such a shame that insects destroyed his penis before he ever got a chance to use it.'

'I take back everything I said about her,' Lively muttered to Salter.

'Don't do that,' Connie said, slapping him on the back as she moved past him to get into the bedroom area, snapping on gloves as she went. 'I much prefer my male underlings to dislike me. Keeps everything that little bit more edgy.' She gave Salter a wide grin as she began pulling out Abnay's bedside drawers. 'Man, for a guy with no chance whatsoever of getting laid, this guy was holding onto a lifetime supply of condoms. It's good to know he didn't die without hope.'

'What was the party he was planning, ma'am?' Salter asked.

'It's Christie, right?' Connie asked. Salter nodded. 'You don't have to call me ma'am. We're equals here. In my hometown, if you get called ma'am you're either past your eightieth birthday, you teach at the high school, or you've really pissed off law enforcement.'

'The latter might well apply to you to be fair,' Lively smirked.

'And that's why *you* get to call me ma'am every time you speak to me,' Connie countered. 'The WATFOR group have spent the last six months contemplating how to kidnap multiple prostitutes at the same time on the same evening, delivering them to rural woodland and engaging in what they call a rape-chase.'

'Holy shit, it never ends,' Salter said. 'Aren't those women's lives hard enough without people planning to do that to them?' She pulled the kickboard away from below the oven and took out a package wrapped in brown parcel paper, peeling the layers away carefully. 'He's got a Taser and a flick knife here. He was either expecting something or preparing for something.'

'And we have a ball gag, cable ties and a blindfold in the bedside table, although they look unused which isn't surprising in the circumstances. There's not a woman alive who would come in here and not realise immediately that she was dealing with a man who would be as capable of giving her pleasure as a snake is capable of juggling. God, these bedcovers smell disgusting. Lively, see if there's any clue on his email as to his mobile number, and get the tech squad to examine his computer in situ. I don't want to risk turning it off and on again. The hard drive has to be copied as a priority.'

'Actually, ma'am, we shouldn't move the computer at all. If he's accessing those incel sites through a specific network here, we don't want to change his IP address. He might get shut out and we probably won't get back in,' Lively said.

Connie stood, put her hands on her hips, and gave a low whistle. 'Nice, sergeant. Not just a pretty face then.'

'It's called police work, in fact. It's my speciality.' He folded his arms and stared at her.

'Ooh, I'm sensing a challenge. What's your first name, sergeant? I don't think I ever heard anyone use it.'

'Lively,' he said.

'Okay, Lively Lively it is. You're a sceptic, that's fine. I actually think that's a healthy starting point.'

Salter stopped what she was doing and turned to watch. Connie Woolwine sat in the middle of the caravan, cross-legged on the floor, and closed her eyes for a moment.

'Shut the door would you please, Christie?' Connie asked.

When the place was dark, Connie took out her mobile and shone the torchlight at the ceiling.

'Dale Abnay isn't whole. He's not a whole man. Look at the layering of images here. He's plastered over other women, leaving only their sex organs on display in many cases. These are pieces of women. He was craving the idea of a woman, the one part of them he'd never had access to. But it's also a reflection of him not being a whole man. The only piece of himself he could focus on was his penis because there was this huge element of himself that wasn't being used as it was intended. And he knew with absolute certainty that he was never going to get a woman back here willingly, because there's no way the place would look like this if he thought that might happen.'

She switched off the torch and sat quietly in the darkness for half a minute. Neither Salter nor Lively disturbed her.

'Do you smell that, beneath the odour of soiled sheets and the food that's burned onto the bottom of the oven?' She breathed in deeply. Lively and Salter did the same. 'There's musk and sandalwood. Something with a hint of spice to it and warmth, like cedar and cinnamon. Know what that is?'

'Aftershave?' Salter offered quietly.

'Yes and no,' Connie said. 'It's actually something much more toxic. It's hope.'

'The wee fucker still thought he might get some,' Lively said. 'Even with all this shit over his walls.'

'Exactly. It was a delusion, and a dangerous one, because he was still hopeful, and every time that hope was unfulfilled and his attentions went unrequited, Abnay grew more angry and more lonely and more desperate. He turned to his incel groups online to find men like himself because misery loves company.'

'Was he dangerous? I mean, given the opportunity, would he have been a threat to a woman on her own?'

Connie stood and moved across the caravan to open the door. Fresh air flowed in with the daylight and as one they drew in a new breath.

'It's possible that's what he was trying to figure out,' Connie said. 'Given what we know about Dale Abnay now, I'm not sure he strikes me as the hiking and art appreciation hobbyist that Jupiter Artland normally attracts.'

'So what was he doing there?' Lively asked.

'That's my question too,' Connie murmured. 'Maybe fantasising about how it would feel to chase women through woodland? The question is, did he go there with someone, or did someone follow him, or did something happen while he was there that enraged someone enough to kill him?'

A uniformed officer entered at a run. 'Something's happening in the centre of the city,' she blurted.

Chapter 16

1 June

'That escalated fast,' Lively said. 'Salter, this one's yours.'

'Oh no, you've got that man-of-the-people thing going on,' Salter replied. 'Plus, you're more senior than me by long service. This is definitely on you. Go ahead and show me how it's done.'

They looked out of the window of the police van at the crowd stopping traffic in York Place. It was a centre point for traffic flow, with access to Edinburgh's newest shopping centre on one side, a multiplex cinema on another, and a variety of restaurants, shops and cafés scattered around. The protest was a flashpoint waiting to explode. On one side, men, women and children held banners with Divya Singh's name printed in bright letters, some with a photo, others with slogans. In their midst, a man was standing on a makeshift stage and shouting into a loudspeaker.

'Justice is white!' he yelled. 'Where is the hunt for Divya Singh's murderer? What do we have to do to be seen? What do we have to do to matter? It's time to make our voices heard! It's time we demanded action! Divya deserves better – we all do. Because next it will be your wife or mother or sister. Divya Singh must be avenged!'

The crowd roared, raised their banners and fists, and pumped the air.

In response, an equally large crowd yelled back and began pushing against the barrier of uniformed officers that had been hastily assembled as part of the city's crisis management protocol. Those were largely men, but there were a handful of women in the throng, and they used their voices and their faces in lieu of banners. No one needed their perspective put in writing to comprehend what was going on. The far right was out in force, the racist name-calling had begun, and it could only be a matter of minutes until someone threw something. There were paramedics standing by, but Lively didn't like their chances of intervening once the blue touch paper was lit.

'There's going to be blood spilled,' Lively said. 'How many more officers can we get out here?'

'We've got extra bodies coming in from Glasgow now but they won't be here for an hour. Any off-duty units are being asked to come in to field calls beyond this event, and armed units are getting in place in concealed vantage points in case anything happens,' Salter said. 'If you're going to do something, sarge, now would be the time.'

'Right, get me the organisers of the Divya Singh rally. Make it clear they're in no trouble and that we agree the community needs answers. If we can turn down the gas a little, we might just be able to disperse this thing. And I want cameras – publicly positioned but in safe zones – recording the faces of everyone in the anti-protest. I want them to know we mean business. Anyone gets out of hand, we'll be able to identify them.'

He took another look out of the window as Salter began issuing commands. Within the growing crowd, the more savvy of the troublemakers were already wearing balaclavas, which was all the evidence Lively needed that the call had gone out across the city to get there fast and be prepared for a fight. Edinburgh was a good place, a city that took pride in inclusivity, tolerance and kinship, but there was the same undercurrent everywhere that whipped up discontent and turned it into hatred faster than you could get out your ASP.

Lively climbed out of the van with his stab jacket and helmet on, much as he'd have preferred to do things the old-fashioned way, with a wing and a prayer. It seemed to him that putting on armour gave the impression that you wanted a fight, rather than doing your best to avoid one. He made his way round the back, through a corridor of uniformed police, to where the Divya Singh protestors had their centre of operations, and saw Salter ahead of him, figuring out who to speak with. He was shoved from one side and elbowed from another, but the contact was accidental or careless rather than malicious. A couple of minutes later, a man and woman were brought to him. He extended a hand, which they stared at rather than shake.

'I'd like to talk, if we can find a better place to do so,' Lively said. 'I appreciate how you're feeling, and my officers are in attendance for your protection. We have no desire to escalate this and we're not planning any arrests. What I am keen to do, is hear you out. I might have information that will help, and you might have some ideas as to how we can better serve your community.'

Salter was looking at him strangely, and Lively felt the warm, slightly sickly glow of approval. Had he not been mid-negotiation, he'd have told her to sod off, even if there was some strange part of him that was enjoying the moment.

'Why did it take this for you to listen to us?' the woman asked. 'And why should we believe that you're interested in anything other than getting us out of the public eye? We've got journalists coming, including at least one TV station. They're going to be interviewing us.'

'I'm glad. Anything that brings attention to the case might help us resolve it sooner. But it's not fair to be doing this in public view. We have a duty to Mrs Singh's family, and I don't want them getting the impression that we're discussing the case without their knowledge or consent.'

'This isn't just about Divya. Our community is consistently ignored when it comes to policing and nothing changes until—'

The missile hit Lively square in the neck and cut through flesh.

He went down knees first, followed by the muffled thud of a body hitting tarmac.

Chapter 17

1 June

Brodie Baarda walked a little behind Connie Woolwine as she strode through the hospital corridors, leaving a wake of some perfume he couldn't name and a slipstream of purposefulness.

She had legs long enough to catch the attention of most men and plenty of women, hair that she most often wore in a ponytail, swinging in rhythm with her footsteps, and a smile that could disarm pretty much anyone. But all of that was just window-dressing.

Beneath her favourite jeans, worn so often they were thinning and faded, and the suede jacket that really wasn't fit for Scotland's changeable weather and propensity to rain even when the sky appeared cloudless and blue, was a person so intuitive and intelligent that she took his breath away not just daily but sometimes hourly. Connie was a force of nature.

'If you walk behind me like that, people are gonna think you're my bodyguard. Something on your mind?' she called over her shoulder.

'Just thinking about the cases,' Baarda lied. In truth, the

cases they were in Edinburgh to help with were relatively straightforward compared to their usual projects, and he was grateful for that. Connie and he had been living life at rollercoaster pace for the two years since she'd asked him to take retirement from the Met and partner with him. They'd seen their fair share of trouble in that time, and more than once Baarda had believed that he was going to lose her. More than that, far more worrying in fact, was his bubbling subterranean stream of belief that Connie Woolwine did not fear death.

She'd stared it down often enough that he had begun to think she relished the fight, and what he knew (and she refused to be told) was the fact that it was a battle you could join only so many times without taking a mortal blow. Connie, he believed, was someone who needed to stare death down perhaps to persuade herself that being alive was the better option.

So a slowdown was good. Taking a breath was good. The opportunity to see his children other than through a video call from an airport or on dodgy hotel Wi-Fi was amazing. He'd had a whole week with them immediately before heading up to Edinburgh while his ex-wife was on honeymoon with her new husband, a former Met police colleague of his.

He hadn't imparted that gem to Connie yet. She had an unnerving way of taking one look at him and telling him how he felt about things, before he'd even started to admit such feelings to himself. Sometimes that was therapeutic, sometimes it was necessary, and occasionally it was just plain annoying. If Baarda had to choose a single phrase to sum up Connie's USP it would be her ability to cut to the chase. He just preferred her not to do it to him – not that his feelings on the matter would ever stop her.

'You wanna take point on this one? Lively might respond better to some good old-fashioned male banter than to my method of communicating.'

'Because I'm so good at engaging in "over-a-pint"-style machismo?' he replied. Connie laughed and paused so they were walking in step. 'I've met officers like Lively too often to play tactically with them. He only gives people grief if he thinks they're up to the challenge. If he doesn't bother with you, that's when there's a problem. The detective sergeant really rather likes you, but you knew that already.'

'You're awfully serious today, Brodie. Tell me what's going on in that Old Etonian head of yours.' She slipped one arm through his to walk closer by him.

Baarda stole a glance at her profile as they walked. It wasn't like Connie to initiate physical closeness. She kept her distance most of the time, reaching out psychologically rather than bodily whenever she could manage it. There were dark circles beneath her eyes he was unused to, and her smile seemed fixed rather than organic. His stomach turned to a hard knot in his abdomen. She wasn't herself and he didn't like it.

'My wife remarried. She's encouraging the children to call him Dad. I've always been Daddy, and apparently that's enough of a distinction for her.'

He hadn't meant to tell her, but his concern for her, and his need to hide that from her, had forced the revelation from his mouth unguarded.

'Wow. She finally did something that made you genuinely angry instead of feeling like you should be angry even when you didn't really care.'

'Connie, now's not the time,' he said as she tightened her grip on his arm.

'Now's exactly the time. Want me to help you process that? You know you didn't really care all that much when she cheated on you. The love was already dying. Your children, on the other hand, are strictly off-limits.'

Baarda let her do it. When they'd first met he'd mistaken Connie's therapy sessions for either precociousness or over-intensity. It had taken a while for him to understand that part of it was Connie's method for self-soothing. She had found her identity in psychology – in being able to read and decipher other people's innermost thoughts and channelling them into the open where she could transform them into something that could be handled or come to terms with. He had long since suspected that it was the way Connie had coped when she herself had been committed to a psychiatric ward aged eighteen, when she'd found herself unable to communicate courtesy of a misdiagnosed brain injury.

How terrifying it must have been for her, locked inside a fully functioning brain. She rarely talked about it, and when she did, it was usually by way of an aside or a joke. The price she'd paid for recovery via neurosurgery was the loss of her colour vision. Her post-hospitalisation life was entirely lived in black and white, both literally and metaphorically, Baarda thought. She had dedicated herself to trying to rid the world of the mad and the bad, and it was as though if she ever stopped, she might end up back on that ward again.

'Things really must be serious if you're not going to tell me to mind my own business,' she nudged him.

'Okay then, mind your own business,' Baarda murmured, not even attempting to suppress his smile as they approached a door. 'Lively should be in here.'

'Saved by the grumpy detective with glass in his neck,' Connie raised her eyebrows. 'You know this conversation isn't over, don't you?'

'I'd be disappointed if I thought it was,' he said. 'After you.'

He held the door as she went ahead, catching himself once more in the grey zone between being gentlemanly and being patronising.

They were worlds apart. Connie was a hummingbird, perpetually in motion, flitting this way and that, sharp and purposeful, beautiful and elusive. He, on the other hand, was a Labrador. Loyal, trustworthy, constant, with the possibility of fierceness only when called for. He belonged to her now.

The sudden realisation was disconcerting. He would take a bullet for Connie Woolwine. Any number of bullets, in fact. Part of that was his job. Part of it though – the larger part – was something more primal and undefined. Baarda took a deep breath and followed her in. Had he been able to take his eyes from the figure of Connie disappearing behind a curtain, he might have seen the man who had been following them down the corridor.

The opportunity slipped past unrealised, and a chance to protect Beth Waterfall went unclaimed.

Chapter 18

The Watcher

1 June

Hospitals were about as secure as supermarkets, only with less CCTV for patient privacy. He liked them for that reason, but also because there were endless options for foolproof disguises that ensured he wasn't noticed going there too regularly. He could buy the same scrubs from the internet that matched the ones worn by various medical staff, and the ID tags were so easy to replicate – at least on a superficial level – that it was a joke. Not only that, but there was a non-stop stream of public transport to a hospital so he didn't have to risk parking his car where the number plate could be recorded. The icing on the cake was the numerous entrances and exits, and he was careful to use a different one every time. Pretty much the only places he'd never been able to access were the surgical area and the maternity and paediatric wards. They'd actually thought about the need for cameras where there were babies and children, terrified of the prospect of someone deviant making off with a child. The greatest threats, though, were always those presented in plain sight.

The protest in York Place had been a blast. It was always

fun seeing people whipped up into a frenzy, and a bit of light relief away from both home and following Beth. He'd attended with fake tattoos on his arms and neck, tinted glasses, a cap that covered his upper face and disguised his hair, and clothes that positioned him squarely within the far-right brigade. He'd foreseen much of what came to pass but not the arrival of Detective Sergeant Lively, who'd been getting far too friendly with Beth Waterfall. They'd had dinner together at least twice, and that was just when he'd been free to follow them. He'd been planning on doing something about that even before the protest, but then fate had intervened.

Hidden deep within the crowd, he'd been able to help the violence along a little, starting some chants that inflamed the perceived injustice of a single group being given a moment of necessary priority. The glassing of Lively's neck by some random protestor with an impressive throwing arm, however, he couldn't have set up no matter hard he'd focused on manifesting it.

That had caused him some internal conflict initially. He'd been unable to resist going to the hospital, but didn't have enough time to be sufficiently cautious about his approach. He couldn't risk being recognised by Beth, but how could he resist seeing her man, pale and fading, in a hospital bed? That's if he hadn't already died. There was enough blood flowing from the wound at the protest to have police and paramedics yelling at one another to move. Who knew how Beth would react if she lost another soul? Imagining her pain made him salivate.

The tattoos, he figured, would be disguise enough to get him through the hospital without being recognised from his previous multitude of visits, but there would be police in situ too and he didn't want to draw their attention. To reduce the impact, he'd pulled on an old denim jacket from his boot, left his car on a side road, walked in using the x-ray department entrance then took the convoluted back corridors to get to where he figured Lively would be. There was security to get through into accident and emergency, but attaching himself to a group of other visitors being allowed in had never been hard. Experience had taught him that if he simply looked terribly upset, no one wanted to ask him hard questions about his purpose.

As luck would have it, a man and a woman were walking ahead of him in exactly the right direction. There were two entrances to A&E. Using the normal route required you to go past reception, electronic check-in machines, and a waiting area full of the coughing, sleepy, groaning sick. The rear entrance, used by staff coming and going from the surgical wards and pharmacy, was only accessed by members of the public allowed to accompany their loved ones who were being taken elsewhere. It was rare to approach A&E that way, but not unheard of.

He followed the couple up the corridor, the man hanging back slightly, staring intently at the woman. If they hadn't been exchanging the odd sentence, he'd have thought the man was stalking her. The woman was striking and well aware of the fact, tossing her ponytail around and taking long strides to highlight her perfect legs. He felt sorry for the man who was in her thrall. She was teasing him as she walked, preening and peacocking, even slowing down to make physical contact with him, threading her arm through his.

Women wanted all the attention they could get from a man, until they actually got it.

The poor bastard even held the door open for her, standing back to give her plenty of space. She just breezed through without a thought.

He might have made a comment, if it hadn't given him the perfect opportunity to enter directly behind them as if part of their group.

They were ahead of him now by only a few metres, looking between curtains for whoever they were visiting.

And it seemed the universe wasn't done with him for the day. The man and woman stepped between curtains to greet a patient. It was only when he got close that he could hear Beth Waterfall's voice providing them with the details of Lively's injury.

He raised his hand to his face instinctively, covering the move with a rub of his eyes and turning his face away.

Not before he'd seen Beth perched on the edge of Lively's bed though. Not before he'd seen her holding one of his hands. Not before he'd realised that the man and woman who'd been walking in front of him were not normal visitors at all, but investigators involved in Lively's cases.

The sole upside had been Lively's face, as pale as the white plastic curtains either side of his bed, and his neck wrapped tightly in dressings. His eyes were barely open, and there was more than one bag attached to the drip stand at his side. One for saline, another for painkillers, was his non-medical guess. Lively's former larger-than-life presence had been diminished to a mere whisper.

That was good. That made him happy. He walked on through A&E not stopping, not speeding up, aware only that he should keep his head down to avoid any cameras and make his way home as soon as possible.

His old-style digital watch was beeping at him, and that meant his father needed him. He had responsibilities to discharge. Playtime was over.

Chapter 19

2 June

They gathered outside the police station, behind the main building, between smokers' corner and the bike racks. June was proving to be elusive in terms of sunshine, so they huddled in coats and wished the wind would die down. Present were not just the Major Incident Team's detectives, but civilian support staff, uniformed officers who'd been assigned to the day-to-day tasks murders threw into the standard policing mix, and a couple of senior officers including Detective Superintendent Overbeck. She was the only person completely unaffected by the low temperature. Baarda was at the back of the pack and Connie was waiting inside, delaying her appearance just long enough to make sure she'd have everyone's attention.

She walked out with the sleeves of her white cotton shirt folded up and her ankles bare between her three-quarter-length jeans and tennis shoes.

'Due respect, ma'am, this isn't California. You should maybe go on a continuing professional development course to prepare you for the Scottish weather,' someone shouted.

'Does everyone want to stand here while I waste your time being witty and sarcastic to the officer who thinks Scottish weather jokes are still funny?' There were a few muttered 'Shut the fuck up's from the vicinity of the offending idiot. 'Good. Now you can all come back in. Briefing room please, two minutes, and make sure y'all exhaust your venting on the way. Anyone who doesn't take me seriously will be filling in for Superintendent Overbeck's assistant for the next month.'

The immediate silence was gratifying. Every pair of eyes slid towards Overbeck for a response which was nothing more than a nod of quiet touché in Connie's direction.

Connie held the door open for the herd, who jogged half-heartedly along the corridor and up the two staircases to the briefing room and the board that was separated into three segments, each with a picture of one of the deceased in its centre.

'Walk with me,' Overbeck purred at Connie as she went inside. 'I gather you saw Lively in hospital. Am I losing yet another of my squad or is he salvageable?'

'The problem isn't getting him back to work, it's stopping him,' Connie said. 'The surgeon's concerned about how weak his blood vessels will be for a while. He should really stay on a desk for at least a month after he's back. He was adamant about discharging himself against medical advice.'

'The man's a liability.' Overbeck sighed. 'You and your sidekick had better come up with the goods quick-smart.'

Connie flashed her a dazzling smile. 'My sidekick. Gosh, now I feel like I'm entitled to some sort of cape or maybe a flying car. Hey, I like your nails. That's quite some signal you're sending out.'

Overbeck instinctively glanced down at the false nails she kept long and pointed, with a burnished gold polish.

'It's called finishing. Apparently, in spite of your impressive

CV and list of accomplishments, that's not something you concern yourself with.'

'I really don't, but that isn't finishing. As mammals go, we're pretty underwhelming in terms of physical prowess. Most dangerous animals retract their claws because they're purely functional. Human females, and a few males, have evolved nail-signalling only relatively recently. Whether you realise it or not, you're flashing a sign that says I'm a great lover but I also bite; submit or beware. Very much how you present at work.'

'Kill me now,' Overbeck muttered.

'Is that something you think about often? Being killed?' Connie asked. Overbeck took the depth of breath she reserved exclusively for either screaming or sacking someone. 'I'm kidding, but that was fun. Note to self – you're not a fan of self-exploration. Let's do this.'

She walked into the briefing room and let Overbeck slip inside to lean against the door she closed behind them both. Connie walked to the board, pulled out three sheets of paper from her pocket and, next to each murder victim's living photo, added an image of them taken at the mortuary.

'Good morning. I've added the above images as a constant reminder to us all of what was done to them and what was taken from them. It's easier for us to look at living images, but what we need is a visual reference of what death looks like.' There were some coughs and shuffles, but most people simply looked at the board in silence. Connie gave them all a minute to take it in. 'Thank you for joining me outside earlier. By now, you should all be feeling a little more alive. This room is overheated, the windows are stuck, and while we try to find the murderers of Dale Abnay, Archie Bass and Divya Singh, I'm banning all egg, fish and cheese products from the room.' That produced a round of cheers that Connie waved away. 'It's not even a joke. I need you all focused and anything that makes this room feel less than fresh and inspiring is stopping you from working effectively. Environment is important. Minimise your sugar intake while you're here, get outside on your breaks, reignite your brain, shift some blood around your bodies.'

'Never mind the air quality, what we need is proper pay for all the overtime we're having to put in,' a uniformed officer commented.

'I agree, and I'm pleased to be able to tell you that Superintendent Overbeck has confirmed that every hour you spend here will be fully recompensed and there'll also be a package to make sure you're offered vacation to make up for the interruption to your home and family time.' Connie looked across to Overbeck whose lips were pressed so tightly together the muscles in her jaw were visibly quivering.

DS Christie Salter got to her feet. 'We all appreciate that, ma'am. Both ma'ams. I'm not sure what the plural is.' Salter allowed a beat for everyone to smile and, just like that, even Overbeck relaxed again. 'Could I add to your ingredient list an obligation for everyone to wear an additional layer of deodorant as we've more bodies than usual in this room?'

'Done,' Connie agreed.

'So what do you need from us in return?' Salter asked.

Connie could have kissed her. Not that she was afraid to give orders, but being invited to do so always made for a softer landing.

'Lively will be missing for a few more days, and when he comes back he'll be restricted to desk duties only. In his absence, DS Salter will be in charge of police operations, and Baarda and I will be heading up intelligence and investigation structure. The superintendent will be overseeing, of course, but given that we've just hit the start of the summer, the city will be soon be flooded with tourists and the crime rate will soar. That means we have to maximise the resources we have to resolve these three murders quickly and efficiently.'

The door opened behind Overbeck and a woman pushed in past her. Her hair and clothes were dishevelled, her face was flushed dark and she was breathing as if she'd just run up several flights of stairs.

'Who's in charge here?' she demanded, staring straight at Connie who was the obvious target, front and centre of the room with everyone focused on her.

'Are you all right, miss?' Salter asked. 'Do you need help?' The woman ignored her.

'It must be you. You're the one they're all looking at.' She jabbed a finger in Connie's direction.

'I'm Dr Connie Woolwine,' she said. 'You look distressed. I'd like to help. Shall we find—'

The woman stepped forward, swung her arm back and slapped Connie full force with an open palm. Connie staggered but didn't fall and turned to face the woman again.

A millisecond of pause followed, then every chair scraped and feet stampeded in an effort to rush forward and grab the offender.

'No!' Connie yelled. 'Stay where you are.'

'Not in my police station,' Overbeck overruled her. 'This is a security threat. How did you get through from the public area?' she demanded. The woman said nothing. 'Restrain her and arrest her for assault.'

'My fault, ma'am. Ever so sorry,' PC Biddlecombe panted from the corridor. 'This lady's your ten a.m. meeting. I only left her alone in your office for a minute, because I was bursting—'

'Biddlecombe, how the hell have you not been fired yet?' Overbeck hissed.

'Could we just take a beat?' Connie shouted. 'Biddlecombe, who is this woman?'

'This is Jane Bass, ma'am. Archie Bass's sister.' Biddlecombe's voice was little more than a mutter, but the import of it carried through the room.

'Let Ms Bass go, please,' Connie said. Overbeck didn't argue and the officers released her and stepped a good distance away. Salter picked up the handbag that had been on Jane Bass's shoulder and handed it to her gently before stepping silently behind her and pulling the mortuary photo of her brother from the board.

Jane Bass was panting like a bull about to charge, shoulders high, knees slightly bent, chin down to her chest.

'Slap me again,' Connie said, so quietly that only those at the front of the room caught it.

'Don't even—'

'Thank you, superintendent, but I don't need your intervention,' Connie said, equally quietly. 'Ms Bass. You're not going to get in any trouble here today. I'm asking you to put your faith in me and let me help you. Slap me again. It's all right. You have more than fifty witnesses.'

Jane Bass raised her right hand in front of her face and stared at it as if unsure what it might do. Baarda had moved forward so he was positioned just behind Bass, and was staring intently at Connie.

'No one else moves,' Connie said. 'No one,' she directed at Baarda. 'Ms Bass, I promise that if you do as I say, we can make some progress. I know you don't know me, but I do know quite a lot about what I'm asking from you. Slap me ag—'

The woman didn't wait for Connie to finish the instruction. The noise of the impact ricocheted off the bare walls like a bullet. Connie's head turned with the blow, but her feet stayed where she'd planted them. There was a mass intake of breath.

Jane Bass, rigid and trembling, opened her mouth to speak but emitted only a fading squeak. Connie held firm as Archie Bass's sister tried, and failed, to breathe. Sobs made her chest convulse but wouldn't exit through her mouth. Her hands were balled into fists as she brought them to either side of her face like a boxer on guard.

Connie extended her arms but did not approach. It took a full minute for Jane to stagger forward, falling into Connie's embrace, head on her shoulder, letting out a shriek that made every other person in the room look away. They didn't move until she'd finished crying, and that took time. No one spoke. No one left the room. Connie's decision to play the confrontation out in front of them all rather than having Jane Bass removed when she had the opportunity to do so was a very clear message: you must all bear witness to this.

When Jane finally pulled away, Salter stepped up with a box of tissues. Jane Bass grabbed a handful and wiped until her face was dry. The effect of the tears was shocking. Her swollen eyes blazed red, her cheeks were blotched, and her lips were bleeding where she'd bitten them. Someone moved a chair so she could sit before she fell. She was panting like a marathon runner and doubled over to drag more air into her lungs.

'You have questions,' Connie said. 'We'll do our best to answer them.'

Jane gulped but nodded.

'There were all those protestors in York Place and police everywhere. It was even on TV. I'm not saying that lady who died didn't deserve the support, but no one's protesting for my brother. Does he matter less because he was homeless?'

'Homeless isn't who he was, it's where he lived,' Connie said. 'We haven't updated you only because we've made no progress on your brother's case. Usually when progress is slow it's because of a lack of forensic evidence. In Archie's case, there's too much. It's a regular problem with people who move around, frequently stay in hostels, and use second-hand clothes and bedding. We haven't found a weapon and there were no witnesses. We've canvassed the local homeless community to ascertain if Archie was having trouble with anyone in particular, but those enquiries also proved negative. By all accounts, your brother was an amiable man who kept himself to himself and who had no known enemies on the streets.'

'So . . . what are you going to do? Is that it?'

'No. That's just the start but I won't tell you it's going to be easy. Figuring out motive is key,' Connie said.

'It does seem to me that we've failed to provide you with the support you need,' Overbeck interjected. Her voice was soft and Connie noted that the long nails had been deposited in pockets. 'I apologise on behalf of Police Scotland for not liaising with you closely enough. Your brother is as much a priority as any other victim of crime. We have no other agenda than to ensure his murderer is brought swiftly to justice. Why don't you come to my office? I'll have someone bring us a pot of tea and some biscuits. We can talk privately there.'

Jane stood, gripping a desk for support as she found her feet.

'Okay,' she muttered. 'I'm . . . I'm sorry I hit you. I didn't even know I was going to do that.'

Connie stepped forward and took her by the hand, gripping it hard as she leaned in to whisper in her ear. 'Don't apologise. It was the only thing you had left. When men hit, it's usually because they hate. When women hit, it's often because they love. You were entitled to wake us up.'

Overbeck escorted Jane out of the room and along the corridor towards her office. No one spoke until they were out of hearing distance.

Baarda returned to his place at the back of the room, folded his arms and leaned against a desk. Salter took up Overbeck's position at the door, making sure it was firmly shut. Connie sighed and looked up at the board where she'd pinned the additional photos of the victims.

'Why no progress in any of these cases?' she asked. 'What are we missing?'

'There's less to go on forensically than we're used to,' Salter said. 'It's become a pattern of late. Everyone's watching those police investigation documentary series, so all the drug dealers and robbers have started leaving their mobile at home meaning we can't trace their movements. There's been a real uptick in purchasing latex gloves. Even teenagers stealing bikes are careful not to leave traces these days.'

'We just have to double our efforts,' Connie said. 'Let's go back to the beginning. Find me someone who was in contact with Dale Abnay shortly before his death. That should be possible given he was in employment. And someone spend more time with Jane Bass when she's finished with the superintendent. I want a history of Archie's regular hangouts. As for Divya Singh, put together a map of possible vehicular routes away from the place where she was killed. At some point that car passed a CCTV camera, and if it didn't, the killer either ditched it or made it home. There's no such thing as no evidence. We just have to look a bit harder.'

Chapter 20

Two Years Earlier

The canvas that Mol had intended to be full of light and blossoms had turned into a muddy mess. She'd mixed in too much red and been clumsy with the tree line, at which point her foreground figure had been thrown into shade and by then she was simply wasting paint. She quit and began cleaning her brushes instead. Her mobile started to ring, and while she hated to be bothered, it was the music from *Grey's Anatomy* that signified her mother was calling – their not-so-subtle private joke from long evenings in front of the TV with cheese and crackers, commiserating over how few doctors in real life were as dreamy as McDreamy.

Mol grabbed a towel then answered.

'Hey Mum, you okay?'

'I am, but I just wanted you to know there'll be a delivery there momentarily. They need a signature. I didn't want you to be concerned if there was a knock at the studio door, sweetheart.'

'You gave them the code?' Mol asked, gripping the towel hard enough to make her knuckles ache.

'I did, and you don't have to answer the door unless they get it right. I don't want you stressed, you hear me?'

'I'll be okay, Mum, but thanks for calling to let me know. I can hear a car pulling up. That'll be them. Gotta go.'

'Message to let me know you're okay?'

'I will. Love you.' Mol rang off and took her rape alarm from her bag together with one of her mother's scalpels. She put the rape alarm in her pocket and kept the blade in her left hand, tucking her fear away where it didn't stop her living her life and forcing herself to act as if everything was normal.

Standing half behind the studio door, she opened up but left the two chains on, staying far enough back that no one could reach a hand inside to grab her. Outside was a young man, his moustache little more than a line of fluff, looking flustered.

'You have the code?' she asked.

'Shit, yeah, er, I've got it in my pocket. Give me a sec.' He started rooting through his overalls and finally pulled out a scrap of paper. 'I taste a . . . sorry miss, what's the word?' He turned the crumpled paper towards her.

'Liquor.'

'Oh yeah, liquor. I taste a liquor never brewed. That's proper weird.'

Mol's pulse slowed fractionally. 'That's fine. You can set the box down there. Pass me your tablet and I'll sign.'

'Sorry, new company rules. I have to keep hold of it while you sign. Could you open up? It'll only take a couple of seconds.'

The lurch of her stomach was familiar but the prickle of adrenaline remained uncomfortable. He had the code. It had been written down for him. They changed the Emily Dickinson poem every week. It was perfectly safe.

'Fine. Wait there,' she said, pushing the door closed and

setting down the knife so she could slide the chains across to detach them.

Her fingers didn't want to obey. They fumbled and missed, then wouldn't let go. It was ridiculous to be so scared, and impossible not to be.

'Sorry, I've really got to be off,' the delivery man called.

Mol was a child again, at the top of the slide with her father at the bottom, all impatience, telling her to let go. Telling her there was nothing to be afraid of.

'Damn it,' she said. 'I have to live my life.' Opening up, she was pleased to see he'd taken a step back and was holding the tablet out for her to scrawl a digital signature on before he took a photo of the box at her feet.

He left and Mol took the box inside, ignoring the fact that her hands were shaking as she bolted the door and slid both chains back across. She checked her watch. Still five hours until her mother's shift ended and she could get picked up. Until then she was a prisoner in her own studio, knowing perfectly well that all hope of creating anything beautiful on a canvas was done for the day. A year ago, there would have been endless other tasks to complete. Her life had been glorious chaos, with never enough time for cleaning up, ordering supplies, answering emails or booking events into her diary.

Now she had nothing but time. There was no mess to be seen, and some empty shelves where there would previously have been canvases drying or waiting for extra touches or needing to be wrapped and couriered. Recently, the studio had become an empty shell devoid of creativity.

As had she.

Mol moved robotically towards her little paint-spattered kettle and flicked the switch before opening the delivery box. The contents confirmed how much her life had changed.

Nestled in the cardboard was an external post box that her mother had ordered so they could have the mail slot in their front door sealed once and for all. There were things you didn't want landing on your doormat. Even if all you could do was reject them before they could violate your doormat and hallway, that was still an improvement.

Mol's stalker – she refused to say his name any more, even inside her own head – was the sort of person who could have been extraordinarily successful in life if only he'd chosen to commit the same level of devotion and hard work to something other than making other people's lives a misery.

She let the kettle billow its steam, gave up on the idea that a chamomile tea would soothe her corroded nerves, and sank to her knees. It was where her stalker wanted her, after all. There had been times when she'd thought that it might be easier to give him what he craved and could have done so had her mother not been there to keep her defiant.

Karl Smith, Carl Smith, Carl Smyth, Carlos Smit, and more recently Cal Smee might have been an army rather than just one man. That army had waged a hate campaign against her that a New York public relations agency would have been proud of. Social media accounts, many and varied, told stories of her private life, from sleeping with husbands of unnamed friends, to having cheated in exams. There were doctored photos of her that claimed she'd long had an illegal drug habit which both fuelled her creativity and implied that any funds from her art sales would simply be snorted at the end of the day. Names, dates and details were lacking from any of the posts, and friends did their best to counter the accusations, but it was like trying to stop a flood with a child's fishing net: everything but the odd twig sailed straight through.

In the beginning, there was fury. Mol raged at it all as if she could overcome the wreckage being made of her life by sheer force of will. Then came quiet determination. Good always triumphed over bad, didn't it? She was an intelligent, well-respected, amiable person. Surely no one would believe such scurrilous rumours, let alone repeat them?

For the first couple of months, Mol managed to keep it from her mother. Keep it, not hide it. Her mother spent that entire period asking what was wrong. Did she feel unwell? Had something happened? Was Molly under too much pressure with all her commissions? Only when a family friend had called her mother to ask about a rumour that Mol was in a rehab unit for drug addiction did her secret bubble burst.

Beth Waterfall, exceptional surgeon and brilliant mind, had assumed there would be a way of dealing with it. A system with built-in accountability. They would just report the fake posts to the people who ran the social media sites. That should deal with it instantly. Mol had explained patiently, then less patiently, how it all worked. Beth's disbelief and outrage didn't help the situation. Once the horrible reality of how social media worked had sunk in, Beth had suggested that they engage a lawyer. Said legal expert had considered the case in detail and at no small expense then concluded that there was very little that could be done. Contacting the social media companies was useless, and nothing Mol hadn't already tried. Trying to identify the source of the defamatory posts was a joke. The accounts disappeared as soon as they'd done their intended damage, and only years of fighting for court orders with international effect would obtain further details. In the end, Beth Waterfall had become just as frustrated, desperate and angry as Mol, and that hadn't helped either of them.

Requests for newspaper and magazine interviews dried up. There were no more places on awards lists. To be fair, Mol knew that might be because the quality of her work was suffering rather than the judging panels falling prey to prejudice. With the reduction in publicity – the good kind at least – went the commissions. Her paintings still sold but tended to sit on display at the galleries far longer than they had before.

Mol had withdrawn from social media and stopped looking to see what was being said about her. Her true friends had rallied but Mol found it increasingly hard to communicate with them, wanting their support without wanting to see their pity on display. Only her website remained. It was the only way members of the public or galleries could reach her unless they wanted to go to the trouble of sending a letter.

Her studio was her sanctuary. She would drive there, country music blasting, certain in the knowledge that there were better times ahead, and free her mind of anything but positive thoughts.

She was well aware that a single man was behind that smear campaign. He might have assumed many forms, become people with different skin colours and unfamiliar names, might have opened new email accounts to fool the very basic social media security, but he hadn't fooled her. Mol had found herself caught in the headlights of a sociopath, an obsessive one at that, and now there was nothing to do but wait until he was so bored of her that he finally moved on to pastures new.

Then the first package arrived.

Left outside her studio door on a hot summer's day, it was nothing more threatening than a box of fruit if you discounted the flies. She heard it before she saw it, the frenzied buzzing making the air hum as she climbed out of the old Datsun 240Z that was her pride and joy. She'd bought it with her first big cheque and had washed and polished it weekly ever since. The first of the flies had splattered juicily on her windscreen and she'd stupidly thought that was going to be the most annoying part of her day.

The box had been positioned directly in front of the little door to the studio, so it was impossible to avoid the parcel if she wanted to get in. She couldn't even simply kick it open to see what was inside, because of the lengths of Sellotape involved. Nudging it to the side so she could open up, her gut was already telling her to do the sensible thing. Put on gloves, shove it in a bin bag, and throw it into the industrial unit's commercial waste bin. But her name was neatly printed on the top and there was a postage stamp and there was a chance, just a chance, that one of her clients had tried to do something lovely for her, and that if she didn't open it up, she might fail to send a thank you. Perhaps, after all, it was just a huge mistake.

Mol slashed at the packaging with a Stanley knife, having donned gloves and a mask, and threw open the lid. Inside was a feast fit for a horror movie. A mountain of once-luscious grapes sat at one side, balanced by past-life peaches that had formed a sodden yellow mass. Between them a grey-green orange was surrounded by plums from which new life was bursting in the form of maggots. The whole of it was a bed of flies not at all bothered by Mol's intrusion. She grabbed her stomach and vomited to one side, narrowly missing the box and tripping to land painfully on her hip. Picking herself up, refusing to cry, refusing to scream, refusing to feel anything else at all, she wiped her mouth on the sleeve of her old painting shirt before ripping it off and throwing it down on top of the stinking box at her feet.

She stormed into her studio, grabbed a bin bag and an old shovel, and marched back out, teeth gritted.

'Fuck you,' Mol muttered as she scraped together the detritus and ejecta that so appropriately represented her life. 'Fuck you.'

Another spadeful in the bag. 'Fuck you.' And another. She didn't care what she looked like. It wasn't as if anyone in the industrial unit would care either.

'Fuck you.' The final, grotesque remnants slid from shovel to bag with slimy finesse. She threw the shovel down and it clattered and clanged on the paving slabs as she grabbed the bag and tied the top before stomping towards the huge bins and thrusting it inside, slamming the lid. She bared her teeth at it.

Enough.

Mol Waterfall stayed awake for the next two days, painting non-stop.

By the time her mother pulled her bodily from the studio she was dehydrated, freezing, ranting and senseless.

On her easel was a painting of a box of rotting, insect-ridden fruit so life-like it made Beth Waterfall gasp in disgust even as her fingers reached out to touch.

'Beautiful and terrible,' Beth murmured.

The gifts, in all their rotten majesty, did not stop coming.

Chapter 21

5 June

'I feel like a fool,' Lively grumbled. 'I'd have been perfectly all right going back to mine.'

Beth Waterfall put his bag down in her hallway and took off her coat.

'Call me judgemental, but I saw your flat when I went to pick up your things for the hospital, and I'm not convinced your kitchen hadn't been leased out to a laboratory breeding new strains of bacteria. Would you sit down, Sam? You're making me nervous.'

He lowered himself onto the sofa and leaned back gingerly. He was conscious of his neck every second. In his imagination, the covering on the wound there was no more sturdy than the skin on a bowl of custard left too long.

'This is ridiculous. You've work to be doing for people who need you more than me.'

'I've leave to take that I'll lose if I don't do something with it before the end of the month, and I give enough of myself to that place without giving extra for free, however much I love my job. Will it be tea or coffee?'

'Ach, coffee, black and strong. Tea's for women.'

She put her head around the sitting room door and gave him a look that made him wilt.

'Coffee it is, but that'll be the first and last reference to women being weaker than men while you're under my roof. You're not at the station now, and you've no one here who needs you to prove that you're one of the boys.'

Lively reddened to an extent that would have permanently ruined his credibility with the team had any of them been around to witness it.

'I'm sorry. That was out of order. Just goes to show I should be in my own home, not bringing my bad manners into yours. Will you just drive me to mine? I really . . .' He struggled to get up and failed.

'Oh for goodness' sake, can you not be told when you're in the wrong either, without needing to run away? Samuel Lively, I'm a single woman who's looked after herself for years, a surgical team leader, something of a loner these days, and chief cook and bottle-washer under my own roof. I'm asking you to mind your mouth, that's all. Among those things, though I say so myself, I'm also something of a baker. So if you'll sit down and swallow your pride, there'll be coffee and Victoria sponge brought to you in just a few minutes. Can you live with that?'

She smiled at him, and Lively thought that surviving long enough to see the beauty of her face in that moment was worth every bit of the pain he'd experienced. And fear. There had been plenty of that too. Perhaps it was the fact that he was no longer a young man that had made it worse. He'd suffered plenty of injuries before, and more than a few moments of true peril. But the warm, wet wash of his lifeblood into his collar, drenching his shirt and dripping thickly onto the bulge of his stomach, had been an awakening into a world where he was suddenly mortal and where the precipice into forever was no longer a distant feature but part of the foreground. He had not liked the feeling. Not one bit.

'Cake,' he nodded. 'I'd like that. Thank you.'

Beth busied herself in the kitchen as he looked around. It was the first time he'd been inside her house, their tentative few preliminary dates having taken place on neutral ground, bumbling between small talk and figuring out how to hold hands as if they were fourteen all over again. Everything they'd done together so far was a first, and as wondrous as it was excruciating. They had knocked noses trying to kiss. Argued over restaurant bills. Been befuddled by the art of holding open doors in the twenty-first century, until Lively had decided that there were some things men should be able to do that were just plain good manners and not at all insulting to a secure, intelligent woman.

The sofa was comfortable – much more so than the old tatty thing at his place with cushions so worn you almost sank through to the bottom of them – and there was a television. He was relieved at that. Beth Waterfall was the sort of woman he'd imagined might spend her evenings reading literary tomes or handwriting lengthy letters to friends abroad. Bookshelves filled an alcove, the upper shelves displaying a variety of fiction and reference books, the bottom section packed with jigsaw puzzles and board games with Sellotaped box sides and battered edges.

'Here you go.' She entered and set a tray on the coffee table, the sponge cake on a marble slab, two plates next to it.

'Just a wee slice for me though,' he said. 'I've been meaning to lose some pounds. Started running again, in fact. Need to up my game if I'm going to keep up with the youngsters on my squad.'

'Sam,' Beth said as she handed him a more than generous slice. 'If you want to get fitter, then as a doctor I say go for it. We live better when we look after our bodies. But as your . . . I don't know, whatever this is at our age . . . I can only tell you that I'm here for your smile, your sense of humour, and because you make me feel safe in a way I haven't known for a while. I'm not here for a six-pack. Now eat your cake and enjoy it. The jam's homemade and I grew the strawberries myself.'

'Where do you find the time?' he asked, torn between wanting to eat and wanting to ask questions.

She shrugged and toyed with the sponge on her plate. 'I have to fill the hours when I'm not at work. Plus, I find it hard to sleep. If you hear me walking around at night, don't be surprised, but I'll do my best not to wake you. Your bedroom's at the back of the house where it's quietest.'

Lively found it necessary to suddenly concentrate very hard on his plate.

'Sure, yup, right.'

There was a long pause.

Beth closed her eyes. 'Oh.' It was her turn to blush. 'Did you think—'

'No, not at all. I'd never presume. We just hadn't discussed it and I felt awkward for asking. The back of the house sounds perfect. And I don't sleep all that much either, so you'll not be disturbing me.'

Beth laughed so hard she had to put her plate down. 'Aren't we a pair of awkward dafties? Embarrassed to talk about such things at our age. I didn't think we were ready for anything more intimate yet given that we've still to perfect the kissing stage, and your neck's not going to be up for much for a month or so.' She reached out and took his hand gently. 'I'd like to look after you, Sam, if you'll stop being such a stubborn old goat and let me.'

'I will, Beth. In fact I'd like that very much.' He stroked the back of her hand with his thumb. 'I was looking at your photos earlier. Is that your daughter with you? She's the spitting image of you.'

She slipped her hand slowly from Lively's and wrapped her arms around her waist.

'It is,' she murmured.

'Does she live locally? I'd love to meet her. What's her name?'

Beth took a breath in through her nose and let it out through her mouth.

'You can't, I'm afraid. That's Molly. Mol to her friends. She's gone.'

Lively put his own plate down, the sponge cake forming an unswallowable lump in his mouth. 'How long ago?'

'It's been more than a year now. I should have told you before, there's just never really a right time to announce something like that.'

'Was it an accident or was she ill?' he asked softly.

'There were pills involved. A lot of them. I hope you won't find it too disturbing but you should know there's an urn in my bedroom with her name on. Well, at least that's over. So you see, I invited you for my own sake as much as yours. Perhaps the company will do us both good while you recuperate.'

Sam Lively, Police Scotland's notoriously grumpy, most irascible detective, found that he needed to look away and blink hard to clear the blurriness in his eyes. Dr Beth Waterfall was more than he deserved, and the sort of woman he'd long since given up any hope of meeting. And there she was, putting her faith in him, a man who had consistently screwed up every close relationship he'd ever formed. She needed someone consistent, more open. She needed a man she'd be proud to be seen with, who could entertain her with clever conversation over the Sunday papers. He wasn't that person. He never could be.

He opened his mouth to destroy the thing that had been offered to him. He would leave straight away, go back to his own place, get out of her way. It was good that she was trying to move forward after such a devastating loss. It was extraordinary that she hadn't simply given up on life completely. And now here he was, catching criminals and being sarcastic his only two real skills in life.

'I'm going to look after you, Beth,' he said.

The words were not the ones his brain had been preparing. They weren't the retreat he had planned. He had no idea where they came from.

Beth Waterfall, slowly, carefully – mindful of his wound – sank against his good shoulder as Lively realised that for once, when it mattered most, he'd managed to speak with his heart instead of his head.

He closed his eyes and held her.

The man watching the house from the car across the street closed his eyes too, and let his imagination run wild.

Chapter 22

6 June

Connie walked into the private hire pub basement first, followed by Baarda, Salter and some additional muscle. Outside on Craigentinny Road, a squad of uniformed officers were poised to help if it was needed, but more importantly, they were armed with video cameras to capture images for facial recognition. It was time to figure out who Dale Abnay's friends were. Police Scotland's online intelligence service had confirmed that, unlike most incel groups, WATFOR had a chapter that met once a month in person, in Edinburgh.

There was some American rock playing in the background and a bar offering only beer, whisky or Irn-Bru. A pool table was in use at the far end, but most people were sitting around tables, talking and drinking. Along one wall were three dartboards upon which had been stuck posters of naked women, with men proving just how powerful they were by throwing darts at them from a few feet away. Connie didn't know whether to laugh or yawn.

In the centre was an area of clear floor that had been reserved for the evening's speaker, a man who'd been campaigning for the reversal of the law that made it illegal for a man to rape his wife. The basement was rammed. Connie headed for the centre of the room as Baarda requested that the music be shut off.

In response, every man present stood at once, and the sound of the chairs on the concrete floor was the world's worst orchestra tuning up. Connie made a show of protecting her ears.

'Guys!' she said grinning. 'Y'all really didn't have to be so polite as to stand, but I sure do appreciate ya.' The mock drawl of sarcasm was lost on them. Several hands went to pockets that could only have contained concealed weapons and all Connie did was smile brighter. 'Oh, you don't want to do that. We're not planning on taking any of you in, unless you make it your business to be difficult. In fact, we need your help.'

A few of the men dropped back onto their chairs and began drinking again. Others remained standing, although most hands had the sense to distance themselves from their pockets.

'You lot got a court order or whatever it is to say you can come in here?' a woman shouted from behind the bar. Connie turned and nodded at Baarda who quietly walked to the bar and whispered in the woman's ear. She reddened, huffed, then declared, 'Fair enough,' and exited sharply. Baarda nodded at her and Connie briefly raised one eyebrow in his direction. People underestimated Baarda all the time. She'd learned long ago that the Old Etonian reserve and propriety was a carefully polished veneer beneath which was something far more lethal than she'd initially seen. When Baarda decided something was going to happen, it got done.

'All we need is a little information about one of your . . . associates.'

'Would ye fuck off already?' one of the men shouted, perching – arms folded – on the edge of the pool table.

120

'The sooner I get what I want, the sooner we will indeed fuck off,' Connie replied cheerily.

A group of men began making their way to the exit. Salter moved to block their path.

'Listen, cunt, get out of our way. You think I won't smack a little bitch like you just because you're polis?' the biggest said.

Salter said nothing but stood her ground.

'So here's the thing,' Connie called to them. 'I have a number of officers waiting outside. I didn't bring them in because who needs to be heavy-handed, am I right? Also, those officers are carrying video cameras, the footage from which will be run through face recognition software. If those are your vehicles in the car park, the details have already been recorded. If anyone's got anything outstanding – bail, probation, fines, child support payments – then you're going to want to sit your asses back down. If I get what I want, none of that footage is getting processed. You have my word.'

She glanced at Salter and hoped the plan was going to work. Her word meant nothing given that she wasn't actually a police officer, but unless and until someone asked her identity, that was their problem. Christie Salter, on the other hand, would be checking the identities and backgrounds of every 'involuntarily celibate' member of WATFOR and making sure an intelligence file was opened for each one of them.

'I bet you've got a right tight pussy on you!' a man as wide as he was short yelled at her.

'And yet your penis, even fully engorged, still wouldn't touch the sides,' Connie said.

Short and wide lurched forward as if to go for her but a wiser man next to him yanked him back into his seat, saving Connie the trouble of humiliating him further.

She didn't need to look at Baarda's face to know he'd be

121

shaking his head. He'd cautioned her against interacting, against winding them up, against scoring points, and yet somehow – in the middle of a room of men who most certainly did not have to be celibate if only they could figure out what it meant to be a decent human being – Connie just could not stop her mouth from running. She braved a quick glance at Baarda and shrugged, at which he only raised his eyebrows.

'Dale Abnay,' Connie said. 'He was a local chapter member and he'd registered on your strangely well-organised digital list for attending this lovely celebration of not getting laid.'

There were some shuffled feet and a few coughs in the uncomfortable silence.

'What about him?' the man who'd restrained short and wide asked.

'Well, he's dead for starters,' Connie said. That comment won her some wide eyes and a few sharp intakes of breath. 'So I want to know if any of you knew him personally. Who he talked to when he came here. If he had any enemies, if he was in trouble, any details at all that might help us find his murderer.' *That is assuming it wasn't one of you*, were the words she didn't say, not that it seemed very likely. The only stink she was picking up was of teenage boy's bedroom rather than anything more organised and effective.

Baarda raised his chin and got her attention, tipping his head towards two men leaning against the bar who were whispering quietly. Salter had turned her gaze towards another near the door to the toilets who was already sending a text message.

'You've already hacked into his computer, clearly, so I wouldn't have thought you need us, girlie. On your way, and take your wee performing monkeys with you.'

Connie didn't have a chance to respond before some brave

soul with little neck and even less judgement took the speech as carte blanche to prove what a big man he was, and reached out and gave Christie Salter's backside an almighty slap.

The room was still collectively drawing in breath when Salter began to turn, grabbing the offending idiot's still outstretched right hand with hers, and pulling him forward. As she completed her spin, she thrust her left knee down onto his forearm, pulling him off his chair and to his knees on the floor, following through by pushing the back of his neck down with her left hand. In one fluid movement, she wrenched his right arm up behind his back, pushed his hand down so the wrist was at ninety degrees to his arm and kept pressing, shifting her right foot onto the back of his neck with his backside up in the air.

As funny as the sight would have been under any other circumstances, absolutely no one laughed.

'DS Salter, did you want to press charges? I can have an officer come in to take him from you, if you'd like,' Connie offered.

'God, no, I'm not bothering to press charges on this soggy biscuit,' Salter said.

Connie opened her mouth to ask for an explanation when Baarda stepped in.

'You two gentlemen at the bar, you next to the toilets, and you in the cowboy boots, out now. If there's no argument about that, we'll accompany those people out and the rest of you can stay and enjoy your evening. DS Salter, in your own time.'

Salter gave Baarda an obliging nod, releasing her foot first, then letting the man's arm drop. He took a moment to get upright, leaving his face-shaped dignity in the dust on the floor.

'Bitch,' he muttered.

'That'll be Detective Sergeant Bitch to you,' Connie told him as she walked past, escorting the line of quietly obliging men through the door.

'You never told us what happened to him!' someone yelled as she was heading for the exit.

She thought about the confidential aspects of the murder, and about the information she should and shouldn't give out, then took one last look at the posters of women with dart holes in them.

'He got whacked on the back of the head with a blunt object, dragged along a pathway in the woods, then buried alive but unable to move. What can I tell you? It's a dangerous time to be an incel, apparently.'

They left in silence and no one tried to follow them, the men they'd removed from the scene walking straight into the arms of officers waiting to take their details.

'Hey, Brodie,' Connie called to him across the car park. 'What's a soggy—'

'No,' he said firmly. 'Absolutely not.'

'My bad, ma'am,' Salter said, running up to her. 'I shouldn't have said it. It's not like me. I've been spending far too much time with DS Lively, is all.'

'I'll get one of you to explain it to me, sooner or later. Nice moves, by the way, Salter. Martial arts background?'

'I got injured a while back, badly. I spent my recovery time, once I was physically able, doing endless defence courses. These days, it's an automatic response. Wish I had your verbals though, ma'am. I can never think of anything clever to say like you.'

Baarda stepped into the conversation. 'Not something to aspire to,' he mumbled. 'Only makes a heated situation even hotter.'

'Feels like I'm about to get sent to the school counsellor to try to figure out the roots of my disruptive behaviour.' Connie grinned. 'Come on Brodie, that was just too good to resist.'

The young man in the cowboy boots appeared in front of them, tears in his eyes.

124

'Was he really buried alive?' he asked.

The smile dropped from Connie's lips.

'I'm afraid so,' she said.

'Where?'

'Jupiter Artland.'

'Makes sense. He loved it there. Went there a lot.'

'Was Dale a friend of yours, Mr . . . ?'

'Wolfe. Leslie. My mates call me Wolfie. And Dale was more than a friend. He'd—' The next words got caught in his throat. He took a shuddering breath and tried again. 'Dale had agreed to donate a kidney to me. I'd been waiting on a match for a year. I thought he'd dropped out of contact because he'd changed his mind and didn't know how to break it to me. I was so angry with him that I didn't—' He began to sob. 'I didn't report him missing. Figured he was being a coward, not just telling me to my face. I didn't know his family or anything. We only met through WATFOR. It's not fair.'

Connie wasn't entirely sure if it was Abnay's death that wasn't fair or the loss of the kidney, but it definitely wasn't the right moment to ask.

'When was the transplant operation supposed to take place?' she asked.

'It was scheduled three months ago. Now I'm back on the transplant list. For all I know, Dale might have been my last hope.'

Chapter 23

7 June

'Makes no sense,' Connie said. She lay on the floor of her hotel suite, stretched out on her stomach, knees bent, waving her feet in the air, in the centre of a circle of scattered pieces of paper. In one hand she held a stick of celery that she was dipping in and out of a tub of humous.

'Any particular bit or just the whole damned mess?' Baarda asked, pouring himself a glass of vintage Fonseca and loosening his tie.

'Stop peering at me from the sofa like some disapproving professor and get down here with me,' she demanded.

Baarda sighed but gave in. It was already 1 a.m. and he knew Connie wouldn't sleep until they had some sort of breakthrough. It was going to be a long night. He'd shared plenty of them with her before and he was equally certain that there were plenty more to come. He sat down next to her, stretching his legs out and trying not to be disheartened by the amount of paperwork on the carpet.

The Balmoral Hotel next to Edinburgh's Waverley Station

resembled a grand, petrified wedding cake and it was Connie's go-to when they were in Scotland, for its spacious suites and the pool where she could be found at 5 a.m. almost without exception. Once an island girl, always an island girl, was her mantra. The water called her. Baarda was happier with an extra hour of sleep and a session in the gym before breakfast. He'd sworn off 5 a.m. starts when his children finally grew out of their toddler years. These days, getting them out of their bedrooms at all when they stayed with him was something of a miracle.

'Hey!' She nudged his leg with an elbow. 'You're miles away. Want to help me solve a murder or three?'

'Why aren't you doing your thing?' he asked.

'My thing? I train for years, work my ass off chasing criminals across the world, occasionally getting down and nasty with the odd serial killer, and you reduce it to my "thing"?' She rolled onto her back and threw the end of the celery stick at the bin, scoring a perfect shot. Baarda knew better than to talk too much. Connie wanted to think. She just did it better when he was next to her. 'Okay.' She flexed her neck and got comfortable. 'Let's start at Jupiter Artland. I liked it there. Can you hit the light switch from there? My imagination works better in darkness.'

He reached up and hit the switch. The hotel lamps faded to black. Baarda settled down, careful not to brush Connie's legs, painfully aware of their proximity and how much he never wanted to do anything she could misconstrue. Connie putting her trust in him was a shining light in his life and he wasn't about to do anything to risk dimming it, even inadvertently.

'Lie next to me,' she said. 'You're going to be my dead people.'

Baarda rolled his eyes, aware that Connie would know he was doing so, whether she could see it or not.

'You've gotta let me be me. Open your mind. It's science, not voodoo. This is how my brain makes connections.'

'Oh for God's sake,' he muttered as he lay on his side, one hand propped on an elbow.

In the minuscule amount of light from the hotel's smoke alarm on the ceiling, he could see Connie do the same next to him, washed red by the flash every thirty seconds.

'Ready?' she asked.

He could hear that she was smiling in spite of the gravity of what they were trying to do. This was what lit her up – travelling into the minds of killers, reaching out with her absurdly advanced intuition and perception; it was like watching a maths genius work out a seemingly impossible sum in their head.

'Be Dale Abnay for me,' she said.

Baarda let go of his reservation – in for a penny, in for a pound – and dived in. Abnay, thirty-three years of age, unable to make connections with women, living alone in semi-squalor, but somehow – amid his many failings – the man had offered to be a kidney donor for a friend in need.

'I'm confused,' he said. 'I tell myself I hate the thing I want more than anything else, because hate is so much easier to live with than loneliness. And you can't tell other men that you're lonely because men don't like seeing weakness in others. It's a reminder that it's there inside them too. So we get together online and at the pub and talk about how much we hate women. But we don't really. We hate ourselves for not being able to get one or keep one. We hate ourselves for not even being man enough to tell the truth about our feelings. Then after a while we hate just because we got lazy and gave up even contemplating changing our lives for the better. Then you wake up one day and you're a shell. You're just going through the motions. Might as well be dead.'

Connie didn't speak for a long, long time.

Baarda wondered if she'd finally fallen asleep, until she asked, 'Is that why you agreed to donate a kidney to Wolfie? To try to feel something good again?'

It was Baarda's turn to pause.

'Yes?' Another pause. 'Yes. It was a connection. Maybe even a lifeline. To have someone need me. Be grateful to me. It was one pure thing, and I sort of knew that if I didn't say yes, if I didn't at least try to reach out to another human being, then it was game over.'

'But you didn't hate everything,' Connie probed. 'You liked Jupiter Artland. You went there often. What was it about that place that attracted you?'

Baarda shrugged in the darkness, his shoulders brushing the carpet and making a brief shushing noise. 'It was like a reset. The city only offered girls I couldn't have – girls going shopping, wearing short skirts, getting drunk, looking at me like I was nothing. The beach is full of kids screaming, couples walking hand in hand like a poster for a life that wasn't mine. Artland is an escape. I like the structure, the symmetry, the simplicity and patterns. You can stay away from other people most of the time. It was like offering my kidney – something good that I could cling onto.'

'And the Weeping Girls – did you ever stand there and imagine it was you who'd made them cry?' Connie asked.

Baarda found his mouth suddenly dry. 'I . . . I don't know.'

'Think about it,' she pressed.

'Maybe,' he said. 'They're very young though.'

'Young like when you first met Lucy Ogunode?'

'That's a low blow,' he said instinctively.

'Ah. So you weren't a completely hollow shell. There was still something happening in the soul, in spite of all the porn and posters.'

'Mmm,' Baarda murmured noncommittally.

'Dale, who do you think killed you?' she asked. Baarda could feel her closer to him, her breath on his cheek, the smell of the Chanel No.5 she'd dabbed on that morning that had faded to an almost-memory on the skin of her neck.

'I have no idea,' he said. 'I was just walking. I know Artland so well now I never have to check the map or the path signs. The blow came from nowhere. It makes no sense.'

'Did anyone want you dead?'

'I don't think I was worth enough to anyone to want me dead,' Baarda said slowly. 'I don't think I ever made enough of an impact on anyone's life for them to care whether or not I lived or died.'

Connie sighed.

'Did you mind dying?' she whispered.

'I never got the chance to be better. I wanted to give Wolfie his kidney. I thought that might be a new start for me. And I never knew what it was like to have a woman care about me. It's sad dying, like that, knowing there's no girlfriend or wife who'll miss you or cry over you. Whatever else I did wrong, it would have been nice to have had someone that missed me. Other than Wolfie, of course, and I doubt that he'd have bothered with me either if I hadn't been a match.'

Connie made a tiny noise that Baarda couldn't decipher.

'I'm sorry,' she said. 'I'll do my best to make it up to you now.'

Before he could respond, Baarda felt the soft, light gift of a kiss at the furthest edge of his lips and found that he could neither move nor speak, his transition into Dale's last moments complete.

'We should take a break,' Connie said. 'I need coffee. You want anything from room service?'

The light came on before Baarda registered that she'd moved.

130

'Tea, please,' he croaked. 'And mineral water, still. Connie—'

She was already dialling and began talking immediately, putting in their order. Baarda got up, walked to the desk and poured himself a trickle of Balvenie whisky that he knocked back as Connie replaced the receiver to room service.

He watched her stretch, tumbling over the right words and wrong words in his mind.

'Connie,' he said, his voice no more than the rumble of a distant earthquake across a mountain range. 'What was that?'

'Role play,' she said. 'And you, my repressed English oak tree, were nothing short of a revelation. I can't wait to see what you'll do with Archie Bass's persona.'

'No,' he said. 'Not again. That was not . . .' His voice trailed off.

'Comfortable?' She grinned. 'Normal? Sane, even?'

'I was thinking, appropriate.' He poured a second measure of whisky.

'Oh, I see. You're freaking out. Come on then, ask it.'

'It's not a joke, Connie. We work together. It's one thing, you being utterly unpredictable, and yes, sometimes really rather abnormal. But that was beyond the scope of, well, of anything.'

'Ask the question, Brodie,' she repeated softly, sitting on the edge of her bed and leaning forward, elbows on knees, chin resting on palms.

Baarda put the whisky tumbler down and folded his arms. 'Who was it you kissed, and why?'

Connie put her hand behind her head and pulled the band out of her customary ponytail. 'Oh, okay, you mean, was it you or was it Dale?' She shrugged. 'Does it matter?'

'It certainly changes the conversation we should have.'

'What if it's neither? What if it was just the result of everything

131

I've seen and heard today, maybe especially tonight? Maybe it was sadness for Abnay or admiration for you, or a need to vent in a way that's an antidote for the anger and frustration I feel. Maybe it was a moment of human connection in the middle of three goddamned murders. That's a lot of maybes, Brodie. Don't we have enough answers to find already, without you adding another one to the mix?'

Baarda ran a tired hand through the tangle of brown curly hair that he was all too aware had recently become edged with salt. Connie made him feel both older and younger than his years, and as if he knew nothing. She was impossible.

'There have to be boundaries,' he said.

'Legal ones? Is this a human resources problem?' She laughed but the smile in her eyes was diminished, and he could have cursed himself for that.

'Boundaries for us. Working boundaries. I know you express yourself in a way that is entirely your own. I also understand that your brain doesn't work the same way as anyone I've ever met. But me lying on a bedroom floor in the middle of the night becoming a dead man . . . that's more than just a little fucked up. And that's before I factor in the fact that I think you kissed the embodiment of a murdered incel because you felt sorry that he'd never been loved.'

'You think that's what I did?'

There was a knock at the door. 'Room service.'

'You were amazing tonight,' Connie said, standing up. 'I know things about Abnay I hadn't seen clearly before. And I also know some things about his murderer. Whatever happened on my floor, it was a breakthrough, not an issue.'

She went and opened the door, holding it for an exhausted-looking woman to carry a tray through.

'That's my cue, I think. I'll skip the tea,' Baarda said. 'See you at breakfast.' He slipped out and let himself into his own bedroom next door, painfully aware of Connie just metres away, and knowing with absolute certainty that neither of them would be getting any sleep in the few hours left before dawn.

Chapter 24

The Watcher

7 June

Karl put on his father's favourite music then ran warm water into a bowl and fetched a clean, soft flannel. The carer had been in that morning, and washing his father's face and chest was on her list of duties, but he'd caught her more than once on her phone, tapping away at a text message or social media post, so how could he possibly trust her to do everything on the list?

He'd worked his way through too many carers to risk losing this one, though, so he bit his tongue and did all the tasks again when he got home, stewing privately over the carer's tiniest faults: not fully raising the blind to allow maximum sunlight in, washing the lunch plate and cutlery but not drying them properly before putting them away, putting a new toilet roll on the holder the wrong way round. She was infuriating. He'd really wanted a male carer, but they were few and far between, and the only one he'd engaged had spoken virtually no English. His father, in his few moments of lucidity, would have been horrified, not to mention confused, so that was never going to work out.

As Lee Marvin sang 'Wand'rin' Star', Karl ran the flannel over his father's face with all the care of handling a newborn.

'Here you go, Dad. Hope that's not too warm for you.' Dip in fresh water, squeeze the excess, wipe again. 'I had a good morning. Was Sandra nice today? I hope she let you listen to your music. Sorry I was out for so long.'

His father responded by jerking his head towards the window, more likely a twitch than a meaningful movement, but Karl stood anyway and pulled the blind down.

'Too bright? I get it. I nearly went straight through a red light earlier cos I couldn't see it properly. Hey, I've got you a treat.' He dried his father's face with a towel softer than a plush teddy, and smoothed the few hairs left on his scalp. 'You warm enough, Dad? I'll put the heating up a little. Don't want you getting cold.'

He pulled the blanket up closer to his father's chin and unwrinkled the fabric. The thermostat was in the upstairs hallway at the end furthest from Karl's bedroom. He'd long since moved his father downstairs into what used to be their dining room. When his father was still able to walk around a little, the idea of him falling down the stairs was just too stressful. The move had made everything easier, and really, who still used a dining room anyway? Karl ate his meals on his lap in the armchair next to his dad's bed, and his father only ate baby food these days.

The change had made the upper floor of the house even more lonely and creepy, but his father's safety was more important than his own insecurities. He moved into the hallway, took a deep breath and gripped the lower banister hard enough to blanch his knuckles, at least in those patches where he hadn't picked the skin off. His mother used to slap his fingers every time she saw him sitting there, scraping at one hand with the other while he was watching TV or reading a comic.

'Stop it, Karl,' her voice said inside his head. 'You'll get blood on your school shirt if you carry on like that, and I'll have the devil's own job getting it out.'

'Stop it, Karl,' Karl said out loud, his falsetto impression of his mother eerily close to her actual pitch. 'Get upstairs and sort out that thermostat.'

'Okay Ma,' he said, his head so low his chin was almost on his chest.

Up the stairs he went.

'Up the stairs to Bedfordshire!' Karl/Ma sang as he plodded, as she had always done. He'd assumed Bedfordshire was some wonderful, made-up place until he'd asked her about it, aged ten. It had never seemed as magical after he was given the answer.

At the top, he paused, gave his shoulders a shake, and stared along the hallway at the thermostat clinging to a once-cream-now-yellow wall, and reminded himself that his mother was gone gone gone. He'd visited her body in the hospital when she'd passed, the whites of her eyes much the colour of the jaundiced wall. Then he'd made arrangements at the funeral home. Once her body had been moved there, he'd taken one long last look at her with his father as they said their until-we-meet-agains. She'd lain in the coffin with a pale blue silk lining. It had been her favourite colour.

So she couldn't possibly be in the room at the end of the hallway now, perched on the edge of her bed, brushing her hair. She couldn't be, because he'd watched her coffin as it was lowered into her grave. And the grave hadn't been disturbed because he visited it every single week on a Sunday afternoon, come rain or shine. Which meant that the woman in the room at the end of the hallway was either his mother's ghost or a figment of his imagination.

'Just my imagination,' he said, his voice all his own again, low and gravelly, as his father's had been when he still spoke, before the stroke had dissolved the man he had been and left only a quivering dad-shaped shell. Karl forced one foot in front of the other. The thermostat was a million miles away at the end of gluey brown carpet that did its best to keep his feet stuck to it.

'Would you hurry up, Karl!' his mother called from her bedroom. 'You always were a slowcoach.'

'Coming, Ma,' he mumbled. 'I'll do better.'

He forced himself to pick up speed, wondering if he'd left the door to her bedroom open himself or if Sandra – stupid, lazy, nosy Sandra – had been poking around where she wasn't wanted.

Karl made it to the thermostat and cleared his throat. It would be better if he just got on with it and cleared out his mother's stuff. She wasn't coming back, and no one else wanted any of it, so leaving all those patterned dresses hanging in the wardrobe and all her tights turning to dust in the drawers was simply an exercise in denial.

Karl put his hand to the dial and turned it up to twenty-one degrees.

'Going to ignore me, are you?' his mother called, her voice thick with extra disappointment. She'd always been disappointed in him. It was her default maternal disposition.

'I'm busy,' he muttered. 'Got to go look after Dad.'

'You'll go when I say you can go, son. Come in and sit wi' me. You never come in my room any more.'

'Not now. Later. I've washing to do.'

'Look at me, Karl,' his mother insisted.

His head turned of its own accord, in spite of Karl willing it not to.

There she was, craning her neck to peer at him, her skin so dry and flaky there was a haze around her in the sunlight. A different woman might have appeared as an angel. Not his ma, though. She was all demands and instructions.

'Ignore her. She can be a bully, but she doesn't really mean it. That's just the way her own folks were with her,' Karl's father had once whispered to him when his mother had told him he'd amount to nothing if he didn't step up and do more of the household chores. He was seven years old at the time.

Somehow his feet had carried him to the doorway of his mother's bedroom. He stood, head down, fighting the urge to stare at her disintegrating face.

'Have you done what I told you yet?' she asked. 'You haven't, have you?' He knew without looking that she was pointing at him with her gnarled right hand, the nails too long, the tips of her fingers the sepia shades of an old photo.

'I'm trying, Ma. I watch her. I'm just waiting for the right time. And now she's got some policeman living with her, so it's hard.' He gave a defeated shrug and shoved his shaking hands deep into his pockets. 'And she hurt me before. I nearly died.'

'Oh, it's hard,' his ma mocked, her voice reedy and whining. 'It's hard and I can't do it. I nearly died. I'm too scared. I'm too weak.' She screwed up her face and more of her skin fell in dusty rivulets to the carpet.

'I'm trying,' he said. 'I can't take risks. What'll happen to Dad if I get caught?'

'You won't get caught if you're clever and careful, but I suppose that's too much to ask.' His mother rose from the bed as if pulled by invisible puppet strings. He heard her knees pop as she straightened and did his best not to let her see the tears forming in his eyes. 'Lazy boy. Stupid boy. Careless boy.'

'Please don't tell me off, Ma,' he whimpered. 'I'm doing my best.'

'You're doing your best for your father,' she hissed. 'Always loved him, didn't you? Clung to him. Asked for him when you were hurt or scared, you pathetic little shit!'

'I loved you both,' he cried. The tears were impossible to hide now, and he knew it would only make her worse, but there was no way of stopping them.

He could hear her feet scraping across the carpet and knew there'd be a trail of ash for him to clear up later.

'Are you scared now, cry baby? You should be. Do you know what I'll do if you don't put that bitch Beth Waterfall down like the dog she is? I'll creep into your bed while you're fast asleep and—'

He screamed and bolted before she could reach out and touch him, tripping over his feet, stumbling, hitting the floor with one knee but getting straight up and clambering like some giant spider missing a leg or two, not even caring if he fell down the stairs. He just had to get away from her. From it.

He made it into the safety of the former dining room, threw himself down at his father's side and pulled one of his dad's arms over his neck, burying his face into the old man's chest.

'She's coming,' Karl sobbed. 'She hates me. Nothing I do is ever good enough. I did everything to Molly that she asked, but even that wasn't enough.'

His father said nothing.

Karl cried until his eyes were raw.

'You won't let her hurt me, will you? I'll sleep down here with you from now on. The chair is all I need. It'll be nice and cosy with the two of us. And I won't have to worry about you as much. She can't get down the stairs yet. We're safe here.'

He pulled his father's arm a little tighter over himself.

'And when Beth Waterfall is gone, Ma will go away too. She promised she will.'

His father groaned then let out a long, rattling sigh.

'You and me, Dad, like we always were. We were the best team.' Karl forced himself to sit up. 'I never knew how much she hated us being together all the time.'

Overhead there was nothing but silence from his mother's bedroom. He hoped that meant she was done for the day. He'd have to run upstairs later and grab his toothbrush and a change of clothes for the morning, but she almost never called to him in the evening.

That had been her special time. His father would come home from work at 5 o'clock, his mother would put tea for them both on the table, then she'd disappear up to her room with a bottle of something cheap but strong and a pack of twenty cigarettes. They'd hear her television go on, she'd pull the curtains closed, and the next time they'd see her would be the following morning. It was an arrangement no one ever complained about.

Not until the night with the ambulance, the trip to the hospital, waiting on the cold, hard chairs while Karl's mother was under the knife. Everything changed after that.

Chapter 25

8 June

Christie Salter and Connie Woolwine walked side by side down the stairway to the cells where their presence had been requested by the custody sergeant on duty.

'Do you know what this is about?' Connie asked.

'He wouldn't say. The custody sergeants here are notoriously tight-lipped and unimpressed. It's a tough job. They're the gatekeepers to the drunk, the drugged, the villains and the falsely accused, and I wouldn't want to be locked up with any of them.' Salter flinched as they turned a corner and her hand went straight to her abdomen.

'You okay?'

'Old wound,' she said. 'The scar tissue mended pretty tight. Gets me when I least expect it. I'm fine now but it was touch and go when it happened.'

Connie saw the shadow draw across Salter's face.

'What else happened?' Connie asked.

Salter gave her head a tiny shake that ran down her body as a shiver.

'Do you mind if we don't talk about it?' Salter asked. 'It's personal and still painful.'

'Did you not get therapy?'

'Counselling, we call it here. And no. Never much saw the point of talking for hours. Time heals, right?'

'Not at all. Time can sometimes make things substantially worse. And the point about therapy isn't that you have a chance to talk, it's that you're listened to. Otherwise you could just sit and spill it all to the mirror. What happened?' Connie paused on the landing and stepped back into a concrete corner.

Salter blew out a long breath and stared at her. 'Everything I heard about you was true, then. You're unstoppable and intrusive.'

'And still you don't really seem to mind. You're perfectly relaxed, your facial muscles aren't drawn in at all. You never let your pain affect you. How have you done that?' Connie asked.

'I adopted a baby to ease the pain of the one I lost,' Salter replied quietly.

'Except it didn't work like that. You still have all the grief and, on top of that, you have all the exhaustion, tumult and exhilaration. I'm surprised you can even get out of bed in the morning.' Salter said nothing. 'There's a thing I do that freaks people out, which seems to be a theme with me right now. But could I see the scar? It would help if I could touch it.'

Salter frowned at her. 'We're in a corridor.'

'Sometimes it's best to make yourself utterly, uncomfortably vulnerable. Often that's the only way to start to heal.'

Salter swore softly beneath her breath, but she was already pulling her T-shirt out of her jeans as she stepped in close to Connie.

They stood, silently, as Connie stared at it before touching it.

'Someone stabbed me with the broken shard of a pottery

cat bowl. Are you not going to comment on how red it is? My husband tells me at least once a week that it looks almost like it's still bleeding,' Salter said.

'I can only see in black and white, or shades of grey to be precise,' Connie said.

Salter paused and cleared her throat. 'How's that possible?'

'Another scar. Mine's inside my brain.' She reached out cool but firm fingertips and ran them over Salter's scar, exploring the map of jagged edges, twists and branches of hurt flesh.

'You could have asked a surgeon to improve this. It would have helped dramatically. But the pain helps with the guilt, right? You feel like you have no right to be happy when your baby is dead. You're using your scar like an offering to the gods. If you keep feeling the pain every day, nothing bad will happen to the child you've adopted.'

'I should have listened to Lively. He told me not to let you get inside my head.' Salter stepped away and pulled her top back down.

'Do you want to know what you're actually doing, or do you want to keep hitting an emotional brick wall?' Connie asked. She rubbed her hands together gently as if she was memorising the scar.

'If I let you tell me, will you stop?' Salter asked, already heading towards the staircase.

'I will,' Connie said, following after her. 'That scar and the pain it gives you aren't just reminding you to grieve the baby you lost, they're actively stopping you from bonding with your adopted child. You feel obliged to hold a part of you back so that the betrayal you've imagined isn't complete. Because guilt is the real monster that lives beneath every adult's bed, and generally it has more teeth for women than it does for men. So here's my prescription. See a surgeon. Let them improve

143

your scar. Grieve your loss by loving more, not less. Heal by feeling joy, not pain. Motherhood is hard enough without deliberately keeping yourself ripped in two for something that wasn't your fault.'

They reached the corridor into the cells as Salter turned to face her.

'Why do you do that – get into people's heads? It doesn't make you feel awkward?'

'It's how I learn. My job is like being a psychological dictionary or thesaurus. An encyclopedia. Every human being I can understand makes me better able to understand all the ways people break. Also, I hope I can help along the way. People always know what's wrong with them really, it's just that they fight the urge to admit the truth to themselves. Having someone else do it simply forces a reality check that hopefully leads to progress. Shall we?'

She walked past Salter and opened the door into the cells and the custody sergeant who was pointedly looking at the enormous clock on the wall.

'Took your time. You'll be glad to know that madam in cell two has vomited twice in the last fifteen minutes, so if you're lucky her stomach will now be empty. In any event, I should stand well back and run if she starts groaning,' he instructed.

'What's she in for?' Salter asked.

'Shoplifting. Haven't seen her for a few weeks, but Mandy's a regular. This time, the off-licence is insisting we prosecute as she knocked over several bottles of expensive wine on her way out, so the total damages run to about three hundred quid. Mandy, however, seems to think she has an ace up her sleeve. Said she wants to talk to whoever's investigating Archie Bass's death. I gather that's you.'

'It is indeed,' Connie said. 'Let's go talk to Mandy.'

Mandy MacGill smelled worse than a student nightclub toilet at 4 a.m. She had a tattoo on her forehead that at one point must have said 'Fuck you' but it had such a deep wrinkle running across it that it looked more like the forces of nature had attempted to redact it. It was impossible to guess her age. Either she was much older than she looked and been pickled by all the alcohol, or it had aged her by a couple of decades. Connie felt a rush of sadness at Mandy's vulnerability and let Salter take the lead, introducing them before getting down to it.

'You wanted to tell us something, Mandy?'

'I've got demands, I have. They've gotta be fuckin' met, right, before I'll say a bloody word. I've got important in-for-ma-tion!' She punctuated the word with a pointed finger.

Salter sighed and folded her arms. 'Your demands are?'

'Bottle of vodka, not cheap shit, fish and chips, deep-fried Mars bar, a four-pack of Irn-Bru, and impunity in fuckin' writing from all prostitutions.'

Salter rubbed her eyes. 'You can have the food but not the booze. I'll do what I can about *immunity* from *prosecution* but first you have to make us believe you've something to bargain with, or we walk and you don't get so much as a sniff of deep-fried fat.'

'Na, I'm not fallin' for that. You'll take the gold and disappear and I'll get nuthin',' she shouted. 'I want a fuckin' lawyer in here!'

'Mandy,' Salter said. 'I'm going to need you to shut the hell up. You don't need a lawyer because Dr Woolwine and I are not here to charge you with anything. I can and will get you the food. You know the rules about alcohol in the cells and you never expected me to say yes to that. But if you don't start talking, I'm leaving because I'm not in the mood to be messed around. You have one chance, and this is it.'

Mandy huffed and kicked at the badly stained floor before nodding.

'Aw right, aw right. But I want curry sauce wi' the chips. I was there, see, the night Archie got murdered. I seen it all.'

'Tell us,' Salter said.

'We was both round in the road behind the back of them big shops, the electrical store and whatever. They've got the big bins out there that's good for finding cardboard and you don't get kicked by the fuckin' passers-by like you do in the city centre. Less chance of being thrown cash, but less chance of getting fucked over, too, know what I'm saying? I was there first and I seen Archie come in but I was already in my boxes and I didn't want him stealing my bottle, so I didn't call out to him.'

'What time was that?' Salter asked.

'Do I look like I wear a fuckin' watch?' Mandy replied. 'Anyways, he's over the road from me, wrapping himself up in his sleeping bag or whatever so I say nuthin', just make sure I'm covered up and start to fall asleep. I wake up when I hear him moaning. He never screamed. Like it all happened so fast that he didn't have the chance.'

'Did you see the person who stabbed him, Mandy? Think hard, and don't just tell us what you think we want to hear. It's too important for that,' Salter said.

'It were just one person. Big coat, hood up. I only saw them from behind. I just know they were in front of him when I looked up, and he was groaning when they walked away. Didn't say a word. I figured it was just like a fight or something.' She put her head down. 'I didn't know he'd been fuckin' stabbed, did I? I'd have done something. Told someone. He just sat there, and I thought he'd fallen asleep again.'

'Was it a man or a woman? What were they wearing on their legs? Anything else, like skin colour or age?'

146

'Dunno. Never saw anything except the back of the big coat. Wearing trousers, I guess, or I'd have noticed. They walked away normal pace, though. Didnae run. I've seen kids do that sort of thing before. Kids run away, like they've been brave wee bastards for a few seconds then they start to shit themselves.'

'You didn't go over to Archie, check on him?' Salter asked.

'To be honest, I was tired. Had a bit to drink, you know? And you get used to a bit of violence on the streets. Archie was all right, but he wasn't a pal. I just thought he owed someone some cash or somethin' and they were teaching him a lesson. I only found out a few days later that he was dead. When I left in the morning, I didn't give him a second look.'

'All right,' Salter said. 'We'll get you your food, I'll talk to the off-licence and see if we can get the charges dropped. You should see a doctor while you're here, too. Anything else we can do?'

'Na, s'awright. Just the food. But I could do with a new pair of socks if you've got any. Some bastard nicked mine.'

Salter and Connie made their way back upstairs.

'Well that was a waste of time,' Salter said. 'I thought we might finally get a break.'

'It might not have been a break, but it definitely wasn't a waste of time. We know Archie wasn't killed in some random drunken fight, we know the assailant was a lone operator, we know the stabbing was planned and calculated, we know it wasn't done by some kid trying to prove how hard they are. That's quite a lot of extra knowledge. Can I just ask, what on earth is a deep-fried Mars bar?'

'Imagine a visual representation of every possible lifestyle cause of a heart attack,' Salter said. 'It looks and tastes exactly like that.'

Chapter 26

Eighteen Months Earlier

The painkillers were all she could think about taking for breakfast. She didn't even want to wash them down with her usual cup of peppermint tea or a glass of orange juice. Just two extra-strong headache tablets and mouth under the tap for water. Molly didn't even know why she was taking them. She didn't have any identifiable pain that needed relieving. They just made her feel more in control, somehow.

They gave her chronic stomachache as well, but that was fine because she got rid of that with . . . well, more pills. The woman in her local chemist had started giving her funny looks and suggesting she should visit her doctor if she couldn't get her pain under control, so the supermarket had become her go-to for the tablets now. Never the same till two days in a row.

The plus side was that she'd lost her appetite completely, so she was saving money on food as well as losing weight. It was every twenty-something's dream. More cash in her pocket, less weight on her hips. Not that she'd had any excess in the first place.

Mol stared at the canvas, half-finished, in front of her. She could barely remember starting it. Insomnia had claimed her nighttime hours so she'd begun a fresh painting to get through the small hours and here, now, was a dead rabbit in a tiny coffin, attended by a procession of teary-eyed woodland creatures. There was plenty left to do, but it had taken shape as if a demon had possessed her paintbrush. The thought of it made her laugh. There were no demons inside her studio, but there might very well be one outside, watching the door to spy on her comings and goings, leaving little things to rip her heart out and violate her peace.

The police had been keen at first, taking statements, making sure she felt heard. But Karl Smith was a common name. All the social media posts disappeared as soon as she'd seen them. The email addresses he'd used were a pathway to nothing. And the gifts weren't harassment if she couldn't prove they were all from the same person. The rotting fruit might have been a simple mistake. The dead rabbit on her car windscreen might have been dropped there by a bird of prey. The silent calls to her work phone were all from different numbers so no pattern could be established. And she'd never actually been threatened, had she? He'd never approached her in person. She wasn't afraid for her life.

Mol lost count of the times she heard an apology followed by the words, 'but there's really nothing we can do at this time. Call us if things develop.'

'Develop,' she mumbled to the sad animals in glorious oils. 'What's that even supposed to mean?'

There was a whole website dedicated to explaining all the reasons why her work was substandard with a domain name hosted on a Russian server, no traceable owner, and in any event, that apparently was the exercise of free speech.

149

Everywhere else her work could be reviewed, it had been, the negative pile-on losing her the few regular clients she had left, and reducing the value of her work to nothing more than hospital corridor prints.

He stalked her in a million tiny ways that couldn't be caught on camera or forensically proven. The online world, Mol discovered, was as toxic and mad as a bag of vipers, but removing yourself from it brought soul-destroying isolation.

Seeing her mother so worried about her didn't help. The constant glances across the table at mealtimes to see if she was eating enough. The messages, hourly, if she wasn't in surgery. Did she need anything? Want anything? Had there been any more 'events', as they'd come to call them? Was she sleeping? Should they move house? There were cameras everywhere, at home and at work, that should have made Molly feel safer but that only ever succeeded in reminding her that she was being watched.

In a moment of crazed fury, she'd signed up for internet dating – daring him, almost wanting him, to find her and ask her out so she could look in his eyes and spit her grief at him for destroying her life. Instead, she'd made contact with a nice man, good-looking but not showy, who taught English literature to children who'd rather be playing football or watching TikTok videos. They'd spoken on the phone then agreed to go on a date and, while she was genuinely terrified and wanted to do nothing but hide, she'd gone out of sheer bloody-mindedness, promising herself that it would be the dawn of a brave new era, where she would reinvent herself and start living again.

Her date had turned up but found it hard to look her in the eyes, been polite but formal, and when she suggested they move on from the bar to the restaurant they'd agreed on, he coughed a few times and found a reason to speak to her while looking exclusively at the floor.

'I'm very sorry about this,' he'd said. 'Really, I am, because you seem lovely. But the thing is, I did a quick search for you online. I know that's shallow but when I found out you were an artist I wanted to look at your work. I wasn't looking for personal details, I promise.' He cleared his throat another dozen times. 'Um, so there were some videos. Private things that I'm sure at the time you hadn't dreamed would be made public.'

'Oh,' Mol said. 'Oh no. They're deep fakes and I thought they'd all been taken down. I would never . . . I mean, I have never—'

'And the problem with that is,' he continued as if she hadn't said a word. It was the only way, Mol thought, that he could get through the speech he'd clearly prepared earlier – ever the teacher – and escape. 'I'm a teacher at a private school. That's no excuse and it sounds all wrong. But I can't be in a relationship with someone who has that sort of online presence. It wouldn't be tolerated. The parents, you see.' As if that was a complete sentence.

Mol's stomach had sunk so low that she thought it might be in her shoes. There was nothing left to say. No point explaining or defending herself to the very nice man who was shrinking away from her as if the mess of her life might be catching.

She picked up her handbag, pushed her chair back without it scraping the floor and making a noise, took out £5 and laid it on the table to repay him for the drink he'd bought her because at least he'd had the decency to show up and explain things to her face, then left without a word. As she walked past the window she could see him in the bar, staring sadly at the banknote.

And that was that.

Her mobile rang twice then stopped, then four knocks were hammered out on the door to her studio, one-two pause three-four. It was her mother.

Beth Waterfall put on her best happy face as she held up a bag of baguettes and lemonade.

'Surprise!' she sang.

'Mum,' Mol's voice was the gentlest of warnings. She didn't want anyone in her space. It was the one place she didn't have to pretend to be okay. 'We talked about this.'

'It's lunch. There's a norovirus alert at the hospital so most surgeries have been cancelled and I've done more hours than I should have this month, so they took me off the rota and told me to go home.'

And you didn't come home last night – those words hung in the air, unspoken. *I'm worried sick about my daughter. I know you're drowning. Why won't you hold my hand to pull you out of the water, when I offer it to you?*

Molly didn't invite her in but knew there was no way of stopping her, so Beth walked close, hugged her daughter with her free hand, kissed her cheek, and bustled past.

'Gosh, this place is cleaner than I've ever seen it. And you've been busy! So many new canvases. Are they all completed? Why are they covered? I've never seen you do that before.'

Before Mol could stop her, Beth walked up to the nearest one and pulled away the sheet covering the painting. She gasped, stared, frowned, looked at Molly then back to the picture. When she was finally able to tear her eyes off the image, she turned to Mol aghast.

'What is this?'

Molly shrugged.

Beth strode to the next covered canvas and pulled the sheet away. And the next. And the next. There were nineteen in all, a few unfinished but most were complete works that could have gone straight into a gallery if they wouldn't have horrified the patrons.

'Molly,' Beth whispered. 'We have to talk about this.'

'You're overreacting,' she replied, already picking up sheets off the floor and starting to re-cover the paintings.

'Stop,' her mother insisted, pulling the sheets from her hands. 'Darling, these paintings are . . . they're—'

'Just say it,' Molly told her.

'Concerning. Disturbing, even.' Beth walked back to look at the bowl of rotting fruit in the first picture. 'Brilliant, too. Quite extraordinary. As good as Adriaen Coorte's gooseberries but a nightmare version, and the hyperrealism is as exquisite as Christiane Vleugels'. Mol, I know things have been awful. I know it feels like life will never get better, but this goes way beyond a dark frame of mind. Everything on these pictures is rotting, disintegrating. And as for the dead animals, birds and fish . . .'

'I'm just processing what's happening to me. It's good for me, I think.'

'But you've done so much. Oil paintings of this size and this detail – this would be a lifetime's work for some artists. Have you been sleeping at all? I've never known you produce work this fast.'

'It's better for me to be busy,' Mol said, but her voice made it more question than statement.

'Oh sweetheart, let's just move. We've talked about it. I think it would be best. We'll put the house on the market, and I can get a job anywhere in the UK. The south coast is nice. Maybe the New Forest. Cornwall, even. We can go as soon as I've got a new job. We'll rent until the house is sold—'

'You can't move away from the internet, Mum. It's everywhere. He's destroyed my reputation, my work, my personal life. My name. Cornwall can't fix that.'

'Then we'll go back to the police and we won't stop until they find this bastard.'

'God, Mum, would you wake up? I know you mean well but it's not your life he's destroyed. I don't even know what's real any more. I see a dead pigeon in our driveway and I'm convinced he threw it there. If a letter arrives with a ripped edge, I think he's been going through our post. I walk along the street with my phone camera pointed over my shoulder so I can see who's behind me. I can't see beauty any more, that's why these paintings exist. I never knew the meaning of the word corruption until this started. My life is over!'

'It's not—'

Molly screeched. 'Yes it is! I can't date, I can't go online or go to galleries, I can't sell my work, I can't sleep and I can't eat. I tried fighting fire with fire and announcing online that I was being harassed but I was just shouting into the void. He's launched a hate campaign against me, and he's very, very good at it. No one can help me. Not even you.' She clutched her stomach and fell to her knees. Beth moved towards her, but Molly held up a warning hand. 'Don't.'

Beth looked around at the canvases filled with death and decay, decadently and extravagantly portrayed, so realistic that it was impossible not to want to reach out and touch each scene. Her daughter, her beautiful, talented adult daughter, was curled up on the floor, forehead touching the cold concrete floor of her studio, broken. Utterly, utterly broken. For the first time since Beth had become a mother, she was powerless and terrified. And she knew in her heart that they hadn't hit rock bottom quite yet.

Chapter 27

9 June

Connie and Baarda were on a video call from their temporary office at the police station. On the screen was a young woman. In the background were patio doors that opened onto an orchard, and in the distance two figures could be seen wandering around and occasionally picking something off a bush or a tree.

'I'm not sure how soon we're going to be finished here, Midnight,' Connie said. 'So don't accept any new consultations. This is proving harder than I thought it'd be. The lack of evidential leads is confounding.'

'Confounding?' Midnight laughed. 'Either you've spent too long in the UK or Baarda is brainwashing you. Did you get the request I sent for a series of training workshops with the FBI in October?'

'I did, and we'll do it as long as nothing serious comes into the diary that's a conflict. Could you reply with that caveat?'

'Sure,' Midnight said, making notes as they spoke.

Midnight Jones was their human hub, dealing with all the vital admin that Connie hated and that she insisted Baarda not get sidetracked by. She was organised, astute, available to help twenty-four hours a day, and was an impressive profiler herself albeit with a more technological leaning.

'And Brodie, we had a solicitor's letter delivered here for you.' She frowned as she spoke and they all knew it was bad news before she delivered it. 'I opened it in case it was urgent. It's from your ex-wife's lawyer.'

'Go on,' Baarda said.

'Now that your ex has changed her name since remarrying, she's asking your agreement to change your children's surname too. Something about maintaining the family unit so things are less confusing for them.'

Connie opened her mouth to speak but Baarda held up a hand.

'Thanks, Midnight. Could you scan the letter and email it to me, please? I'll deal with it.'

'Brodie, she can't just—'

'I said I'll deal with it, Connie,' he interjected. 'Can we talk about the Edinburgh murders instead?' His voice was giving nothing away, but there was no mistaking the clenched muscles in his jaw and the narrowing of his eyes.

'Of course,' Midnight said. 'I started with Dale Abnay's body. There are no other missing persons in the Edinburgh area who seem to have similar interests to Abnay regarding the incel group, so it doesn't look as if his disappearance is part of a wider plan or group retribution. I checked in with DS Salter who let me have his mobile messages and emails. There was nothing there to suggest any active threat, no planned liaisons with people who are red flags, and no debt. However, he did have an app on his mobile confirming that he was a hiking enthusiast – it shows the trails he'd walked previously – so it looks as if he was genuinely at Jupiter Artland for recreation.'

'That's a diverse CV then. "In my spare time I enjoy hiking and imagining the violent repression of women." Mr Abnay was just full of surprises. Do we have verification of the planned kidney donation?' Connie asked.

'We do. There are emails from the donor service, proposed dates for the operation, advice for recuperation and a request for him to take independent medical and legal advice before he signed the documentation. Things never progressed that far, though.'

Another woman burst into the room holding hands with a much older lady. The younger of the two was a carbon copy of Midnight but grinning from ear to ear, and waving into the camera.

'Wooly!' she cried. 'Look!' She held up a handful of early summer fruit from the garden then popped a raspberry into her mouth.

'Dawn,' Connie said. 'That looks nice. And hello Doris. You two look like life is treating you well.'

'It certainly is that, dearie,' Doris said. 'The garden's giving us so much fruit and veg, we don't know what to do with it all. I've got jam coming out of my ears! We miss you down here. Time for a visit before you two go gadding off again?'

'Wooly!' Dawn said again. It was her pet name for Connie, and she was the only person in the world who could get away with giving her a nickname, but Midnight's twin, though fate had been cruel at birth and left her with severe special needs, had the sweetest of souls. Doris, in her seventies with purple hair and huge, colourful earrings and beads, had left London to live with the sisters as the mother figure they so badly wanted. Together, the three of them had created a home as full of joy as any Connie had ever visited.

'We'll make sure to visit you in the beautiful West Country

157

before we leave the UK,' Connie said. 'A proper visit this time, not just an hour.'

'Careful, Dr Woolwine, we'll end up domesticating you if you're not careful. You won't want to leave,' Doris said. 'I need to cook for you for a few days, anyway. Put a bit of meat on those bones. You do look thin, lovey.'

'Thank you, Doris,' Connie said. 'I will eat whatever you put in front of me.'

'Okay, that's enough chatter, back to work,' Midnight said, giving her sister a kiss on the cheek.

'Righty ho, time to bake some tea loaf, I think. Come on, Dawn. Let's leave this lot to it!'

They left in a burst of chatter and laughter.

'As I was saying,' Midnight continued. 'Dale Abnay's offer of a kidney appears to be real and valid. Also, I couldn't find any suggestion that money was going to be exchanged, although that's not something I'd expect to see in writing anyway.'

'Okay. What about Archie Bass? Has anything turned up on him?' Baarda asked.

'No. Edinburgh had a spate of murders of homeless people a few years ago, but nothing recently. This one is much less puzzling than Dale Abnay, though. Homeless people can be prey to drug users, mentally ill people, or just someone with an amount of rage who feels like finding an easy target. Without CCTV – the only cameras there were focused on the rear doors of the property to catch burglars going in or staff removing goods – it'll be hard to pin down a suspect. Interestingly, neither Abnay nor Bass had any close, regular ties in the community other than Bass's sister Jane, who saw him only sporadically, and Leslie Wolfe, who wanted the kidney. Both men would have appealed to a killer who wanted victims where there would be minimal public outcry.'

'That's a good point,' Connie said. 'Let's move on to talk about Divya Singh.'

'Different set-up, really impersonal modus operandi. Whoever killed her really didn't want to get their hands dirty, same as using a gun but without the possibility of having to look a victim in the eyes,' Baarda noted. 'There are a lot more possibilities here. We can't exclude people who knew her. There was an insurance policy on her life, it could have been a personal vendetta, potentially she was a victim of a racist attack. It could even have been mistaken identity or a thrill-killer.'

'This killer certainly doesn't have poor impulse control,' Connie said. 'The scene looks chaotic but the kill was the opposite. They attacked her away from CCTV, away from witnesses, not even with a view from a window. It was fast and left no possibility of survival, and they didn't leave a forensic trail. That's a perfectly executed murder. In terms of categorising it, it's more like a professional hit.'

'An assassination?' Midnight asked.

'It's as clean as a professional hit, although there would have been ways of killing Mrs Singh that might have looked more like suicide. Brodie, how much was the insurance policy worth?' Connie asked.

'Only a hundred and fifty thousand, which isn't nothing but it's not a lot compared to others I've dealt with.'

'Most hits cost in the region of thirty thousand depending on how high-profile the target is, so the profit is relatively low given the risks. Still, it's an area to look at,' Connie noted.

'So you have three separate cases: one dead incel, a homeless man and a person of colour,' Midnight said. 'If they were linked, I'd say this was looking like a far-right evangelical murderer who thinks they have a divine right to rid the world of anyone not in their chosen societal group.'

Connie played along. 'If it were a far-right evangelist psychopath, Dale Abnay's death could even be because he agreed to a kidney transplant. Presumably that goes against the will of God.'

Baarda sat forward.

'It's not impossible,' he said.

'Brodie, I was kidding. There's nothing linking these deaths,' Connie said.

'Not all links are positive in nature. Sometimes similarities are found in the things that are missing. There's a lack of ritual, no torture, every crime scene is left immediately, it's forensically clean, no weapons have been found, out of reach of CCTV.'

'Archie Bass didn't die immediately though,' Midnight noted.

'Not for want of trying, and he was only saved by excessive layering of clothing,' Baarda said. 'Maybe they couldn't risk opening the clothing to check the wounds or find a pulse because of trace DNA. Rather than carelessness, it might actually be more evidence of good practice.'

'Serial killers choose one method and stick with it, almost exclusively, not to mention the fact that you can usually find a link between the victim types,' Connie said. 'What's the motivation? The gratification element of these deaths would have to be something like a god-delusion or a power play. But surely then they'd want some recognition of their work. I'd expect the killer to have at least kept a trophy.'

'A photo, maybe,' Baarda suggested. 'Something easy to erase, without risking any transfer of DNA material onto the body.'

'But a photo would be a definite link to the murders if the mobile phone was found, and this killer has done only one thing the same at every crime scene – they've made themselves untraceable. A photo would be too risky. Deleting it fully isn't the same as hitting a button. Even teenagers know that,' Connie said.

'I feel like I've started something that I can't justify,' Midnight said, starting to type. 'I have some statistics here. Scotland's homicide rate is at an all-time low. Last year there was only one homicide in the whole of Scotland where a single perpetrator killed more than one victim. As for Divya Singh, women being killed by strangers account for an incredibly low proportion of deaths in Scotland. And in the last year, sixty-seven per cent of all homicides up there happened inside residential premises. All of which means that the chances of this being the work of a single killer is statistically almost impossible.'

'Goddammit,' Connie said. 'You know that as soon as we declare something almost impossible, it becomes the most likely scenario, right?'

Midnight and Baarda thought about it, and neither commented.

'So in terms of a profile, we have someone purposeful, careful, capable of learning, someone who is aware of what not to do. Intelligent, but driven and single-minded,' Midnight said.

'And flexible. Able to adapt to kill however best suits the moment or the victim. It would, at least, explain the sudden rise in Edinburgh's homicide rate.' She sighed. 'All right. Do we agree, then, that in the absence of any leads indicating individual killers, we should proceed to consider the possibility that a single person has committed all these deaths?' Connie asked.

Baarda and Midnight nodded.

'Then we need to brief the rest of the squad,' Connie said. 'We should do that sooner rather than later. Brodie, gather the troops. I'll deal with them, you go and break the news to the superintendent.'

'I feel rather as if I've drawn the short straw,' Brodie said. 'Any particular reason why that's falling to me?'

'It's that Old Etonian charm.' Connie winked at him. 'You're

161

hard to resist when you decide to switch it on. Also, for some reason, I feel as if she's less likely to be sarcastic to you.'

'Because I don't provoke her.'

'And that is why you're my perfect secret weapon. And I'll buy you dinner if you do it.'

'Not worth it,' Baarda said, already knowing he'd do it anyway. It was impossible to say no to Connie Woolwine.

Chapter 28

10 June

Connie ran faster.

Jogging at 4.30 a.m. was always fraught with unspoken risks, but she figured the majority of society's detritus had to be asleep at that time. She loved the empty streets and the sense that the world was neatly tucked away, giving her brain the space to expand on all the theories she had bubbling away.

Back home on Martha's Vineyard, her parents' house had been situated south of Oak Bluffs and out on Seaview Avenue that ran for miles down towards Edgartown. They didn't get as many tourists as Edgartown with its film locations from *Jaws* and upmarket art galleries, but Oak Bluffs was still booked up from Spring Break through the long summer vacation and into September. The shifting population was just something you got used to, with people camping out on the beaches or sleeping in utility vehicles. All of which meant one thing – you had to be careful what you did, where you went, and who was around. Martha's Vineyard was low crime but not no crime, and girls jogging along the beach early in the morning and late at night were targets for the wrong sort of men.

It was the rape of a fifteen-year-old holiday-maker that was the real wake-up call. At sixteen, Connie had been a sensible enough teenager, and her parents were naturally protective, but the idea that girls weren't safe in their hometown was a shock to the system. Her best friend's father, an engineer by trade, had responded by designing a weapon that his daughter and all her friends could have on them as needed, even without bags or pockets, and that no one ever needed to be aware of. Fast forward almost two decades later, and Connie still wore it whenever she went out jogging or looking for answers in the sorts of places where you probably didn't want to find them.

Edinburgh was darker than Martha's Vineyard at that time in the morning, but it had the benefit of there being many more places to turn off and hide, which was what she was planning on doing just as soon as she found the right place.

It had begun the second she'd exited her hotel. Connie had been awake for an hour and knew full well that she wouldn't get back to sleep. Calling Baarda to start work had been tempting but unfair, so jogging it was. The city had been a friend to her on previous trips. The people who lived there were kind and welcoming, and visitors seemed, on the whole, friendly and well-meaning. So to start with, when she'd sensed eyes on her as she'd left the hotel and paused to stretch, she'd decided that she was being ridiculous.

A couple of minutes later she was off on her usual Edinburgh route, turning behind The Balmoral and heading over North Bridge then left down High Street. Whoever the shadowy figure was behind her, they were wearing super-soft trainers and were fit enough that she wasn't losing them. The question that bothered her wasn't who, but why?

Her career could be drawn on a map, from a dangerous criminal in one city to another dangerous criminal in the next, either serial killers or serial rapists, occasionally kidnappers or torturers, but never anything less. Most had been captured and were either dead or behind bars, but there had been those who'd escaped. Connie lived with the knowledge that she had enemies worldwide. That was why she was careful.

In Edinburgh, she felt sure there was someone on the prowl who she was struggling to form a picture of in her mind. The random killings made no sense. The lack of torture or ritual was completely unfulfilling within the normal parameters of serial offender behaviour, unless the kill method wasn't the point. Perhaps, she mused, it was as simple as a release of energy, like a solar flare from the sun.

An assassin in training was another option, but most assassins were experts in low key. Whoever was following her now was good but definitely not an expert. Connie wasn't sure yet if it was a man or a woman, but they were a few inches taller than her, slim build, dark hoodie and joggers, and they ran with their feet slightly turned out.

Connie turned right on St Mary's Street then took another left into Boyd's Entry and hid behind the high wall of the private parking area at the top of Gullan's Close.

Hiding was the sensible option. She wasn't stupid nor was she careless with her own life. There had been poor decision making in the past when she was stressed and under pressure, but she'd never thrown her safety away and she wasn't about to do that now. If she let her pursuer go, however, it was a missed opportunity.

Was it the person who appeared to be choosing odd victims for no other reason than to take a life? It wasn't impossible. Connie had only seconds to make a decision. It wasn't that she was brave – her pulse rate was alarming – but she just couldn't let the chance pass. And talking dangerous people out of doing terrible things was her speciality. Plus, she was wearing her secret weapon, and she'd already undone the popper that kept a tough leather band over the top when it wasn't needed.

Stepping to one side, she not-accidentally knocked a bin then took a sharp intake of breath at the noise. The person who'd been following her stuck his head around the wall and came face to face with a woman who'd assumed the persona of someone with a will of steel.

Connie went straight for the throat just as the FBI had trained her, smashing her elbow into his Adam's apple then using her forearm to shove the man against the wall as she brought up her right wrist and pushed her bracelet into the side of his neck.

'Don't move,' she said. 'And before you speak, whatever you've got in your hands to hurt me with, know this. Pressed into your neck is a piece of surgical steel with hundreds of tiny hooks embedded, a little like insects' claws. All you'll feel right now is a prickling sensation from the miniature bed of needles, but if I fall or I'm hurt or I have to defend myself, those little hooks are going to keep hold of a section of your flesh and pull it right off, and you don't want that on the side of your neck. That would be very dangerous indeed.'

'You're . . . you're a fucking psycho. I'd heard you were weird as shit, but you're actually out of your fucking mind!'

He was Scottish, Caucasian, late twenties or early thirties, five foot eleven tall, with carefully plucked eyebrows and a neatly trimmed beard. He was also starting to cry, so unless he was the best actor in the world under severe pressure, Connie deduced that whatever else he might be, he certainly wasn't a killer.

'Get it out of my neck,' he shrieked. 'That's assault!'

'Are you kidding me? You were waiting for me outside my hotel, you've been following me, I perceived you as a threat, I hid from you and gave you a chance to move away, then you actually followed me into the area where I was hiding from you. Now I'm no lawyer, but I think I'm going to get away with telling them I was acting in self-defence.'

'It hurts!' There were proper tears cascading down his cheeks now and his nose was starting to run. Connie rolled her eyes.

'Only because you're pulling. If you stand still, it'll be fine. I'll lift the hooks out when you've answered my questions. Let's start with the obvious ones, who are you and why are you following me?'

'Journalist. I write for *The Daily Essay*.'

'Never heard of it,' she said. 'Speed up.'

'We're mainly online because of paper costs. But I was told to follow you and keep track of your movements. It was my editor's idea, not mine, I swear. I didn't have a choice, I just go where I'm told. I'm not getting paid enough for this.'

'Name?' Connie demanded.

'Kev,' he said, the crying reducing to a mere snivel.

'Okay, Kev. I'm going to take my arm away from your throat but you need to stay very still so that I can lift the hooks out of your skin with minimal damage. You're going to stay put for the remainder of our conversation.'

He screwed his eyes tightly shut as she removed the barbed bangle, and even Connie was a little concerned about the damage, having never used it before. Fair play to her friend's father, though, who'd designed a mostly legal weapon that could be worn as a fashion accessory. She was impressed.

Kev was left bleeding and raw but not in need of medical treatment, so that seemed reasonable.

'Walk with me,' she said. 'We need to talk.'

167

They retraced their steps with Kev gripping his neck as if he was bleeding out.

'Does it look bad? It feels bad. Should we call an ambulance?'

'I try not to be rude to people I've only just met, Kev, but would you grow a pair? Now, tell me why your editor would think I'm an interesting enough person to have me followed.'

'It's the cases you're investigating.' He paused and looked at her in a way that suggested he'd practised it in the mirror. 'We know.'

Connie fought the urge to slap him.

'You *know*? God, this is exhausting. I'm just calling the police. I work with them after all. I'm pretty sure I can have you locked up for harassment or intimidation or something like that, and that's if they don't plant some drugs on you just because you're annoying me.'

'You can't threaten me,' he wailed.

'You're right, it's so easy it's beneath me. I'll play nice. So what is it that I'm supposed to know?'

'That you believe there's a serial killer operating in Edinburgh, that your whole squad has no leads and no clues, and that absolutely anyone might be the next victim because, in spite of the fact that you're supposed to be some shit-hot profiler, you can't find any patterns at all in the killer's behaviour.' By the time he'd finished the sentence, his voice was so high that it was painful to listen to.

Connie stopped still in the middle of North Bridge and stared at him.

'And how in the name of all that is precious to you, did you happen to come by that information, Kev?' she asked quietly.

Had Kev been a snail, he'd have retreated the soft parts of his body back into his shell. Instead, he just looked like he was sucking himself inwards.

168

'We never reveal our sources,' he said.

'Suppose I said you're completely wrong and that if you print it, we'll sue you.'

Kev shook his head frantically. 'It's a good source. Anonymous but we have detail.'

'Give it to me fast,' she said.

'Three murders, no suspects, no torture, no accidents, clean crime scenes, lack of motive, resemble assassinations. Someone in MIT dubbed him the Joyride Killer yesterday because it looks like he's just enjoying himself for no particular reason.'

He was right. Someone had shouted the nickname in the briefing room as Connie was explaining the latest theory, although she hadn't seen who. All of which meant that she had two choices. Lie and deny, or take the facts as she believed them to be and try to turn the situation to her advantage.

'So a member of my team took a theory from yesterday's briefing and presented it to you as fact,' she said. 'That's not good. It means I'll have to look at everyone's phone records, emails, messages, social media—'

'So you don't deny it,' he said, emboldened.

'That someone's getting disciplined, fired and might end up in court? Nope, don't deny that at all. Keep walking. There's someone I want you to meet.'

Connie greeted the early shift reception team at The Balmoral cheerily as Kev plodded along behind her still gripping his neck with bloodied fingers. If they wondered what was going on, they were well trained enough to simply smile and wish them a good day.

Baarda opened the door on the second knock, looking as if he too had already been awake and was in the middle of exercising.

He stared from Connie to Kev and back again, then sighed.

'Come in,' he said. 'I'm not even sure I want to know what's happening here.'

Connie filled him in as she put the kettle on. They took Kev's mobile from him before letting him clean up in Baarda's bathroom.

'You realise we're pretty much holding a journalist hostage right now?' Baarda whispered.

'Well, I can't deny what he said, so we need to figure out a way to make this work for us before we can release him into the wild,' she said. 'And after that we need to figure out who gave the story to the press.'

'All of which is far less worrying than the fact that you were running around with a weapon that you actually used on him. I never even realised what that thing was!'

'That's exactly the point!'

Kev emerged from the bathroom holding a makeshift toilet roll bandage against his neck.

'Coffee?' Connie asked him cheerily.

'I don't do very well on caffeine. Is there any hot chocolate?' he asked. Baarda trod on Connie's toe before she could say whatever was in her head, and a few minutes later they sat down together to talk.

'Here's what we're going to do,' Connie said. 'You can print your story but only in the form of an interview with me. I want this to be in my words, not through some third party who'll miss all the nuance and rationale. You can have the exclusive.'

'We'd want to do a photoshoot with you,' he said. 'Properly, of course, hair and make-up, the works.'

'Absolutely not,' Baarda interrupted. 'It's too dangerous. You might as well paint a target on your back.'

'It's not as if there aren't plenty of pictures of you available on the internet already,' Kev said. 'You've got a bit of a following.

Mainly conspiracy theorists and nutters, of course. Hey, maybe that's who the killer is, someone who wants to mess with you and see if they can beat you at the profiling game, but the key is not to leave a pattern,' he added with a disturbing level of enthusiasm.

'There's always a pattern,' Connie replied, 'even if it's only the fact that it looks like there's no pattern. Brodie, could you get him out of here, please? Give him Midnight's phone number and email. She'll make all the arrangements.'

'Midnight?' Kev asked.

'Our remote research assistant and head of operations,' Baarda said. 'And it sounds to me as if Dr Woolwine has had enough, so best be going now.'

Connie stretched out on Baarda's bed and closed her eyes. Either the early start was catching up with her or she was getting a migraine.

'I'm making you a mint tea,' Baarda said. 'You're pale.'

'It makes me unhappy,' she said. 'Not mint tea, the publicity stuff.'

'The idea that people are getting to know who you are? It was inevitable at some point. You've become a global expert in serial killers. It's the modern obsession. People want to know what the secret of your insight is.'

'It shouldn't be about me. That's insulting to the victims and their families.'

He put the tea next to her on the bedside table.

'That may not be up to you to decide. But this interview will only put you more in the spotlight. We don't want the killer coming after you, Connie.'

'We have to do something. The bodies are piling up. Mmm, this tea is lovely, thank you.'

He sat on the edge of the bed as she sipped. 'You think that

171

giving an interview will force the perpetrator out of hiding? Maybe appeal to their ego? Get them to write to the newspaper or contact us directly?'

'It's worked before. If these are the efforts of a single person then they're adapting as they go. Most psychopaths get set in their ways. It's the repetition that trips them up. And most of them at some point express a desire to be profiled or some pleasure at the attention it brings them. The majority of serial killers have asked to meet with their profiler after capture. It's as if they want someone to look into their soul and explain their whole psychological chemistry to them. Kind of why some people buy books about the meanings of dreams, because they think there's some code in there that will uncover their secret inner self.'

'Is there?'

'No. It's just your brain putting everything into a filing cabinet, only some of it needs to go in the stressors section, and those dreams are almost always bad. You think the interview is a mistake?'

'I don't know,' he said. 'But I don't think Superintendent Overbeck is going to sign off on it, and I'm fairly certain she'll go for the "don't make yourself the story" angle.'

'I think you might be right,' Connie said, putting the cup down and getting herself comfortable on his pillows. 'Do I have time for a nap? I got up way too early.'

'You do,' he said. 'I'm heading down to the spa for a swim. You can stay here then we'll get breakfast together. Sound good?'

'Sounds like heaven,' she said. 'I was thinking today about when I used to run along Seaview Avenue at sunrise. You like the sea, right? You'd love it there.'

Baarda grabbed his swimming shorts and his mobile, and moved to the door.

'Will you visit Martha's Vineyard with me, Brodie, when we're done here? I've stayed away too long. It feels like it's time to go home, but I'd rather not go alone.'

'Of course I will, if that's what you want.'

Connie smiled and closed her eyes.

'I'll take you to the beach every evening. We'll light fires and make hot rocks that you hold in your hands so you never get cold even after the sun's gone down. And when it's been really hot all day, the shallows are like a warm bath. We can go skinny-dipping if you think your aristocratic English self can bear the indignity.' Her voice was drifting into a murmur. 'We'll eat lobster and get hot fried doughnuts at midnight. And I can show you who I really am, Brodie, when I'm not doing this—'

She tumbled into sleep. Baarda watched her for a few more seconds then left, making absolutely sure the door was locked behind him and that Connie Woolwine was completely safe.

Chapter 29

The Watcher

10 June

Karl sat on the edge of his father's bed and tried to spoon-feed him some soup. His father was getting weaker, no point pretending otherwise. The man had hated soup before his stroke, now it was almost all he could eat. Karl stirred the beef broth and wondered if everyone's life played such ironic tricks on them or if it was just the unlucky few. He spooned another few drops into his father's mouth and wiped the drips from his chin, aware that his mother was coming down the stairs again, the swish of her nightie bringing a cloud of a freshly smoked cigarette with it. He turned back to concentrate on his father. He couldn't pretend she wasn't there any more, but he could ignore her if he tried really, really hard, except now she was humming, and that had always set his teeth on edge. Today it was the fucking 'Birdie Song', of all things, not because she liked it but because she knew he'd always hated it, and that tune – no coincidence – was the one she'd been humming when she'd suddenly clutched her chest, cried out then fallen to her knees.

They'd all been at home together that day. His parents had

produced a baby rather later in life than the norm, so both had been retired for a few years, but Karl had a job back then in the investment department of a pension fund. It wasn't electrifying work but he was a fast learner and understanding how to grow money was an underrated skill.

Karl thought it was a Sunday, but perhaps it was a Saturday, not that it mattered. His father had been watching TV, Karl had been playing a game on his mobile, and his mother had been watching the new neighbours from the corner of the sitting room window. They'd arrived a month earlier carrying a toddler his mother hated on sight, having instantly decided that it would be screaming at all hours of the day and night, that they'd all have to pretend it was gorgeous, and God help those parents if they thought they'd moved into the sort of road where people were going to babysit their wee brat while they went out on the piss.

Neither Karl nor his father had said a word during his mother's continuous spew of undeserved hatred. They both knew better. There was no point interjecting. If they agreed with her, she'd ignore them, and if they disagreed then life wouldn't be worth living for the next few days. His father had developed the skill of nodding occasionally in all the right places while simply carrying on with whatever he was doing. Karl didn't have it perfected quite, but he was getting better at it.

'And look at that crappy plastic swing-set and slide they've put up on their front grass,' his mother was saying. 'Fucking red and yellow, like we need any more tat in this road. Shouldn't be allowed.'

Karl's father made a 'mmm' noise in the general region of agreement that avoided becoming an active part of the discussion.

'Someone should put some fuckin' razor blades on there is what I think. That'll have 'em moving out pretty bloody

175

sharpish.' She laughed, and Karl winced. 'See what I did there? Razor blades . . . sharpish.'

Karl couldn't bring himself to make a single sound, and his father was looking in the opposite direction at a blank wall for no apparent reason.

'Oh yeah, that's right, the two of you sayin' nothing again. Better than me, are you? Is that what you think? That I'm mean, that I'm nasty to the poor bairn.' She screwed her face up and held up her hands like claws. 'Want to see the nasty old witch-lady bite that little child, do you? What are you going to do, burn me at the fuckin' stake?'

'Stop,' Karl said. He hadn't even known the word was going to come out of his mouth. His father's face was horror and disbelief.

'What . . . the actual . . . fuck?' his mother said, dropping the witch act and standing up straight, window forgotten.

'I just meant—'

'Aye, you tell me what you just meant. That'll make everything better,' she said quietly. Karl, taller than her, heavier than her, stronger and faster, felt the contents of his bowels liquidise under her furious gaze.

'They should stop, is what I was trying to say. Not you. I'd never—' The excuse was pathetic and they all knew it. His father turned away to stare at nothing again.

Karl's mother took a step towards him across the sitting room. She was almost within striking distance, and now he needed to go to the bathroom really, really badly, but trying to leave the room, letting her see his desperation, would be disastrous.

'Would you like a cuppa?' he blurted. 'I can put a whisky in it, if you like. A double. Treat you, maybe. Do something nice for you.'

His mother stopped dead, all the emotion gone from her face,

176

hands dangling at her sides. If she ever became a zombie, like in one of those TV shows, Karl thought, in the first few seconds after she turned, that was how she'd look, with only the memory of having once been human. Still maintaining the shape of a person, but the soul having already flown.

'Is that what you think I need, now, son?'

Karl finally managed to stop talking.

'Is that what you think of me? Offer me a drink and I'll shut up. Put some whisky in my tea and I'll be good. Say it.' Her voice was so soft he almost had to strain to hear it, but some ancient, self-preserving part of him didn't let him stretch his neck out in her direction.

Karl said nothing. His father was actually shrinking into the cushions of his armchair.

'Come on, boy. Don't stop now. Cup of tea with a double in it at eleven o'clock in the morning. That's what an alkie would want, am I right?'

Karl's brain was on a mental merry-go-round: fight-or flight, fight-or-flight, fight-or-flight. At that point, he couldn't have said a word even if he'd wanted to.

'You tell me what I am, then, if you're so clever now, Karl.'

She said his name, his actual name rather than boy, son, or idiot, and it made his testicles retract painfully. Karl thought it was entirely possible that he might be about to die.

'I love you, Ma,' he muttered.

It was the only thing he could think of.

His mother laughed and Karl wished she would stop. He wished she would fall down dead, then and there. He wished never to see her again. More than that, he wanted his father not to be scared of her any more. He wanted some joy in his life. If that meant his mother collapsing to the floor, never to bother them again, or threaten them, or spew her hatred for every other person who happened to walk into her line of vision, then bring it on, he thought. Please die. Please just die right here. A slip, a choke or a stroke, I don't care which, but please do the world a favour and end her, he'd begged the universe. I'll do anything. I'll pay any price. Just fucking kill her!

'Do you really love me, Karl? I'm not so sure. I don't think your father loves me any more. Maybe he did once, when all he wanted was to dip his wick, but time kills even the dirtiest of desires. As for you loving me, why don't you prove it? Give me a hug, dear. A good, long, hard hug.'

She took another step towards him, arms stretched out in his direction. He could smell the sweat from her unwashed dress, with a heady combination of sour booze and cigarette butts, and saw the devil in her face. Not just a deranged addict who'd long since lost her humanity, but something much darker. Something evil. A many-legged, always-hungry beast who really would put razor blades on that slide given half a chance.

What would she do if he let her hug him? Would she try to snap his neck with some unearthly strength? Would she touch him in ways that made him feel like screaming and crying and cutting himself? Would she bite him? He thought that might be it.

'Leave me alone,' he muttered.

'Oh, little Karly-Warly, Mama wants a cuddle.' She smirked and stepped in closer.

'Don't touch me,' he said, louder now and bolder. He was panting, hands in fists at his sides.

'You're crying' his mother mocked. 'Do you want to suck my titties like you used to when you were a baby?'

She reached out and put her hands either side of his face.

Karl erupted, whipping both his arms up and sending his mother's arms flying outwards.

178

'Fuck you, you fucking bitch!' he screamed. 'You freak! You evil cunt!'

She began laughing again, a proper belly laugh as he yelled in her face.

'I wish you were dead! We'd be happy then. We never wanted you here.'

She was clutching her chest with it now, her face contorted with the terrible joy she got from his distress.

'Yes, you're an alcoholic. You're an addict. And you stink! Every fucking day I hope you won't touch me cos I don't want to smell you on me!'

His mother wasn't laughing now, she reached out a hand to him as she swayed on her feet.

'Don't you dare,' he warned. 'Don't you touch me. I'm leaving. Dad can come with me if he wants, but I'm going anyway.'

His mother was making an odd choking noise, like a duck that's swallowed too big a chunk of bread. He watched her sink to her knees, and felt a burst of glee. She was down! He'd finally found his voice and the words and, God, it felt good.

'That's right,' he screeched. 'That's where you belong. I hope you never get up. I hope you—'

'Karl,' his father said.

He glanced across the room to where his father, standing now, was pointing one shaky finger in his mother's direction.

She'd slipped down and was lying on her side clutching her chest, and if Karl wasn't mistaken her lips had turned a shade of blue that reminded him of cheap red wine lip stain.

Her breath was staccato bursts of pure agony. Karl frowned. What was happening, exactly?

'Do you think we should maybe call an ambulance?' his father asked.

Karl heard it as a whisper from a hundred miles away.

'Ambulance?' he asked.

'I suppose we should.' His father answered his own question and plodded out into the hallway.

Karl looked down at his mother and saw the hand that had been clutching her chest had fallen away, and now her whole face was a pale blueberry.

It hit him like a freight train.

In a second he was on his knees trying desperately to find a pulse, laying her out so he could make sense of what was going on. He could hear his father saying their address and confirming that no, they didn't have any dogs in the house, and that yes, the front door would be unlocked.

And now his mother wasn't breathing at all. It was his fault. He'd wished it and wished it, had even told her that he wished she was dead. He'd all but done a deal with the devil to make it happen.

His father appeared in the doorway.

'The lady says if she's not breathing, you're to do the kiss of life until the ambulance turns up,' his father said. 'I can't do it. My asthma's playing up.'

'I don't want to,' Karl whined. 'Dad, I can't.'

His father shrugged uselessly and looked down at his slippers. Karl knew the choice was his to make, and his alone.

'Oh Christ,' he said.

He had no idea how to do it, had never done a first aid course, but he'd seen it on TV and that would have to be enough.

He slid one hand under her neck, pinched her nose shut with the other, closed his own eyes so he didn't have to see her up close, and blew hard into her mouth. She tasted like crap, and the air that came back out was vile, but on he went.

She couldn't die because he'd wished it on her. He couldn't pay the price for that with whatever he had in the way of a soul. She needed to live so that he could leave properly, as he'd intended. She had to live so that he hadn't been the one to kill her. On he went. Pushing oxygen into her lungs, then stopping to lace his hands together, one on top of the other, pumping her chest.

He had no idea how much time had passed when the paramedics entered, but they took over from him, telling him well done, good job, how brave, what a difficult thing to do, and that he might just have saved his mother's life. How little they knew.

It was a heart attack, they said. No time to lose. Then she was in the ambulance, lights and sirens, the whole nine yards, him and his dad following on behind to the new hospital, St Columba's. There, they had to park in a multi-storey that was far too tight and far too busy. He helped his father out and held his arm as they walked down three flights of stairs to the main concourse and followed the signs to accident and emergency. Then there was another delay as they signed her in, and finally they were taken through to a waiting area until a doctor could come to speak with them.

His mother had been taken into surgery, they were told. It might be a long wait. If they wanted to go home, someone would call them. No, they said, they would wait there. Directions were given to the cafeteria and the multi-faith chapel, as if that was going to help. The surgeon operating, they were told, was the very best. If anyone could save his mother's life, it was her.

Two hours later, Karl told his father he was going to buy coffee and sandwiches from the shop. He'd be right back. No news was good news. Not to worry.

Karl went outside and stood in the rain to wash away the memories of that day, to take away the taste of her mouth and wash clean his grubby guilt. The rain, it turned out, was useless.

By the time he went back inside, Barbara Smith was dead.

Karl took his guilt, wrapped it in so many layers of blaming others that the original emotion was impossible to locate, then coated it in a murderous fury and polished it until it shone.

Chapter 30

Body Four of Eight

12 June

Vic 'The Belt' Campbell had been occupying half of a double room at St Columba Hospital on a high-dependency ward. He'd been dropped off three weeks earlier at the entrance to A&E, literally pushed out of a car that barely stopped moving by a mate with whom he'd done some meth then chased it with some cocaine while sharing a bottle of home-brewed vodka.

When he'd started foaming at the mouth, his friend had responded by taking a video of it. Then Vic had started fitting, and that was less entertaining. His friend, a fellow gang member, had started calling round for advice, and the consensus had been to get him to the hospital but to get the fuck out of there as fast as possible without drawing too much attention.

He'd drifted in and out of consciousness, tried to focus when they'd slapped his face, been vaguely aware that some brighter member of his crew had grabbed a handful of dirt on the way out and obscured both number plates, then they'd squashed and squeezed him onto the back seat and, in the words of the man in the front passenger seat, driven like fuck.

CCTV avoidance necessitated hoods up as they'd tried to push him out onto the pavement, and by then Vic was so out of it that he hadn't heard the car as its wheels screeched on exit. Most of his new brothers were wanted for something or other. There was always a violence charge or a drugs investigation, a theft, housebreaking or failure to pay a bloody fine. The place where they lived was as anonymous as they came and owned by the sort of landlord who only wanted cash, nothing in writing, and who had his own unpleasant way of dealing with people who didn't deliver on time.

Vic was all in with the gang. They were the family he'd never had. Coming from a failing care system, he'd needed some people he could rely on. And if sometimes he had to do some crappy things to pay his dues, then that was life. No one else had ever been there for him.

He'd been found outside the hospital almost immediately, taken inside on a stretcher, and from that moment on, he had no memory. Later, he'd been told that he had actually died at one point but the resuscitation team had worked their medical wonders and brought him back. Then he'd been hooked up to various anti-opiates, had his system flushed out, and left in a semi-comatose state for his body to either mend or give up the ghost.

A week later, he'd come round. There'd been a visit from a police officer, a social worker, a counsellor and a drug rehabilitation worker. For the first day, he was too weak to get up to use the bathroom. If nothing else could persuade him that he should never touch drugs again, the humiliation of having a young, beautiful female nurse turn her head from the stench as she wiped him after he'd crapped in a cardboard bowl was a powerful argument for abstinence.

The same nurse had held up a mirror up in front of his face as she'd cleaned his teeth and washed his face, and he'd finally seen the damage – the toll – his life choices were taking. His skin was a mess, but that didn't matter because he had enough face tattoos that you couldn't really see much else. His regularly shaved hair was growing back in rough patches, and several of the piercings in his ear had ripped as he'd hit the pavement, causing additional infections. He was also, apparently, substantially underweight. Scotland's gangs, he'd thought but not said, weren't known for the nutritional value of their catering. You probably had to go to Italy or Mexico for a gang with those skills.

The police had decided, in the circumstances, not to charge him, and there was nothing anyone could do if he declined to engage with drug rehab, which was how the day had come when he could finally walk out, with the help of crutches anyway, to meet his mates in a pub a few streets away. The hospital desk had let him make the call to arrange it given that he'd been dropped off with literally nothing.

The clothes he'd been found in – jeans and a sleeveless T-shirt – had long since been consigned to the hospital incinerator. Instead, Vic had been gifted some porter scrubs in a dull shade of grey, and they were remarkably comfortable on areas where he'd been tubed, prodded and poked for so long. Also donated had been a pair of plastic sliders. No one seemed to know where his trainers had ended up, and in the grand scheme of things, Vic wasn't going to make a fuss about that.

His favourite nurse, the one he had something of a crush on in spite of the fact that he'd seen how she looked at one of the junior doctors, brought him his discharge papers.

'There's a rehab meeting here on a Wednesday night,' she said. 'It's free. All sorts of people go. No judgements. Why don't you give it a go?'

'I'm not an addict,' he said, as he signed three different pieces of paper and accepted a bag of the drugs he was going to need for the next month given the mess he'd made of his stomach lining.

'You don't need to label yourself to understand that it would be good to get help,' she said. 'Next time, we might not be able to save you, and if we do, you might not like what's left of your body.'

'Because I'm so gorgeous now?' He grinned and was painfully aware of the two teeth he was missing.

'Because we all have only one body and one life, and the people here who've looked after you care very much that you don't waste it. Will you at least think about it? If you're not ready now, maybe in six months.'

Vic wanted to say something clever or glib but all he managed was, 'Yeah, sure. Thanks.'

The nurse turned to leave. 'You'll be okay then? Someone's going to look after you, I hope. Life'll be tough for a while yet.'

She was kind and genuine, and it brought a lump to his throat that he'd thought he was past feeling. Vic nodded. He wasn't quite sure how his voice would sound if he tried to answer.

'Well then, I'll leave you to it. Remember, call the nurses' desk if you're worried about anything, and you have a follow-up appointment in a fortnight that you really must keep. Swing by the ward, why don't you, so we can see how you're getting on?'

She left, and he wished he'd been able to say something – anything – in reply.

He shuffled out of the room, still getting used to the sliders on his feet, taking it slow with the crutches. Just outside his door, he paused. The one thing he could do was walk off the ward with his head held high, looking like a man. Perhaps it was because he resembled someone with a responsible job in the porter scrubs, or maybe it was three weeks without drugs and with regular meals, but he felt like a different man, or at least as if he had the potential to become a different man.

He exited the ward, took a deep breath, balanced the crutches in a corner where they could be found and returned to the store, then slowly made his way to the lifts.

'Excuse me, can you tell me the way to the café?' an elderly lady asked him.

She thought he worked there, he realised. He smiled and pointed to the far end of the corridor. 'It's that way, through the double doors and across the courtyard.'

'Thank you, darling,' she said.

He watched her go, feeling an odd pressure under his diaphragm, a sort of fizzing. It was happiness, it hit him, natural rather than drug-induced, and it had come from the sense that someone saw him as responsible, helpful. Human. Someone had needed him, even if it was only to answer one little question. She hadn't even been scared of how he looked. The scrubs, it seemed, had erased all the other shit – his past misdemeanours, his drug abuse and his failure to look after his body.

An idea occurred to him, silly no doubt, a pipe-dream maybe, but was there just a chance that he could pull something good from the wreckage of his pointless existence?

He stepped into the empty lift that had just arrived with a ghost of a smile on his lips, unaware of the person directly behind him who slipped a needle into his neck before he could move and exited again before he could react.

By the time the lift had been summoned to the ground floor, Vic Campbell's late-come dream of turning things around and becoming a hospital porter was no longer viable.

Chapter 31

Body Five of Eight

Sixteen Months Earlier

It wasn't sound that woke Beth in the middle of the night, but the absence of it. She'd grown used to her daughter's small-hours wanderings, so much so that they had become like white noise to her. Molly in the kitchen rummaging in the fridge, running a 3 a.m. bath, pacing in her bedroom just before dawn.

They'd reached an impasse of sorts that on days when Beth couldn't pick her up, Mol would make her way home from the studio by 9 p.m. to ensure that she ate one decent hot meal, changed her clothes, took her eyes off the canvas for a while and generally decompressed. Beth was aware that what she was asking was as much for her own sanity as for her daughter's but that didn't matter. The only important thing was establishing some boundaries, a routine from which a new normality could grow.

Then two days ago a school friend of Mol's had got in touch to say there was a photo on social media that showed her hurting an animal. Beth had got home to find Molly in her wardrobe crying in the dark. The forty-eight-hour spiral had forced some decisions. She'd called an estate agent, put the house on the market, made enquiries with friends about jobs that might suit her far away from Scotland, and turned off the Wi-Fi in the house so that Molly wouldn't be tempted to seek out the image.

If her surgical team hadn't already been short-handed, she'd have simply taken the time off, but instead she'd ended up in a twelve-hour surgery trying to save the life of a motorcyclist who'd hit a patch of oil. Mol had seemed better when she got home. Calmer, at least. And now she was silent. That was good, Beth told herself, as she listened in the darkness. Perhaps her daughter was actually sleeping for once. Even if that sleep was born of exhaustion rather than a desire for rest, it was better than the awful half-awake half-nightmare existence of the previous year. She got up quietly, anxious not to disturb her daughter, and padded across the hallway, opening Mol's door a couple of inches to peer inside.

All the breath left her body.

She rushed forward, grabbing Molly by the shoulders and shaking her, spilling the pill bottles her daughter had emptied across the carpet.

'Oh my God, oh my God, what are these?' she shouted, grabbing bottles and reading labels. 'Painkillers, sleeping tablets, more sleeping tablets . . .'

'S'okay,' Molly groaned. 'Let me.'

'Don't you fucking dare!' Beth yelled. She charged back into her own bedroom and ripped her mobile from its charging cable before running back to Molly, feeling for her daughter's pulse with one hand as she dialled 999 while trying to count in her head as she asked for an ambulance and gave their address.

Mol's pulse was sluggish, weak and erratic. The woman who'd taken the emergency call was trying to give advice she didn't need, but Beth couldn't form the words to explain that she was a doctor. She left the call line open but set the phone on the floor.

'Stay awake, Molly,' she insisted, lightly slapping her daughter's face. 'Don't even think about doing this to me.'

An ambulance would take at least fifteen minutes. Molly had stopped groaning and her tongue was lolling from her mouth where her head had fallen to one side.

'No, no, no,' Beth chanted. 'No you don't.'

She couldn't get Mol to vomit up the drugs while she was nearly unconscious, but she could be ready to perform resuscitation if it was needed, and it was better done on the floor than a soft mattress.

'Come on,' she said, hauling Molly's dead weight out of bed, then getting her into the recovery position on her side. 'How long?' she shouted into the phone.

'They're on their way. See if you can keep her awake and don't leave her side except to let the paramedics in.'

'Damn it, the door's locked and bolted,' Beth muttered. 'Molly, you hold on. Just a few minutes. Help's coming.'

She ran downstairs, mindful not to trip and make things even worse, fumbling the lock and the bolt three times before getting it open and leaving the door ajar for the ambulance crew to enter. Sprinting back up the stairs, she was already calling Molly's name as if she could make her conscious again through sheer force of will. Back in the bedroom, Molly's eyes were rolling and her breath had slowed to just a few times per minute.

'Molly, do you remember when you were four and you got lost at the supermarket? You just stood still and called my name, and I found you and you were safe again. That's all I need you to do now, sweetheart. I need you to concentrate on me. I need you to believe that if we can just find each other again, I can make you safe. I can make everything better, Mol. I promise I will. I'm your mum, so that's my job.' She cradled Molly's head on her lap and stroked her hair. 'I know you're in there, I know you can still hear me. Please just come back and I'll make you safe again, baby. Let me try. I can't lose you.' Her tears splashed down onto her daughter's face.

As the paramedics charged in, Molly's pulse faded into nothing.

'You have to help her!' Beth said. 'Please! Please? You have to bring my baby back.'

'Defibrillator,' one said to the other. 'Make sure her airway's clear.'

The pads were held to Molly's chest and Beth let her daughter go.

'Clear.'

The charge made Molly's body convulse.

'Still no pulse. Let's go again.'

Another charge.

Beth looked at the young woman on the floor and saw her baby crawling for the first time. She saw a toddler crying because her favourite toy, Lambie, had been dropped in a shop and tossed into a bin by someone who didn't understand that a toy, no matter how old and tatty, was still precious. She saw the little girl who looked ridiculously tiny in her uniform on her first day at school, and the young woman who'd long since outgrown the need to wear a uniform by the end of it. And most of all, she saw the girl-woman who had become her best friend, her confidante, her companion, as they had grown together, just the two of them.

Finally she saw the ashen face of end of life, and knew she had failed as a mother. She hadn't seen the chasm of her daughter's despair, had underestimated the need for it all to be over. She saw how thin, how emaciated her daughter had become, and understood the lies she'd failed to decipher about how Mol was okay, doing better, learning to cope.

And before she could be told anything more, Beth Waterfall fell to the floor, unconscious.

Chapter 32

14 June

'So you're sure his death isn't linked to his drug abuse?' Connie asked. 'One hundred per cent?'

Dr Nate Carlisle had the decency to consider his position once more before answering.

'One hundred per cent,' he said. 'Mr Campbell's cause of death was an air embolism in the heart. It takes a bit of work to confirm it, and we were lucky the hospital was careful about not just writing it off as a natural death.'

'I'm guessing they didn't want to be responsible for discharging a man who died five minutes later. That would have raised some eyebrows,' Baarda said. 'How soon did they call you in after he was found?'

'That evening,' Carlisle replied. 'They didn't know what they were dealing with initially. The deceased's body was taken down to the hospital morgue and there was no obvious cause of death when the patient notes were checked. A nurse had spoken to him as he was being discharged and said it was the best she'd seen him. Apparently he even left the ward without needing to use his crutches. The one thing that had been noted was a puncture wound on Mr Campbell's neck that ward staff said they hadn't put there, and that hadn't been seen previously.'

'You think that was a mechanism for murder?' Connie asked.

'I think the air had to get into his body somehow, a needle had to have been used, and the neck is perhaps the fastest, most obvious point of entry. You want to take a look?'

'I really do,' Connie said. 'Brodie, you sticking around?' She turned to Carlisle and faux-whispered, 'He doesn't like the thing I do with bodies. Very old school.'

Baarda cleared his throat and folded his arms. 'I'll stay. And for the record, no one likes the thing you do with dead bodies. Nothing old school about it.'

Nate Carlisle raised his eyebrows, directed Connie and Baarda to where they could put on coveralls, and prepared Vic Campbell's body for viewing.

'You can take pictures but please don't touch the body without me in here. I'm just going to give my staff a few instructions. I'll be back,' Carlisle said.

Connie got suited then went to Campbell's body and tried to get a sense of who the dead man was by staring intently at his face.

'You like him,' Baarda said.

Connie frowned theatrically and tutted. 'I hardly think that's appropriate. He's dead, for goodness' sake. There are laws, you know.'

'I meant Nate Carlisle.'

She laughed. 'Yeah, I got that. Do you *not* like him?'

'He's reputed to be an excellent pathologist, and yes, there's nothing to dislike. I shouldn't have said anything. I've . . . not been sleeping. Shall we get on with it?'

Connie gave a mock salute and cartwheeled her arms over her head, limbering up. 'You want to have a go?'

Baarda raised his eyebrows. 'This is your specialisation, not mine. I'm on sidekick duties only.'

The smile fell from her lips and she tipped her head to one side.

'That's not how you really feel though, is it?'

'Just a joke,' he said. 'We're not communicating very well today. The lack of progress on this case is frustrating. It's like trying to fit pieces from several different puzzles together. Nothing fits.'

'*We* fit.' Connie walked back over to the body and immediately broke Carlisle's rules by taking hold of one of Vic's hands in her gloved ones. 'Has something changed?'

'No,' Baarda replied softly. 'Tell me about the boy.'

She sighed. It didn't take her skills to read the victim like a road map. 'The tattoos are all standard gang stuff. Allegiances, challenges, something that might be a badge of rank. They're supposed to look kind of scary, I guess, but the funny thing is, gang tattoos are as much a uniform and a symbol of compliance as wearing a political party pin or a boy scout scarf. These tattoos aren't well done. I'd say most are amateur. Almost all gangs now have their own preferred tattooist.'

'Someone in MIT will be able to tell us which gang,' Baarda noted. 'There's plenty of undercover intelligence. He has some previous convictions.'

'Anything of interest?' Connie asked, rolling down the sheet that was covering Vic's torso.

'Petty theft, but he was acquitted of one serious charge of violence because the victim failed to attend to give evidence. He's supposed to have put a chain around their neck until they passed out.'

'That makes me feel sad,' Connie told Vic's body. 'Why on earth would you do that to another human being?'

Baarda flicked through the file. 'Looks like his drug use was long-term. He might have become violent when he was under the influence, or if the gang was dealing, it might have been a rival supplier. Alternatively, it's the sort of thing they ask you to do for a gang initiation. Then there's the possibility that he was just bad.'

'I know,' Connie said. 'But at twenty-four? You've barely lived enough to be bad by choice at that age. Not without something happening to you.'

'He has some peculiar markings on his buttocks,' Carlisle offered as he re-entered and closed the door. 'I'll turn him over and show you.' He removed the sheet completely and carefully manoeuvred Vic. 'Here, here and here,' he pointed to three small, round markings, faint with darker pink at their centres and rough skin around the edges. 'You know what these are?' he asked Connie.

'Unfortunately, yes. They're scars from cigarette burns, right?'

'They are. There's a lot of healing tissue around them so I'm guessing they were infected for a while indicating a lack of medical treatment, but the outside edges are quite pale now. I'd say these are old, probably from wounds that occurred during childhood.'

Connie hung her head for a few seconds. 'Brodie, what do we know about his early years?'

'Taken from an abusive home aged nine, although the parents didn't contest his removal in the family court. After that he went into the care system, both children's homes and foster placements, until he was sixteen when he ran away.'

'So either one of his parents did that to him, or someone he was placed with to keep him safe from his parents did it.' Connie shook her head. 'I'm not sure which of those two options is worse. You poor thing.' She stroked the side of Vic's face. 'Nate, what can you tell me about the needle entry wound?'

'You can see it best from here, in fact.' He turned Vic's head so it was facing right. 'I made a small incision to the side of it during the postmortem. It must have been a very fine needle. There was almost nothing left of the entry, and no visible bruising at the entry point. I can tell you, though, that the needle went from the entry point forward slightly towards his chest.'

Connie ran her fingers over the incision that marked the spot.

'Someone approached him from behind,' she said. 'How much air does it take to cause a lethal embolism in the heart?'

'As little as one to two millilitres, but the more that's injected, the faster it works and the more certain you can be of causing death. In this case, I'd say it was substantially more. His assailant wasn't leaving anything to chance.'

'Not in terms of timing or outcome,' Baarda noted.

'And there are no signs of a struggle, a fight, no self-defence?' Connie asked.

'Nothing,' Carlisle said. 'But he was lucky to have survived the overdose and his system would still have been weak. If someone wanted to kill him, they picked the best possible time.'

'Oh, Vic.' She folded her arms as she considered it. 'Who wanted you dead so badly that they'd do that inside a hospital? You can't have seen anyone you recognised or you wouldn't have turned your back on them. That's gang training 101.'

'He was found in a lift,' Baarda said. 'So he must've been injected from behind when entering. No one would have risked dragging him along the corridor. Footfall is too heavy for that.'

'Okay. So you've been discharged, having nearly died. You've been looked after, you've healed, you're back on your feet. Those moments can be life-changing. There's no way of experiencing that and not lying in your hospital bed thinking about who you are and what you nearly lost. Can you turn him back over, please?'

Carlisle did as she asked, while Connie read the hospital file. 'The notes say he was given new clothing as his had to be destroyed. Do we have it?' Connie asked.

'Yes, it's in the bag on the counter waiting to be picked up for forensic testing. Please don't touch it, even with your gloved hands, Connie, given that you've been handling the body.'

'I'll do it,' Baarda said, stripping off his original pair of gloves and taking a fresh set before opening the bag and peering inside. 'They gave him a work uniform. Do you remember who at the hospital wears grey scrubs?'

'Porters,' Carlisle said. 'Amazing people.'

Connie's eyes flew back onto Vic's face. 'Well, that's much more interesting. Perhaps this had nothing to do with your gang life at all. Who decides to kill a hospital porter? There would have to be some very sick individual wandering around to just randomly take the opportunity to kill.'

'And who's taken the time to learn how to do it quickly and effectively,' Baarda added. 'Connie, could it be?'

She was silent and back to staring intently into Vic's face. 'Give me a minute with him, would you?'

'Sure,' Baarda said, immediately making his way to the door.

Carlisle hung there a few seconds more. 'You won't touch him? More than you already have, I mean. At least not with anything other than gloved hands?'

Connie smiled slowly. 'Dr Carlisle, I recognise that my behaviour strikes some people as odd, eccentric even, and that I take a bit of getting used to, but what exactly are you worried about me touching this body with if not my hands?'

Carlisle put his hands on his hips and shook his head. 'Honestly, Dr Woolwine, I have no idea. I've never met anyone like you.'

'Fair enough. I promise not to contaminate the body in any way, nor to behave in an unseemly manner.'

He looked towards the door but still didn't move his feet.

'Would it help if I pinky promised?'

'Hmm. Can you maybe just explain what exactly you intend to do that you can't do with me in the room?'

'I need to have a conversation, just like I did with Divya Singh,' she said. 'But this time it's private.'

Carlisle shrugged. 'I can live with that,' he said. 'Take all the time you need.'

Connie waited until the heavy postmortem suite door had clicked shut, then pulled up a chair next to Vic Campbell's head, gently turned his face in her direction, and sat down holding one of his hands in both of hers.

'Not how you thought it was going to end, huh? All the drugs, the violence, gang rivalry, life on the edge, then your soul leaves your body on the floor of an elevator in the place where your life had already been saved once. No gun, no knife, just some sneaky fuck with a hypodermic who didn't even have the guts to look you in the face as he did it.'

Connie gave his hand a squeeze and closed her eyes.

'I'm so sorry. I knew people like you in my life before this one. I was in a hospital for a while too, only the doors there were locked and we were only allowed plastic cutlery. I'm guessing your experience was a little nicer than mine. But I was in there with some people who'd been messed up by narcotics and addiction. And by their parents. Christ only knows where those cigarette burns came from, but I think you spent every day with that gang just happy that someone had your back.'

She released his hand and stood, cupping his shoulders in her palms.

'You never had a chance to show the world what you could have made of your life. I guess, if you had a few seconds where you truly believed you were dying, that was what you were thinking about. I'd have been wondering where I might have ended up, and who with, and all the other, better ways there were to die.'

She leaned over his face, not quite touching, mindful of Carlisle's warning and slightly resenting it, as much as she knew that contaminating a body in a murder investigation was the very last thing she could risk doing.

'I'm going to find the person who killed you. I know you did some shitty things in your life. I have, too. But the very least you should have had was the chance to put them right. You keep watching, okay? Stay with me. If I can't get legal justice, we'll see what kind of natural justice floats to the top. Sleep well.'

Connie wanted to leave him with a kiss on the forehead, forced herself not to, and had to be content with imagining it instead.

Vic Campbell, twenty-four years old forever, waited for resolution in the last place in Edinburgh that anyone wanted to call home.

Chapter 33

15 June

'I shouldn't have stayed off work so long,' Lively grumbled. 'Every time I switch on the news, there's been another murder. And are you serious that there are no leads in the ones we already had?'

'It's not that there are no leads, it's that the killer is leaving no trace. You can't find something that doesn't exist,' Connie said.

'Oh aye, your serial killer theory. I read all about that in the fuckin' newspaper. How the hell did you get the Evil Overbitch to sign off on that one?'

'Superintendent Overbeck gave me free rein to run this investigation as I see fit, so I didn't ask her. But she isn't going to be throwing me a tickertape parade any time soon. Now, what do you make of this?'

They were standing in the corridor, staring at the lift door Vic Campbell had entered before his death.

'You have to be pretty ballsy to kill someone you think works in a hospital while they're still in the building,' Lively said.

'Easy enough place to find a hypodermic syringe, though. Just find an empty treatment room and look in the sharps bin.'

'Possibly. But gangs who run drugs have access to needles too. Someone must have known he was getting discharged. It might have been a rival gang member he'd never seen before who did it, which is why he didn't panic when someone was right behind him stepping into the lift. It's even possible someone in his own gang wanted rid of him and sent a stranger to do the deed. Who's checking the CCTV?'

'We've got four people on it, but the bulk of the cameras are situated on the ground floor at the exits and entrances. A&E is well covered because of regular issues with violent patients, and the car park has cameras to prevent theft. Up here, waiting rooms and wards have no CCTV for patient privacy and there's nothing in the lifts until the alarm gets pressed. We're obviously checking all the CCTV for the time period, but we've no point of reference as to who we're looking for.'

'Hey you two,' Beth Waterfall called from the end of the corridor. 'Do you really have to have that discussion so publicly?'

'You should run,' Lively said. 'She's cross with you and I don't blame her.'

'Wait . . . your surgeon friend is pissed at me? I have no idea what I did.'

'In there, please,' Beth pointed to a side room as she approached. Her words were uncharacteristically clipped.

They filed into the examination room and Beth pointed to a chair for Lively. He sat.

'Woah . . . that's impressive. You could offer yourself out as a man-trainer and make a fortune.' Connie whistled appreciatively.

'You live in my house, you follow my medical recommendations. He should still be in bed, but he insisted on coming in to meet you. I read your article, Dr Woolwine. A heads-up would have been nice.'

'I promised the paper an exclusive,' Connie said quietly. 'Is there a problem?'

'A man was killed in this hospital. You recently gave an interview to the press saying there's a serial killer operating in this area, so of course everyone is now concerned that this latest death is the work of the same person. Is that what you think?'

'I think it's very likely. It's certainly the most compelling conclusion to draw when we look at all the deaths together.'

'All right. You're clearly someone who thinks long and hard about these things. But we have patients confined to their beds, the elderly, the terminally ill, cancer patients too weak after treatment to move very far. Those poor people are already dealing with so much, now they've to wonder if they're about to get attacked out of nowhere. We can't afford to have security guards walking the halls. And as for the staff, they're already rundown, overworked and underpaid. The man who died was wearing scrubs. It's a miracle that any porters turned up for work at all.'

'Oh Christ,' Connie said. 'You're right. I can see how this must be affecting the hospital. The article was a tactical move to try and force the killer to communicate with us. I'm sorry for the fallout.'

'I appreciate the apology,' Beth said. 'But can I ask, what makes you so certain the attack on poor Mr Campbell relates to the other deaths? I operated on Archie Bass myself. That was an outdoor stabbing at night. Please don't think I'm questioning you. I just need to do all I can to make sure our patients and staff remain safe.'

'It's not that there's a link so much as the absence of—'

'There is a link,' Lively said, standing to make a call from his mobile. 'Salter, it's me. Yes, I'm back from sick leave . . . oh, for fuck's sake, I've enough women telling me what I can and can't do without you joining their ranks. Just look this one thing up, would you? In what hospital was Dale Abnay going to be donating a kidney? No, don't hang up. I'll wait.'

Beth Waterfall's mouth was hanging open. 'I don't believe this. You're making it worse. Please don't tell me you're linking not just one murder to St Columba's, but two?'

'I'm actually trying to solve murders rather than making anything worse, but I get how it probably seems unhelpful right now.' He smiled apologetically.

'But Archie Bass was only treated here *after* getting stabbed,' Connie said. 'So that can't be a link in terms of choosing victims.'

'It was the nearest A&E,' Lively said. 'So the rough geographical centre might be this hospital. And we'd need to check his records to see if he'd been treated here in the past.' He looked hopefully at Beth who sighed.

'I suppose you want me to do that,' she said. 'Give me five minutes, and don't go back out there discussing murder. Like the NHS doesn't have enough problems right now.'

'Thank you, and sorry again,' Lively said.

Connie stared at him and folded her arms.

'Detective Sergeant Lively, I do believe you are head over heels in love. Well, who'd a thunk it?'

'Would you mind your own? Beth and I barely know one another. I'm sure she'll come to her senses soon enough and kick me out of her home. Probably just feels sorry for me.'

'Don't do that,' Connie said. 'In spite of your endless sarcasm, questionable sense of humour and intense dislike of learning, I'm sure Beth Waterfall has seen something in you that ticks all her boxes. You deserve to be happy, you know.'

Lively stared at her, and slowly shook his head. 'Did you just . . . give me a fuckin' pep talk? Because I think I'd prefer to be given a hot tar enema than explore my feelings with you.'

'You're adorable,' Connie said. 'Your cell phone's squawking.'

He put it to his ear.

'Hi Salter. Yeah, I'm ready.' He listened for a few seconds. 'Right. Got it. Find the dates Dale Abnay was here, the name of the transplant doctor, where in the building he went, see if they've got the CCTV on file and check every second of it. I want to know who he bumped into, who he passed in the corridor, who he sat next to in the waiting room. Everything. Then cross-reference it with Vic Campbell's stay. Yes, I know it's a long shot, but it's better than the grade A jack shit we're shovelling at the moment. I'll be in later.'

'You will not, Sam,' Beth said as she entered. 'That wound is still healing. Why would you take the risk?'

'Because,' he said, walking forward and kissing her tenderly on the cheek, 'apparently I left a bunch of bampots in charge of multiple murder investigations, not dissimilar to you letting one of the cleaning crew perform open heart surgery. They need me to go and save the day.'

'He has a delusional hero complex,' Connie said. 'It's been known to happen after a near-death experience.'

Lively waved a dismissive hand at her. 'Did you find anything in Archie Bass's medical records?'

'I'm afraid to say I did. Mr Bass attended here for various vaccinations – Covid, flu and tetanus – but also A&E following a fall down some steps when he sprained his ankle quite badly, and once when he was found unconscious in a public toilet. That looks to have been alcohol poisoning, and there was some suggestion that he'd drunk some sort of chemical mixture. So all in all, it's fair to say he's been here a number of times.'

'Not Divya Singh though,' Connie said. 'I've seen her medical records. She'd had no hospital treatment for years, long since before St Columba opened. I don't think she'd even seen her GP for three years.'

'Doesn't mean to say she hadn't visited another patient here,' Beth noted. 'And sometimes we offer anonymous advice clinics which wouldn't have shown up on her records.'

'Come on,' Lively looked impatient. 'You've got to admit, it's the closest thing we've found to a connection.'

'Oh, I'm conceding that one,' Connie said. 'But making it work for us is another matter. Thousands of staff and visitors, the population changing on a daily basis with different appointments and clinics. How do we find the killer?'

'More importantly, how do you find them before another of our patients or a member of staff gets killed?' Beth asked. 'We can't shut down, and we can't make patients too scared to come here for the treatment they need. So I'm begging you, do your jobs fast, because there are no good options for us.'

'I'll get uniformed officers posted downstairs in the public areas,' Connie said. 'We'll call it a community outreach scheme. And we'll brief your security team and the hospital board in the meantime. But I agree. Panic is likely to make our job harder. If every visitor or staff member starts acting skittish, it'll be even harder to spot someone acting out of the ordinary.'

'We can divert some undercover officers on a roving basis too,' Lively said. 'The more eyes the better.'

Beth's eyes were suddenly full of tears. 'I wish you didn't have to go back to work,' she said. 'I'll be worried about you.'

'It's not me who's working at a hospital that seems to be attracting a serial killer,' he said. 'I don't suppose you could take some time off?'

'No.' She shook her head. 'We're short-staffed. And wouldn't that be awful, me running away because I know something other people don't? I don't think so.'

He reached out his arms and she walked into his embrace. 'Then you'd best be careful,' he said. 'I've only just found you, and we've already nearly lost each other once.'

Connie smiled and looked at the floor.

'You'll stay living with me though, even now you're back at work?' Beth asked.

'You try getting rid of me,' he said. 'I'm going nowhere.'

Karl Smith, at that precise moment gazing into the fridge at Beth's house and wondering what he could do to the contents, had a different idea.

Chapter 34

The Watcher

15 June

That morning, Beth Waterfall had left home mid-morning and taken the obviously malingering Detective Sergeant Lively with her, which meant that Karl finally had the opportunity to do some mischief at the doctor's house. Not that he had the guts to do anything when push came to shove. He'd made it as far as the kitchen, appraising the contents of her fridge, before deciding that he was testing his luck and retreating to his car. Now that he had a key, copied from the spare that Beth kept in her utility room drawer after breaking in through an unsecured window, getting in and out was easy. What he hadn't banked on was the bastard copper moving in for so long.

Lively might be injured, but he was a police officer with a reputation. The more Karl had looked into him, the less he liked what he found out. Lively was old-style, not afraid to take on Scotland's gangsters, not afraid of getting hurt, and – reading between the lines – not afraid of getting a bit dirty when it was needed. The newspapers told hyperbolic stories of his heroics in apprehending several serious criminals, most of which stretched credibility a little far, but still Karl couldn't be sure Lively hadn't decided to increase the building's security now that it appeared he was getting settled there.

'Spoiling my fucking fun, is what he's doing,' Karl muttered.

'Fun?!' his mother screeched from the back seat, slapping Karl hard around the back of his head and catching the scar that was barely concealed beneath hair that had failed to grow back properly.

Karl screamed and clutched his chest.

'Ma!' he half-shouted, half-whined, not so stupid that even in moments of shock he would dare shout back at her. 'What are you doing here, out of the house?'

He slid his eyes over the rearview mirror, not quite letting them stop for his sanity's sake. His mother had rarely been out of her bedroom, only venturing down the stairs on a handful of occasions. Now she'd figured out a way to get into his car, too. Was he to have no peace?

'There's no one in, so why are you still sitting here? Coward. Lazy fool. No better than your father in that bed all day.'

'Ma, he's had a stroke! You know he can't get up.'

'I know he's better when you're not there, and when that silly wee bitch who comes to watch him is out the back sneaking a fag. He grabs the TV remote, changes the channel, fluffs his pillow. Oh aye, quite the mover, he is, when he wants something.'

'That's not true,' Karl griped, although hadn't he noticed things moving around now that he thought about it? And surely the whisky in the bottle at his father's bedside was evaporating faster than was scientifically possible. No, his father wouldn't be duping him. Not when he changed the man's adult nappies and gave him a bed bath every evening. 'You're lying,' Karl dared to say, flinching as soon as the words dribbled from his downturned mouth.

209

He expected another slap but what came was worse: silence at first, then the creak of the faux-leather rear seats, the smell of mints wafting across, just barely covering something rancid and ancient on her breath.

'Am I now?' she growled at him.

Karl could feel her bottom jaw hitting his shoulder with each word and imagined her drooling something viscous and foul but couldn't bring himself to check. Better that he kept his eyes tight shut. Better to pretend she wasn't real at all.

'Here you are, telling me I'm lying, when just last night you found yourself wi' a cushion in your hand, wondering if anyone would investigate your father's death given the mess he's in.' Her voice was gravel and razor blades.

'Didn't,' Karl squeaked, fourteen years old again and fighting the shame of a disobedient voice box.

'There it is, that's what a lie sounds like. You know it and I know it, son. I was there. I saw the look on your face. You wanted to look it up, too, to figure out if they'd do one of them post-mmm . . .' she couldn't quite get the word.

'Postmortems,' he filled in for her, hating himself for the tacit admission. 'I didn't want to do it! I thought it might be kinder. I love my dad. You know I do.' He was crying now and rubbing his head against a pending migraine.

'Oh, does it still hurt, baby?' she mocked. 'Were you not strong enough to defend yourself?'

'I did what you told me!' he yelled.

'And yet you're still here, sitting outside her house, crying, and she's still at her important job, cutting people open, being paid a fortune, then coming home to fuck that no-good, nosy-parker policeman of hers. What are you going to do about that, boy?'

It was all he could do not to vomit onto his own lap, her

210

mouth up against his cheek, able to smell her dead-animal breath.

'I've got to go,' he said. 'Someone'll see me.'

He turned the engine over and raced away, his mother flying backwards in the rear seat as he fled the road where Beth Waterfall lived. Twenty-five minutes later he was home, shouting a half-hello to the carer who wasn't due to leave for another hour and racing up the stairs to the bathroom then bolting the door behind him and running a bath.

He hadn't had a bath in years, and it wasn't clear to him why he so desperately needed one now, but all he could think of was immersing himself in water as hot as he could get it. Karl dropped to his knees and scrabbled through the cupboard beneath the sink.

'There's some in here. I know there is,' he muttered. 'Yes. Here.' He pulled a yellowing plastic bottle from the back. Top off, he poured bubble bath into the flowing water, holding his head in the steam and breathing in. 'Nice,' he murmured. 'That's better.'

He ripped off his clothes and stepped in, hopping from one foot to the other until he got the balance of the taps right and the cold water stopped the scalding of his ankles. As he sat down and sank into the tub, he felt better. He needed to wash off the stink of his mother.

Ducking his head beneath the surface, he relaxed. The lavender bubbles worked their magic. He was clean again. His skull had stopped aching. He was at home and safe, and his mother was dead. He sat up and took a deep breath.

'Dead as a dodo,' he said, giggling. 'Dead and gone. All in my head. Got to get a grip.' He slapped his forehead with the base of his palm enough times to see bright lights in his peripheral vision. 'Got to dead a grip. Dot to dead a dip.' He carried on

211

hitting his head, lost in the rhythm of it, happy for the pain then the numbness to take over.

The fingers that grabbed his ankle had not been made slick by the water or the bubble bath. They were as dry as topsoil in a drought, and just as crumbly.

Under the water he went, splashing, reaching for the sides, gasping for air and drawing in soapy lavender. Karl thrashed, his feet meeting his mother's flesh where she sat opposite him at the far end of the bath. He shrank backwards, drawing his knees up to his chest to cover his own nakedness as he turned his head to one side to avoid looking directly at his mother.

'You never minded bathing with me when you were a wee thing. You'd climb all over and tickle me until we were both laughing ourselves senseless. Until you'd pee, of course, then we'd both have to get out and shower together instead.'

Karl gagged and swallowed the bile that rose in his throat, inadvertently glancing at his mother as he tried to control his cramping stomach.

'Ach come on, you've seen titties before, haven't you? Not very often maybe, and not the ones you wanted to. You had a thing for her, didn't you, that Molly Waterfall girl?' Karl felt his face flush. 'But you still did right by me in spite of wanting her, and I won't forget it, son. Just a little more. Beth Waterfall can be pushed over the edge, too. You just have to find a way to do it, and for that you'll need to make sure she's alone.'

'But that policeman . . . he's there all the time now.'

'You can deal with him. He's not a young man. You're fitter and stronger, and he's had an injury. I bet if you pressed on that, your fingers would just sink right in where the glass got him.'

Karl sighed.

'Then when he's disposed of you can take your time with her. Imagine the look on her face when she sees it's you. You should do it in the middle of the night, when they're at their most vulnerable. You want them confused and sleepy.' She peeled her lips back from brown, sharp-edged teeth.

'It's too risky going to their place, Ma. The best way to kill is always outside. Less forensic evidence, easier to get away, no chance of any hidden cameras or silent alarms.'

He was picturing it already. In spite of what his mother thought, in his opinion a death was best carried out swiftly. A fast kill was cleaner, more professional. It rang with nothingness and disdain. Kill and go. Now that was power.

His excitement rose, unbidden, and his mother began to cackle.

'There's my boy!' she said, waving her loose-skinned arms in the air – a ghoulish version of jazz hands – and Karl stood up, past embarrassment at his arousal and past the fear of consequences for what he intended to do to Beth Waterfall.

Because killing the doctor was an ending.

If Karl only did as his dead, disintegrating mother wanted, she would disappear from his life forever. And this time, there would be no coming back.

Chapter 35

16 June

Brodie Baarda sat in an unmarked police car in a side road from where he could see the entrance to the hospital multi-storey car park. It also offered a view of one of the entrances to the main building, although the whole site sprawled across acres and acres, with separate buildings for some specialties.

The footfall through the hospital was unimaginable, and it wasn't even just staff, patients and visitors. There were deliveries turning up, people ordering food, others visiting a legal firm that had set up shop somewhere inside. Then came a minibus full of nuns in wimples and habits that Baarda realised would be an absolutely ideal costume for a female serial killer. Finally, a school bus came in, unloading at least forty children and five teachers, presumably for a work experience talk. Brodie stopped looking at the main doors and concentrated on the idea of the best vantage point that offered the least chance of being noticed.

The road he was on had no CCTV. There were no traffic lights with cameras either, and no businesses nearby that would have their own security cameras. It was the perfect place to park, but spaces were limited. Hospital parking had to be paid for, so it was likely that nearby free spaces got taken early. That only left more distant side roads, which meant walking a few minutes to get to the hospital, but without the benefit of being able to sit in a car to observe.

Baarda dictated notes on his mobile as he watched. 'Team of plain-clothes officers to conduct door-to-doors in roads local to hospital to check for repeat sightings of pedestrian watching hospital or hanging around area.'

He got out of the car and walked towards the hospital, checking for visible camera locations inside the grounds as he went. Some were obvious – mounted on poles or positioned at doorways – but there were others, he already knew, that looked like street lighting or alarms. All in all, the security set-up was substantial, and it would be enough to put most intelligent criminals off using the hospital to identify targets.

Unless, of course, they had cause to visit the hospital regularly anyway. That made much more sense. Baarda walked through the main doors and looked around. Serial killers got sick too. They had sick relatives. They had jobs in healthcare.

There was no magic to psychopathy. Serial killers were from all walks of life. They didn't only hunt at night or have a third nipple. Quite often, in his experience, they were really very boring.

'It's impossible,' he muttered. 'Too many variables.'

A female nurse walked past and gave him a broad smile. 'You okay?' she asked. 'You look miles away.'

Baarda gave a small shake of his head and laughed. 'Guess I've got a lot on my mind. I have a friend who's agoraphobic and they have to come in for a minor procedure. I was trying to figure out which door they could use that gets the least foot traffic. I need to keep things quiet for them to avoid stress.'

'Now that I can help with.' She beamed. 'My shift doesn't start for half an hour so I can show you myself. Follow me.'

They walked away from the doors of the main building and back out towards the road before turning around the side of the block.

'So do you live in Edinburgh or are you just visiting your friend?' she asked.

'Just visiting,' Baarda said. 'Although I've always loved Scotland. My parents used to bring me here for holidays as a child. It gets in your blood.'

'That it does,' she said. 'I could never live anywhere else. What is it you do when you're not travelling around being a good Samaritan?'

'I'm in close protection,' he replied automatically. 'Bodyguard work for politicians and VIPs.' It was his standard line.

'Gosh, how exciting. Have you worked with anyone I'd know? Just down the pathway and the door's on the right.' She pointed.

'Elton John, Kate Moss, Gordon Ramsay. Honestly, it's not as glamorous as it sounds. Lots of late nights standing around in hotel lobbies and outside restaurants.'

'Sounds thrilling to me. I'd love to hear a bit more about it. This is the entrance. It's the external route into our geriatric rehabilitation unit. Most of these patients have been there a while but we're still trying to get them well enough to go back to independent living. The double doors on the right go into their lounge, the corridor straight ahead goes past the nurses' station and towards their bedrooms and physiotherapy rooms, but if you turn left here, you end up going through radiology then into A&E. The external door saves visitors to this unit from going through the main hospital with all the bugs and bacteria. Keeps our geriatric patients that little bit safer, but if they need x-rays or treatments, they can be taken straight through.'

'That's so thoughtful,' Baarda said. 'How clever. And yes, this does seem like the perfect entrance for my friend.'

'I wish I had a boyfriend as thoughtful as you. Not many people would come to do a recce.' She blushed slightly and Baarda was suddenly aware that she was looking at him with more interest than a simple desire to help. He wished he hadn't had to lie. It was a part of the job that always made him feel uncomfortable. 'You know, I still have just enough time for a coffee if you'd like one. I can show you the route through to the main block.'

'That would have been lovely, but I'm on something of a deadline.' Her face fell. 'Plus, I don't think my partner would appreciate me getting coffee with anyone as attractive as you. Thank you, though. Under any other circumstances, I'd have said yes.'

'I suppose I'll have to forgive you, then.' She smiled. 'I hope your friend has a stress-free visit. I work on the paediatric ward, just in case things change.' She shrugged. 'A girl can dream.'

Baarda watched her walk away and wondered what his life would be like had he never met Connie. Simpler, that was certain. Less exciting too. Definitely less confusing.

He constructed a rough map of the hospital grounds in his mind and tried to figure out what the view was from the unit he was in back towards the main entrance. The best way to check was to go into the residents' lounge. That door, he found, was not locked. Baarda wandered in.

At the far end of the lounge was a wall of glass, with multiple sofas and armchairs overlooking a lawn and flower beds, beyond which were the main car park and the road where Baarda had parked. Soporific music played through tinny speakers and the few residents who were using the lounge looked unimpressed. Other than that, the light was good, there was an enormous television at one side, plenty of games stacked on a table, and a packed bookshelf for readers.

Baarda went to the corner with the best view and looked out.

'You'll be police, then,' a man said. 'I can never quite put my finger on what makes you all stand out like you do.'

Baarda looked across the room at the man who was speaking to him. 'Sounds like you know a few.'

'I was in the fire service for forty years. Some of my best friends were police officers. It was always easier to be around people who understood what the deal was with the job. I'm Charlie Stott.' He offered a hand to shake and tried to stand but was struggling.

Baarda went to him instead. 'Brodie Baarda. It's nice to meet you, Charlie. What's landed you in here?'

'Too much time up ladders carrying hoses, and eighty-year-old hips. It's a bad combination. I don't suppose you could just pull the wires out from that speaker, could you? I could tolerate this place much better if I didn't have to listen to this dirge all day.'

'I suspect that would be criminal damage, but I can ask them to change the music if that would help?'

Charlie had clearly once been a hulk of a man. He still had an impressive head of white hair, a voice that came from the depths of his chest and a determined set to his mouth that Baarda knew would put him at odds with being dependent on others. Ageing was slow torture, and that was if you were one of the lucky ones who made it that far.

'Ach, don't bother,' Charlie said. 'They'll change it for half an hour then put the same drivel on again. I think it's supposed to encourage us to want to leave.' He gave Baarda a wink. 'You'll be here about the murder, I suppose.'

218

Baarda took the seat next to Charlie and relaxed into surprisingly comfortable leather.

'We've done our best to keep the details out of the public eye. What have you heard?'

'I listen. People's tongues are the best newspaper you'll find. Some of the nurses were talking about it during drug rounds yesterday – they assume we're all deaf or past caring. One of them said everyone thought it was natural causes when the lad first collapsed in the lift, but then the police were all over it and now there are special security measures in place. Is that right?'

'The security measures have obviously not been put in place here,' Baarda noted. 'I was able to walk straight in.'

'Well, really, what's left to kill in here?' Charlie grinned. 'A few old folk who're already infirm. He can come in here and have at it, if he likes. He'll have to take me beating him with my crutches first though!'

Baarda grinned back.

'Well, we don't know who's responsible yet, so I can't tell you if it's a him or a her, but it was definitely an unlawful killing, and it definitely took place in the hospital. I'll ask that security measures be applied here properly. No one should be put at risk.'

'I'd put money on it being a man. I told the nurses there's been a dodgy chap coming through here a few times. No one takes any notice of me though. They see wobbly hips and act like it's my brain that's rotten.'

'What have you seen, Charlie? And for the record, I can already tell there's nothing wrong with your faculties.'

Charlie leaned forward and lowered his voice. 'They all think it's my imagination, but I could swear there's a man who comes through here once a week, sometimes more, only he looks different every time. Sometimes he's in normal clothes but always with a hat on, and sometimes he's in a hospital uniform.'

'Do you think maybe he just works here and sometimes gets changed in a staff room?'

'That's the thing,' Charlie said. 'He wears different sets of scrubs. Sometimes like a male nurse. Sometimes like a porter. I've seen him in a cleaner's uniform too. And I've seen him leave through this route on days when I've not seen him enter this way. Even when he's wearing scrubs, he's still got a hat or a cap on, or a hood up.'

Charlie sat back in his chair and Baarda watched him for a few seconds.

'You know I've got to ask: how can you be sure it's the same man?'

'It's a fair question. I've seen him shave his hair, dye it, grow a moustache for a while then shave it off again. All his clothes are sort of generic, nothing stand-out. But it's him. I've started looking out for him. I thought maybe he was getting treatment for a sort of multiple personality disorder, then I figured I was the one losing the plot. Then this happened.'

Baarda got his mobile out of his pocket.

'Charlie, do you mind if I record the next few questions I ask you, just so I've got an accurate note?'

'Go ahead,' he said. 'You want to know what I remember?' Baarda nodded. 'Well, he's skinny for one thing, not shorter than five nine and not taller than six foot. Height is harder for me at the moment as I'm always sitting down. White-skinned though, and I reckon around about thirty years old, maybe a bit older, but he changes his look so it's hard to be specific.'

'What was his hair like the last time you saw him?'

'He's growing it again, I reckon,' Charlie said. 'But then I never see the top of his scalp.'

'Anything in particular about the way he walks? Have you ever heard him speak? Does he have tattoos? Does he ever carry anything like a bag or a bicycle helmet?'

Charlie thought about it. 'No tattoos. He brought a backpack with him once or twice. Those are fire doors you came through so I've seen him through these windows and the glass in the doors, but it's soundproof from the corridor into here. As for how he walks, I'd say it's like he's trying to make himself nothing. Not small, exactly, just head down, hands in pockets. Sending out signals like, nothing to see here. Know what I mean?'

'I do indeed,' Baarda said. 'That's a very good description. I don't suppose you'd be able to recall the last time you saw him?'

'I can tell you exactly. It was the twelfth of June. I'd just had a review to decide whether or not I'm fit to be sent home yet. Bastards sentenced me to another month even though I've been on good behaviour.'

'I'm sorry about that, Charlie, but also not sorry, if you'll forgive me for saying. If they'd sent you home, I wouldn't have ended up speaking to you today.'

'That's got to be worth you smuggling me in a bottle of a decent single malt, surely?'

'It certainly is. And when they let you out, I'm taking you for a steak too. I'll be sending an artist to work with you and we'll need to take a formal statement. Is that something you're okay with?'

'More than okay,' Charlie said. 'It's the most interesting thing that's happened to me in eight months, much as I wish no one had died.'

'Don't you worry about that.' Baarda stood and put a hand on his shoulder. 'We all have to make the best of every day. I'll be back to see you, Charlie. In the meantime, you stay safe.'

'What do I do if I see him again?'

221

'I'll have an undercover officer here with you within the hour. If you see this man, tell the officer. We'll take it from there. No running after him and starting a fight,' Baarda told him, mock serious, but not altogether sure Charlie wouldn't have a go if he got the opportunity.

'Chance'd be a fine thing. He's lucky my hips aren't healed. Wee bastard would be wearing his guts for garters.'

Chapter 36

Twelve Months Earlier

'We remember Molly as a daughter, as a friend and as a gifted member of the art community. She left those who love her far too soon and will never fulfil her extraordinary potential. And yet we are grateful for her life and for the time she spent with us, every day a precious gift.' The reverend put his hand out to hover vaguely over the urn that was situated next to a large photo of Mol at eighteen, running up a beach towards Beth who had immortalised her unconstrained grin and shining eyes with a camera.

Turnout to the service was poor. Beth hadn't been expecting many people following the damage to Molly's reputation, and she believed it was better that way. Next there would be a reading, something suitably sombre with an edge of positivity. *Molly is in a better place. Molly's pain is at an end. Molly wouldn't want anyone to mourn for long.* All the true but useless things people say at times like this. Beth had organised the memorial service for public closure. All the other arrangements had taken place with her alone to witness them.

The service was no help to her. Her daughter was gone. She lived alone. There was no one to go home to and no one to start the next day with. Molly's bedroom was almost exactly as it had been the night the paramedics charged in, but different in all the ways that mattered. Beth had cleared up the bottles of pills and stripped the bedding. The photos of her and Molly had been moved from her daughter's bedside table to somewhere they could still be appreciated. Once a day she went in and sprayed Mol's favourite perfume so she could pretend for a few blissful seconds at a time that the room wasn't unoccupied, and that her daughter might come barrelling out at any moment, holding an armful of paint-spattered clothes, a paintbrush tucked behind her ear because she was so used to feeling it there that she could hardly bear to be without it.

As for Mol's studio, Beth had given the landlord notice on the lease and begun the long, painful task of packing up the contents and sending everything to a new home. Molly had left detailed instructions for the completed canvases.

For two weeks, Beth had stayed at home, made arrangements and written articles for local papers about her daughter's life and work. Then, because she could no longer bear the silence and emptiness, she'd gone straight back to work to fill herself up with the all-consuming concentration demanded by scalpels, sutures and surgery.

People sent cards and flowers that only served to make Beth more furious. Former friends, conspicuous in their absence from Mol's life when it mattered, wanted to make themselves feel better after reading the announcement of her death. Members of the art world who'd skittered away and taken shelter when Molly's reputation had taken a battering were waxing lyrical about her talent and potential to anyone who stood still long enough to listen. It was sickening.

But the extremes of Beth's hatred – the Mount Everest peak and Mariana Trench floor of her loathing – were reserved for a single man. Karl Smith was no longer just some probably impotent, sexually frustrated, pathetic piece of shit who had decided that toying with her daughter's life was what it took to get him off. He lived inside her head in every free moment, breathed heavily in her ear as she jogged to pound her loss out on the streets, watched as she adjusted to cooking meals for one, and peered at her from the corner of her bedroom as she tried to fall asleep each night in a too-empty, too-lonely house. The idea of him was literally consuming her, her body weight dropping every few days, as she exercised more than ever and ate less than ever.

Her daughter was not there for her to hug in the morning because of him. She was not there to share a bowl of popcorn with in the evening because of him. Mol could not be heard singing in the kitchen or the garden or the bathroom because of him. Beth's new life was brittle and unsteady, and while not all of it was hopelessly dark, she had lost enough that she hardly recognised herself in the mirror.

While she'd never in her life been violent or vengeful, never wished anyone harm or thought how best to ruin another's life, bringing Karl Smith to justice was all she could think about. Justice, or a timely accident. Beth could only hope.

Chapter 37

17 June

Lively sat on a bench outside the entrance to the geriatric rehabilitation centre with a walking frame in front of him, dressed in pyjamas, a dressing gown and slippers he'd sworn he'd rather die than wear. Salter had purchased the outfit for him especially, and loved every minute of it.

Other similarly camouflaged officers had been strategically positioned around every possible entrance, including the ambulance and morgue doors where undercover officers had been given staff clothing. Lively, as the oldest member of the Major Investigation Team, had been the only choice for the geriatric spot. To be fair, he also still had a bandage on his neck, so at least they hadn't had to fake that part of his disguise.

Lively had met Charlie and had a chat about their suspect's comings and goings, and they'd figured out that they must have crossed paths during the early part of Lively's career, a fact that didn't help him feel any younger, although he'd liked Charlie instantly. He had, however, insisted that Charlie be moved to another part of the hospital for the duration of the operation. As unlikely as it was, if Charlie spotted the suspect first from the lounge window and caught the man's eye with the wrong expression on his face, there was a chance he'd realise the game was up and run. Worse than that, there was a possibility it would make Charlie a target, and that would be unforgivable.

None of the hospital staff had been shown the images of the suspect for the same reason. The alternating scrubs the suspect had been seen wearing made it clear that he wasn't a real member of staff and equally that he was unlikely to be attending appointments, so Superintendent Overbeck's one decision had been to minimise disruption within the environment. Only the police team and hospital security had seen the collection of images to facilitate surveillance.

Sooner or later, Police Scotland would have no choice but to release the image to the press as a 'person they were keen to talk to' or 'potentially an important witness' to encourage an identification, but an undercover operation was everyone's preference.

Connie was staying out of the way after her newspaper interview, and Baarda was off-site too in case anyone had investigated Dr Woolwine and found images of the two of them together. Every other spare body was at the hospital, though, on wards, in the cafeteria, the gift shop, roaming the corridors or hunkered down in cars.

Lively sighed and opened his newspaper, hoping some kind person would deliver him a coffee and a pastry before long. It had been hours since breakfast, and the need to stay in character meant he wasn't able to just pop over to the café and get something himself. Like an angel, Beth appeared through the external doors carrying a Thermos flask and a plastic container.

'I was looking for somewhere to sit and enjoy the sunshine on my break,' she said. 'Do you mind if I join you?'

He loved the fact that even without anyone around at all, she was keeping up the charade of not knowing one another. Beth Waterfall was a singular woman.

'Suit yourself,' he said. 'Bench is a bit hard though.'

'Poor you!' she murmured. 'I can fetch you a cushion if it's that bad. Old age is no fun.'

'All right, that's enough of the piss-taking. If there's no coffee in that flask, you can just leave the food and skedaddle, lady,' he muttered, doing his best not to smile.

'Oh, would you like to share my coffee? I've more than enough for two. There's no sugar, I'm afraid. We do encourage our patients to cut down.' Lively managed not to respond as she poured him a capful and handed it over.

'Lovely day to be catching some rays. You're recuperating by the look of it.'

'I'm starving, is what I am. Don't make me break character and rob you of that carton. What did you bring me?'

'Homemade sausage rolls with a cheesy pastry, some cherry tomatoes and a few Jaffa Cakes. I know they're your favourite but I'm rationing you.' She opened the box and Lively couldn't help but grin.

'Damn, that smells good.' He took a sausage roll and destroyed most of it in a single bite. 'You know I can't let you sit with me for more than a minute, don't you?' He very much wanted to take her hand.

'I know,' she said. 'But I couldn't not check on you, at the very least. You're still a patient here, technically, and I'm in my scrubs after all, so it's not like I shouldn't be here. My shift ends at six. Will you be done for the day by then?'

'We don't really have set hours during operations like this.' He took a cherry tomato to make Beth happy and to justify the Jaffa Cakes he was about to consume. 'Something could happen in the next half hour or nothing could happen for a week. Sooner or later we'll call it a day, but that's down to the superintendent who's watching from the security centre. She's stepped in while Connie isn't able to come onto the site, which is amazing given that the last time she got her hands dirty was probably in the previous millennium.'

'You're rude to her,' Beth said softly. 'Maybe if you were all a bit kinder, she'd soften.' She took one of the cherry tomatoes herself.

'I think probably the superintendent enjoys the banter. She wouldn't know what to do with herself if we didn't give her a hard time. She's good at her job though. You don't last this long in the service if you've got no idea how to lock the bad guys away. And much as I'm enjoying this, you'd better make yourself scarce. I don't want you in the area if anything happens.' He took two Jaffa Cakes from the tub and mentally congratulated himself for not taking all four.

'And you're sure you don't want me to see the image of this person? I hate to think I might walk right past him in a corridor and miss a chance to save a life.' She stood and put the lid back on her flask.

'I know it's hard with us in a relationship and me knowing something you don't, but I think this is best. If you saw him and reacted, he might notice and hurt you. We've got this covered, I promise. St Columba's has never been more secure. My team would lay down their lives, if need be, to protect your staff and patients.'

'Well, let's hope it doesn't come to that,' she said. 'Do try to come home tonight though. You're not at full strength yet. Just a few hours' sleep would do you the world of good.' Her cheeks flushed. 'It would do me good, too. I'm happier when you're around, Sam. It's like a different house.'

'Then I'll make sure I come back. I might be late, so don't get worried about me. If you've not fallen asleep yet we could have a game of cards or watch some TV together. Sound good?'

'Sounds more than good,' she said. 'You stay safe, Sam. I don't like this.' She went back inside.

Lively closed his eyes and turned his face up to meet the sunshine.

He let himself feel the joy of having someone to go home to. He allowed himself to believe that, just possibly, Beth might end up being the someone he would be going home to for a very long time. He didn't want to eat the two Jaffa Cakes that were melting in the palm of his hand, because he wanted to look better and feel better and live longer if he had Beth Waterfall in his life.

All of these thoughts and dreams meant that he didn't see the car driving slowly along the road in sight of the geriatric rehabilitation unit. He didn't know that both he and Beth had been spotted by the very man he'd been waiting for. Lively had no way of knowing that he had been the single worst person to dress up as a patient and position himself outside the doors the suspect preferred to use. And he would never know how close his squad had come to catching the man he would later find out was Karl Smith, without violence, without trauma and without any loss of life.

Karl, wearing a charity shop football shirt for a team he'd never supported and a beanie hat he'd found left on a fish and chip shop chair, simply drove on past. The hospital had been compromised, it seemed, but he himself had been saved so the universe was in balance. He'd known it couldn't last forever. Sooner or later his time following Beth Waterfall around had to come to an end. That was all right. He was resourceful and determined. And after all, there was more than one way to skin a cat.

Chapter 38

Body Six of Eight

The Watcher

By the time Karl got home, he had to acknowledge that everything had changed. His mother was hanging around almost all the time he was in the house now, his father's carer was starting to side-eye him with a look that a freak-show audience might give a performer billed as half-man-half-slug, and he hadn't been paying anything like as much attention as he should to his investments, so their money was dwindling. On top of that, he was out so often that the carer bill was going up and up. Something had to give.

Two days earlier he'd called the doctor out to his now mostly unresponsive father and reported that his dad was increasingly refusing food, often inhaling soup or choking on tiny morsels of bread. He'd also made it clear that there were multiple occasions when his father had seemed to stop breathing for periods of time. Karl had sat dutifully and held his father's hand, looking suitably sombre but hopefully also looking as if the doctor might have some solution to the problem. The doctor had listened to his descriptions of each incident and kindly but firmly explained that it seemed likely that his father was reaching an end-of-life situation, and that strokes did take their toll long-term. He was told not to be afraid to ask for a hospice place if everything was too much. Karl had put on a suitably brave face (turning to dash away what he'd hoped the doctor had assumed were tears) and said he would look after his father at home, where they'd lived so happily as a family. The doctor left telling him what a good son he was, and how he wished all his patients had such doting adult children.

Karl had seen the good doctor out, then sat down with his notebook and pen. He had big plans and there was still much to do, but it all had to happen in the correct order. The first two items on his agenda were complete: *Cancel the carer* (tick), *Make it clear to the doctor that things are getting really very shaky* (tick). Next, it was time for soup. He tipped a can of chicken and vegetable broth into a pan and heated it up. Not too hot. He didn't want to burn his father's tongue. Then he took a slice of white bread from the loaf and carefully cut the crust off it. He placed the meal on a tray with a glass of water, a napkin and a metal straw (better for the environment), taking it into the lounge where his father lay, watery-eyed, sort of staring at the television but mainly at the wall.

'Lunchtime, Dad,' he said. 'Come on now, can't have you getting too weak.'

Karl put the tray on the side table next to his father and stroked back the stray hairs that were hanging down his face. He didn't sit him up for lunch. That wasn't going to work. Instead, he made sure the curtains were fully closed, double-locked the front door, and put the TV up loud enough but not so loud that the neighbours would consider coming round to complain.

The first spoonful of soup he gave his father went down just fine, annoyingly so in fact, given that the old man was on his

233

back. Karl tried again with a fuller spoon. A little of that one rolled down his cheek and onto the pillow and that time his father coughed and spluttered, but managed to turn his head to one side to get control of it.

His father was looking at him now. He rarely made eye contact any more, so much so that some days Karl forgot he was alive at all. It was more like looking after a large and unwieldy houseplant.

'All right, there, Dad?' Karl asked. 'Is the soup tasty? I made sure it wasn't too hot. You just relax and let me do all the heavy lifting.'

Like I've done ever since Ma died, he thought, but he kept his smile in place and filled the spoon again. He could have sworn his father was trying to say something as he approached with the next spoonful, but his father hadn't spoken a word for at least a year so those vocal cords weren't going to be any use to him at that particular moment.

'Here you go, Dad, in comes the aeroplane.'

His father's mouth was stubborn, but it couldn't resist for long. The soup went in, Karl wiped the dribble that escaped, and just like clockwork, his father began to choke. Karl gently but firmly held his nostrils closed with one hand and pushed his chin up to keep his mouth mostly sealed with the other. Not completely shut, because it helped to have his father pulling the soup down with some air, just as long as he couldn't spit it back out.

On the television, a young couple was looking for a second home in Spain and were being shown a place that was more a hutch than an apartment, but nonetheless, they were playing their part and making all the right noises. His father was doing the same.

'Oh no,' Karl said softly. 'Are you struggling with that, Dad? Try not to fight it. That would make it worse.'

He gave a bellowing sputter, then his stomach heaved and he swallowed. Karl released the pressure on his nose.

'Got some of that one down the right hole, did you? Good for you. You're not full yet though, surely.'

Karl got as much of the soup on the spoon as he could, pulled his father's lips open and poured it in.

'How would you feel about coming with me to see our mystery property?' the presenter asked.

'Yes please!' Karl responded. He threw down the spoon, gripped his father's cheeks with one hand and pinched his nose with the other and watched as he breathed in the life-threatening miniature chunks of carrot. 'I'd like to see it. What do you think it'll be like, Dad? I'm guessing, access to a slightly shitty pool, with a kitchen you couldn't swing a cat in and a bedroom that only needs a bit of TLC to make it their dream home!'

His father's body convulsed on the bed, heaving up and down, and Karl kept the liquid in his mouth. There was an odd gargling noise at the back of his throat, like that coffee advert his mother had hated with a passion, something to do with people in a kitchen pretending to make posh coffee with one of those machines but really making all the noises themself. That was it. His father was a posh coffee machine.

'Won't be a minute!' Karl called in a falsetto, suitably posh English accent. 'I'll bring the coffee through in a jiffy!'

His father's body was writhing now, moving more than it had for months. It was amazing what residual fight the human form could store. There was a time when it would all have been too much for him, too horrible and traumatic, but Karl wasn't scared of dead bodies any more.

'Did you not want to come and watch, Ma?' he yelled in the general direction of the hallway. 'This was your idea, after all! Bit squeamish, then. Not your usual cocky bitch self today!'

His father had stopped moving and Karl hadn't even noticed. He released him gently, mindful that there couldn't be any bruising or, God forbid, scratches. Nothing to arouse the suspicion of the paramedics.

'You did ever so well,' Karl told him. 'Just one more little thing to do, then we'll get you taken care of, and not by that monster, Waterfall. I won't let anyone cut you open, don't you worry. It just needs the cherry on the cake.'

Karl bit off a tiny section of bread and chewed it, making it both moist but claggy with his own saliva before inserting it into the end of the straw. He opened his father's mouth, slid the straw oh-so-carefully into his throat, took the deepest breath he could, and blew hard. There was no way of knowing where the bread ball had ended up, but it was a nice touch.

'Oh my God, we love it. It's exactly what we'd dreamed of!' the couple were exclaiming over the cockroach haven mystery property. 'I just don't know if we can afford it.'

'You can't, and you won't,' Karl said. 'Right, let's sit you up. Don't want anyone thinking I fed you soup while you were on your back, do we?'

He got his father into a more seemly position, threw the soup and bread onto the floor as if they'd been spilled in the panic of the moment, then opened the curtains and unlocked the door once more. Finally, he turned down the television and made the call.

'Please, it's my father, he was choking and now he's not breathing,' he sobbed as the call handler asked him what his emergency was. 'Ambulance. Please hurry. I'm all alone.'

He managed to actually cry as he gave out the address, which he hadn't foreseen. Then an ambulance was on its way and he was to stay on the phone, as instructions were given to turn his father onto his side and so on and so forth.

Karl remembered to move the straw in the nick of time, shoving it into the dishwasher as the doorbell went. The paramedics hadn't wasted any time, and he was glad he hadn't called them earlier. Imagine if they actually managed to save the old man?

As they walked into the house and did all they could to revive his father, Karl noticed his mother plodding down the stairs and peering into the lounge with all the grace of a teenage boy trying to sneak a peek at his older brother's porn stash.

It was just him then, he realised. No one else could see her. Her dressing gown was flapping open to reveal a filthy nightie that might have come straight out of the grave with her, crusted in filth and crawling with insects. No way could the paramedics have seen that and walked out of there with their sanity intact.

'I'm so sorry,' one of them said. 'There's nothing more we can do for your father. He died before we arrived and can't be resuscitated. It looks like he's been in physical decline for a while. Is that right?'

Karl nodded and pressed a shaking hand to his mouth. 'Are you sure there's nothing you can do?'

'I'm afraid not. Do you have a family doctor?'

Karl nodded and slowly sank into a chair. 'He was here just a couple of days ago. He warned me that things weren't looking good, but I think I just didn't really want to believe him.'

'I see. In that case, we can arrange to have the body taken away, and we'll speak to the doctor to confirm things. Is there someone we can call to come and be with you? There are some procedures we need to explain and it can be overwhelming.'

'No,' Karl said. 'There's no one. It was just my dad and me. He was my world.' In the midst of his award-winning performance, Karl realised that he'd left his to-do list out on the side in the kitchen. 'Do you mind if I leave you to it for a minute? I'll put the kettle on. I think I need some sweet tea.'

'Great idea. We'll start getting things sorted in here. It's probably best if you leave this bit to us.'

Karl nodded sadly, shoulders down, head bowed. The paramedics shut the door respectfully behind him as they started the paperwork and made calls. In the kitchen, Karl turned on the gas and burned his list, keeping it in his head instead.

Get rid of Dad in a way that won't raise any suspicion (tick). *Prepare to get rid of Beth Waterfall once and for all so that Ma will leave me alone too* (tick). *Put the house on the market. Start again and leave all the death behind.* And if the worst happened, if by some chance it all went wrong and he got caught, at least now his father wouldn't end up being abused or ignored in some awful home. What he'd done had been a mercy, really.

Perhaps he should give Spain a try, Karl thought. There were plenty of apartments going cheap, after all. For now he needed to prepare for the worst and hope for the best. He went upstairs to pack some clothes, his laptop and his passport. It was entirely possible that – much like his father – he would be leaving soon and never coming back.

Chapter 39

Eleven Months Earlier

It began with a sparrow.

It was seven weeks since the paramedics had burst in and found Molly at death's door, and three weeks since the memorial service when Beth became aware that the things Molly had complained of were still happening.

The tiny bird was on the doormat outside Beth's back door. Its neck was broken and one of its wings was badly damaged. She'd found it as she'd opened up to take a bowl of food waste, coffee grinds and loose-leaf tea to the compost heap at the end of her garden. The bird's body was cold but it hadn't yet attracted any flies, and Beth hadn't seen it the previous morning. She scooped it up in newspaper and took it to the compost heap with everything else, hoping it hadn't suffered as she set it down for nature to reclaim it, then went back to the house.

Inside, she took a spray from beneath the kitchen sink, and went back out to wipe away the mark where the bird had hit the door. But as hard as she looked, she couldn't find any evidence that the bird had crashed into the door, and the upper windows were over the kitchen's flat roof so the bird couldn't have landed where it did unless it had literally dropped dead from the sky.

'It's nothing,' she told her garden. 'He got what he wanted. Molly's gone.'

She responded by getting dressed with more purpose than ever and striding out to her car on the front driveway. As soon as she started it, the car's computer notified her of a loss of pressure in the front passenger side tyre.

'What now?' Beth muttered, desperate to be on her way. She climbed out and inspected the tyre, which was visibly flatter than the other three. Her recovery service took an hour to arrive, which wasn't bad in the circumstances, but it was an hour longer than she'd wanted to wait around thinking of all the reasons she hated living alone.

'I can see the problem. You've got a nail in it. A big one too, it's gone right in. That was unlucky. You must have driven directly over it for it to go in at ninety degrees like that. It took some force.'

Beth thought about the sparrow. A small thing designed to have a big impact.

'Could someone have put it in there deliberately?' she asked.

'Yes, but they'd have to be a right psycho to do that. It's a huge nail, they'd have needed a hammer or something like it, and that's proper dangerous. This tyre could have blown on a motorway and then there's no telling what might've happened to you. You're lucky the computer warned you. It's expensive, too. Costs a hundred quid a pop for these. Anyway, I'll have the spare on in twenty minutes, don't you worry.'

Don't you worry.

Beth was sure she'd said exactly those words to Molly when it had all started.

'He'll get bored, don't you worry.'

'We'll track him down, don't you worry.'

'The police will help us, don't you worry.'

And yet worry, Molly had, until it had all become too much for her.

Beth drove to work checking her rearview mirror while simultaneously telling herself that she wasn't looking to see if she was being followed. Behind her was a taxi, although she couldn't see if anyone was in the back. It followed her for three miles then turned off. Was that because she'd noticed it on her tail? She wasn't sure she'd ever used the phrase 'on her tail', even inside her own head. She sighed. It was two things, and two things only. A dead bird and a flat tyre. She was being ridiculous. There were bigger things on her mind without looking for reasons to be paranoid.

You just want something to think about except Molly's absence, her inner voice told her.

'Go to hell,' Beth replied reversing into a parking space and storming out of her car.

She made it to her office without bumping into anyone she was sufficiently friendly with that she needed to stop and chat, then dumped her bag and started looking through the urgent surgeries that had come in overnight. There was a knock at her door before she could open the first file, and her favourite anaesthetist, Sharon, popped her head round the door.

'Hey,' she said. 'You okay?'

It was a question everyone asked before they got down to anything more substantial, since Molly had gone.

'Sure. How busy is today going to be?'

Sharon frowned momentarily then took a deep breath. 'Did you just get in?'

'Yes. Flat tyre, so although I was supposed to be here early I'm now running late. Anything tricky waiting for us?'

'Um, Beth, I . . . something came up. The chief executive wants to talk to you. You're not on the list for surgery today. I'm so sorry,' Sharon said softly. 'Whatever I can do to help.'

'You can tell me what's going on, that would be a start,' Beth said, standing instinctively.

Sharon looked like she'd been picked to play for a team she hated. 'You obviously have no idea, and I wish it wasn't me who had to tell you. There's a video of you. It's gone viral.'

Beth's stomach performed somersaults that an Olympic gymnast would have been proud of, and she realised she should have been ready for it. She wasn't stupid and she didn't have an overactive imagination. The man who had destroyed her daughter's life was coming for her too, and he wasn't playing around.

'What's on the video?' she asked.

Sharon looked her square in the eyes. 'It's you, looks like you're in a pub garden or something, and you're saying that people who smoke, drink and eat too much shouldn't be allowed NHS treatment, and how we should only be saving the lives of the people who look after their bodies. Some of the language you use to describe those people is, well, unfortunate. Lots of expletives too. Ends in a toast, something about saving NHS money and you getting the pay rise you deserve. You get the idea.'

'Is it my voice?' Beth asked.

Sharon shrugged.

'Come on, you've known me longer than anyone else here. If it could fool you then it could fool anyone. Is it my voice?'

Sharon paused for half a second. 'Sounds exactly like you. I wish I could tell you something different.'

'But it's not me,' Beth said. 'You know that, right?'

'I do,' Sharon said. 'But you know what's going to happen.

They're going to have to investigate. They'll suspend you until it's been assessed. It'll all be about bringing the hospital into disrepute and patients losing faith in us.'

'Yeah, I know.' Beth picked up her bag and coat but the door opened again, this time without a warning knock.

The chief executive walked in followed by two men.

'Beth,' she began. 'We need a formal chat, on the record, and you'll need representation, but I wanted to see you before anyone else, although I see I'm possibly too late for that. This is our in-house lawyer and this is the head of human resources.' She indicated who was who.

'I should go,' Sharon said.

'Don't bother,' Beth told her. 'The video's a deep fake. It's not me. I didn't film it, I didn't say those words, I don't agree with the sentiment and I never have. Everyone who ends up on my table gets equal treatment. I don't judge.'

'We shouldn't have a substantive discussion,' the head of HR said blandly.

'Beth, you know how much we respect you here. But the video looks and sounds exactly like you. It appears from items in the shot that alcohol has been consumed, and of course, you've just suffered the worst loss any mother can. No one would blame you.' The chief executive didn't finish the sentence.

'It's a deep fake. It's been put on social media as a form of harassment. My record is impeccable.' Beth's voice was louder now, the effort to control her anger making her throat tight.

'I'm not sure deep-fake technology is that good. And why would anyone do that to you?' the chief executive continued.

Beth sighed. 'We have the technology to perform surgery through computer controls when we're not physically in the theatre, and a couple of years from now, with the right software, we'll be able to do that remotely from anywhere in the world with decent Wi-Fi. Deep-fake technology has been producing videos of world leaders doing and saying ridiculous things for ages. Just how out of touch are you?'

Sharon reached out to lay a hand on Beth's arm who shook the fingers away.

'We're going to give you a week while we get ourselves ready for a preliminary hearing, and you should obtain representation and produce any evidence you'd like to. That will simply be a fact-finding exercise. Please do consult your union. After that we'll adjourn and look at professional outcomes.'

Beth was already walking around her desk and towards the door. 'It's not me,' she said. 'You can have as many hearings as you like, but I'm simply going to say the same thing over and over again.'

'There's a process,' the chief executive said. 'It's unavoidable. No one wanted this to happen.'

'That's not quite right,' Beth said as she opened her door and stepped out into the corridor. 'One person definitely did.'

Chapter 40

Body Seven of Eight

Ten and a Half Months Earlier

Since leaving the hospital, all Beth had been able to think about was getting away. It had taken her a week of sitting around watching and rewatching the horrific video of herself talking cruelly about people whose only crime was getting addicted to products that had been specifically designed and marketed to make them want more, before she'd realised she either had to get active or dissolve in the mire of social media.

There had been television and radio interviews about her, she'd received death threats, and someone had thrown unbelievable amounts of dog excrement at her door in the middle of the night. Even if the hospital found that she'd not been responsible for the video and accepted that it was a deep fake, her relationship with patients was going to suffer terrible damage. Rebuilding the trust would be near impossible.

In desperation, she'd gone online and found a property to rent for a few days near Balquhidder in the Queen Elizabeth Forest Park. She'd packed everything she could think that she'd need – her brain wasn't in great condition for effective planning – then set off, only stopping for a coffee in Stirling because she needed to buy matches and milk. It took her two hours to drive from Edinburgh to Balquhidder, another half hour to locate the cabin that was set a short walk back from the banks of Loch Voil, and fifteen minutes more to figure out exactly where the key had been hidden. Judging by the dampness of the limp curtains and the mossy smell in the air, no one had stayed there for a while.

It turned out that the wood store was drier than the house, which was lucky as the open fire was going to be her only source of heat. It was a two-way fireplace that she could feed from the sitting room at the front and from her bedroom at the back, and the second she struck the match and the kindling caught, the scent of apple wood, pine and heather filled the air. She sat close to the fire and huddled there, staring into the shifting flames.

Beth had no idea how long she'd stayed in that position until she tried to unbend her knees. They protested. She stopped trying to get up. It was all too much effort. The fire was starting to weaken and she couldn't even be bothered reaching out a hand to throw on another log. Her mouth was parched from the heat, but even thirst couldn't induce her to move.

A sob erupted from deep in Beth's gut, as if some invisible strongman had performed the Heimlich manoeuvre on her. Her body was rocked by it and even the flames died down momentarily. Her loneliness was an enormous spider hanging in the corner of every room she entered. She'd thought her career would be enough to save her, but now she knew she was wrong. Then there had been the delusion that the passage of time would make her feel better, but empty rooms were ghosts and eating alone was a virus.

She'd feel better after some exercise, she told herself. That was why she'd chosen a remote hideaway, after all. There were endless trails around the loch, footpaths through the forest, and so few houses for miles that she could go for hours and see no one. All she needed were trainers and a hairband. Just those two things and she might survive the next hour, and if she could survive the next hour then she could probably make it through to the next day. That was as far ahead as she could imagine.

Beth found a band in her coat pocket and tied her hair back before shoving her feet roughly into trainers and dashing out of the door. No need to lock up. If anyone could find her cabin there in the middle of nowhere then they were welcome to the few supplies and the tatty clothes she'd brought with her.

Slamming the door shut, Beth took several deep breaths then set off up the heavily wooded slope, searching out a high point on the crest of the tree line from which to gaze down at the loch. Street running hadn't prepared her for the gradient, though. Her thighs were aching within a minute. Three minutes more and she had a stitch, clutching her side as she pushed onwards and upwards.

At the top, she sought out a place to sit, finding a fallen tree and perching on it, careless of scattering beetles and spiders. Looking down on Loch Voil it was easier to get things in perspective, to understand the smallness of her place in the world. Beth breathed in the scents of earth and mulch, and freshly produced oxygen, and breathed out the city, its pollutants and the bodies that she treated and fixed or treated and lost. She didn't mind the natural cycle of life. That was all part and parcel of her job. What she minded and hated – despised, loathed, a voice inside her whispered – was the interference of man in that cycle.

Beth forced herself to close her eyes and just be in the moment. She was becoming consumed by her hatred and it was festering no less than any physical wound might. Standing, she took one last look at the loch below, superficially beautiful and calm while the current beneath the surface was lethal. The similarity to how she felt wasn't lost on her.

Beth took the return trip slower, the gradient hard on her knees. Twice she slipped, once landing on her coccyx, the next trying to avoid a repeat of that and going down onto her left hip. Still, she could see the roof of her cabin in its tiny clearing below and inside the fire was waiting, along with a kettle and bathtub. Sanctuary.

Taking the slope steadily, going from tree to tree to keep herself upright, she made her way down. Sunset was staining the sky from bitter orange to pomegranate.

He hit her from behind as she paused one last time to turn her face into the dying sun.

'Wha—' was all that came out of her mouth before barrelling sideways and smacking her right temple into a branch then crashing to her knees and falling face first into the dirt.

'Bitch!' the man who'd emerged from behind a tree screeched. 'You fucking bitch. You killed her!'

He pulled back a leg and went to kick her, losing his footing on the slope with the movement and shoving his foot downwards into her chest, sending her rolling over and over, protecting her head with her arms. He slid after her.

The trees weren't the only hazard. There were thorns, roots and rocks to contend with too. As fast as the world blurred when she opened her eyes for a fraction of a second, he was still coming after her, the two of them crying out as they snagged their skin or took a blow.

She had time to wonder who the hell it was who'd jumped out and pushed her, another second to process what he'd screamed at her, and a few moments to finally – in slow motion which was ironic given how fast her body was moving – figure out the identity of the man trying to kill her.

Beth's journey ended when her abdomen hit a tree trunk, her legs wrapping around one side, her arms around the other.

I'm a ragdoll, she thought, as she hung around the tree, her hands feeling nothing but air the other side. She realised the tree that had stopped her was leaning over the edge of a steep drop-off.

She turned her head, the vertebrae in her neck crackling, to watch his incoming body fly down the slope at her, and immediately shut her eyes again. His body was a ball of flesh and cloth hurtling at a speed that would surely end him if he hit a tree headfirst.

'Die,' Beth wished for him, as she braced for impact.

Something snapped.

He screamed, more animal than human, and that cry was pain. Beth had heard it enough times to know. Then there was a crunch, not of impact but the crushing, crumpling sound of tangled undergrowth. And not-quite-silence. A whistling. The sound of moving air.

Beth's eyes flew open in time to see the end of the human cannonball's flight off the edge and into a line of smaller, younger trees below.

Something dripped into her right eye and she wondered how it was raining without a cloud in the sky, until the world turned crimson and the pain in her head became a monster intent on splitting her skull in two. She vomited.

Get up, she told herself. Get up and deal with him, because if he's still alive, he's coming back for you.

She pushed herself off the tree trunk, mentally checking each limb as she went. The pain in her left side was undoubtedly a cracked rib. Breathing was agony. Best-case scenario was no internal bleeding. She'd broken one tooth, possibly more. Her pulse was racing and her head was throbbing. Concussion, almost certainly. Arms and legs though, while scratched to pieces, were not fractured.

Taking the slope in a seated position, she made her way down, with no clear plan what she'd do when she got there.

She paid for the journey in agony and it seemed to take forever. What she found was nothing except a few scraps of black material fluttering from the ends of branches and a scuffed path in the dirt that went in the direction of her cabin.

'Still alive,' she muttered. 'Fuck him.'

Beth looked more closely at his tracks. She was no wildlife expert, but she knew the difference between footsteps and drag marks. The tracks were two long, deep lines, blunt and wide. Her assailant wasn't walking, he was on his hands and knees.

'Badly hurt then,' she told herself. 'Worse than me.'

She had two choices. Head in the opposite direction, get far enough away that he wouldn't be able to find her, then seek help.

But he might find her again. He just might. And she might be more badly hurt than she felt as yet. The body had a wonderful inbuilt pain relief system that kept you going for a while before letting you know just how bad things really were. Worse than that, he might get away. He had to have a car or motorbike in the area, there being no easy way of getting where they were without a vehicle. And it was possible that she'd just get lost. More than possible. Probable. Her head was already spinning.

That left only the prospect of going after him in the direction of her cabin and car. She needed her keys, her wallet and her mobile. That was all. If he really was as badly hurt as she suspected, it was possible that he wouldn't bother her at all.

She moved several metres to the left of his tracks and followed as quietly as she could, clutching the cracked rib and stopping to check there was no blood in her saliva. It was clear. That was good. No wet sounds in her breath, either.

The man she was walking towards had lost someone under

her knife. A woman. Beth hadn't got much of a look at his face, but the glimpse she'd had was all she needed. That, and his scream. He'd yelled that at her once before.

His mother had been brought in by ambulance having suffered a suspected heart attack. She'd been kept alive en route with shocks and drugs, but as soon as Beth had cut her open, the damage was obvious. Such were the perils of decades of smoking topped up with years of alcohol abuse. The woman had been thin, almost emaciated, and it had been clear that all her calories had come from an off-licence and that even when she wasn't actively smoking, the air she was breathing in at home was still tainted with toxins.

A postmortem had confirmed extensive cardiovascular damage, a massive blood clot in her heart and several small tumours forming in her lungs. The cancer would have claimed her, had her end not been quickened by the heart attack. Her body had been a corpse-in-waiting. There had been no kind way to break the news to her family, but as ever, it was hard to tell people that someone they loved had caused their own death, and that there had been nothing medically the team could do to save them.

There had been an older man there, Beth now remembered. Unemotional, almost closed off. The adult son hadn't been in the room as she'd broken the news to his father. It was only as Beth had exited with the two other doctors who'd volunteered to be present to answer questions, that the son had appeared.

'You killed her!' he'd screamed at them.

'Keep walking,' one of the other doctors had warned Beth as she'd turned round to look at him, preparing to go back and talk it through. 'I'll call security.'

'But—' she'd begun.

'You know the protocols. It's dangerous to talk with family

251

when they're that upset. Best advice is to walk away and let them calm down.'

They'd rounded the corner as he was still yelling, but he hadn't run after them. The image in her mind was of a man somewhere between twenty and forty, with mid-brown hair, a sprinkling of moles on his face, with deep-set brown eyes and square shoulders that seemed to jut out from his neck at ninety degrees. But it was the desperate screech of his voice that had stuck in her memory. The sense that he needed to vent at them, that he needed it to be someone else's fault. Grief was a parasite, and its favourite meal was blame.

Still she couldn't summon the woman's name. Working in trauma, there were so many losses that it was a necessary protection of her own sanity to let some of it go. The oncologists she knew all said the same. If you carried every death with you every day, if you could see all their faces and name all their names, you were on a slippery slope into depression that would land you in a breakdown. Beth thought she knew a little more about slippery slopes given what she'd just been through.

As she drew closer to the cabin, her footsteps slowed and her pulse quickened. She could see her car through the trees. The front door of the cabin remained closed, but of course, unlocked, because she was an idiot who'd allowed her need to escape to override common sense. Beth stood still and listened. Distant birdsong, some insect noises. Was that a chainsaw a long way away? The sound could even be echoing from across the loch. But near her position? Nothing. The air was dead. Had that silence been caused by her approach or his?

Part of her wanted to scream that she was there, to get it over with, to make him rush out of the trees or out of her cabin, or from behind her car, or wherever the bastard was. His trail went out into the clearing but she couldn't see further than that without giving herself away.

Do or die, Beth thought. The world was spinning faster with every passing minute.

She took several deep breaths, removed her hand from her side so as not to indicate weakness just in case he was watching her, and stepped out into the clearing.

Time stopped.

Even her thudding heart was quiet.

She wanted to cry with the tension, with the need for it to be over – the waiting, the fear, the danger.

Still nothing.

The vacuum began to fill with a diluted version of hope.

Beth took one more step towards the cabin and forced herself to breathe out. Another step and she breathed in again, unable to control the wince that came with the movement of her ribcage.

The silence and stillness remained unbroken.

The cabin door was just a few steps away now, and inside, her car keys were on a little table that she could reach from the threshold. She wanted her mobile but would do without it if it meant a guaranteed getaway.

Beth tried another step, stumbled but righted herself on her car, then moved forward again. Now she could almost feel the door handle in her palm and remembered it would squeak as she pushed it down, but there was nothing she could do about that. If he was in there waiting for her, she was doomed anyway. Another move forward, still holding the car, but the cabin door was just a metre away. She reached for it, biting her bottom lip, desperate not to have been wrong, not to have signed her own death warrant.

He came at her from the side, running and bellowing, a warrior from some action movie holding a log aloft as he staggered.

Beth lurched for the door handle, gripping it and pushing down. Inside was safety. Inside was life.

She made it a second before he reached her, rushing in and shoving the door shut with all her might, waiting to feel his weight thrust against it as she turned the thumb bolt.

Nothing.

Beth grabbed a wooden chair from the side of the dinner table and pulled it beneath the door handle, not that it fitted the way she'd seen on TV. It was better than nothing though. Clutching her side again, she stepped quietly to the window and gathered every ounce of courage to pull back the curtain. Was he poised ready to break the glass? Had he already gone round the back to find another way in? And where the hell had she put her mobile?

She peeked out.

There he was on the gravel in front of her car, face down. One of his legs was in a position that must have been agony, and his hair was a bloody mess. The log he'd been wielding had rolled out of his grasp. Beth drew the curtain fully back and took a better look, studying the rise and fall of his chest. His breathing was laboured and uneven. She could imagine exactly how it would sound if she held her stethoscope to his chest. The fingers of his left hand were spasming. He was in trouble, more so even than her.

She sighed. It was hard to watch anyone in pain as a doctor. One phone call and she could ensure her own safety and get him help, both physical and psychiatric.

'Barbara Smith,' Beth announced. 'That was your mother.'

And then the world fell away.

Barbara Smith, deceased. Husband's name long since forgotten. But it was her son who'd yelled at her in the hospital corridor. Her son, presumably, surname also Smith.

A synaptic connection snapped into place in her brain, far, far too late.

'Oh God, it was all my fault,' Beth said.

The man who'd started out as Karl Smith, then become Carl Smith, after that Carl Smyth, next Carlos Smit, and at the end of his overt communications Cal Smee, had targeted her daughter for one reason and one reason only. His mother had died on Beth's operating table.

He'd never referenced it, never mentioned Beth, never hinted at it, and so Beth had never made the connection. Not once. How was it possible that she hadn't even considered Molly's stalker might have been her fault? It hadn't once occurred to her, so certain was she that all she ever did in her job was good.

Beth knew that nothing would ever be enough for him. No amount of loss, pain or suffering. He would hate her forever and follow her to the ends of the earth to take his revenge. No one in her life, near or far, would be safe. And Beth had to look after the people she loved. It was all so fragile and so easily lost.

'He came here to kill me,' she told the transparent reflection of herself in the glass. 'He would have done it, too, if he'd caught me.'

She walked to the door, gulped down the nerves that were rising in her throat, unlocked and opened up.

He hadn't moved.

Beth felt her lungs burning and her right eye bulging. There wasn't much time.

She went back to the kitchen area and picked up a knife, holding it out in front of her as she stepped onto the gravel drive and approached him.

There was no horror movie moment. He didn't suddenly leap up or grab her ankle. She prodded him with her toes once, twice, three times.

'You destroyed Molly,' she said. 'You tried to kill me.'

He didn't respond.

How should she do it? Not should she do it, she realised. She'd skipped all the way through to the end of the argument to methodology. No time for philosophy. The sky was warning her that it would soon be lights out.

The knife was the obvious answer and she was good with a blade.

But if it was ever found, there would be no question about what had happened to him. No grey area. It could only have been a murder.

Prepare for the worst, hope for the best, her father whispered from some dim place inside her subconscious.

'Ah yes,' Beth said, as if she'd misplaced her car keys and just remembered she'd left them in the ignition. 'Silly me.' She walked around Karl Smith's body and picked up the log he'd dropped. 'It needs to look like you fell onto this, not that someone hit you with it.'

Beth put down the knife, used Karl Smith's hair to lift his head, and whacked the front of his skull on his forehead hard enough to sound like someone had just hit a six at The Oval. She laid his head back down carefully onto the gravel and waited for the inevitable.

Karl's body convulsed, then lay still again. His breathing grew ragged then shallowed. She made herself wait a full ten minutes before taking his pulse. It was weak, thready and uneven.

'Time to get moving,' she muttered.

She tucked the knife into the waistband of her leggings, rolled Karl onto his back, arms up over his head, and took one hand in each of hers behind her back. Dragging him was slow going and even harder once she reached the trees. Twice she had to stop and hump him up and over fallen branches. Twenty minutes later, she found what she'd been looking for: another drop-off with a ditch below it, and by then the last dribble of bloody light had slithered from the horizon. No phone, no torch, in agony and desperate, Beth hauled him to the edge of the ditch until his jeans got caught on a branch.

She pulled too hard, and she knew it as she was doing it. The pop of her arm from its socket was the last straw in a day that she'd believed for a while would be her last. Even then she couldn't scream and risk some dog walker or camper hearing and calling the police.

The pain was a firework set off inside her body.

'Fuck,' she growled, ripping at the stuck jeans with her good hand and feeling for his neck in the pitch black. No pulse. No breaking sounds. All good. He was done.

Finally, with a last push of her foot, he rolled down into the ditch that would be his resting place. Beth kicked some leaves down after him. It wouldn't do to make it look as if he'd been buried. That, too, would arouse suspicion. But just maybe, if he ever was found there in the middle of the forest, it might be that he'd been hiking, lost his footing, hit his head, and died there in that nowhere, that last ditch.

She said a short prayer for her own soul but did not pray for his. Why should she? He'd brought it all on himself.

It took her forty-five minutes to get back to the cabin in the dark, and more than once she felt that the woods simply did not want to let her go. But she made it, threw her belongings back into her bag, left the cabin exactly as it had been when she'd arrived, and climbed into her car. She paused only to message the letting agent to say there had been a change of plan, that she was stuck in Edinburgh and would not be able to get away for her break after all but understood that she wouldn't be eligible for a refund.

Then she drove back to Edinburgh one-handed, fiercely grateful for having an automatic car, and took herself straight to the hospital. It was a risk, and one she felt bad about. Several times she thought the pain might make her pass out, but she couldn't be found in her car away from the city. Her face in the rearview mirror belonged to a ghost more than a living person. But it was only fair that she suffered, she realised. It was the price she had to pay.

Karl Smith had finally been reunited with his mother. It was a fitting end for him, lying with the skittering, slithering things that he'd driven her beautiful daughter to paint over and over again until madness had taken her.

Beth parked at the hospital, staggered in through the doors and collapsed on the mat before anyone could reach her.

It was another twelve hours before she would open her eyes and know that she'd survived the night.

And another four hours after that, Karl Smith would – unbeknown to her – do the same.

Chapter 41

Ten and a Half Months Earlier

By the time Beth was not only conscious but sufficiently drug-free to really understand what was going on, the first thing she asked for was a newspaper.

'As soon as we've checked you out properly,' the doctor overseeing her treatment promised. 'You've had antibiotics and saline, and your tetanus was nearly out of date so we did that too. Can I ask how the arm is feeling today? It was dislocated. You'll need to keep it in that sling for about a month, and you'll need physiotherapy before you can safely hold a scalpel again. You had a rib fracture too but it wasn't displaced and it should heal nicely, and a dentist is coming in this morning to take a look at your chipped tooth.'

'None of it matters. Given the damage to my career, I'll never hold a scalpel again anyway,' she said. 'Did anyone find my phone? There are some people I need to call.'

'I gather the only thing in your hand when you passed out in A&E was your car keys, but one of your colleagues checked your car, found your handbag in there, and anything of value has been placed in your office and locked up. Can you tell me how you dislocated your shoulder? You have a number of cuts and grazes too. We were concerned that we should call the police.'

'No,' Beth said quietly. 'It was my own fault. I was upset about being suspended from my job, so I went for a run and ended up falling down a slope. I tried to grab a bush to stop myself and dislocated the shoulder.' She tried to sit up and failed. Her shoulder was only mildly uncomfortable. What really hurt was her head. 'Could I get some more pain relief? My head's thumping.'

'I bet. That was a nasty blow to the temple. We've done a CT scan though, and you were watched closely for concussion, but you're out of danger now. The neurologist said there was nothing of concern in the scan.'

Beth rubbed her forehead with her free hand and groaned. 'Yes, sorry. I remember the scan now. Everything was fuzzy for a while.'

'You were given strong painkillers when we found you. I'm not surprised your memory is blurry, but it'll all come back.'

The door opened.

'Knock-knock,' the visitor said. 'Is this a bad time?'

'Not at all, I was finished anyway. I'll give you the room.'

Beth's stomach shrivelled at the sound of the chief executive's voice. She sank as far back into the pillow as she could manage and braced for more bad news.

'I'm not really feeling up to this,' she croaked, shaking her head. 'And if you want to discuss my suspension, I should probably have someone—'

'We know it was a fake,' the chief executive cut in. 'We had the video checked by an expert – no expense spared – who was able to detect some . . . anomalies or something in the code . . . honestly, how these people do this stuff is beyond me. And why, well that's something I'll never understand either. I do hope, Beth, that you ending up in here is nothing to do with our investigation. You appreciate that the steps we took were to protect both the hospital and you.'

'No expense spared,' Beth repeated. That hadn't been for her benefit, of course. If they were going to sack her, they had to make sure they were on solid ground or risk getting sued. 'It's not going to be as easy to fix my reputation as my arm.' Not that any of it mattered, not if Karl Smith's body had been found.

'Don't worry about that. We've already issued a statement and we have a top PR firm on it. I'm doing an interview on BBC Radio Scotland tomorrow about the perils of artificial intelligence, and *The Scotsman* is running an article about medical heroes and how they can become targets because of their work on the frontline. The video has been taken down from all the major social media outlets too. More importantly, what can we get you? Obviously we put you in a private room because we need to protect our staff better than . . . well, before. But what about clothes and toiletries? I can have someone go to your house and pack you a bag.'

'I'd like to go home,' Beth said. 'Apparently the CT scan was clear and the medication won't be a problem.'

'Oh, please, don't even think about that yet. I'm sure we'd all like a chance to look after you for a couple of days. Bit of rest and recuperation. I can always arrange for a couple of meals to be brought in, if hospital catering isn't quite what you're used to.'

'I just want to go home,' she repeated. 'There are plenty of other people who need this bed. It's not right.'

'But we do need to make sure that our most valued surgeon gets all the care she needs to come back on board with us!' the chief executive cooed.

Beth fought the urge to say bad words, choosing instead not to blow up what remained of her career.

'I'm going home, but I'll keep in touch. A taxi would be appreciated, with a driver who doesn't mind carrying my bags in for me. I'll have to leave my car here until I can drive again. I'm grateful for your support.'

'Of course. Take as much time as you need, and if you'd like to come back on reduced hours initially while your arm gets back to full strength, then we'll make that work.' She took a step away from the bed towards the door. 'You're all right, though?' She hesitated. 'It was rather a coincidence of timing, I thought, your accident.'

Beth sighed. 'I was trying to get fit. It felt like good self-care during my suspension, but it seems I'm destined to end up at this hospital whether I'm suspended or not.'

The chief executive was nodding her head as if her life depended on it. 'Ah, yes, very funny. But you're definitely not suspended now. Quite the opposite. And you don't think you need any sort of, er, psychiatric evaluation, before you return to work?'

So that was it. Beth failed to stifle a small smile. They thought she'd attempted and bungled suicide. Or perhaps that the whole accident was some sort of attention-seeking behaviour. Thank God they didn't know the truth. Clearly the police hadn't been in there asking questions. Not yet anyway.

'No psychiatric evaluation needed. Perhaps a raise though?'

'Ah ha ha ha,' the chief executive managed. 'Good one. Very funny. I'll get that taxi for you right away.'

Asking for more money had been the surefire way to get the woman out of her room. At last, Beth was alone.

So much of what had happened was shrouded in mist. Not what she'd done, but getting back in the car and driving to

Edinburgh – unforgivably reckless – and before that, hitting Karl Smith with a log. She knew in her conscious mind that she'd done it but, looking back, the memory wasn't first person at all. It was as if she had watched some stranger, some mad woman, kill in cold blood.

Part of her wanted to go back there, straight away, to find the body and see if it was real or if she'd lost her mind. But it was too risky. Why leave even more of a trail? In her mind, she was already answering questions in some dingy police interview room.

'I had nothing to do with it, officer. He must have followed me up there and had an accident. I had no idea. I cancelled my accommodation when I hurt myself and they obviously got the wrong end of the stick when I cancelled. I didn't mean I hadn't turned up at all.'

On and on the imaginary interview ran in her mind until a porter came in with her bag and the message that a taxi would be there to collect her within the hour. She was given clean scrubs to go home in, and a supply of painkillers from the pharmacy. All very calm, all very normal. As if she hadn't ended a man's life.

Now she had to inhabit her normal body and let her friends and remaining family know that she was fine, nothing to worry about. Beth Waterfall version 2.0. That was who she had to be.

Karl Smith had been too much of a threat to let him go, but all that was behind her now.

It was time to start living again.

Chapter 42

18 June

'So from the snippets of hospital CCTV of our suspect following Charlie's description, we can get no facial recognition because the top half of his face from just below his eyes is always obscured by headwear and he looks down all the damned time. We've got no number plate as he obviously parks away from the site, no mobile number, no means of identifying him, and I suspect he's onto us because he hasn't been seen at the hospital since we've been undercover there,' Connie said. 'It's like this man has superpowers.'

She and Baarda were in his room at The Balmoral, in the dark once more and staring at images projected onto the wall.

'I can't hold the publicity any longer,' she said. 'At nine a.m. tomorrow, the media liaison team will release these photos to see if anyone can name him, but the second we do, it'll be all over the internet and he'll run. It's a hell of a compromise, getting his name but quite possibly losing him into the bargain.'

'If he runs it's an admission of guilt, so that'll be one problem sorted, because all we have at the moment is proximity in time and place to the hospital, disguises, and passing himself off as a member of staff. That won't get a conviction, even if we find and arrest him.'

'Agreed. We definitely need more than that.'

'Like a motive,' Baarda said.

'Like a motive,' she repeated. 'Do you have any snacks left in here? I ate all mine, and I really love those little packets of toasted sunflower seeds.'

'Next to the kettle. You okay? You seem . . . twitchy.'

'Yeah, I'm missing something. I know I am. Makes me want to bash a pan into my head. Here they are.' She opened the pack and sat back down crunching. 'Let's take a closer look at him.'

Baarda increased the image size but the blurring was too much of a distortion, so he decreased it again.

'I like projecting images onto walls. It's better than looking at photos. The light makes the faces more alive. Let's play a game. You tell me something you see in the photo and I'll tell you something. If you name something I haven't noticed yet, you get a point and vice versa. Go.'

Baarda reached across and took some sunflower seeds before answering.

'You can see even through the scrubs he's wearing that his collarbones are quite pronounced. Most people have enough flesh on them that they wouldn't be so noticeable through light clothing. He's underweight, probably running on pure adrenaline, but also I'd say definitely under thirty-five after which the vast majority of people find it harder to shed pounds.'

'Nice,' Connie said. 'And I agree. But no points, I already had that one. Okay, it looks to me as if he used to have an earring in his left ear, and the red dot is still noticeable enough that I

265

don't think he took it out all that long ago. Might be a further suggestion that he's trying to be less easy to identify or to blend in, or it could be that he's going through some psychological changes that are making him want to alter himself, possibly both.'

'Good but I got it,' Baarda said. 'He's tense in every image we captured. Look at the tendons at the sides of his neck. If we don't catch him, he'll have had a heart attack within the year. That's a man on a mission.'

'One–nil,' she told him, screwing up the packet and tossing it across to the bin. 'And I hate losing so give me a minute. What have we got? Pale skin, no tan, he's inside a lot, too obvious. Lips look rough, probably bites his bottom lip but that's linked to tension and you already got the tendons. Make the image a little bit bigger but not so we lose the definition, would you?'

Baarda obliged.

'That's better.' Connie gave her shoulders a shake and licked her top lip. 'His facial skin looks uneven in places, as if he has acne scars, although there's no discolouration. It's all very even in tone, in fact.' She stopped talking. 'All just one tone. More like a woman's skin—'

'Because he's wearing make-up,' Baarda finished for her. 'I think you're right.'

'Bring up the other photos,' she said. 'All of them. I want to see if it's a lighting anomaly in this one image or if it's the same in every one. And that's my point, by the way, even if you butted in at the end.'

'If you're right about this, I concede anyway. Here you go. These four other shots are the best we've got, although not quite as close up as the one we were just looking at. Everything else is too blurry.'

Baarda scrolled through them.

'Go back,' Connie said. 'No, next one. It's the same, right? That even, pale, beige skin tone in every shot.'

'Yup,' Baarda said. 'There's no stubble shadow anywhere, and you can see at the base of his cap that his hair is a darkish brown, so there should be a sense of beard growth even just under the surface. It's completely hidden. The question is, why?'

Connie took in a slow deep breath as she reached out with her left hand and gripped Baarda's right wrist.

'Brodie, go back to the first of the four new images you brought up.' He did so. 'There,' she said, standing and walking to the wall. 'Now make it smaller so that the resolution is as good as it gets and come here.' Baarda adjusted the setting and got up to join her. 'What do you see here?' She pointed to a dot at one side of his mouth.

Baarda squinted. 'There's a mark there, but I couldn't tell you from what. Could be a scab or even some food he hasn't wiped. Maybe part of a birthmark. Is that what you think the make-up's for?'

'I don't think so,' she said. 'On the original image, I thought the bumps looked like acne scarring because they were quite well defined and rounded. This mark isn't scarring, it's too dark, but it's definitely rounded and very noticeable.'

'A mole?'

'Uh-huh. And I'd say it's one of several, looking at his overall skin texture. It's taken a lot of make-up to cover them all up, which is why it looks a bit cakey and unnatural in tone.' She went back to the sofa and flopped down.

'Multiple moles on his face would have made him far too standout to get away with going to the hospital regularly. Damn it. You won again. If we send out this image but we get a visual artist to reimagine it with a few of the moles uncovered, even if they're not exactly in position, it's bound to jog someone's memory out there.'

'I agree. But I think that imaginary pan just hit me in the head. Those moles are much more important than just helping us identifying him. Can you bring up facial images of all the victims, but I need them all at once?'

Baarda created a new image with the four faces in a square.

'Now we can see our killer more clearly, it's so obvious that I can't believe we missed it.'

'It was literally staring us in the face,' Baarda said. 'I get the connection. Tell me what you know about him now that we didn't before.'

She rubbed her hands together and gave a tiny bounce on the sofa before she spoke. 'He's someone who's been self-conscious his entire life. Moles anywhere else on your body can be covered up, but facial moles are unusual. They make people stare. Kids especially, who have no filter and often no socially aware conscience, are cruel and fast to create nicknames. I'm guessing the moles were the first thing anyone ever saw when they met him. The first name calling probably started when he was no more than five years old. Lucy Ogunode mentioned it to Christie Salter in relation to Dale Abnay who had eczema, talked about him being bullied by other kids.'

Baarda switched the lights back on in the room and turned his attention to Connie instead of the images. 'So they all have some form of facial marking. Abnay's eczema, Divya Singh's hyperpigmentation which also resembles tiny moles, Archie Bass has a lot of facial scarring from various wounds and exposure over the years and Vic Campbell has excessive tattooing on his face which has also messed with the texture of his skin. But why choose them as victims? Most people develop empathy from bullying, surely, at least towards people with similar issues.'

'That only works if your psychological set-up allows for empathy. Step into his world for a second. As a baby and a toddler, you're blissfully unaware that you look a bit different. Maybe you notice it in the mirror but not in a way that sets you apart. It's just your face, and that's great. Then you start school and people point at you and talk about it, and make you feel like an outsider. Skip ahead a few years and those kids are a bit older and bigger, and now they're really laying into him, because nothing makes kids feel powerful like excluding someone who's a bit different. Those days you come home and look in the mirror and yeah, you hate those kids, but you also hate the moles. After a while you start hating your whole face. And you're powerless to change it. You can't do anything about it. It never stops, it never gets better, and maybe there are even new moles appearing. Fuck me, you're pissed now. You're enraged. Girls are giggling at you, boys are shitty. It's hard to make friends, and your parents just tell you to ignore the bullying which is bullshit. How much hate are you feeling now? That's got to go somewhere, Brodie, because if it just stays inside it's gonna break you.'

'He's killing people whose faces remind him of himself?' Baarda asked.

'I think maybe he's killing a representation of himself. Perhaps he's someone who's thought endlessly about suicide but who can't do that, hence the lack of torture or the lack of a standard pattern in choosing victims – different genders, different races – and in his head he's killing himself over and over again.'

'I get it. And I need a drink. You?' Connie shook her head as Baarda picked up a glass. 'What's the link to the hospital?'

'I don't know yet. Maybe he's hanging around the dermatology unit? Possibly it's just somewhere with a huge amount of people passing through so there's every chance he'll identify a victim. It might equally well be something personal to him that we haven't figured out yet. But it's the only link between the victims, Brodie, and I can feel it in my bones. This is why they were all chosen.'

He knocked back a whisky and began putting on his shoes.

'We'd better get back to the station then,' he said. 'You ready?' Connie was already at the door.

Chapter 43

Ten Months Earlier

Driving was both painful and against doctor's orders, but Beth couldn't stay home any longer. All she did was wander around finding cupboards to tidy, drawers to sort and things to throw away. The result had been an ever-growing pile of rubbish in her front garden that would never fit in the bin, and that needed taking to the household waste recycling centre.

It had taken a while packing it into her car with the sling on, but it was faster after she'd thrown her sling onto the top of the rubbish stack and used both arms. It had been a little over two weeks, and she was doing all the physiotherapy exercises she'd been set, so there wasn't much point keeping the sling on anyway. That was bad advice, of course, but she couldn't stand the restriction for one more day. The sling made her feel vulnerable and old. Worse, it was a reminder of . . . things she wasn't prepared to think about.

The recycling centre was quiet, unusually so, but that suited her. It was going to take a few trips from the boot of her car to each different container to get rid of all the bits and pieces, especially with only one good arm, and she didn't want people staring. She was still worried about being recognised from the damned deep-fake video.

Reversing her car into a bay, she caught a glimpse of a man leaning against a wall and reading a newspaper. He was wearing a cap and the shadow was falling across his face, but there was something so familiar about him. Something that made her shoulder and head ache anew.

In an instant, Beth was falling again. She was back on the endless slope she'd been so certain would finish her. In the front seat of her car, she folded her arms in front of her face to avoid the trees, branches, brambles and rocks she was hurtling towards.

'Oh fuck. It's him,' she muttered. 'It's him, it's him, it's him.'

She ducked down before he could see her and started her car again, shooting forward then having to slam on the brakes as a van did its best to avoid her. The man was looking up at her now, checking out her car, walking towards her. He'd dropped the newspaper on the ground, no longer walking but striding in her direction as she slammed her right foot to the floor and sped away.

He was yelling now, waving his arms at her, shouting at her to stop. She went faster, taking the tiny roads of the recycling centre like a rally circuit.

Karl Smith was fucking alive. She hadn't killed him. Now he'd come for her again. God only knew how he'd managed to get there ahead of her. She hadn't noticed any suspicious cars or motorbikes following her. Perhaps he'd simply seen her loading up and gone on ahead.

She raced away, checking her mirror every few seconds to make sure no one was coming after her. A few miles later, she pulled onto the forecourt of a small garage she used for MOTs and repairs, and rushed into the tiny office.

'I need you to check my car, Bill. It's urgent.'

'Not a problem, let me see when we've next got a slot,' the mechanic said.

'That won't work. I need help now!' Beth blurted.

Bill raised his eyebrows and nodded. 'I see,' he said slowly and loudly, as if he was talking to someone either very disturbed or a child he needed to humour. 'And can you tell me what you believe the problem to be?'

'Yes,' Beth said, aware that she was almost panting and doing her best to slow her breathing. 'I know how this will sound, but I think there might be a device on my car that, um, you know, would enable someone to track my movements.' Her face reddened as she said it, and she found she could no longer meet Bill's gaze. Still, she held her ground.

'A tracking device,' he said. 'Do you, perhaps, need me to call the police for you?'

'No!' She caught the desperation in her response and forced a smile. 'The police won't help. Listen,' she stepped closer to him and lowered her voice, 'it's an ex-boyfriend. He hasn't moved on, and there's been this car that appears, follows me for a while then turns off. If it's him, it could be dangerous for me. I know it sounds extreme, but when you've been through what I've been through . . .' She let it hang.

'Of course, I get it. Let's get her up on the ramp and I'll check it out. You'll be safe here, I promise.'

Beth handed him the keys and sat on a rickety chair pretending to look at a decade-old magazine as he worked. The guilt she might have felt at her lie was diluted by the knowledge that the truth was much scarier. If Karl Smith had been a threat to her before, just what might he be capable of since she'd tried to kill him?

It wasn't him, her rational voice insisted. It couldn't have been. You checked his pulse and tipped him into a ditch.

Beth wished she could believe her own brain when it tried to reassure her.

At least you're not a murderer, she answered herself. And it was him. She'd seen his speckled skin beneath the shade of the cap, and he'd started watching her as soon as she'd driven in. Who stood around a recycling centre reading a newspaper?

But he died. You're a doctor. No one knows better than you how permanent death is.

Beth stood up, shook her head to silence the duelling voices, and really thought about it. By the time she'd rolled Karl Smith into the ditch it had been pitch black. She'd been exhausted and coping with extreme pain. On top of that, she'd had a serious blow to the head. Then there was the stress, the adrenaline and the panic.

Sometimes, she knew, it was almost impossible to find a pulse. Plenty of doctors had recounted incidents when they'd declared a patient dead only to find them alive an hour later. Pulses were tricky things when patients were unwell. So maybe she'd missed it, or maybe his pulse had temporarily been too weak to find. But she had to accept that it was possible that he hadn't died at all.

'No,' she said. 'I won't have it. That can't have been him. There's no way he got out of that ditch. He's dead, he deserved it, and I've got too much to lose to be driven insane by this.'

She strode out of the office to the mechanic who was shining a light on the underside of her car.

'It's all right now. I think I overreacted. You can stop.'

'Well, there's nothing in the way of tracking devices, but I did find an almighty great nail stuck in your rear driver's side tyre. Lucky you brought it in, to be honest. That could have burst at any time, and if you'd been going fast, who knows how that would have ended up.'

274

Another nail in another tyre. What were the odds? She did her best to keep her face and voice neutral.

'Can you change it for me? I have somewhere to be.'

'I can, but I think you should consider that call to the police. This is a very long nail. Chances of it getting into your tyre from a road or by accident, I'd say are low. If your ex is trying to hurt you, this would have been a clever way of going about it.' He put the torch down and went to a rack of tyres and began looking for the right one.

'I'll bear that in mind,' Beth said. 'Thank you. How long?'

'No more than fifteen minutes. You can use my phone if you need it. The police station's only down the road. I'll show them what's happened if they can spare someone to come down.'

'Now's not a great time, to be honest. If you could just change that tyre for me, I'd appreciate it. But if you put the old one in the boot, I'll call the police when I get home and ask them to take a look.' She checked her watch. Bill got the message and began fitting the new tyre.

Beth waited, paid and got back in the car. Ten minutes later she was at the recycling centre entrance, paused in a lay-by. She had to be sure. If the man she'd seen wasn't Karl Smith, then everything was fine. If it was, then she'd have to come up with a plan for how to deal with him.

Her head was hurting, and she wished she was still wearing the sling because her shoulder was agony too. She closed her eyes for a minute and waited for the pain to pass. When she opened them again, the clock told her it was an hour later. Surely that wasn't possible. Beth checked the clock against her phone. She had to have fallen asleep. The headache had knocked her out. She had just a few minutes left to double-check and get the rubbish out of her boot.

In she went, slowly this time, trying not to draw attention to herself. She parked up, not rushing, keeping it casual.

All the staff members were wearing high-visibility jackets, so it couldn't have been one of them. Most of the visitors were wandering from vehicle to container like a train of ants. But of Karl Smith, or the man she'd thought was him, there was no sign.

She emptied the last items from the boot, finally taking the tyre from where she'd propped it against the side of her car and rolling it to where a sign said she could leave it. Beth ran her fingers over the place where the nail had punctured the surface. The hole it had left when the mechanic had removed it was substantial.

'It's a coincidence,' she said. 'He's dead. He's going to stay dead. I'm not doing this again. And tomorrow, I'm going back to work.'

Longing to close her eyes, desperate for sleep, feeling the exhaustion of not just that day, but that month, that year, and every second since Karl Smith had come into their lives, Beth Waterfall headed for home.

Karl Smith watched from behind a tree in her road as she unlocked her front door, didn't so much as bother turning on a light, and headed straight for bed.

Chapter 44

'DS Salter,' Biddlecombe shouted down the phone line, 'I'm transferring a call to you. It's from a woman who claims she knows the man in the CCTV image.'

'All right, put her through,' Salter said, flexing her neck and wishing she was in bed. Since the image of the suspect had been released in the morning papers, they'd been overrun with calls from people who claimed to know his identity, so much so that the briefing room had become one huge call centre. They were already following up several calls with more detailed enquiries, but the sheer volume of possible names was proving unhelpful in the short term.

'Hello, this is—'

'Karl Smith,' the woman on the other end of the line said. 'The man in that photo is Karl Smith. I'm not just guessing, I know.'

'Okay,' Salter said, 'and in what capacity—'

'I was his father's carer until just a few days ago. I saw that man five days a week and I'll tell you something for nothing,

277

he is absolutely fucking terrifying. I only did that job because I needed the hours, and caring is good money because no one wants to wipe old people's bums for a living. But that house? The agency couldn't get anyone else to bloody go because the few people who had worked there before me hated it. They had to pay me more than my usual rate to do it, and if I hadn't been desperate, I'd never have gone there for so long. When he terminated my contract last week, I swear my blood pressure halved immediately.'

'He terminated the contract this week just gone?' Salter confirmed, waving another officer over and motioning at the notepad she was writing on.

'Yes. Something about not being able to afford it, but he had some money from his mother's death, plus a carer's allowance, and I know he worked from home too. He was always on his laptop if we were there at the same time.'

'And your name is?'

'Mrs Sandra Bissett. The thing you should know is, sometimes I heard him talking to his mother. Like, arguing with her. I don't think he even knew he was doing it. He'd be on his own upstairs then suddenly he'd yell and I'd think, is he hurt? Has someone broken in? Should I go up and check on him? But there was never anyone else there.'

'Okay, I'm just taking some notes, Mrs Bissett. You said you found him terrifying. Was there anything specific he did to make you feel that way or was it something you sensed?'

'Both!' she blurted. 'He would stare at me when he thought I couldn't see him, not directly but using the hallway mirror so he could see into the lounge. I don't just mean for a few seconds. Sometimes he'd stand out there and watch me for fifteen minutes while I pretended not to notice. A couple of times, he got so angry about stupid little things that he'd almost seemed to be baring his teeth at me, then a second later he'd give me this great big smile as if he'd remembered he was supposed to be acting human.'

'And was there anything unusual that happened in the last few months?'

Sandra paused to think about it. 'Only the deliveries, really. We didn't get many of them before, but recently they started coming. Clothes mainly, for him. But there was something going on, because every now and then his father would have an accident in spite of the adult nappies he wore, and then I'd strip the bed and dump the soiled stuff in the laundry. There were at least three sets of doctor's or nurse's clothes in there, the cotton trousers and top, you know? Different colours, and had been worn, for sure. But that man didn't have a job at any hospital that I was aware of. Gave me the creeps, like he's got some sort of fetish.'

Salter was on her feet in a heartbeat and banging on the desk.

'Mrs Bissett, not that I don't believe any of this, but are you absolutely sure, beyond a shadow of a doubt?'

'Oh yes,' she said. 'I'd bet my life on it.'

'Please don't do that,' Salter said. 'But could you give me the address?'

Salter was leaving nothing to chance. At Karl Smith's house, warrant obtained en route, there was a van of armed officers, a crew from MIT and Brodie Baarda.

'We're covering front and back?' Baarda checked.

'We are. Armed units are going in first to clear the place, then we can enter. There have been no signs of life from inside so far, but his father is supposed to be bedridden and not left alone.'

'All right,' Baarda said, motioning to the armed unit leader. 'Let's go.'

279

They knocked, announced themselves, then broke in through the front and back doors simultaneously. A few minutes of shouting followed as they went from room to room, then the unit leader reappeared.

'Property is safe and unoccupied,' he said. 'Nothing suspicious to report and no evidence of a recent or hasty departure. You can go in now.'

Baarda went in first with Salter behind him. They headed directly into what should have been the dining room, only it was taken up with a bed, different types of medication and a tatty armchair.

'I want to know where his father is,' Baarda said. 'He didn't get up and walk out, so someone must have seen something.'

'Uniformed officers are starting door-to-door enquiries already. If anyone's seen anything in the last week, we'll know about it. Look, family portrait. I'm guessing he was about ten or eleven at the time.'

On the wall to the side of the TV was a yellowing photograph of Karl Smith with his father on one side and his mother on the other. Barbara Smith was looking into the camera as if she either wanted to eat it or kill it, it wasn't clear which. Karl's father, on the other hand, was looking slightly away from the lens. But it was Karl who they stared at, his face marked with a spattering of moles, lips slightly parted. Baarda took a photo of it and sent it straight to Connie.

'He looks like he's about to scream,' Salter said. 'I can see why the carer didn't like it here.'

'Ma'am,' an officer said from the front door, 'the neighbours say an ambulance was here a couple of days ago. They were here quite a while and eventually a body was taken away covered up. No blue lights. They got the impression the father had passed.'

'We need to see that body,' Baarda said.

'Any word on where Karl might be?' Salter asked.

'Apparently he was last here the same day, and he hasn't been back since that anyone's noticed.'

'Thank you, constable,' Salter said. 'Well, that's convenient. His father dies, he packs a bag, no one to look after any more. What do you think?'

Baarda walked up to get a closer look at Karl in the photo. 'I think he killed his father because he had no intent of ever coming back here. And that means he's either left the country because he doesn't want to get caught for the things he's already done, or he's got something else in store and doesn't want to be interrupted before he can do it.'

'I agree,' Salter said. 'I'll have a scenes of crime unit go through everything. What's your priority?'

'Getting an up-to-date photo of his face. DVLA will have one or maybe the passport office if there's nothing here. See if we can find his mobile number and get a trace on it. I want Nate Carlisle inspecting Mr Smith's body for signs of foul play. Also a number plate, see if we can figure out where his car is, and a ports alert throughout the UK.'

'On it,' Salter said. 'And the carer mentioned something about his mother, who's deceased. The carer thought Karl used to talk to her, even argue with her sometimes. He sounds delusional.'

'Let's see what else we can find,' Baarda said, heading for the staircase and taking care to touch as little as possible on the way.

The bathroom door was wide open.

'No toothbrush or toothpaste there,' he noted. 'Karl is definitely taking a trip.'

Next was Karl's room, bed unmade, drawers open. Baarda moved on. Next door was a bedroom with no bed in it, and a single wardrobe with a few pairs of trousers and a couple of shirts. At the far end of the upstairs hallway was one last bedroom. Baarda pushed open the door and immediately covered his nose and mouth with his hand.

Everything was yellow, from the wallpaper to the sheets and curtains, to the stained mirror.

'It's like a pub taproom from the 1970s,' Baarda said. 'It must have been hard to move on when they were able to smell this room every day.' He walked to a dusty pile of paperwork on the rickety bedside table, picked up a letter and opened it up, reading it from top to bottom before turning to Salter.

'What is it?' she asked.

'It's the end of a complaints process,' Baarda said quietly. 'The board at St Columba hospital concluded that there had been no negligence or mistreatment of Barbara Smith, and that everything possible had been done to attempt to save her life. They were notifying Karl that his complaint against the hospital would not be upheld and they suggested that if he felt the need to take it further, he should get independent legal advice. They've also asked that he stay away from the hospital unless he had a legitimate medical reason for being there, and that any further contact should be made only through lawyers. Sounds like he was causing them something of a problem.'

'So maybe that's what he was doing there,' Salter said. 'It was a vendetta, and he was collecting victims along the way.'

'We should go straight to St Columba's. I want to speak with whoever handled this complaint and I want immediate access to the files. I'll call Connie and Midnight from the car. If Karl Smith isn't there already, I'm sure whatever he has planned involves someone from the hospital. We just need to figure out who.'

Chapter 45

19 June

'Midnight? You still there?' Connie asked.

'Give me a minute,' Midnight said. 'The electronic file is vast. I'm using AI to strip out anything that looks procedural and get me to the bones of it. Is Baarda not with you?'

'He's at St Columba's which we've made a temporary command centre until we can locate the suspect. We're lucky the hospital gave us access to the complaint file at all. Their first response was that it was privileged and we could only get it by court order or – get this – with Karl Smith's consent.'

'So how did you get it?' Midnight was tapping keys furiously as she spoke.

'I let Superintendent Overbeck handle it. She knows all sorts of people, and they tend to be deeply afraid of her, which is questionable ethically but useful when it really matters. I suspect she called in a favour with a member of the hospital board.'

'Okay, well this is what the superintendent got you. I'll summarise. Karl Smith lodged a complaint following the death of his mother during surgery. She was taken to St Columba's by ambulance having collapsed. Paramedics confirmed that she'd had a coronary event. Long section of medical history here. Okay, she was operated on and efforts were made to save her but her heart muscle and arteries had suffered severe damage. Attempts were made to revive her, but there was literally no route for repair of the heart muscle. A full review of her medical history was undertaken and a postmortem was performed.'

'What did that find?' Connie asked.

'Hold on, let me take a look. That's in a separate folder. Here we go. Postmortem undertaken by Dr Ailsa Lambert.'

Connie sighed. 'She was Nate Carlisle's predecessor. I met her,' she said. 'Wonderful woman.'

'I can tell – the notes are incredibly thorough. The conclusion was that not only had it been the original heart attack that killed Barbara Smith, but that there would have been literally nothing surgery could have achieved. In spite of that, the surgical team clearly tried for a sustained period to find a way forward.'

'Pretty cut and dried then,' Connie said.

'There's more. On inspection of the lungs, the postmortem showed multiple small tumours. It looks as if the cancer had also spread to Mrs Smith's lymph nodes. The conclusion was that had the heart attack not caused her death, she only had a matter of months to live, it was just that the lung cancer hadn't been diagnosed.'

'So what did the hospital do?'

'Everything I've seen indicates that a medical review is undertaken first by a consultant within the hospital who has not been involved with the case. If there are any red flags from that, the hospital undertakes a full review with interviews of staff members by an external committee. Barbara Smith's case was open and shut, so it stopped there. I can see, however, that Ailsa Lambert invited the son and father to meet with her so that she

284

could explain all the physical evidence, and for them to ask any questions they wanted. It looks as if there was no response to that invitation. The notes from the postmortem file indicate that no such meeting took place.'

'So they just laid the blame at the hospital's door, didn't get the answers they wanted from the preliminary enquiry, then decided it was all some conspiracy,' Connie said.

'You think they hid themselves away and let their anger fester until one day Karl decided to start visiting the hospital and found people to kill there? It feels like there's a piece of the puzzle missing,' Midnight said.

'It really does, because none of the family's anger was directed at the hospital itself. Nate Carlisle has confirmed that a cursory look at Karl's father's body showed that he had inhaled liquid and choked on a small item of food. Do you have access to those notes?'

'I do,' Midnight said with a new flurry of tapping. 'Dr Carlisle's assistant sent them over a few minutes ago. He'd been bedridden for a long period of time – the mortuary managed to get access to his medical records. Looks like his stroke occurred just a few weeks after Barbara Smith's death. It would have been while the hospital's preliminary enquiry was taking place, in fact.'

'So Karl is at home grieving his dead mother, presumably, when suddenly he ends up also having to care for his father. His whole life was upended. That's a lot of emotion to have to put somewhere. You'd need someone to blame for that, right? Midnight, are you able to get me the names of all the people on the surgical team who treated Barbara Smith?'

'Two seconds, here it is. The anaesthetist was Giles Polgood and the trauma surgeon on duty was Elizabeth Waterfall. They then called the duty cardiac surgeon who was—'

'Stop,' Connie said. 'Elizabeth Waterfall also known as Beth Waterfall?'

'It's an unusual surname, so if you know of a surgeon there called Beth Waterfall, then I'm guessing it's one and the same. Do you know her?'

'Yes, we've met a few times. She's newly in a relationship with one of the officers from MIT. If Karl Smith is stalking her, though, he must be doing a good job of hiding it or I'm sure she'd have said something. Could you check police files to see if she's made any sort of complaint since the date of Barbara Smith's death about anything happening either at the hospital or at home that she was worried about? I'm going to call DS Lively while you do that.'

Connie rang Lively's mobile but got only his voicemail recording, then she tried Baarda but got the same.

'Connie,' Midnight said. 'I've got something. A couple of years ago, there was a complaint to the police but not by Elizabeth Waterfall, it was by someone called Molly. She would have been in her early twenties, but she was accompanied to the station when making the complaint by Beth Waterfall, her mother.'

'Go on,' Connie said.

'The complaint was about a stalker, mostly online stuff. Damage to reputation, deep-fake videos, posting untrue allegations about her private life. It's pretty nasty but the investigating officer reached the conclusion there was nothing that could be done. The videos were posted anonymously, websites would pop up then disappear, the servers were international and social media sites wouldn't disclose user information. Overall, it was impossible to prove it was the work of just one person. Several names came up during the investigation.' She went quiet.

'Midnight?'

'Yeah. One of the names listed was Karl Smith, no other

details known. Various spellings of it and alternative surnames were also used. No other identifying details and it's a common name. Police were unable to trace where the harassment started so no suspect was ever found.'

'Oh crap. I take it there was never any arrest?'

'Nothing. The file was closed when no further complaints were made after a year. It was him, wasn't it?'

'I think so. And because the complaint Karl made about his mother's death was decided during the preliminary enquiry, Beth would never have been made aware of the complainant's details. Stay right there. I need Beth's personnel file.'

She called DS Salter.

'Christie, you're on speaker with Midnight and me. Are you at the hospital?' Connie demanded.

'Yes. All quiet here, nothing coming up on the surveillance. You okay?'

'Has Lively ever mentioned Beth's daughter to you?'

'Only once. I asked if it was just him and Beth at the house and apparently she had a daughter who passed a while ago. Lively hadn't wanted to pry but he got the impression it might have been a suicide.'

'Oh, hell. That's why the complaints stopped. Listen, I think Karl's real target is Beth. He believes she was responsible for the death of his mother, and it looks like he started out targeting Beth's daughter as revenge. Do you have someone from the hospital admin team with you now?'

'I do.'

'Good. Is Beth working right now or should she be at home?'

There was a pause.

'She's not on duty. I have her mobile number on the screen. We're trying to contact her,' Salter said.

'Don't scare her. She needs to either get straight to the hospital

287

or the nearest police station, or stay at home and lock all the doors and windows.'

'Have you told Lively?'

'Couldn't get hold of him. I need you to email Beth Waterfall's HR file over to Midnight immediately, and don't take any shit from anyone about privacy. This could be a life-or-death situation. Midnight, stay on the phone to me while I drive. I want to know everything about Beth Waterfall that might help me negotiate with Karl when we find him. Christie, get me Beth's address. I'm getting in the car now. Tell Baarda to meet me there, and make sure you have a team ready to go in but not until I say so. Keep trying to get hold of Lively.'

'On it,' Salter said. 'And Connie . . .'

'Yes?' She was already running for the door, car keys in hand.

'Two things. The carer said she could sometimes hear Karl talking to his mother, arguing, as if she was still alive. He sounds really deranged. And second, Lively's in no condition to fight. I know he's acting tough, but I've known that man a long time. He's in pain and he hasn't recovered. If it comes down to it, I'm not sure he'll be any match for a younger man who's out for blood.'

Connie reached her hire car and started the engine.

'Then we'd better get to him before Karl Smith does, because if he could kill his father, he really didn't plan on making it home.'

Connie fed the address into her satnav and raced off as Midnight received and digested Beth Waterfall's personnel file.

'How long have we got?' Midnight asked.

'I'll be there in seven minutes. What have you found?'

'Beth Waterfall is fifty-five years old. She trained and has always worked in the Edinburgh area. She's been at St Columba's since it opened four years ago. Let me see . . . divorced. She's involved with two charities at the hospital. There's a mentoring scheme for female staff that she set up to encourage women to apply for promotions and new opportunities. That won an award from Women in Business.'

'Anything about her daughter?' Connie asked.

'Beth reported that her daughter had died – no details other than that it wasn't at St Columba's – this was thirteen months ago. She took some leave but ended up coming back really quickly. The HR department was concerned about it and asked her to consider getting counselling. There's no note about the outcome of that.'

'Anything to do with being harassed at work?'

'Ooh,' Midnight said. 'Not exactly, but this is weird. Beth was suspended on full pay pending investigation about a year ago because a video went viral of her talking about certain patients not deserving NHS care because of their lifestyle choices. Looks like a big deal. There are several entries about it. Beth's reaction was to explain that it was a deep fake—'

'Like the ones her daughter was subjected to,' Connie said.

'Exactly. The hospital brought in an expert who confirmed it. Beth's suspension was stayed but by then she had to go off sick. She'd dislocated her arm, fractured a rib and had a head injury requiring a CT scan from an injury when she was out running. She spent a brief period in hospital for that. She needed physio before she could operate, but again, she got herself back on her feet and returned to work. She's tough.'

'As tough as they come. I can see why Lively's fallen in love with her. Anything else in the records that might help me?'

'Only that a few staff members expressed concern for her over the past year, having lost her daughter and still working at full capacity. It seems she took virtually no compassionate leave, went back to work and just never talked about it. She's obviously been through hell. No pressure, Connie, but you have to save her. There's a limit to what anyone should have to endure,' Midnight said.

'I agree, but also because Lively will never forgive me if I don't. I can't be the person who lost him the chance of true love. Everyone deserves their happy ending. Wish me luck,' Connie said, slamming on the brakes and throwing open the car door.

Midnight never got the chance.

Chapter 46

Lively had been caught with his pants down, literally. Beth had taken his blood pressure the night before after his surveillance shift had ended and taken a look at the wound. She wasn't happy with either.

'Too much stress on your body, and in particular your neck,' she'd declared. 'The superintendent won't mind you taking a day off, Sam. It's not like you're having any success at the hospital.'

'We're nearly there, I can feel it,' he'd said. 'Sometimes when you've been in the job long enough, you just know.'

'So that's your professional experience talking then?' She smiled at him.

'Aye, it is.'

'Good. I'm glad you put so much store by professional opinions. Mine is that you need rest. If anything does happen at the hospital, that wound of yours is a real weak point. One day off, that's all I'm asking. I've done too many hours this month too, so I can stay home with you. We'll put our feet up and I'll cook you something that involves potato. Deal?'

291

She'd beaten him again, not that he minded. For the first time in . . . well, forever . . . the job wasn't the most important thing in his life.

'Deal,' he said. 'Can I have gravy with those potatoes, whatever form they come in?'

'Even if it's chips?'

'Even if it's chips.'

'I'm not sure I'll be able to sit at the same table as you eating chips and gravy, but if it keeps you home and resting, I'll agree to almost anything.'

Just like that, he'd forgotten all about his sense that they were about to get a breakthrough in the case, gone to bed, and slept as if he hadn't a care in the world. True to her word, not only had Beth let him sleep in undisturbed, but lunch was already in the oven by the time he'd padded down the stairs, and it smelled like heaven.

'Far be it from me to say I told you so, Sam, but you definitely needed the sleep. How are you feeling?'

'Like I could eat a horse,' he said.

'None of that on the menu, I'm afraid, but I went to the butcher and got some nice lamb chops that I'm doing with mash and an onion gravy. Why don't you go and shower? It'll be ready when you come back down.'

They'd eaten in the back garden then picked raspberries together from the lane behind the house, leaving Beth's arms covered in a web of scratches and tiny thorns. Lively had run her a bath and lit the candles she liked, then made her a cup of tea and told her he'd do the washing-up while she relaxed for an hour. It had been perfect. So perfect that he'd forgotten to turn on his mobile. So perfect, in fact, that he'd even thought – without immediately touching wood, like the idiot he was – that it had been such a wonderful day that absolutely nothing could spoil it.

With Beth happily soaking, he'd gone to use the downstairs toilet. They were still at that stage of the relationship where he couldn't bring himself to ruin it with the less pleasant aspects of biology, so made sure he only did the necessary when she was busy elsewhere. Almost every aspect of his new life would have reduced his squad to hysterical laughter. He knew it and he couldn't have cared less.

So it was that Lively found himself just starting to pull up his trousers when there was a creak on the floorboards outside the toilet. He considered staying there quietly until Beth had gone back upstairs, but he'd just flushed and he didn't want her thinking he was doing anything weird. He opted for opening the door in a casual but upbeat fashion and being done with it.

The shovel he saw inbound towards his face was the one he'd turned the compost with as they'd thrown away any raspberries not fit to eat. He noticed one stray berry go flying onto the cream stair carpet. His last thought as he went down was that the stain would be an absolute bugger to get out.

He couldn't have been out for more than a few seconds, he realised, because the suspect was still hauling him into the lounge as he came round. The spade had hit him full in the face, and Lively knew his nose was broken – not the first time that had happened, and he was long past assuming it would be the last – but he could feel shards of his front teeth crumbling onto his tongue and he was struggling to get his eyes to focus.

The spade had been thrown down in the hallway and now the man was getting something out of his pockets. Lively knew that if he didn't act fast he'd be all tied up and completely unable to help Beth when she emerged from her bath. The main thing was for Lively to stop the man from getting both his wrists in the same place.

'Who the fuck are you?' Lively asked as the man rolled him over and tried to get him sitting up with his back against the sofa.

'Fuck off, old man,' he said.

'Na, na, that's not the way this happens,' he made sure to slur his voice just enough to seem dazed and harmless. 'If you're going to be the wee bastard who actually kills me, then custom dictates that I at least get to know your name.'

The man got Lively sitting up then sat on his legs as he cable-tied his ankles together. Lively wasn't able to move or think fast enough to stop that from happening, but his eyes were focusing well enough by then that he'd got a look at the man's face.

'My name's Karl,' the man muttered. 'Not that it'll help you. You're going to die, you and the doctor bitch, but I want her to watch you die first.'

Karl, Lively thought, was without a doubt the man he'd waited outside the geriatric rehabilitation unit for. What a waste of time that had been, when he could simply have stayed at home.

'That'll take a while,' Lively said. 'She's out at the shops.'

'And yet her car is on the driveway and there's only one shop within walking distance, so even if you're telling the truth, which I doubt, she won't be long.' He climbed off Lively's legs who tested the restraints to see what movement he still had. The answer was little to none.

'Lean forward,' Karl said, 'and put your hands together behind your back.'

'I'm not sure I can,' Lively replied. 'I've a problem with my shoulders.'

'Then it's your problem, not mine. Hands behind your back. And don't try any stupid policeman tricks. I know who you are. I've read all about you. All that tough guy shit with the Scottish mafia. I don't care about that. I've got a knife and if I have to I'll just cut your throat. Won't take much given that you've already got a hole in it.'

So he really had done his homework, and the knife hadn't been a bluff. Lively could see the handle poking out of his pocket, and it was one of those big American hunting knives by the look of it.

The options were (a) grab the knife and hope to get the advantage from his position on the floor, (b) grab Karl by the neck when he was leaning down to cable-tie his hands, or (c) shout a warning to Beth, hope she'd locked the bathroom door, and that she had her mobile phone with her to call for help. Given that his head was swimming and that Karl knew his neck was a weak point, he didn't like any of the options much.

Karl kicked him hard in the upper thigh as he was considering what to do.

'Hands . . . behind . . . your fucking . . . back!' he hissed, punctuated by additional kicks.

Lively sighed but began moving his arms slowly backwards. Karl took the hunting knife from his pocket and deposited it on the bookshelves before returning with a cable tie in his hand.

'If you stay still, I won't pull it so tight,' he said, kneeling next to Lively and reaching round.

You got one chance, Lively knew. It had taken him a few years of policing to really understand the importance of that, but once learned, it was never forgotten.

Lively braced his neck as best he could then reached out to grab Karl's collar and smashed his forehead into Karl's. It was a stupid move given the spade injury, but his head had never failed him yet and he'd given out his share of Glasgow kisses in the previous decades.

Karl, though, was less chaotic than he seemed, reacting by reaching out and digging his fingers into Lively's neck until he hit the injury. Lively let go of Karl's collar, screaming, as Karl scrabbled for the bookshelves, standing to grab the knife and pulling the blade open at the exact moment Beth ran into the room, wrapped in just a white towel, though her face was even paler.

'Get out!' Lively yelled, but Karl was already reaching for her, catching her by the hair and shoving her to the floor on her knees, the long knife edge at her throat. 'Don't hurt her!'

'It's you,' Beth said.

'Jesus, Beth,' Lively groaned. 'You know him?'

'Does she fucking know me?' Karl screeched. 'Do you, Dr Waterfall? You want to tell him how you know me?'

Beth's voice was calm. 'This is Karl Smith, Sam. He thinks I killed his mother.'

'I don't think so, you did! You put her on that operating table and she died. She was still alive when they put her in the ambulance, and ever since then she's . . . she's—'

'Your mother's right behind you,' Connie said, walking in from the kitchen. 'I can see her too, Karl. You're not going mad although it probably feels like it.'

'How did you—' he started.

'I broke a pane of glass in the back door while you were all shouting, which is why you didn't hear. You should know, though, that I'm not alone. There are other police cars beyond the driveway and officers in the back garden.'

'I don't give a shit.'

'I believe you. I think that when you killed your father, you made a decision about how things were going to work out. I think you mean what you say about wanting to kill Beth, too.'

'He's always wanted to kill me,' Beth said. 'And he just keeps coming back to try again.'

'If you don't want to die with them, you should stay back,' Karl told Connie, his face twisted into a snarl.

'Sure. Can I just ask, were you close to your mother because – sorry to be blunt – the woman I can see behind you doesn't look all that loving if I'm honest. If you were my son and I could see what you were about to do, I'd be concerned for you. She just looks kind of . . . angry.'

'Shut the fuck up!' he screamed. 'I know you can't see her! You're just saying it to fucking freak me out!'

'Sorry, I should have introduced myself. My name is Connie Woolwine. I'm not a police officer. I'm not exactly what other people think of as normal, either. Most people say I'm a bit weird. They think they say it behind my back, but I have a sixth sense about that shit, so I know what they say and who says it.' She tried not to look at Lively who was shaking as he stared at the knife digging into Beth's flesh.

'So fucking what?' Karl laughed.

'So I see things other people can't see, too.' She dropped her voice so it was little more than a whisper. 'Dead people talk to me. We're the same, you and I.'

'Did they teach you to mind-fuck people when you trained with the FBI? I read all about you. I know you're a psychologist. I know you're here to get me to roll over and let you lock me up without making a fuss.'

Connie ignored his rising anger. 'Was it your mom who told

you to do all this? You looked after your dad really well for a long time and that can't have been easy. I don't think you'd have chosen to hurt him unless your mom had persuaded you to do it.'

'He . . . I didn't . . . he just died.'

'There was certainly food and liquid in his airway, but you'd been caring for him a long time. You're more careful than that. How did your mom get you to do it?' She looked over his shoulder. 'Mrs Smith – can I call you Barbara? No. Okay then – how did you persuade Karl to hurt his father?'

'She's not there right now. I'm doing this on my own. If I do it, she'll leave me alone! I just have to finish it. I have to.'

'Beth didn't end your mom's life, Karl. I think you know that. She's a doctor who cares about her patients. She helps other members of staff and does charity work. That's not someone you want to kill, is it?' Connie took a step towards him.

'My dad had a stroke after my mum died! She didn't just kill my mother.' He pulled Beth's head up to fully expose her throat and stepped in close so her back was hard against his legs. 'And she tried to kill me.'

'You stalked my daughter and drove her half-mad,' Beth said softly. 'Then you came after me and you'd have killed me if I hadn't fallen down that slope. All I did was defend myself.'

'Then you should have made sure you finished the job,' he said. 'Because now I'm going to.'

'No, Mrs Smith,' Connie said to the far corner of the lounge with so much certainty in her voice that everyone followed her gaze. 'Don't blame Karl. I don't accept that. I think you're responsible for the things he's done. For all of it.'

'Stop talking to her!' Karl shrieked.

'She's saying it is your fault. She's saying you were always an angry teenager, that you were bullied. I think she bullied you too, though, Karl. That's the impression I get of her. She seems angry, unforgiving. You must have felt so furious at the world when she reappeared. Even after she died, she just wouldn't leave you alone, would she? I can understand completely why you killed all those other people.'

'What?' he stared at her.

'You knew about it, didn't you, Mrs Smith?' She paused and nodded.

'You stop talking to her!' He pointed the knife away from Beth's throat and waved it towards Connie instead. 'She's not here. She wouldn't come here and she wouldn't talk to you! She always hated people like you, people who thought they were better than her!'

'Hold on, Karl. I want to listen to your mother a bit longer. She's telling me some very interesting things about you. Nasty things. Honestly, I'm not sure your mother even liked you.'

He charged at her, knife out front. Beth grabbed at the backs of his knees and he crashed to the floor. Lively, ankles still tied, managed to move far enough to throw himself onto Karl's feet and keep him down.

Karl rolled halfway over, thrashing, holding his hunting knife to his own throat as Beth got up and ran into a corner.

'Don't do that,' Connie said. 'Karl, I think you need help. I believe you've been seeing your mother and that she's been influencing your behaviour.'

'Fuck you,' he sobbed.

'I mean it,' she said. 'I think the people you killed – Dale Abnay, Archie Bass, Divya Singh, Vic Campbell – they were reflections of yourself. It seems to me that it was you who wanted to die, and I give you my word that I will make sure there are psychiatric reports prepared—'

'What the fuck?' Karl said, lowering the knife without even

thinking about it. 'You're not pinning that on me. I didn't fucking kill anybody. What I did with my dad was a mercy not a murder. Don't you even fucking think about saying I killed those other people. That's bullshit and you know it!'

Lively punched him hard, once, to the side of the head.

Karl Smith was down.

Chapter 47

Body Eight of Eight

19 June

'Get the team in,' Lively shouted. 'We need him restrained.'

'Hold on,' Connie said.

'No, this bastard needs stringing up for what he's done.'

Connie checked Karl's pulse and breathing then took out her mobile and dialled Salter. 'Christie, could you come in here, alone please. No current threat to life.'

Salter appeared within the minute. 'Is everyone okay? What happened?'

'We're all fine,' Connie said. 'Could you stay next to Mr Smith, please? He'll be coming round soon. And he's probably lying on a hunting knife that'll need processing.'

Salter found the knife under Karl's stomach then cut the cable tie around Lively's ankles and sat back down next to Karl on the floor.

'I'm getting Beth out of here,' Lively said. 'We can give our statements later on.'

'Sam,' Connie said. 'I need a word with you and Beth first. Christie, you can stay.'

'Of course,' Beth said. 'Did you want me to take a look at Mr Smith? You hit him pretty hard, Sam.'

'He'll be okay. We'll get him checked over by a doctor while we're processing him. But Beth, you said something earlier, about Karl coming back again and again. What did you mean?'

Beth frowned and shook her head. 'I'm not sure. Just that . . . he seems to be everywhere. First when he was stalking Molly, then me with that video, then he followed me to the cabin up at Loch Voil. And I've seen him since, I think. He was at a recycling centre once. And since then I've suspected he was around, but . . . I can't give you any specifics.'

'At the hospital?' Connie asked.

Beth's eyes filled with tears. 'I don't really know. Whenever I see him, it's like I get so panicked that I can't remember it clearly later.' She walked to the sofa. 'I'm sorry, Sam. When he attacked me, I was so scared. I believed I'd killed him, and after the police didn't help when Molly was being harassed, I didn't feel I could go to them and explain. I knew then, it was him or me. I hurt my arm, and he'd given me a fractured rib and a head injury. I got back to St Columba's for treatment then just blocked it all out. If I'd known it was him you were looking for . . . if I'd seen the photo . . . I feel so responsible.'

She was trembling. Lively went to sit next to her, putting an arm around her shoulders.

'I think that's enough,' he said. 'I think that's enough,' he said. 'We've had our home invaded and a knife held to our throats, surely this can wait.'

'I don't think it can,' Connie said. She went to sit down in an armchair opposite Beth. 'Because I believed Karl when he said he didn't kill those other people. He's going to prison, of course, for what he did today and for killing his father. But he

302

was genuinely surprised, outraged actually, when I mentioned the other deaths.'

'Aye, well I've never seen a killer put his hands in the air and say, "It's a fair cop, you got me,"' Lively said.

'Me either, but they usually find it hard to fake surprise well. And normally they don't need to do any acting. They just deny it and make us prove it in court. This was different, Sam, and I think even you know it.'

Lively stood up. 'Where are you going with this?' His voice was cold and hard.

Connie's heart sank. 'Will you bear with me a minute?'

'I will not. This is ridiculous. It was you who told us what Smith's motivation was, and you were right, too. Look at his face. It's exactly what you thought. The similarity to the victims is right there.'

'Sam—'

'Don't Sam me. You're not my fucking colleague.'

'Then I will, because I am,' Salter cut in. 'Sam, would you sit down and listen for a minute? If Dr Woolwine has something to say, she's going to say it sooner or later. Better to hear it now.'

'Sit down, sweetheart,' Beth said. 'I don't know what you're so worried about.' He took a seat. 'What is it, Dr Woolwine?'

Connie cleared her throat and kept her voice gentle. 'Beth, have you needed any repairs to your car recently?'

Beth shrugged and thought about it. 'Yes. I managed to get a dent in the front. I don't even know what happened. I think someone must have hit me when I was parked either at the hospital or while I was shopping. Took them a day to beat it out and respray it, and it cost a fair bit. What's the relevance?'

'It's an electric car, yes?' Connie checked.

'That's right. Do you know something I don't about how that happened?'

Connie sighed and Lively balled his hands into fists.

'No,' he said. 'I don't care what mumbo-jumbo bullshit you're about to spout, but this is absolutely fucking outrageous!'

'Sam, you're scaring me,' Beth said. 'You're all scaring me, and I've been through enough.'

'Yes, you have,' Connie said. 'Beth, how did you feel when you saw Karl again today?'

Beth looked down at her hands, then drew her arms around herself. 'Scared. Terrified, in fact. Like it was all happening again.'

'But you didn't overreact. You stayed calm, handled the situation, like you did at the cabin?'

'I suppose so,' she said.

'Can I ask, what did they find when they did the CT scan at the hospital?'

'Nothing of note. They believed I was concussed but not badly. I was kept in briefly for them to check on me, mainly because a dislocated arm can cause lasting damage if it's not corrected professionally.'

'Did they do an MRI?' Connie asked.

'No. There was no indication that one was needed. I'm afraid I don't understand, what does it matter if I had an MRI or not?'

Connie rubbed her forehead. 'You treated Archie Bass. That's where you two met, if I'm not wrong. I believe you spoke to him, Sam, before he was anaesthetised. How did he react when he saw you, Beth?'

She shrugged. 'He was losing blood fast and confused. Patients are often distressed directly before surgery.'

Lively's jaw dropped.

'Sam?' Connie asked. 'You just remembered something.'

He shook his head. Beth reached out gently and put her hand on top of his. 'Whatever this is, it seems to be important. I'd like you to just say it.'

Lively dashed a sleeve across his eyes. 'All right. Fine.' He glared at Connie. 'But you'd better have a bloody good explanation.' He looked at Beth. 'Bass was okay for a moment. Then you came in. He started freaking out when he saw you.'

'I really don't understand any of this,' Beth said. 'I'd never seen Archie Bass before that moment.'

'I believe you,' Connie said. 'I think you saw Karl Smith, and I think your brain told you he was in disguise. I believe you felt that you were being stalked again. Persecuted, and with good reason. And I think your brain told you to do exactly what you did in the woods. It was him or you.'

Beth dropped Lively's hand and stood.

'No,' she whispered. 'No! You're saying you think I killed him. That I stabbed him! That's insane. I'd know – I'd remember.'

'Were you at the hospital the day Vic Campbell died?'

Beth turned to Lively, tears streaming down both their faces, and Connie wished she was on any other case, anywhere in the world.

'I was,' she said. 'But I didn't hurt that boy. Tell me I didn't. Please?'

'I need you to look at some photos for me and tell me what you see,' Connie said. She took out her phone again, tapped in a search term and got a series of images up. 'Here.' She handed the phone to Beth.

Beth took it and breathed deeply before casting her eyes down on the screen.

'Is this a joke?' she murmured. 'Why would you do this to me?'

Lively took the screen from her and flicked through the different photos as Beth moved across the room.

'What's the matter?' Lively asked. 'Who are all these people?'

Connie looked at Beth. 'Who do you see when you look at the photos?'

'Well, half of them are him. I mean, he's disguised, but you can see him clearly. Are you trying to catch me out, because—'

'I'm not,' Connie said. 'I promise. Would you show me which ones are Karl?' She stood up, took the phone back from Lively and walked it to Beth.

'Here,' Beth pointed. 'And here, this one, that's him again—'

'What the fuck is going on?' Lively asked. 'There are no photos of Karl on there.'

Beth put her hands to her mouth and shut her eyes tight.

'I'm so sorry,' Connie said. 'It's not your fault.'

'I didn't do it,' Beth muttered from behind her hands.

'In all the ways that count, you didn't,' Connie told her. 'Have you heard of Fregoli syndrome?'

Beth shook her head.

'She didn't kill anyone! Are you insane? Fuck me. Christie, tell her. This is some science fiction bullshit,' Lively said.

'It was probably caused by the injury to your temple,' Connie said. 'Fregoli syndrome often results from a lesion, the one that caused your concussion, but a CT scan wouldn't have been detailed enough to show it. With Fregoli delusion, your brain tells you you're seeing the same person over and over again. You see the real faces but believe wholeheartedly that you're seeing someone usually very important in your life, often someone associated with a trauma. People who suffer from Fregoli delusion feel victimised, and in your case, I think you were transported directly into that moment of fight-or-flight when you felt you had to kill Karl Smith to survive.'

'She'd remember it,' Lively said. 'There'd have to be some sign of what she'd done.'

'Actually that's why I think it was you, Beth,' Connie said.

'You're a surgeon. You know how to kill fast and efficiently. You didn't leave any forensic trace, not because you were being devious, just because your natural intelligence kicked in, and you never hurt anyone more than was necessary to kill. The whole case has been quite unlike anything else any of us have ever seen, and that's why.'

'But those poor people,' Beth sobbed. 'I worked so hard to save Archie Bass. Why didn't I see him as Smith again if I'd tried to kill him the night before?'

'Probably the sterile setting or the fact that he had all sorts of tubes, wires and a mask on. Fregoli delusion is very rare, but it also tends to mess with your memory. It's like the rest of your brain knows it's not possible, so everything gets jumbled. You were just reliving that day with Karl at the cabin over and over again, and fighting for your life each time. You'd have been a in fugue state during each attack and for some time afterwards.'

'But Divya Singh,' she cried, doubling over. 'How could I have done such a terrible thing?'

'Your conscious brain had no idea it was Divya Singh. It's unlikely you knew you were killing at all. You were, to all intents and purposes, fighting a ghost,' Connie said.

'Her family won't care about that,' Beth sobbed. 'I wouldn't. It was so violent, so brutal.'

'I know this is hard,' Salter said gently. 'But we need to establish the facts before we explore Dr Woolwine's theory in any more depth. Dr Waterfall, do you remember visiting Jupiter Artland?' Salter asked.

Beth dashed tears from her cheeks and nodded. 'Several times. It's a place I love. But I couldn't give you the dates.'

'Did you ever go home and find yourself more muddy or dirty than usual after a trip there? Have to wash your clothes or really scrub your hands?' Salter continued.

Beth gasped. 'I couldn't figure out why. I thought that maybe I'd fallen over, something to do with my head injury, but I didn't have a headache and my vision was fine.'

'You fucking did it!' Smith moaned from the floor. '*You* are the killer!' He looked across to Connie. 'I told you she was a murderer. I told everyone at the hospital too. No one believed me.'

Salter twisted his left arm behind his back and put her other hand on the back of his neck while pushing his head back to the floor, then got her weight on top of him to keep him down. 'You need to shut the fuck up, right now,' she told him. 'Because the truth is that you caused all of it, whether you meant to or not.'

'We need to get you to a hospital,' Connie told Beth. 'Salter, can we move Beth without making an arrest?'

'Oh God,' Beth sobbed. 'What have I done?'

Connie went across to her and wrapped her in a tight embrace. 'You'll get through this,' she whispered. 'I know this feels terrible and I know you're going to be in a very dark place for a long time, but this wasn't you.'

'Please don't tell Molly,' she cried. 'I'm so sorry, Sam. I didn't know. Please just don't tell Molly what I did.'

Connie stepped aside and let Lively take over.

'She doesn't even remember that her daughter's dead. What'll happen to her?' Lively asked Connie over Beth's shoulder.

'We'll do all we can to unravel it,' Connie said. 'It might not be easy and it won't be fast, but don't lose hope, okay? Beth's going to need you.'

Everyone's attention was elsewhere when it happened.

Karl slid the knife into his neck with no fuss and no sound. It hadn't occurred to any of them that he might have been carrying a backup blade. He'd taken it from his pocket with his free right hand, slowly, gently, and slid it into the soft tissue at the side of his throat.

'Fuck!' Salter shouted. 'That's so much blood. How do I stop it?'

'Oh God.' Connie ran to her side and pressed hard on his neck. 'Lively, run out and bring in the paramedics!'

Beth stepped over and got down on the floor.

'Apply pressure here and here,' she instructed them. 'Let's get his head raised. Wait there.' She raced into the kitchen, slamming cupboards before running back with her hands full of gauze and bandages. 'Let me work.'

She did her best to stop the flow of blood, packing the wound and holding it until the paramedics got there.

'Don't give up,' Beth said. 'Karl, stay with me. Listen to my voice.' She was still checking for a pulse with her free hand as the paramedics took over.

The puddle on the floor had become a small lake.

'Beth,' Lively said, trying to pull her away. 'Darling, he's gone.'

'No, I can still save him,' she said. 'Do you have emergency blood in the ambulance?'

The paramedics looked at one another.

'He's passed,' Connie said. 'You weren't responsible.'

'But if I could at least have saved him . . . just one life—'

'That one wasn't yours to save,' Lively said. 'Come here.' He took her in his arms again and held her until the paramedics moved Karl Smith's body and they began the long, painful process of processing a woman for crimes she had no memory of committing.

Chapter 48

30 June

'I do hope you're not planning on claiming too much in the way of glory, given that you were pursuing the wrong suspect until the eleventh hour,' Overbeck said, lighting a candle on her desk and sitting back in her chair.

It was the first time Connie had seen her relax.

'I'll leave the glory where it's best placed, with Police Scotland, but in my defence, there have only been around one hundred cases of Fregoli syndrome identified since it was first diagnosed in 1927, so I'm guessing most profilers would have struggled to get it right. But point taken, it could all have gone horribly wrong.'

'Is it real, then, this Fregoli thing? Only you'll forgive me for saying it sounds like a poor excuse for murder and I'm answerable to both the Police Scotland board and the general public.' Overbeck kicked off her stilettos and put her feet up on the desk.

'It certainly is real, and it's also very disturbing and upsetting. But most importantly, it's a recognised delusion. Dr Waterfall could no more have avoided what happened to her than anyone else with a chronic mental illness. She had a CT scan to check her head injury after Karl first attacked her, but it didn't show the lesion on her brain that caused the delusions. It's been picked up in an MRI scan since then, but those things are hard to spot unless you're looking for them. Hers, thankfully, can be improved with surgery and medication.'

'That doesn't help the families of the deceased come to terms with their loss, unfortunately. Give me something, Dr Woolwine. You seem to be the queen of the snappy one-liner. What am I supposed to say to the press?'

Connie shrugged. 'Just the truth. That a young man had a mental breakdown following the death of his mother. He sought retribution against the family of the surgeon he wrongly perceived to be at fault, injured that surgeon causing a traumatic brain injury, and she then developed a syndrome that had disastrous consequences.'

Overbeck stared at the ceiling. 'It's not very snappy,' she concluded.

Connie stood. 'If you want snappy in this case, you'd best stick with Shit Happens. Sometimes it's just a circle of trauma that destroys everything in its path.'

'That'll do,' Overbeck said, sitting upright then grabbing a pen and writing down Connie's last sentence. 'Do we know how she came into contact with each of the victims?'

'We believe so. It was the hospital connection that actually threw us off course, even though Beth worked there. She bumped into Dale Abnay by chance while they were both hiking at Jupiter Artland. Now that we know it was Beth, we were able to trace her vehicle on CCTV the evening of Divya Singh's murder. We think Mrs Singh approached her car in the supermarket car park. The CCTV footage is poor quality, but it all ties in time-wise. Archie Bass we believe she saw exiting the hospital after an immunisation. She followed him back to one of his regular night bases. Vic Campbell she also saw in the hospital as he was being discharged. We'd asked every local garage to report front collision damage to electric cars, but how could her regular mechanic, who only knew her as a lovely woman doctor, possibly have thought anything other than to believe her when she said another car had hit hers in the car park?'

'So you're claiming that profiling failed in this case because fate conspired against you.'

'I'm saying that it was a case in a million. Also, given how much more I now know about the delusion, I'd say we're lucky there weren't more victims. There are cases when sufferers end up seeing the same person several times a day. And it was all to do with the moles on Karl Smith's face. Anyone with a skin complaint or scarring, Vic's tattoos even, was enough for the lesion in Beth's brain to kick in and convince her it was Smith and that she would be killed unless she killed him first.'

'And how am I supposed to spin Karl Smith's death? Somehow he managed to take his own life with one hand behind his back and an experienced detective sitting on him.'

Connie rubbed her eyes. 'Everyone's eyes were off the ball. We'd taken one knife away and it didn't occur to any of us that he might have another. I'll take responsibility. We should have processed him immediately but I'd only just figured out what had been happening and I didn't want to break the spell. You want me to say sorry? I am. But Nate Carlisle has confirmed that Karl did kill his father, and he also attempted to kill Dr Waterfall. Doesn't make it okay, but it's context.'

Overbeck tutted. 'Well, what a grade A, bound to be turned into a true crime fucking podcast, nightmarish shitshow you uncovered.'

'Amen to that,' Connie said.

'You'll come back should we need you again, Dr Woolwine? It's taken some doing, but I'm almost used to you now.'

'If I come back, will you teach me how to walk in stilettos? I never got the hang of that.'

'Absolutely not,' Overbeck snapped. 'No one gets to walk around taller than me in here. I will give you the number of my manicurist though. Your nails are a disgrace.'

Connie laughed and made her way to the door. 'It was nice working with you again, detective superintendent. Good luck with the press. I'm sure your natural charm and warmth will win the day.'

Chapter 49

14 July

'There's someone to see you, Beth,' Lively said. 'Are you feeling up to a visit?'

'I'd rather not' she said.

Her head was bandaged from the neurosurgery that had repaired the lesion in her brain causing Fregoli syndrome, and tests to establish success were still ongoing, but the surgical and psychiatric teams were hopeful. The more concerning issues were depression and anxiety. Lively was encouraging her to work with a therapist, but it was too soon. Going through her mobile and emails to assess the case, though, Salter had found something she thought might be far more useful than counselling.

'Mum?' a voice called from the corridor, then the uniformed police officer stationed outside the door moved out of the way and a young woman ran in.

'Oh my God,' Beth sobbed. 'Molly!'

Mol ran in, throwing her bag down and rushing to her mother's side, crying before she even reached her.

'Mum, it's okay now. I'm here. I'm back.'

They wrapped one another in a desperate embrace.

'I didn't want you to see me like this. I didn't want you to know what I've done. Such terrible things, Molly. I killed people!'

'No, Mum,' Molly said softly, rubbing her mother's back, and rocking her gently. 'That wasn't you. It was brain damage. It was broken cells that had become wrongly wired. You had no idea what you were doing.'

Beth looked at Lively over her daughter's shoulder.

'How did you find her? We were so careful. I'm sorry I had to lie to you about her death.'

'Molly explained everything,' Lively said. 'Her going back to Australia to find her father, you both not knowing if Smith had accessed your emails. No social media, no visits, Molly changing her name. It must have felt as if she really did die.'

'I did, briefly,' Molly said. 'They revived me in the ambulance, and I knew I had to leave and never come back. It was me who persuaded Mum to tell everyone I was dead. Thank you for looking after her, Sergeant Lively, and for protecting her from Smith. I'd never have set foot back in Scotland while he was alive. He did kill me, in lots of ways. If I hadn't had an Australian passport through Dad, I don't know what I'd have done.'

'Call me Sam, please,' Lively said. 'Stalking is one of the least understood, hardest to prosecute crimes, but it's devastating. I was able to go through the complaints you filed, and I'm sorry nothing could be done to help you. Karl Smith was a severely mentally unstable but very intelligent young man. For what it's worth, I think leaving the country may have saved your life. There's no way of knowing what he'd have done if you hadn't.'

'I held a memorial service for you,' Beth said. 'And I have an urn with your name on, full of newspaper ash in my bedroom

315

in case he broke in. Some days, it was like living in a parallel universe.'

'He had to believe I was dead,' Molly told Lively. 'Not just so he wouldn't follow me, but so that I could restart my life. Mum would only talk to me from the bathroom with the shower running once a week in case he was bugging the house.'

She let her mother go and sat back on the bed.

'How are you feeling after the surgery? Does it feel different?'

'It's so hard to explain,' Beth said, leaning back on the pillow. 'I can't remember the things I'm told I did. It's like my brain wiped them out of my memory, yet when I was doing them, I used all my knowledge and skill. All those years as a surgeon, and still I underestimated the power of the human brain.'

'I don't even like to ask, but what's the police position on the deaths of those other people?' Mol asked, voice shaking, gripping her mother's hand.

'I'm not allowed to be involved, for obvious reasons, but I've heard on the grapevine that Superintendent Overbeck has been consulting with the families of the deceased, explaining the situation and giving them full background. The position is very much that Smith was really the one responsible. It just needs a lot of careful handling. If it were me making the decisions, I'd just want to be sure the surgery had worked, then I think the Procurator Fiscal could be convinced not to prosecute at all, but only if there were no risk whatsoever of the problem coming back. You can expect several more months of being asked to voluntarily comply with psych evaluations, interviews, handing over of evidence, then there are questions about getting your car repaired after the Divya Singh incident.'

'Her killing.' Beth nodded and folded her arms. 'Let's call it what it was.'

'Don't do that, Mum,' Molly said.

'What if they can't fix me?' she frowned. 'What if some psychiatrist somewhere concludes that I'm still a risk? And even if everyone puts all those deaths down to my skull injury and bloody Fregoli syndrome, how do I even start to learn to live with myself? How can I ever look in a mirror again and not hate myself?'

Lively went to sit the other side of the bed from Molly and took hold of Beth's hand.

'One day at a time. No mirrors if that's what you need. With people who love you there to hold you and tell you that it wasn't your fault, and that although you survived, you were a victim too,' he said.

Molly reached out with her free hand and took his, completing the circle.

'We'll both be there, Mum, every day. I'm home for good. I can put a little studio in the garage and paint from home. The collection did rather well in Australia. I made some serious money. I had a show in a gallery in Sydney and called it "Beautiful Terrible". All the awful things he sent me, all those rotting packages, I made something from it. You won't need to worry about money even if you can't work. And you're already due your pension if you can't operate any more.'

'You didn't tell me about your art show,' Beth said. 'Why not?'

'I thought you'd worry about me, remembering all the bad times with me painting out my memories. But it was therapeutic in the end. I got it in perspective, and it gave me some power over what happened to me. You need to find a way to do the same. Maybe we can set up a charity, a support network or advice centre, for other women who are being stalked?'

Beth smiled. 'I think that might help,' she said. 'Balance the scales in some small way.'

'And I'll move out, of course, to give you two some space. But

317

I can be there at a moment's notice, whenever you want me or need me,' Lively added.

'No way,' Molly said then looked at her mother to double-check. 'Mum needs you as much as she needs me. When she first started talking to me on the phone about you, I couldn't believe that she'd actually met someone. I'm glad you found each other, in spite of everything else. We have to grab hold of the good bits of life, however we find them.'

'Yes,' Beth said. 'Say you'll stay, Sam. I think that there was some part of me, buried deep in my subconscious, that needed you to save me from what I was doing. I saw that strength in you the first time we met. And there's plenty of space in the house for us all. Only if you want us, of course. I understand that the two of us together might be a little overwhelming.'

'Will there be cake?' Lively asked, grinning.

'As much as you can eat.' Beth sat up and kissed him on the cheek.

'And invitations to art galleries with my girlfriend's ridiculously talented daughter?'

Molly burst out laughing, and the air in the room felt several tons lighter.

'Yes!' she cried.

'Am I your girlfriend, then, after everything? After all you know about what I've done?' Beth whispered.

'Aye, Beth Waterfall, you are. We'll take one another as we find each other, and be grateful for it. And I'll carry on protecting you, both of you, with every ounce of strength in my body.'

Molly leaned across and kissed Lively's other cheek and Beth smiled in a way that Lively had, for a time, given up hope of ever seeing her smile again.

Chapter 50

10 August

The hallway was quiet as Lively reached the top of the stairs. It was his first day back after taking leave to settle Beth at home, and he'd been looking forward to it and dreading it in equal parts.

'And so,' he could hear Detective Superintendent Overbeck's voice bouncing off the briefing room walls like hailstones off a car windscreen, 'we've been left with a substantial budget deficit at the end of this operation. The result is that there's no capacity for overtime pay for the next three months, requests for special training will be put on hold, and—'

Lively walked in.

'Ah, my life is complete. Ladies and gentlemen, feast your eyes, if you will, on the team leader whose intimate friend was responsible for all the murders we were investigating, while he sat on her couch making eyes at her and eating her home baking.'

There was a round of laughter and applause from the squad and Lively could feel his face turning purple.

'Right, that's it,' Lively bellowed, 'Dr Waterfall is not a killer. She's been the victim of a sustained and vicious—'

'Sergeant Lively!' Overbeck cut through his rant. 'There's no doubt in any of our minds that Beth Waterfall would never have done anyone any harm but for the brain injury she sustained at Karl Smith's hands. What we're all wondering, is what the incredibly successful, intelligent, hard-working, capable, level-headed, sophisticated and normally peaceful surgeon sees in a loser like you?'

Lively frowned and tried to think of a comeback. In more than thirty years of policing he'd never once been stuck for a sarcastic retort, and there he was, wanting only to rage about how amazing Beth Waterfall truly was, and yes, how he too could not understand what on earth she saw in a scruffy, earthy, no-frills cop like him.

Just as Lively was about to protest, Overbeck said, 'But you're *our* loser, Lively. You belong to the Major Investigation Team, and while I may, frankly, be flummoxed about the reasoning, everyone here appears to adore you. So they insisted we buy you a cake and stop any form of work temporarily to celebrate your return.' She stepped aside to reveal an enormous cake that was a cartoon robber sneaking away with a bag of swag. 'They also wanted to shout "Surprise!" when you walked in, but I put my foot down at that point, assuming that you would prefer the tradition of me giving you a hearty Police Scotland ribbing.'

'Oh, fuck me,' Lively said. 'In the circumstances, ma'am, I think I'd have preferred the surprise party.'

'Come now, sergeant, has falling in love made you lose your edge? What pleasure would there be in the job without a stone like you for me to sharpen my blade on each day?'

But Lively heard nothing after the word 'love'. Someone, thankfully, had produced a knife and was handing slabs of chocolate cake (his favourite) out on paper plates, while some other genius had remembered to bring canisters of squirty cream (the only thing that could improve a slice of chocolate cake) and still Lively couldn't seem to move a muscle or say a word.

Love. Was that what he was feeling?

It had been such a long time, and he'd become so hardened and set in his ways, he'd forgotten that love even existed beyond tacky greetings cards and the reality TV shows that had perfected the art of everyone faking the emotion.

Love. It felt strange in his head, like an idea that was too big to contemplate. It was Brian Cox explaining how the universe was expanding or describing the concept of superposition.

Someone thrust a plate of cake and cream in his hand and slapped him on the back, and still he stood there like a lemon, wondering how he was supposed to eat when he'd just found out that he was, in fact, not only in love, but in love and happy, in love and becoming part of a family. In love with someone who loved him in return, he hoped.

'Y'all right there?' Salter asked. 'You're looking a bit lost, sergeant. Shall we take our cake somewhere quieter?'

Lively managed to nod, so that was something. Salter took him by the arm, across the corridor, and into an empty consultation room.

'Bit much?' she asked.

'Just wasn't expecting it,' he said. 'How did you persuade the super to sign off on it?'

'Ah, that's the thing, Overbeck actually ordered and paid for the cake. I wouldn't go quite so far as to say she likes you, but I think she understands that the squad is happier when you're around. You don't seem exactly happy to be here, though. Not ready to get back in the saddle yet?'

'I'm just very aware that I've got folk at home who need me.

I'm not used to the pull, Salter. How do you do it every day, get up and leave your wee girl with someone else? What happens if she needs you?'

'I get a call, and if we're not too busy on a case, I go,' Salter said. 'Is that all that's bothering you? Looked to me more like you'd been hit by a busload of emotion.'

'Ach, you spent far too long with that doolally American woman, always wanting to talk about how people are feeling. It's enough to make me feel sorry for the criminals.'

'Connie Woolwine is unconventional and also invasive. Bull in a china shop might be a fair analogy when it comes to getting in other people's heads. But she knows something about something. What advice do you think she'd give you now, if she were here?'

Lively ate a mouthful of cake with a dollop of cream as he thought about it. 'Bloody woman would tell me that trying to stop myself feeling things only intensifies the experience because it becomes all you can concentrate on. She'd probably say that the easiest way to process all my emotions is to let them come and go freely. Be like a sapling and bend with the wind, or some such shite.' He put the plate down. He had Beth to think about now. She needed him. And he needed her to need him.

'Some such shite, indeed,' Salter said. 'Right, I'm away. You'd best go in and convince your squad that you're happy to be here. Probably all that's needed is for you to insult a few people, be a bit grumpy, and pick a fight with the boss.'

'Good advice,' Lively said. 'And where are you off to? Bit early for end of shift.'

'I've an appointment with a surgeon of my own.' She rubbed her stomach without realising she was doing it. 'I've decided it's time to let them repair the scar. No point living with pain if I don't have to. You never know, one day I might even get a holiday from this bloody place and end up somewhere hot with a beach. Got to look good in that bikini, right?'

'Good for you,' Lively said. 'It's been a journey, Christie. Nice to be moving on.'

She gave him a hug that lasted longer than Lively would have been comfortable with a few months earlier, and he returned it with the fierceness of a father dropping his daughter at an airport alone for the first time.

'You'll be all right,' Salter murmured. 'And so will I. Let's face it, Police Scotland would fall apart without us.'

'That it would,' Lively replied. 'Now off you go. And kiss that little one for me when you get home.'

He picked up the plate of cake and walked back through into the briefing room, and life – the new and improved version of normality – began again.

Behind him, a man and woman entered and the room fell silent. Those who'd been sitting, stood. Anyone who'd been eating put down their plate. She was painfully thin, but her eyes were bright and her smile lit up the room. The man with her, half his face a map of scars, the other almost unbelievably handsome, gave Lively a simple nod.

'About fuckin' time you two showed up,' Lively said.

Chapter 51

10 August

They hired a car from Heathrow to drive southwest towards Dorset to visit Midnight. Connie was leaning out of the window, drinking in the summer air.

'England's gorgeous in August,' she declared, as Baarda turned into Midnight's driveway. 'You have cider, scones, ice-cream cones with sprinkles, cyclists who take over the entire road system, and street parties with buns and bunting!' She said the last two nouns as if she were auditioning for the part of head girl in a 1950s play. 'It's a wonder I ever persuaded you to travel the world catching killers with me, Brodie.'

'Yup, well, the UK's a little less appealing from October to March unless you're a plant who likes very little light and excessive watering. We're here.'

'Wooly!' Dawn was shouting from behind a little gate where a springer spaniel puppy was bouncing up and down as if on a tiny trampoline. 'Wooly hug!'

'You go ahead,' Baarda said smiling, 'I'll bring the bags.'

Connie raced across the driveway to grab hold of Dawn and

hug her tight. Midnight picked up the puppy and went to meet Baarda at the car.

'It's lovely to have you here,' she said. 'Connie looks well. You look a bit drained, if I'm honest. Long drive?'

'Long couple of months,' Baarda said. 'Goodness me, I can smell the orchard from here. How do you get anything done except fruit picking?'

As if summoned, Doris appeared wearing an apron smeared in reds, oranges and pinks, with a bowl still in one hand as she stirred with a spoon in the other.

'Just in time, dearies,' she said, the south London accent at odds with the surroundings, and all the more lyrical for it. 'We've chicken and cucumber sandwiches, rhubarb scones with strawberry or blackcurrant jam, a summer berries sponge pudding with homemade custard – none of that tinned nonsense – and elderberry ice cream.'

'Doris, you are a marvel,' Connie cried. 'No wonder Midnight begged you to come live with her. I'll be stealing you for myself if they're not careful.'

'Not me, sweetheart. I'm staying put. Picked out my burial plot in the churchyard up the lane and everything. Much as I loved London, I can't believe I stayed there so long. This place makes up for all the holidays I never went on. It's a little slice of paradise.'

Midnight took Connie by the arm. 'The burial plot will have fallen into the sea before she's ready for it. Doris is stronger than the lot of us. And you'll have to fight me if you think you can poach her. Come on through to the garden.'

Baarda put their overnight bags inside before joining them all in the shade of an ancient oak tree. Midnight and Doris were in deckchairs and Connie was lying out sunning herself on a picnic rug with Dawn.

'How did you leave things in Scotland?' Midnight asked. 'Please tell me they're not prosecuting Dr Waterfall. Poor woman has to live with the things she's done, surely that's punishment enough.'

'They've agreed not to,' Connie said. 'All the psychiatric and medical reports concluded the same thing, and because she was in a fugue state for the killings Beth wouldn't have been able to get a fair trial. The surgery and medication were successful. She's not a threat any more.'

'My loves, can we keep the conversation away from such brutal stuff in front of Dawn?' Doris asked in a hushed voice. 'She might not understand much of it, but I can't stand any talk of death around her.'

'What would I do without you, Doris?' Midnight asked. 'Except that I'd be thinner, of course. My waistline hasn't been the same since we moved here.'

'Wooly stay,' Dawn said, reaching out to hold Connie's hand.

'Just for tonight, sweetheart,' Connie told her. 'But I'll do a puzzle with you, and I'll read you bedtime stories and I'm sure there's a present for you tucked into my bag.'

Dawn grinned and started playing with the multicoloured laces on Connie's trainers.

'Brodie, did you get the issue with your wife sorted out, about the children's surnames?' Midnight asked.

'I did,' he said, closing his eyes as he leaned back on a sun lounger. 'I left it to the children. They're teenagers, and frankly one can't do anything without their consent these days. They were both very clear that they weren't prepared to change their names, and that they weren't the least bit bothered by their mother changing hers.'

Midnight grinned. 'And how did your ex take that?'

'For a woman who's been used to getting her own way, surprisingly well. We even managed to have a half-civilised telephone conversation about it.'

'You didn't tell me,' Connie said.

'We've been rather busy,' he replied. 'I should add that I need to take a look at our diary. I was thinking about reducing my travel and staying put in the UK for the next year. You don't need me on most of the jobs you do. If there's a security issue, I can find cover.'

Connie looked away and Midnight stood abruptly.

'Let's go and get tea on the table, shall we? The thought of those scones is making my mouth water. We'll call you when it's ready.' Midnight helped Dawn to her feet and they went with Doris into the house.

'You didn't think to discuss that with me first?' Connie asked. 'Since when did we start not discussing our plans? We're partners.'

'Not really,' Baarda said. His voice was warm and deep. 'You're the person our clients pay for. It's your expertise they want. I'm just part of the package. I'm not saying I want out, just that a bit of distance with the added benefit of being around more for my kids seems like a good idea.'

Connie got up and wandered over to a nearby pear tree, reaching out to pluck one from the branches. She held it to her nose and breathed in deeply.

'I shouldn't have kissed you,' she said. 'I made things messy, and I know you don't like mess. I knew it was wrong when I did it.'

'Then why didn't you stop yourself?'

She shrugged and took a bite of the pear, wiping juice from her chin, chewing and swallowing before answering.

'I honestly don't know. Sometimes this feels like a marriage, Brodie. Not that I've been married but for me our relationship is how I imagine all the good bits of a long-term relationship. I can trust you. I never get sick of you. And you get me, right? Like, no one has ever really gotten me before? There's this . . . continuity with you. You're my anchor.'

'An anchor is designed to weigh you down. It feels to me as if you're not making other connections in your life because of us, except that we're not married. You should want your own life, a private life, a partner.'

'I have you,' she said.

'Connie, for the brightest person I've ever met – the brightest person anyone I've met has ever met, in fact – you are startlingly dumb.'

She threw the core of the pear into a compost pile and wiped her fingers on her jeans.

'I kissed you because you smelled good,' she said. 'It's that Mont Blanc aftershave. The dark and the late night, and you really engaging with me, I just couldn't stop myself.'

'That's not what this is though, this thing with us. It would destroy everything.'

'Me losing you would destroy everything,' she said. 'Don't leave me, Brodie. Not even for a few months. I do what I do well because when I turn around, you're there. I never have to be distracted by anything because you're next to me, and I don't mean travel arrangements or security or driving – I can pay someone to do any of that. It's my head and my heart that need you. When you're not there for a week, it's like I can't think straight. We're a machine that only works when you fit both parts together.'

'I'm not a machine, Connie,' he said.

'Believe it or not, neither am I. I can break, and I can run slow, and parts of me can get worn out.'

She sat down next to him in a garden chair. 'Come to Martha's Vineyard with me for a few days and decide then. No work talk. And I won't try to pressure you. Will you at least do that?'

Brodie Baarda looked at her face in the light of the blossom pink late afternoon sun, and knew he would never be able to say no to Connie Woolwine.

'All right,' he said. 'Martha's Vineyard. Beyond that, we'll just have to wait and see.'

Author's Note

In the usual way of truth being stranger than fiction, I can tell you that Fregoli syndrome is very real and absolutely terrifying for the sufferer. It was named for Italian actor, Leopoldo Fregoli, who was famous for his extraordinary ability to mimic other people.

The delusion was first properly documented in 1927 by Courbon and Fail. They described what has become the best-known case of Fregoli delusion, wherein a young Parisian woman became convinced that two well-known actresses – Sarah Bernhardt and Robine – were following her. The actresses were apparently taking the form of people she knew or encountered in the street, including acquaintances, doctors, and people with whom she had worked.

Unlike other delusions, it doesn't involve a generic sense of persecution or paranoia. Instead, it's very specific to one or two individuals. Usually, the sufferer can physically see that someone looks different to the individual they think is following them, but is convinced that disguises are being worn. It often comes with a sense of being deliberately followed – these days, we would say stalked – often with ill intent. In many cases there are also memory issues noted relating to neurological disease or traumatic brain injury.

The causes of Fregoli syndrome are many and varied, from types of psychosis, such as schizophrenia and psychotic depression, to stroke, epilepsy and head injuries. Data collated for a 2020 *Neuropsychiatry Conference* report (Blackman, Bell, Dadwal & Teixeira-Dias) listed the recorded identities of the person perceived by Fregoli patients to be tormenting them as family members, acquaintances, romantic interests, famous people or people related to a trauma the patient had suffered.

It is often the case that a brain injury might be so slight that it is missed by a CT scan alone, and an MRI scan is always required in cases where Fregoli delusion is suspected. For this reason, it can remain undiagnosed for long periods of time.

It is, in many ways, a baffling disease with very specific but very strange symptoms. From the moment I first read about it, I was fascinated. Thus, the idea for a book was born. As fantastical as the scientific elements of the book may seem, all of it is possible. If you're interested, there are a few articles to read online with some case studies. My research did make me wonder whose face I'd see if I suddenly developed a lesion to the wrong part of my brain. Someone famous who I'd once admired in a film, or someone from my past who I might find terrifying? Either way, Fregoli syndrome has to be one of the most bizarre delusions I've come across in all of the crime novels I've written.

Acknowledgements

Books are hard to write. I thought, rather naively, that as I wrote more of them it would get easier. Boy, was that a steep learning curve! The one thing that does make the process more bearable is working with amazing people who know what they're doing. And so my very sincere thanks go to everyone at Team Avon, my champion Helen Huthwaite in particular, but also to the people whose quiet work in the background is everything, Maddie Wilson, Francesca Tuzzeo, Claire Ward, Sarah Foster, Katie Buckley, Emily Hall, Jessie Whitehall. Angela Thompson, Hannah Lismore, Emily Gerbner, Colleen Simpson, Rhian McKay and Anne Rieley. Also to HarperCollins for taking my little ideas and helping me grow them into something much bigger.

As ever, my agents have been there for headaches, administration, my stupid questions, self-doubt and pep talks. Thank you Caroline Hardman, Joanna Swainson, Hana Murrell and Lucy Malone.

To Sharon Avery, who is back in my life at last, albeit that I wish so many years hadn't passed. Thank you for the medical advice that helped get this book moving in the first place (the mistakes are mine and mine alone) and for the lunches, walks, child disaster support and the memories.

Last but never least, thanks to my gang. To Gabriel, Solomon and Evangeline, without whom I would be richer and less grey, but rather sad and less fulfilled. And to David – you are my Sergeant Lively (with the six-pack he always dreamed of and just as much sarcasm). Without them, I'd have nothing to write about.

Looking for your next explosive crime thriller?
Don't miss *The Profiler*!

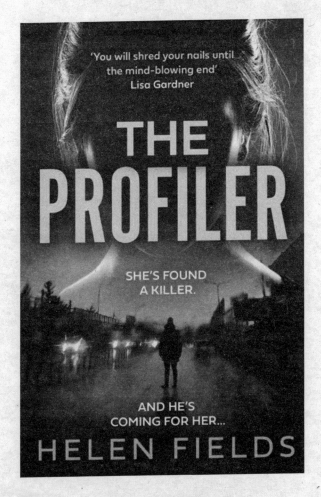

'You will shred your nails until the mind-blowing end'
Lisa Gardner

THE PROFILER

SHE'S FOUND A KILLER.

AND HE'S COMING FOR HER...

HELEN FIELDS

He's going to kill you.
He just doesn't know it yet.

Why not try the twisty locked room thriller
The Institution?

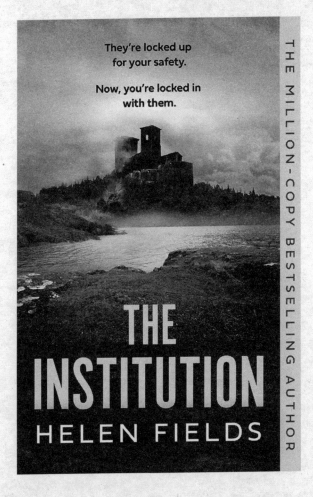

They're locked up
for your safety.

Now, you're locked in
with them.

THE MILLION-COPY BESTSELLING AUTHOR

THE
INSTITUTION
HELEN FIELDS

How do you find a murderer in a prison full of killers?

Have you read Helen Fields's iconic DI Callanach series?

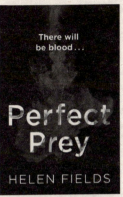

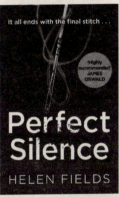

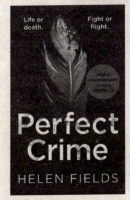

And if you enjoyed the DI Callanach *Perfect* series,
we think you'll love these fantastically twisty
crime thrillers . . .

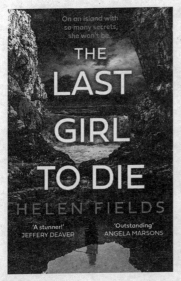

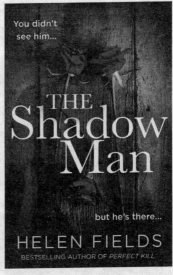